THE
SECRET KEEPER

THE
SECRET
KEEPER

PAUL HARRIS

DUTTON

bar

DUTTON
Published by Penguin Group (USA) Inc.
375 Hudson Street, New York, New York 10014, USA
Penguin Group (Canada), 90 Eglinton Avenue East, Suite 700, Toronto, Ontario M4P 2Y3, Canada (a division of Pearson Penguin Canada Inc.); Penguin Books Ltd, 80 Strand, London WC2R 0RL, England; Penguin Ireland, 25 St Stephen's Green, Dublin 2, Ireland (a division of Penguin Books Ltd); Penguin Group (Australia), 250 Camberwell Road, Camberwell, Victoria 3124, Australia (a division of Pearson Australia Group Pty Ltd); Penguin Books India Pvt Ltd, 11 Community Centre, Panchsheel Park, New Delhi - 110 017, India; Penguin Group (NZ), 67 Apollo Drive, Rosedale, North Shore 0632, New Zealand (a division of Pearson New Zealand Ltd); Penguin Books (South Africa) (Pty) Ltd, 24 Sturdee Avenue, Rosebank, Johannesburg 2196, South Africa

Penguin Books Ltd, Registered Offices: 80 Strand, London WC2R 0RL, England

Published by Dutton, a member of Penguin Group (USA) Inc.

First Printing, April 2009
10 9 8 7 6 5 4 3 2 1

LIBRARY OF CONGRESS CATALOGING-IN-PUBLICATION DATA

Harris, Paul, 1972–
The secret keeper / Paul Harris.
p. cm.
ISBN 978-0-525-95102-5
1. War correspondents—Fiction. 2. Human rights workers—Crimes against—Fiction. 3. Murder—Investigation—Fiction. 4. London (England)—Fiction. 5. Freetown (Sierra Leone)—Fiction. I. Title.
PR6108.A766S43 2009
813'.6—dc22   2008022393

Printed in the United States of America
Set in Adobe Garamond
Designed by Leonard Telesca

PUBLISHER'S NOTE

For my mother, father, and brother, Mark.
And for Moira.

THE
SECRET KEEPER

You lament not the dead, but the trouble of making a grave.

—A traditional African proverb

PROLOGUE

HE RAN HIS TONGUE over his swollen gums and tasted blood. His Torturer was gone for now, but had left him with this memento. A taste of bitter iron in his mouth where two of his teeth had been and a numbing pain that gripped his jaw so tightly he felt it might shatter if he spoke.

The Torturer's final words hung in his mind.

"What would she have wanted you to do, Danny?" the man had asked, leaning into his face. Danny had smelled his breath as the words came out, the aroma of fresh mint wreathing his head, carried to this place from some pristine bathroom downstairs. He had asked him the question just after he had stuck the pliers in his mouth and yanked out his teeth.

Danny had never suspected it before, but he realized now how shockingly intimate torture was. He felt as close to the Torturer as to a new lover, freshly exposed, naked and raw. It was an intimacy born of the power to inflict pain, bonding them together in a slow, hurtful dance. A vision struck Danny of the Torturer, standing in front of a mirror, gargling with his mouthwash and spitting into the sink. Then heading upstairs, pliers slipping into his back pocket. Heading to work. The hate clenched in his stomach and mixed with a tight knot of fear making him feel suddenly sick. He fought down the urge to throw up as the world swam in front of him.

"You fucker . . . you fucking bastard," he spat, spraying a fine red mist with each forced word, staring down at the brown tiles of the terrace on which he crouched, hands tightly bound behind his back.

No one heard him. The door onto the terrace was shut. The Torturer was gone. Leaving only his questions behind.

"What would she have wanted you to do? Ask yourself that, Danny," the Torturer had repeated, leaning even closer. He emphasized the "she," his lips rounding as he said it, as if by mentioning her, he could summon her presence. Then he had cupped Danny's face firmly in one hand and smiled sympathetically, lovingly even, before his other hand hit him hard across the jaw. There had been no need for a balled fist. Just a tiny touch jarred his ruined gums and sent rivulets of hot pain through his head. Then the Torturer had left, wiping his bloodied hands clean with a towel, which he tossed into a corner as if he had just taken a piss.

"Think about it for a while. I'll give you half an hour," he had said as he walked out the door. He closed it behind him with a soft click.

Danny coughed as his mouth filled with phlegm and blood, aware that a stream of red goo was dribbling down his chin, onto his shirt and then to the terrace's dusty tiles. He knew the Torturer was downstairs, but the whole house felt empty. It sat unmoved and silent in the thick, humid air that hung over Freetown—as it did every night of the year—like a dense blanket of invisible fog stifling the lives of everyone trapped in it.

Danny bent his back and hauled himself into a sitting position, then he pulled his knees in and looped his tied hands over his legs. His arms ached from having been bound behind him and now he stretched them forward, forcing what movement he could from the plastic cords that cut into his wrists. Then he sat, panting heavily and trying to calm himself.

From his new position he could see out over the low wall of the balcony. He did not know the time, but it must have been almost midnight. Not that it mattered. All that mattered were the thirty minutes given him by the Torturer. It was pointless to think too far into the future beyond that. Freetown's city lights shone and winked down the hillside, growing brighter as they clustered in the slums of downtown and the port. No noise reached this far up the hillside, but he could imagine the hustle and bustle below, even see traffic on the old highway leading out of town. A line of scattered red dots were heading upcountry, a thicker line of white ones coming in. Farther out still was the snaking path of the river, widening its mouth out to Freetown bay. And beyond that was the blackness of the ocean, like a pool of ink on the horizon, illuminated only by the lights of passing ships far out to sea.

He felt calmer. The initial panic and terror were ebbing away. He smelled now for the first time that he had pissed himself. His crotch and leg were damp with it, and the sodden material of his trousers clung to his skin. The realization brought a short stab of shame, the sudden transport back to a childhood feeling long forgotten. He desperately wanted to take his trousers off, to get them away from him. He kicked and wriggled his legs but quickly realized the impossibility of it. It was futile. His whole situation was futile. He would just have to sit here, waiting for the Torturer to come back. He began to cry. It was not a panicked sob, just tears welling up in his eyes, blurring his vision. What would she have wanted me to do now? he asked himself.

He was not sure if he had spoken aloud or just framed his thoughts into the question. How could he know?

Maria had been dead for three months.

He sat and stared at the floor and tried to conjure something of her before him. He thought of her skin, her smell, the touch of her hand on his cheek or ruffling his hair, the sound of her voice. Anything. He wanted her vivid in his mind so he could imagine her reply. But his memory did not answer. He took deep breaths, spat out the fresh blood that had gathered in his mouth and looked out at Freetown again. The lights still twinkled far away. He could think now, think clearly of what to say when the Torturer returned. Danny did not really care anymore what she might want. He just knew that he wanted to live. I want to live, he thought. I want to live.

Each word slowly.

I—want—to—live.

He wanted to rejoin the world of shining headlights and passing ships down below. He stared at Freetown as fat drops of rain began to fall from the sky and splattered against the ground. They felt warm as they hit his skin, warm and welcome and alive. Soon they would pour down in a waterfall, mingling with his blood and tears, running down his cheeks together and washing them clean.

1

[London, Three Months Earlier]

THE LETTER LAY on Danny's doormat, its gray blank ordinariness standing out among the garish colors of unwanted bills and junk mail. It bore a smudged handwritten address that jarred on his eyes as he bent down to pick it up. It was an unexpected human touch amid so much typed print.

Danny blinked, feeling the tiredness of the early morning still sticking his eyelids together. His mind had yet to register real puzzlement, but there was a flicker of curiosity. He could not remember the last time anyone had written a genuine letter to him. Then he saw the stamp and he knew where the letter was from.

Sierra Leone.

He stared at it like it was a stranger knocking at his door, arriving mute and uninvited at his London home. He turned the letter over. There was no return address; just his own on the front, sketched out in a slightly feminine hand slanting far to the left. He didn't recognize it.

But then again he did not expect to. Already his thoughts had clustered around one name. Maria? It felt familiar to him again in an instant. He let his mind repeat the name, feeling the vowels and consonants like a body's curves. Maria, Maria, Maria. He turned the envelope over again, almost afraid he would see a new name and address appear on the worn paper. But no. His was still there. Then he heard a soft pad of footsteps behind him, coming down the hallway in slippered feet. An arm snaked around his stomach from behind.

"Hey, sweetheart?" came his girlfriend's voice. "Anything in the post for me?"

He turned quickly and in one move, flushed with unexpected deceit, he pushed the letter into his back pocket and tossed the other post onto a sideboard.

"Just bills and other crap," Danny said.

Rachel looked back at him, smiling tiredly but happily. Her pretty face was framed by the blond hair that straggled across her eyes. They were caressed by the need for more sleep but still bright blue in the hallway's gray morning light. She was wearing her tattered red dressing gown; the same one, she said, she had had since college. For luck and comfort.

"You want me to deal with them?" she said. She clutched an outlandishly large mug of steaming coffee and leaned forward to kiss his cheek, standing on tiptoe to reach him. "I've got a free hour this morning."

Danny shook his head and kissed her. Her skin felt good to the touch. He knew without seeing it that she had shut her eyes. She always did.

"No. I'll do it," he said.

"Okay. Have a good day at work, honey." She smiled. It was her little joke, playing at fake homeliness. Though each day the joke was becoming a little more real.

"Will you have the dinner on by the time I get home?" he asked, responding in kind.

"You've forgotten. Bad boyfriend," she mock admonished him with a smile. "I've got a plane to catch at noon to make my conference in Edinburgh. I won't be back until late."

He leaned over and held her face for a moment, kissing her on the mouth, lingering for a moment to enjoy her warmth. She squeezed his elbow in return and he could feel her light up inside.

"I've got to go. Have a safe flight," he said. He walked out the door, shutting it behind him. Then he felt the weight of the letter in his pocket. It didn't feel like paper. It felt like lead. He glanced at his watch. It was 8:30. God, he hated mornings. He was late already.

AS THE TUBE TRAIN SHUDDERED to a halt, Danny's eyes snapped open. Over the four years since he had got back from the war in Sierra Leone the rattling of the train had become a rhythm as familiar as his heartbeat and he had taken to falling asleep on his morning commute. Before the war he had used the time to read his notes, to pore over newspapers, to prepare for the day. Now he preferred to snooze away the thirty minutes in blissful ignorance.

The train had stopped deep in the tunnel. A delay. He glanced around at his fellow passengers crowded in their anonymity. Few registered anything but slight annoyance. To Danny's right was an older man, dressed primly in a pin-striped suit, staring blankly ahead like he was in some sort of trance. He was on the wrong side of middle age, and his jowly face sagged as it began to lose its long battle with gravity. For an unkind moment Danny thought he looked like a melting candle.

The man's nose was red and bulbous, crisscrossed with exploded blood vessels that marked a dedication to liquid lunches. It was a nose common in Danny's newsroom: a mark born by veterans of Fleet Street's glory days when booze was as vital as ink to bringing out a newspaper. It was a face Danny's father proudly wore. He had seen his father just yesterday in a strained and painful Sunday lunch marred by two familiar Kellerman vices: red wine and honesty. Both always led inevitably to his father making disapproving comments about the liberal newspaper Danny wrote for. Danny's standard response—his counterattack—had been to raise the reliably explosive subject of his parents' divorce.

"So much for your own 'family values,' Harold," he had sneered, trying to combine condemnation of his father's politics and personal life in one go. The use of his father's first name had been an unnecessary touch. It reeked of the trendy liberal parenting that was one of the bugbears of his father's right-wing polemics. It worked too. The elder Kellerman had exploded into a monologue against modern Britain, sounding off with phrases that Danny had read in his father's columns a thousand times before.

Danny hated those columns. But they had made Harold Kellerman a Fleet Street legend. They were stocked with familiar, unexciting prejudices, yet had won many journalistic awards in a marked contrast to Danny's own plodding career of modest scoops in crime and politics. Then his father had rambled on about his true heroes of journalism: the foreign correspondents he admired for their dispatches from trouble spots around the world. If he had his time again, he spluttered, he would have taken that path himself just like several of his contemporaries from back in Oxford had done. Danny took the observation as yet another dig at his own career and a further reminder of the gulf between father and son: a distance unbridged these days by anything resembling love. The row had been an ugly scene, raising the eyebrows of fellow diners at one of London's better restaurants. It had been made even worse by his father's obviously declining health. Not even alcohol and rage had put color back into cheeks that now always seemed pale.

With a shudder the train pulled forward another ten feet and the movement jolted Danny's thoughts to a man farther down the carriage. He was young, with skin so dark it was almost blackish blue. He was tall and thin, dressed in ill-fitting jeans and a neatly ironed shirt. He was from Africa. Danny was sure of it. Suddenly he thought of the unopened letter in his pocket. He could feel it press against his flesh through his clothes. The thick air of the tube took on a tropical whiff. It was close and stifling, clinging to the skin like it had always done back in Freetown, impossible to escape its damp hug. Danny began to sweat.

He did not want to think about Maria just yet. He was already puzzled as to why he had hidden the letter from Rachel. It was, after all, just a note from an ex-lover. Nothing more. He felt a pang of guilt but told himself he had done nothing wrong. Rachel would not want to know an old girlfriend had written to him, whatever it was that Maria had to say. It would just confuse her, just like he would not want to know about Rachel's ex-boyfriends, though, unlike him, she had an uncanny knack for remaining friends with them. Her good nature seemed to bandage over any ex-lover's wounds. No, he'd been right to palm the letter away. After all, everyone had a right to a past. He looked again at the man opposite him. Who was he? A refugee from Uganda? A Ghanaian sending precious dollars back home? Was he the focus of some unknown clan's ambitions or a lone migrant, severing all ties to fulfil dreams first felt on the floor of some dusty hut? Dreams that had never imagined a stalled tube train waiting to get to King's Cross.

It was the shoes that really gave the man away as not being British, Danny thought. They were a neat pair of old-fashioned black dress shoes, of the type Danny might once have worn to school. They had been polished to an impossibly bright shine. They were village shoes, worn as a badge of pride by their owners back home, but garishly out of place among London's fashionable crowds.

Danny fought down an urge to wave, and as the train finally began to move again, the man opened his eyes and stared straight into Danny's. Danny looked away, missing a puzzled but friendly smile. Suddenly this was London again and no place to meet a stranger. A few seconds later, as the crowds poured out onto the King's Cross platform, the African disappeared from view. Danny glimpsed his back being swallowed up by the rush hour crowds, his village shoes carrying him into the city above.

RUNNING LATE, Danny walked into the newsroom of *The Statesman,* nodding a good morning at his colleagues. The clutter on his desk left behind by last week's stories greeted him. It was piled with Styrofoam cups containing cigarette butts stranded in a dank brown liquid that had once called itself coffee. Danny tipped each one into a bin, catching a smell of sodden, stale tobacco. He didn't know why he smoked anymore. He didn't enjoy it and morning coughing fits had started to hurt his chest. Quitting would come, but even as the thought crossed his mind he felt a pang of nicotine desire. He fished in his pocket for a crumpled pack of Camel Lights and extracted a cigarette as bent as a boomerang. He straightened it and popped it in the side of his mouth. As he did so he could feel the burning gaze of the health editor, Janet Ellis, who sat opposite him.

"Morning, Jan," Danny said, lighting up the cigarette and taking in a deep lung full of smoke. He took a drag and winked at her. She narrowed her eyes and turned back to her computer. Why and when had he become so sour? It seemed to be something he just couldn't help, something he had turned into while he wasn't looking.

He took another drag, sat down, and picked up his phone from under a pile of notebooks covered by his spider-like scrawl. The dial tone beeped loudly, indicating he had messages. He punched in a few numbers and began to scan the headlines of the papers in front of him.

You have one message, a metallic voice intoned from the phone. Then his father's stilted accent filled his ear. Even while leaving a message the old man still had to clear his throat before he spoke.

"Daniel. It's your father here. Look, I feel very badly about yesterday." His voice was its pompous self but weaker than usual, as if pausing for breath between words.

"I think we both said some things that might have been a little, well, misplaced. I know the situation between your mother and I has never been easy for you, but it wasn't easy for us either. . . ."

Danny felt a rush of anger. Not easy for him? Bastard. He was the one who had run off with someone half his age. He was the one who had abandoned his wife after thirty years of marriage for a secretary at his own newspaper. Danny pressed the delete button before the message ended and put the phone down with an unintentional slam. Again he felt the eyes of the health editor upon him. He took one more deep drag on his cigarette and then he stubbed it out in an overflowing ashtray.

Then he remembered the letter. He dug in his pocket and fished it out. He stared at it again, looking at the colorful stamp and the postmark. He noticed that it had been sent more than four weeks ago. Even by the vagaries of the West African post, that was a long time in limbo. He opened it and pulled out a single sheaf of paper. For the faintest of moments, not sure if he imagined it, he caught the smell of a familiar perfume, a message from a distant continent and a different time. Then he saw the word that he had been both hoping and afraid he might see. Not a word. A name.

Maria.

He began to read. The letter was written simply and bluntly, just a few sentences. But they were all that mattered in the world.

> *Danny,*
>
> *I need you. I'm in trouble. I know it's been too long. I'm sorry. It's my fault and I hope you forgive me. I can't use the phones or email to ask you this. They are not safe. I need you to come to Freetown to help me. I'll explain it all then.*
> *All my love as ever,*
> *Maria.*

Danny sat in stunned silence and then laughed out loud. He noticed Ellis jerk her head in his direction, but he ignored her. He could not believe the words he had just read. What the fuck was she thinking? Four years of silence, four years of nothing, and then this? He read the letter again. What sort of person could send a letter like that, so full of melodrama and secrets? And why couldn't she use the fucking phone or an email like everyone else? Did she think sending a letter would summon him up from the past, casting off his present life for a trip to West Africa? He laughed again, though it was a sound devoid of humor, like the bark of a jackal. He shook his head to expel the vivid memories of her that were starting to well up in his mind.

He read it again. And, gradually, a different emotion began to rise in his chest. It was a hint of fear. Maria had been the most unflappable, determined woman he had ever met.

But there it was: *I need you. I'm in trouble.*

Christ, the way he remembered it, Maria had never needed him for anything. He would ring her. He would call her right now. He switched on his computer and pulled up the home page of Maria's old charity War Child International. Images of Sierra Leone filled his screen, smiling children, crying children. He searched around on the site for a contact number. But there was nothing. Just a post box address in Freetown. He sighed in frustration. This was ridiculous.

He typed in her name on Google and pressed search. The results flashed up onto his screen in a sudden waterfall of text.

Later he would look back and wonder at how simply clicking a mouse could change so many lives. He could have thrown away the letter then as a message from the past unheeded. But he did not. By searching for her at his desk he had already started to answer her call. He gazed at his screen. Maria's name was everywhere and the top entry's headline told him everything he needed to know.

"U.S. Aid Worker Killed in Sierra Leone. Body to Return Home." It was dated three days ago.

Maria was dead.

He felt a stab of shock that left him dizzy, and an inky blackness crept into the sides of his vision. He clicked on the headline and read the story.

FREETOWN—The body of American aid worker Maria Consuela Tirado was yesterday brought back to Freetown, the capital of this once war-ravaged West African nation, in preparation for its return to the United States.

Tirado, who was killed last Thursday in a suspected robbery or kidnapping attempt, had been working for a charity that rehabilitated some of the country's thousands of ex–child soldiers. She was 36 years old.

The story was just two quick wire paragraphs. Succinct and soul-less: the facts and little else. Frantically he reread the words. Body to return home? Maria was a "body"? That was an impossible concept. He looked at the letter lying on his desk and could feel his breath coming in quick, sharp gasps. There was no hint of perfume now. Nothing at all apart from dead air that felt cold around him. He looked at the words again, tracing her flowing handwriting, its arcs and curls.

I need you. I'm in trouble.

He clicked on another story. He saw now that Maria had been news for several days. Just not in London. But in America. The first story had come out of Freetown three days ago. It was more wire copy but it was longer, and most of the main U.S. papers had run it.

U.S. AID WORKER KILLED IN SIERRA LEONE

FREETOWN—An American aid worker was killed today in the West African nation of Sierra Leone in what local police said was an attempted robbery or kidnapping.

Maria Tirado, 36, had been traveling with local companions on a road between the capital, Freetown, and the central town of Bo. Police said it appeared her car was stopped by bandits at a roadblock. Jewelry and money were reported missing.

A hospital official in Bo said Tirado had been shot at least three times at close range. Three Sierra Leonean aid workers traveling with her had also been killed by gunfire, the official added.

Tirado had been working for War Child International, a charity that helped rehabilitate child soldiers traumatized by the country's 10-year-old conflict that ended in the summer of 2000 after an intervention by British and United Nations soldiers.

Police said that a unit of government soldiers had later shot and killed six bandits in the bush near Bo that were believed to have carried out the robbery. All were suspected to be former members of the Revolutionary United Front, a ruthless rebel group in the country's civil war.

A spokesman for the U.S. embassy in Freetown paid tribute to her work in the country, noting that she had lived there for eight years during some of the most difficult times of Sierra Leone's long-running civil war.

Tirado was originally from Puerto Rico but had grown up in Toledo, Ohio.

(AP)

There was more. Several Ohio papers had picked up the story and run a piece on her family. Danny read it, the familiar victim's relatives' quotes bouncing around his mind.

"My baby is gone," said her mother. "I keep thinking she will be walking through the front door to tell us all it was just a big mistake," said her father.

Danny read the words and felt numb. Lying in bed together just before they had parted she had once talked about her parents. It had been a typical immigrant's tale of America, given an extra gloss by the undoubted pride with which Maria told it. How her mama and papa had left "the island" as teenage lovers and ended up in Ohio. They had created a slice of middle-class life in Middle America, ignoring the whispered word "spics" around them. Maria had been the culmination of their hopes.

Danny stared at the words. Then, without thinking, he got up. He printed the stories into a bundle of papers and walked across the newsroom to the news editor's office. He felt like he was on autopilot, watching himself detachedly from above. He would go back to Sierra Leone. He had to.

He knocked on the glass door once and walked into the news editor's office. Tom Hennessey looked up. Danny put the printouts on Hennessey's desk.

"I knew her," he said more bluntly than he intended.

The words just blurted out. It hadn't been what he had wanted to say but it was all that was on his mind. A simple truth. I knew her. This name in the story. I knew her as a real person, not a headline. Now she is gone.

Maria is dead.

Hennessey picked up the papers and scanned them. "Shit," he said. "I'm sorry, Danny. Did you meet her back in 2000?"

Danny nodded. Hennessey seemed at a loss for what else to say. Danny broke the silence and put Maria's letter on the top of the papers, staring up like an accusation.

"I got that through the mail this morning," Danny said.

Hennessey read it and whistled through his teeth. Now he was interested.

"Fuck me," he breathed. Then his eyes narrowed. "Is this for real?"

Danny ignored him. "I need to go to Freetown, Tom," he said.

He felt it like a physical urge, like a thirst that needed to be quenched.

Hennessey looked again at the papers and the letter and then he put them down on his desk and pushed them back toward Danny.

"Look," he said. "I know what happened in Sierra Leone in 2000 was tough on you. Fuck, it would have been tough on anybody. I know you feel strongly about the place and now your friend has been killed there."

Hennessey put the slightest of stresses on the word "friend." Not too much. But just enough to let Danny know he was no fool.

"But I'm not sure this is a big story for us. I'm sorry to have to say this, but she's not even British, for God's sake."

For a moment Danny felt he was about to explode. Not British? But he controlled himself, let Hennessey stew, let him understand what he had said. It worked. Hennessey's expression softened and he grimaced slightly.

"I didn't mean that, Danny," he said eventually. "She was your friend. Sorry."

Hennessey sat back in his chair and put his hands behind his head. "Sell it to me."

Danny thought for a moment.

"Look, four years ago thousands of British troops went to Sierra Leone to stop a war. That was exactly what they did. I was there. But we all left that country thinking that it had worked out and Sierra Leone had a bright future. But look at the place now. If you've got this sort of thing still going on, if you've still got ex-RUF roaming around killing aid workers, then what was it all for? This was the biggest story in Britain four years ago, and we've not been back to look at it since. It's a follow-up, a long-overdue follow-up."

Hennessey considered it. Danny could tell he was wavering. He just needed an extra little push. Danny gestured at the letter on the desk.

"I can use this as a way in," he said. He looked at the letter, sitting between him, its words speaking of fear and need and now cut off by a bloody death.

"Maria was in some sort of trouble," Danny said, as much to himself as to Hennessey. "I can't imagine what it was. But it can't be a coincidence. She had not spoken to me for four years. Then she writes asking for my help but before the letter even gets here, she's murdered. She says she is in trouble. She says she needs me. That she can't even use the phones. I don't know what that means, Tom, but some bastard has killed her."

Danny winced at the words coming out of his own mouth and the wire stories came back to him, their sparse language masking what his imagination could easily fill. A winding road, sweltering in midday heat and surrounded by thick green bush on all sides. A lone car traveling north, its passengers chatting or perhaps silent, sleeping in the face of a long journey. Unafraid and unaware of the seconds ticking off on their lives. Maria among them. The killers waiting, watching, deciding to strike. The sudden crack of gunfire . . . He stopped himself. And forced himself to speak.

"Maria was never afraid of anything. She never needed anybody. This is not just a robbery, Tom. She was in trouble and someone had her killed. I want to find out who. I want to find out why," he said.

Hennessey shrugged.

"I don't know, Danny. Sometimes things are what they appear to be. Sierra Leone's a tough place still. It could just be she was in the wrong place at the wrong time."

"Either way, it's a story," Danny snapped. "It's a personal way in, to make it more of a magazine-style piece."

The words were already out when he realized what he was doing. He was selling Maria's death as a story. But the rush of guilt was quickly replaced by determination. He would do what it took to get back to Freetown. At last she had needed him. In a way he had never felt when they were together in Freetown. Suddenly the last four years in London, his job, his flat, even Rachel, seemed like a gray dream he was waking from. They seemed like the memory. Freetown and Maria was his real world.

"Do I need to worry about you?" Hennessey asked.

Hennessey leaned forward.

"You were never quite the same since you came back," he said quietly. "I'm not the only person to think that. Is this actually about a story or is it about you?"

"I'll get you a story, Tom. Give me the space and I'll give you the story for it."

Hennessey considered it, but Danny already knew he was hooked. Danny waited and suddenly Hennessey lit up a cigarette.

"Oh, fuck it, then," Hennessey said, and then paused for a moment.

"Look, Danny. Don't misunderstand me. You've got to come up with the goods here. I can't afford you going on some sort of extended therapy session in the jungle."

Danny felt a surge of relief. He was going back to Sierra Leone.

He turned and left. Hennessey watched him go, not moving for a long while after, not noticing as his cigarette slowly burned down to ash in his hand.

BACK AT HIS DESK, Danny, for the first time, allowed himself to remember Maria. Her long dark hair, the birthmark on her right shoulder, the way she narrowed her eyes when she thought he was getting out of line. Her touch. How could someone like her die? It felt as if the universe was out of sync. He had to get over there. Had to see where it had happened, to see that something so wrong could be real.

He wished Hennessey had not been so frank about his career dive. He knew he had stalled since coming back four years ago. London seemed to have taken everything out of him, like a vacuum, sucking up all the light. He remembered the day he had returned after the war had ended, fleeing Sierra Leone, fleeing Maria . . . fleeing what had happened. . . . He stopped himself. He did not want to think about the events at the end of the war. How everything had spiraled out of control. They had left him deeply shaken, like a vivid red scar across his life: before Freetown and after. He realized now that he had been suffering from some form of post-traumatic shock. He had been angry, bitter and prone to unpleasant outbursts. It was like the world had suddenly leached itself of color and sunk into a grainy black and white. He drifted, put in the hours at work and began to sour.

Rachel had rescued him from that.

God knows what she had seen in him back then, he thought. Perhaps her caring nature meant she was drawn to those she sensed were wounded. He had met her at a dinner party—seated next to each other by a married friend—and been surprised when she had taken an interest in him, lightly resting her hand on his knee as he spoke. It had been so long that it was only after several hours and two bottles of wine that he realized she was flirting. She was an editor working for a small publishing house in Bloomsbury and seemed entranced by his tall tales of journalism, badgering him into talking too much about his job. It was only later she realized she was actually working on his father's upcoming—and soon to be best-selling—biography of Winston Churchill.

"You're Harry's son? You're Danny!" she said in amazement. "But I've heard so much about you."

For once, looking into Rachel's eyes, sparkling with life, he hadn't minded the mention of his father's name. Indeed, he had relished the hint of private praise. For a while it was like a fog had lifted, revealing a clear road ahead. He had plunged down it, rediscovering his charms, laughing and joking. His wooing had been swift and aggressive—something Rachel might have taken as a warning sign but instead took for an intense passion—and within six months they were living together. He had bullied her into it, sending flowers to her at work every day for a whole week. And yet he remembered the moment they walked into their flat together as the first sign of something wrong. They had stood, holding hands in the bare living room. She had been feeling relief that she had made the right choice, overcome her doubts, but he—inside himself—suddenly knew that something unexpected had happened: that domesticity now stretched ahead. He dismissed it then as natural male nerves. But instead it had been the beginning of the fog returning. Life with Rachel was good—he knew that, he really did—but as he looked back, now it seemed true color only existed in Africa; in Freetown; in the arms of another lover.

Now he wanted to feel alive again. Sierra Leone had been a story that mattered beyond all others and Maria had been a part of that. The real world, and his life with Rachel, all seemed like a shadow flickering on the walls, a mere suggestion of what life should be.

His phone rang. He picked it up.

It was Rachel. She sounded faint and he could hear the sounds of an airport in the background.

"Hey, you," she said, her voice shouting brightly above the hubbub of sound.

"Have you got a flight back?" he asked.

"It's delayed for an hour. You know the weather in Edinburgh is never going to be predictable."

She began to talk of her conference and the talk she had delivered. Rachel was a rising star now in the field of popular biographies, catching the latest publishing trend. But she sounded a little tired from the rushed journey and the speech. He knew he should offer a bit of sympathy, but his mind was too full of the implications of his decision to go back to Sierra Leone. "Look, I've got to go away on a story," Danny said. There was no point in beating about the bush.

"I'm heading back to Sierra Leone."

There was a silence on the other end of the phone.

"An old friend of mine got killed over there. I want to find out what happened and make it into a piece. It'll be good for me. Get me back out in the field again."

"Danny . . . ," Rachel said. He could picture her in the airport, shifting her weight from one foot to the other, which she always did when something unexpected happened. He could hear her breathing, close in his ear, despite the hundreds of miles between them. He wanted to reach out to her and hold her.

"I'm sorry about your friend," she said softly. "How well did you know them?"

Danny ignored the question.

"Look, I'll see you tonight when you get back. I'll explain more then," he said.

"I'm worried, Danny. This is so sudden," Rachel said. If he had got away with being vague, it was a temporary respite. Rachel was a good editor, with an eye for detail. His dad had testified to that a thousand times. He knew her mind would be racing with questions, and maybe, just maybe, the beginnings of doubt.

"I'll see you at home," Danny said.

"Wait a minute," Rachel said hurriedly, shutting off his attempt to end the call. "You know your dad's ill. He'll worry himself sick about you."

Danny shut his eyes. He doubted that very much. "I'll call him. I saw him yesterday. He seemed in good shape and we had a nice chat."

Danny knew that lie would probably not hold. But it was the easiest thing to do. Rachel would relent now. She hated the fact that Danny and his father didn't get on. Her work with him had been her pride and joy, made doubly so by the Churchill book's enormous success. They made a good pair. The elder Kellerman had been strangely susceptible to her suggestions, his usual stubbornness melting. They had become close, like father and daughter, even before Danny had known her. Danny knew any sign of a thaw between himself and Harry—even a false one—was always too precious for her to waste.

"Okay. Look, let's talk later," she said, suddenly distracted by some announcement in the airport. "I think they're talking about my flight."

Danny put the phone down. He probably should call his father. At least say good-bye. It was, after all, some sort of peace overture and they were rare enough from either side. He began to dial. For a moment he believed he was actually ringing his father's house. He'd dialed the paper's travel agent instead.

He can read about it in the paper, he thought, as he began to book his flight.

2

EVEN IN THE heaving crowd churning outside the chopper, Kam was easy to spot. He looked like a great obsidian rock, arms folded across his chest, unmoving in the sea of people ebbing and flowing around the helicopter landing ground in Freetown. With a touch of familiar arrogance he nodded at Danny as he emerged. Then he barged his way forward. Danny put down his luggage and threw his arms around the tall Senegalese. Kam was his old driver. His old friend. It was a joy and a relief to see him and to return his embrace. Relief that a few hasty calls from London to the desk of the Cape Sierra Hotel had summoned this African genie to be his eyes and ears again. But also simple joy at seeing the man who had guided him through the war.

Danny was back in Sierra Leone.

"It is so good to see you," Danny said. "I was worried you did not get my messages."

Kam grinned.

"A friend of mine at the hotel came to my house and found me. He said you were coming as soon as possible and looking for a driver again. But you know, you could have called me on the mobile phone," he said.

With a flourish he plucked out a tiny little handset and proudly showed it off.

Danny looked at the technological marvel. "Last time I was here, there was barely a mobile phone in the whole country," he said.

Kam shrugged.

"Things have changed, Mr. Danny. Everything has changed in Sierra Leone."

Danny already knew this was going be a different kind of trip from when he had arrived to cover the war. The airport was still chaotic but it was chaos with an orderly heartbeat. Kam looked different too, no longer wearing a ragged T-shirt but decked out in a bright blue silken shirt with a weave of colorful patterns of gold and green. On his head he sported a tiny white cap, a symbol of his Muslim childhood back in Dakar. His shoes were shiny and black though Freetown's dust had dulled the gleam of the toes. His car too, was new. The old, beaten-up little blue Renault with the sticky door was gone. In its place was a gray Mercedes. Danny ran a hand down the bonnet and clucked his approval.

"What happened to your car? I liked that old Renault."

Kam snorted in mock disgust.

"I sold her for a good price. She had been good to me, but . . ." His voice trailed off as he looked at the Mercedes and searched for the right words.

"She was like a girlfriend when you are a young man. She was right for the moment, but a man moves on. He must find a woman that more suits his station in life. This is more my sort of car now," he pronounced.

The Mercedes was an old model, secondhand. But Kam had a

boundless pride in it. Its gray paintwork was polished even down to the rims of its wheels. "I drive this special lady mostly for Mr. Ali," Kam said. "I only drive her for a few people now. Only exclusive people. Kam works for the Big Men in Sierra Leone now."

Mr. Ali was Ali Alhoun, a Lebanese businessman with fingers in pies all over West Africa. It made sense that Kam would do work for him. If anyone would prosper in postwar Sierra Leone it would be Ali. Danny smiled at the thought of Ali's talent for survival—no, for prosperity—in even the worst of times. God alone knew what Ali was up to now there were no rebel armies to slow his ever-expanding interests.

"How is Ali? I hope to see him again."

"You will do better than that," said Kam, opening the passenger door of the car and gesturing for Danny to sit down. "When I told him that Mr. Danny was coming back to visit our little corner of Africa, he insisted that you stay in his villa. He is away up-country for a few days, but he said you should make yourself at home and he will come and drink with you when he returns."

This was almost too good to be true. Danny had not really wanted to go back to the Cape Sierra. Or any of the refurbished hotels that had now grown up around it. Staying at Ali's house would save on costs, but also give him a grounding in the country better than the sterile environs of the hotels.

Danny gazed out of the car as Kam steered it onto the traffic-clogged streets. At first glance they seemed unchanged. The roads were still potholed and Kam had to steer around some of the bigger divots, where it seemed a giant golfer had scooped out the tarmac. Other cars also weaved around in an elaborate waltz that had no respect for which side each vehicle was meant to be driving on. The pavements were still crowded too, crammed with people walking to and fro or hawking goods in front of buildings that mixed and matched the derelict with the rebuilt. He rolled down the window, letting out the cool air of the car, and breathed in the heat and smell of the street. The smell of Freetown. Ripe and dirty, it tingled the back of his nose with the aroma of cooking fires, sweat, rotting food and cheap perfumes. It smelled of life. It smelled of death. Kam glanced silently at him.

"How is Freetown these days?" Danny asked without turning from the streets outside.

"It is better," Kam said. "Foday Sankoh is gone now. Dead. They say he had gone mad by the time he died. Even more crazy than before he was caught. He caused so much shit for this country."

Kam paused, as if thinking about his next remark.

"The other RUF leaders are not so bad, you know," Kam said quietly. "There is no trouble. Business is good."

Danny turned to look at his old friend. He could not really believe what he had just heard. Kam had never been one for judgments; he was a survivor, trying to earn a buck. But he had always loathed the RUF, hating their mindless brutality as they waged their doomed rebel war that had reduced the country to ruins.

"You're joking, right?" Danny asked. Kam kept staring ahead, but he shook his head.

Kam leaned forward.

"You know they pay better than the Lebanese too. Better than Mr. Ali. The RUF are Africans. They know we must look after each other, not send African money out across the ocean."

For a moment a dark cloud seemed to enter the car. A lot of Sierra Leoneans had always resented the Lebanese and their riches. It was a natural enough feeling, he supposed, born of envy and exploitation and race. But he had never heard Kam utter such sentiments.

"You work for some of the ex-RUF?" Danny asked. Kam laughed and patted the dashboard of the Mercedes.

"Of course!" Kam said. "Mr. Danny, this is the new country. We are at peace now. I work for all. So I work for ex-RUF. Who do you think it was that gave me this car?" Kam asked the question as casually as if talking about the weather.

"Minister Gbamanja! That old bastard General Mosquito! He gave me this car and now Kam is a much-respected man in Freetown," Kam exclaimed.

This was almost too much. William Jusu Gbamanja was the new Information Minister in Freetown. But that was just his official title. It meant nothing. Gbamanja's real power came from the reputation he had won during the war. He was better known by his RUF name from those days: General Mosquito. It was a bizarre name, like so many other nicknames adopted by RUF soldiers as they shed their old identities as peasants to become killers. Mosquito was an obvious choice: a bloodsucker. Mosquito had been one of the bloodiest RUF commanders during the war. Gbamanja had been a thug and a brute at the head of a band of drugged-up, psychotic child soldiers. Danny felt disorientated. He felt his skin shrink away from the car seat, as if reacting to the fact it had been earned with Gbamanja's blood money. Kam sensed his unease.

"I just do some driving for him. I know he was a bad man during the war. A very brutal man. But this is new country now. No point in holding grudges. We forget the past."

He slapped the dashboard again and put his foot down on the accelerator.

"Besides, you like my new car, yes?"

Danny gripped his seat as the car swerved around the bend and drifted into oncoming traffic. He heard a horn blast from an irate driver behind them. At least Kam's erratic driving still had the ability to scare him witless. That was the same.

"You don't want to go back to Senegal? What about your wife?" he said hurriedly, changing the subject.

"Mr. Ali, Minister Gbamanja and others have too much work for me here. In Senegal it is still tough for me. The government there do not like my people, the Jola."

Then Kam winked. "Besides, here I have girlfriends to keep me warm. And I know my girlfriends would not like my wife. No, they would not get on at all well," he said.

Despite his new white cap, Kam had always worn his Islam lightly. He was as fond of a drink as the next man and four years ago he had always been at the tender mercies of a harem of Sierra Leonean beauties. It was good to see that, too, lingered on.

Gradually the car crawled out of Freetown's lower suburbs where the poor masses lived and up into the foothills above the city. In the days of British rule many colonial officials had chosen these shaded slopes for their houses, high enough up the mountains to catch a lucky breeze. The area had been given the name Hill Station, an echo of the Indian Raj that no doubt most of the officials posted to Sierra Leone had secretly longed for. After the British had left, the area had become home to Sierra Leone's ruling class: whether Krio politicians, army generals or Lebanese and Greek families. The suburbs' fortunes had waxed and waned along with the city's. Some of the houses were shells, staring at the world through windows empty as eye sockets, their gardens as overgrown as unkempt hair. Others boasted tall new security fences with guards standing outside in little sentry boxes. Their weapons seemed to hint at the state of the family fortunes within. One was guarded by a solitary old man dressed in blue overalls and holding a gnarled wooden stick. While next door two young men lounged in military uniforms, cradling semiautomatic rifles and guarding a fluted metal gate.

It was through this gate that Kam sped, nodding at the guards who looked puzzled as they glimpsed Danny's white face. The car pulled up outside the villa's front door. It was a rambling angular bungalow built in the seventies, squat and concrete but with huge windows and bay areas, all sharp corners and blank cement walls. It had been given a fresh coat of white paint, but that could not entirely disguise the harsh effect the humid climate had had on the concrete, cracking and rotting it from the inside.

Kam handed Danny his luggage.

"I have a few errands to run for other clients. But I'll come by tomorrow. I have arranged for you to meet a few people. I do not know exactly what you want to do here, but we must start somewhere," Kam said.

Kam's words were a kind of reproach. Danny had wanted to tell Kam everything as soon as he saw him, but he had felt too unnerved by the changes. Ex-RUF had killed Maria. But now Kam worked for some of them. And not just any of them, but Gbamanja. One of the most brutal men in a country full of them. He needed to be careful. Danny shook Kam's hand and ignored the implied question.

"Thank you, my friend," he said. Kam smiled, letting the matter drop. Danny walked inside the villa. The air-conditioning was not on, but each room had a ceiling fan. Pictures littered the desktops, a visual history of the Alhoun clan. Behind many of the faces stood the mountains and cityscapes of Lebanon, but looming over others were the thick green forests and white beaches of Sierra Leone. As Danny stared at them he heard the sound of footsteps behind him. He turned to see a portly young Lebanese man walk into the room, a short, heavyset figure with a round face below an untidily cut fringe. He was sweating profusely and dabbing his forehead with a handkerchief.

"Fuck me, it's hot today. Too hot for a fat man," the man said cheerfully, and then thrust his hand out in front of him. "I'm George, Ali's cousin," he said.

Danny smiled a hello.

"Where is Ali, by the way?"

George did not know for sure.

"I spoke to him two days ago and he was driving to Bo. After that I think he was off east to Kono. Some sort of trouble in the diamond mines."

Driving to Bo? Business in Kono? Four years ago, both would have been as impossible as going from Freetown to the moon. They had been RUF strongholds or surrounded by those killer soldiers. It would have been suicide to try to reach them. Only the poor and the desperate, drawn by family or circumstances, would have attempted it.

Danny expressed his amazement at how things appeared to have changed. George's sunny demeanor dimmed and he sank into a chair with a sigh.

"Yeah. But it's a more complex place now. Things are getting difficult here for us. Now that there is peace, people don't want the Lebanese around. Ali spends half his time up in diamond country, just trying to keep hold of what we have. We've worked there for years and some of these new types think they can just take it all away. Just because they've got black skin, not brown."

George seemed to appreciate the opportunity to vent. He described the resentment against them as being because they were outsiders even though the Alhouns had first come here more than one hundred years ago. Danny listened patiently and expressed his surprise that Kam was working for ex-RUF, driving for Gbamanja.

George laughed.

"Old Kam will work for anyone. He has a price, like every African, and there's a lot of money in Freetown now," he said. Danny felt lost all over again. The things that had been solid during wartime seemed to be fracturing during peace. George shrugged.

"But Kam's still the best driver in town. What are you doing back here anyway?"

Again Danny felt tempted to say everything. To ask about Maria. It was almost an explosive urge. But he stopped himself. Instead he just asked when Ali might return.

"A few days, I hope," George said, and he got up to leave. He scribbled on a scrap of paper. "Here's my mobile number. Call me if you have any trouble," he said.

Danny watched George's portly figure waddle out of the door, still mopping his forehead. Then he stared back at the photographs on the wall. It was family life: people smiling and laughing into cameras, arms draped around each other. He thought of Rachel. What was he doing here? He should be in London, trying to be happy with her, with his job. Even with his dad. Practically everyone in this whole country would kill to have his life back in England and he was running away from it.

He went into a back bedroom and slowly began to unpack, unfolding his clothes, a mobile phone and a laptop, and a pile of blank notebooks. He was back. Freetown again. He wished the city felt like a second home. But it did not. It felt like a place he had never seen before.

He took out Maria's letter and—for what must have been the hundredth time—he stared at the words on the page. He didn't need to read them anymore. He knew them by heart. His eyes just followed the script, the letters, the ink they were written in. He wondered when Maria had written it. Had she sat in her bedroom, hurriedly composing the panicked note? Had she been at work, at the orphanage? Or stuck, in some other place, the source of her fear, and only managed to snatch a few moments to write. The words had no answer. They sat, caught in a lost moment of time, mute except for a simple message. I need you. That was enough. He knew why he was here.

DANNY AWOKE the next morning to the sudden sound of the ceiling fan dying. He opened his eyes. It was already bright outside. As the fan's blades slowed he could feel the hot air clot around him like blood at a wound. It was a power cut. Then he heard the sound of a generator engine roaring to life and the fan began to move again.

He had hoped to dream of Maria, yet instead he had dreamed of Rachel. They had not parted well. She was hurt when he had told her why he was going and he had suppressed his guilt by snapping at her when she just needed some reassurance. Maria had nothing to do with her, he told her, and he felt he had a right to his own past. But he knew why she was confused. He had told Rachel about everything else that had happened in Sierra Leone, but not Maria, keeping her to himself like a secret totem. And now here Maria was, a stranger at the door, calling him away. Danny knew Rachel had a right to be annoyed. To her it looked like an indulgent wild-goose chase after an ex-lover, a rival whose greatest advantage was that she could make no fresh mistakes. Maria's faults were in the past and forgiven, absolved by the bullets that had taken her life. Worse still, Danny could not explain why this mattered so much to him. He could not tell her why this was so important without breaking her heart.

In his dream he had replayed the argument. She had been angrier than she had been in real life. Her soft voice replaced in his head by a shouting and haranguing that perhaps his unconscious thought he deserved. He lay on his back, staring at the circling fan, and stretched out an arm for his watch. It was already nine o'clock.

"Shit," he muttered, and struggled out of bed in the direction of the bathroom.

Walking into the kitchen ten minutes later, he was only half surprised to see Kam sitting at the table, a freshly brewed pot of coffee steaming in front of him. Kam poured him a cup. Danny felt the hot liquid beckoning him to start the day.

Ten minutes later they were driving out of the gate. Kam was in a hurry and he hustled and bustled Danny from the villa, giving him only enough time to grab a notebook, a tape recorder and a couple of pens. Kam announced he had arranged an interview for him that morning. It was with General Foster Hinga, the new chief of staff of what passed for the Sierra Leone Army. Danny was not surprised that Kam had been able to set something up so quickly. Kam's dealings had always been shrouded in mystery and that would only have doubled now that he worked for Ali and Gbamanja. God knows what favor Kam owed Hinga, but there must be some sort of debt to be repaid. There were numerous currencies in Freetown and only one of them was money. They descended from Hill Station at a breakneck pace. Kam muttered under his breath about being late as they drove up to the gates of the main army barracks. The base lay behind a thick, stained concrete wall, shielding it from the crowded slums outside. Kam pulled up to a sullen guard at the gate and was waved through at the mention of General Hinga's name. He drove his car slowly forward through an open space dotted with dilapidated buildings and then pulled up in front of a battered-looking office block.

Kam shooed Danny through the doors, walking slightly in front, approaching a man at the front desk with a swagger he never would have used if alone. Even now it was still a strange thing that the color of

Danny's skin could grant him, and those with him, a special authority. It was a mark of separation, of being elevated above the herd.

"This is Danny Kellerman," Kam said. "We are here to see General Hinga. For an interview." He pronounced the word "interview" carefully like it was a physical thing.

The man looked down at his ledger and picked up a phone. He tapped the receiver several times, trying to get a dial tone. After a minute of useless prodding, he looked up apologetically.

"The fourth floor," he said. "Just go upstairs."

They plodded up the stairs, working up an unwelcome sweat. At the fourth floor Kam led Danny down a dim corridor and stopped at a door on which Hinga's name was printed. He knocked softly once and opened it slightly.

"Ah, Kam!" boomed a voice.

Kam opened the door and Danny followed him inside. The general sat behind a cheap-looking desk piled with sheets of paper. He was a big man with a waistline that stretched the front of his green military uniform. He was pouring out a cup of tea and Kam walked over and limply shook his hand. Kam's swagger was gone now. The usual rules of deference applied again.

The general looked at Danny.

"You must be Mr. Kellerman. Sit down," he said. "Have some tea."

"Thank you, General," he said. "It is good of you to meet me at such short notice. I know you must be a busy man."

The general beamed. He was clearly enjoying the prospect of an interview.

"It is good that you have come to Sierra Leone. We get very few reporters from England these days. But tell me, is this your first time in Freetown?"

Danny shook his head. "I was here four years ago."

"Good, good," he enthused. "Then you see how so much has changed now. Our government is in control again. The people are at peace."

"And the RUF?"

"There is no RUF." Hinga laughed. "There are some people who were once in the RUF, but they have changed. We are all Sierra Leoneans now. Of course, we are still poor. That is why I am pleased that you have come. You need to let people in England know that we still need their help."

Danny looked at the general's warm smile, but inside he bristled at the platitudes. He was not here to help.

"What about Maria Tirado?" he said calmly. Hinga looked puzzled. He shook his head as if he had not heard the question. Danny repeated it.

"She was an aid worker, killed by ex-RUF a week or so ago. That hardly seems a country at peace, General."

Hinga's face stiffened. Danny also heard Kam shuffle his feet behind him, and a spot in the middle of his spine began to warm as he imagined Kam's gaze burning into his back. Suddenly Hinga's almost jovial tones were gone. Danny could not tell if a mask had fallen off Hinga's face or one had been put on. Either way, Maria's name had just changed everything. Hinga regarded Danny from a distance that seemed far more than just the width of a battered desk.

"The death of that woman was a tragedy. But it was a robbery. Such things happen in poor countries," he said, his voice firm and flat.

"How can you be so sure?" Danny asked. The general ignored the question.

"Why do you ask of this, Mr. Kellerman? It is the opinion of our police that it was a robbery. That would be good enough for you if the victims had been black, perhaps. But because she was a white woman, it is not enough. Our police are not to be trusted with the deaths of white people? It was a robbery. The bandits who did it are already dead. This matter is closed."

"There are rumors . . . ," Danny began, weighing his options as to whether to tell Hinga about the letter. But Hinga cut him off, abruptly standing.

"Rumors do nothing but harm this country. You should not spread them. Write a story about our needs, not this sad death."

Hinga shot Kam an angry glance. Kam flinched.

The general strode around the desk and barked at Kam to get out. He retreated under the general's orders, mumbling that he would go back to the car. Hinga loomed over Danny, his eyes, which had at first appeared so mellow, now glared fiercely. Danny struggled to his feet, unsure of what was going on.

"Come with me, Mr. Kellerman. I will show you why we don't like rumors," Hinga snapped.

The general led Danny downstairs and outside. He saw Kam waiting by the Mercedes and recognized a look of fear on Kam's face. His own heart quickened. He followed the general along a line of low, single-story buildings, half ruined and almost overgrown. Hinga stopped outside one and Danny peered inside. He could see a young woman, wearing a tattered dress, crouched over a cooking fire and, in the shadows, groups of men talking in low tones. Some of them were smoking and Danny caught a powerful whiff of marijuana in the air. Hinga shouted something in Krio and slowly the figures began to get up, emerging into daylight, blinking as if unused to the light. They were a ragtag bunch, dressed in mismatched green uniforms, their hair long and bedraggled. Some of them looked barely teenagers whereas others seemed perhaps in their early twenties. They stared sullenly at

Danny, registering no emotion at his presence but at the same time not taking their eyes off him. They formed a ragged inspection line, a few of them holding greasy automatic rifles, their magazines bound to their guns with black tape. Hinga turned to Danny.

"These are my soldiers," he said. "Some of them are government. Some of them are ex-RUF. But four years ago all of them were out in the bush."

Hinga did not need to continue. These men and boys were killers. The war had destroyed their villages and lives and they had done what they needed to in order to survive. Now they were here, smoking weed in a half-abandoned army base, waiting for a future that had not yet arrived. But at least they had left their past behind.

"Four years ago, these boys were killing people. Now they are not," Hinga said. "That is progress. That is change. So when you ask about your white friend's death, remember that this means nothing to us. What is important is that these soldiers are at peace."

Hinga kept mentioning the fact that Maria was white, a foreigner like him. Danny began to speak but Hinga jabbed a finger in his chest. "These men have all killed. They would do so once again if given the word. If given the motivation. They would think nothing of it."

Hinga stared hard at Danny and let his words hang in the air. It seemed suddenly silent. Danny looked at the men and did not doubt for a moment that what the general said was true. He swallowed hard. He looked into Hinga's face, trying to guess how serious the threat was. He wished Kam were here.

"They have seen and done terrible things," Hinga continued, his voice lowering to a conspiratorial whisper. "Their home villages will not take them back. Some of them killed their own parents, you know?"

"I know," Danny said, surprised at how difficult he found it to force the words out.

He looked again at the soldiers, lined up like suspects against a wall. Danny felt afraid, scared that Hinga would give an order to spirit him away inside that dank, brooding building. Another foreigner missing or dead in Sierra Leone. Another accident.

But then, out of nowhere, Hinga adopted the gentle admonishment of a schoolteacher and wrapped a thick arm around Danny's shoulders. He guided Danny away from the soldiers, walking him back to the main building.

"You see, Mr. Kellerman, these men. They have no uniforms. No training. We need your help. When we were killing each other you in the West cared so much. Now we are at peace and we are forgotten. That is why Maria Tirado's death should be left alone. Such accidents never help anyone."

They were almost back at the car now. Hinga's arm still lay heavily on Danny's shoulder. Kam watched them arrive, his face lined with worry and the corner of his mouth twitching. Hinga looked at Kam.

"You should keep an eye on our friend, Kam," Hinga told him. "He needs help to see all that the new Sierra Leone has to offer." The general turned to go but then stopped for a moment. He faced Danny and let out a heavy sigh.

"I have been to your country, Mr. Kellerman. Eight weeks at Sandhurst as the guest of your British army. And every Sunday I would go to church to praise my God. But it was like a museum. You Europeans brought the word of God to Africa, but it is only here that we still listen to it. I am used to praying and singing with many people, but there I was always alone."

He paused, caught in some far-off memory. "You know, I want to live in England one day," Hinga said. "Do you think that would be possible?"

"All things are possible, General," said Danny. "I would never have thought Sierra Leone would have peace. But here I am."

The general laughed his booming laugh again.

"Yes, Mr. Kellerman, that is the right attitude. We Sierra Leoneans are not all bad people, you know? You must change the world's opinion of us." He shook Danny's hand with a palm that felt dry. As dry as cold, dead bone.

IN THE CAR as they drove away Kam spoke in a fast monologue of reproach.

"That was bad, Mr. Danny. Bad," he said. "If I had known you would ask about Miss Maria I would not have brought you here. This was not the right way to go about this."

Danny looked at the Senegalese. He seemed oblivious to Maria's death.

"She's dead, Kam. Maria is dead. I want to know what happened."

Kam slowed the car to a halt and stared ahead, his hands gripping the steering wheel. When he finally spoke it was in a low tone of voice, tinged with concern.

"Of course, I know that. It was in all the newspapers. She was killed by some bandits up near Bo. They were robbers. Bad men."

"And they too are dead?"

"Government soldiers went looking for them and killed them. They were bandits. . . ."

"Before she died she wrote me a letter, Kam," Danny said. Wordlessly he fished out the letter and handed it over. Kam carefully put on a delicate pair of glasses and unfolded the paper, looking like an arcane professor examining some ancient text. His face was emotionless as he read it. Then he handed the letter back and spoke in a voice that was angry and bitter.

"Maria was a beautiful woman. She loved this country and it killed her. These people can be so crazy."

Kam spat the words out. It was moments like this that reminded Danny that Kam was as much of a foreigner here as himself. That despite his long experience, Sierra Leone had played with his head far more than any Westerner's.

"Will you help?" Danny repeated.

Kam looked at him. His face was tinged with concern.

"Of course," he said. "But Hinga is right too. Sometimes robberies just happen and good people die. We cannot help this. In this way Sierra Leone is no different from any other country in the world."

3

[2000]

IT WAS A TAP on the shoulder that had sent him to Sierra Leone for the first time. He liked to imagine, sitting later in a Freetown bar or, afterward, alone and drunk in a London pub, that it was like a finger from God coming out of the sky to change his life. But it was a tap on the shoulder. That had been all. That had been enough.

He had been at work, just sitting at his desk.

Tap, tap.

Danny had turned to see Tom Hennessey clutching a proof of a story he had just written. An exposé on arms dealers. Good work, Hennessey had said. Do you fancy a trip to Sierra Leone? The foreign desk is short-staffed at the moment and trouble is brewing. We need someone there for a few weeks.

Danny had stared at Hennessey blankly for a moment. He had been lobbying for this moment for a year, pushing and pulling his editor to send him abroad. He'd toiled in the newsroom on domestic news—the crimes of passion, the dirty politicians, the corrupt coppers—but he knew the glamour lay in the wide, wide world as a foreign correspondent. He grinned inwardly so hard it felt it would split his face. But he kept his cool. "Sierra Leone?" he said. "Sure. No problem."

How quickly lives change.

Two days later Danny was sitting on a rickety airplane on the tarmac in Abidjan, capital of the Ivory Coast, and heading to Freetown. There had been no direct flight from London to Sierra Leone and so he had to stop off in this slice of French West Africa. It was disorienting at first. Abidjan had looked like any European city, with its business parks crowned by high-rise buildings faced with reflective glass. The modernity was a surprise. Later, as he had pored over his background notes in his hotel bar, he realized Abidjan was just an illusion. A glossy façade of what lay ahead. He had printed out every cutting he could find on Sierra Leone for the past three years: wire reports, newspaper stories, TV transcripts and magazine pieces. He read them all.

It was a rapid education. Sierra Leone, like many other nations dotted along the West African coast, had been a chunk of the British Empire carved out of the bush by accident. It had washed up on the shores of the late twentieth century as an independent country when the Europeans raced to get out. At the start Sierra Leone had fared well. The country's ruling elite were Krios, the descendants of freed slaves brought back from the Americas by the British. They lorded over a population of native Africans from more than twenty different tribes, who resented their rulers with their British-style manners and names like Wilson, Stevens and Smith. Then it went wrong. By the end of the 1980s a disillusioned colonel called Foday Sankoh formed the Revolutionary United Front. With little or no political ideology, the RUF became a vehicle for Sankoh's personal goals. It took over Sierra Leone's inland diamond mines and recruited members by brutalizing the children of its victims. Its calling card was the "long sleeves or short sleeves" method of cutting off people's arms: short sleeves were above the elbow; long sleeves were above the wrist. Young boys were forced to kill their own families and then join. Their crimes meant they could never go back to their villages. The RUF became their only way of survival.

Danny felt his throat grow dry. He could not imagine the brutality. He read on.

The RUF looted Freetown in 1997 after a military coup. The next year a force of Nigerian-led peacekeepers arrived but they too looted the city, and a year later the RUF attacked again. By the time the United Nations negotiated a peace accord much of Freetown was in ruins, two million people had been made homeless and tens of thousands had died.

But the long nightmare was nowhere near being over. Sankoh had accepted a handful of ministerial posts in a unity government and moved into a Freetown mansion. But he had also whispered word into the bush that the struggle was not over. The RUF had reached for their machetes again. As Sankoh swaggered around the ruins of Freetown, his boy soldiers inched closer atrocity by atrocity and the power of the government shrank like a puddle drying in the African sun. Freetown was helpless, like a rape victim lying bloodied in a gutter, purse stolen, skirt torn, waiting for the final blow.

Later, as Danny's plane began to trundle down the runway at Abidjan, heading to Freetown and its unknown citizens, he remembered the words of a young Kenyan BBC journalist he had met on the flight coming over from London. She was a veteran of covering Sierra Leone, and she had spotted him as a first-timer. "Relax," she said. "The people there are just lovely . . . when they are not hacking each other to bits."

It had been an attempt at gallows humor to initiate him into the club of journalists heading off to cover the unfolding tragedy. He smiled and relished the casual way one could put danger aside with dark humor. But as he put his notes away and the plane began to heave itself into the air, he saw the ground falling away beneath him. Within two hours he would be in Freetown.

THE FIRST THING Danny ever felt in Sierra Leone was a blast of hot, humid air rushing into the plane like an oven had just been opened. One of the plane's pilots, in a thick Russian accent, had clambered back and opened the cabin door.

Danny descended onto the tarmac and blinked in bright sunshine. He could feel a thin film of sweat already breaking out on his skin. A swarm of men in ragged uniforms had opened a door hatch in the plane's belly and were hauling out luggage, like they were gutting a giant bird. Danny was relieved to see his suitcase standing on the ground. He picked it up and found himself next to the BBC journalist.

"How do I get into town?" he asked, suddenly aware he had no clue where he was. She looked up from carefully counting out a pile of silver metal cases packed with equipment.

"Freetown doesn't have an airport of its own. From here you just need to get on the chopper and fly into Freetown. You'll see the signs after you go through customs."

Danny laughed.

"You mean you have to actually catch a flight to get in and out of the airport? That's crazy."

"Well, you could go by car. But given the road is controlled by the RUF, I wouldn't really recommend it if you want to keep your arms attached to your body."

With that she plunged into the seething mass of passengers. Danny dragged his suitcase across the tarmac in the direction of a dilapidated terminal. He walked down a corridor past a rusted and long-defunct baggage carousel and then saw a sign advertising the helicopter shuttle to Freetown. Sixty dollars and ten minutes later Danny found himself inside an old UN chopper. People sat on the floor, clutching their luggage, and scrunched together down the sides. Danny was squeezed onto half a seat next to a Middle Eastern–looking man dressed in a well-cut black suit, his sunglasses proudly bearing a designer name.

"Nice shades," Danny said. The man turned to look at him and for a moment Danny wondered if he didn't speak English.

"The best Italy has to offer," he eventually replied.

"I'm Danny Kellerman. I work for a British newspaper, *The Statesman.*"

"Pleased to meet you, Danny Kellerman," the man said in a tone of voice that suggested the opposite.

"Do you live here?" Danny persisted.

"For most of the time."

"What do you do?"

The man regarded Danny for a moment, weighing up the unexpected interrogation.

"I do business."

His tone was abrupt but Danny did not care. He was excited. "This is my first time here," Danny said. "It's my first time in Africa, in fact."

The man spat out a surprised laugh. Then he took off his sunglasses with theatrical effect. He was smiling now.

"You are kidding me," he said. "Your editor sent you to Freetown for your first time in Africa?"

The man let out a long sigh.

"This isn't a safari in Kenya, you know? The last lions here got killed one hundred years ago," he said.

The man chuckled to himself.

"You must have pissed someone off in your newspaper. Or fucked the wrong person. Tell me, Danny Kellerman, did you fuck your editor's wife?"

Ice had been broken and the conversation was now open and engaging.

"Actually, it was kind of a reward," Danny said.

"I don't believe this," the man answered with mock indignation. "You have been had, my friend. Someone in your newspaper wants you dead and you don't even know it. Come on, tell me, who did you fuck?"

As the man spoke the helicopter engines started to whir and the machine began to haul itself from the ground, battling gravity like some pregnant insect. The man barely noticed, raising his voice as the deafening engines threatened to drown him out.

"This country is really screwed, you know?" the man shouted above the noise without breaking stride.

"Sankoh wants it all and he's going to grab it. It's okay for me. I'll always be fine. RUF and Sankoh or President Kabbah and his crooks. Who cares? I just deal with the winner. But it's these poor bastards I feel sorry for." The man gestured at the Africans on the floor of the chopper, crowded with their bulging bags of clothes and food.

"You really think the RUF are going to try and take over?" Danny asked casually, trying to appear as unconcerned as his new friend.

The man nodded.

"They haven't fought a war for ten years to settle for crumbs from the table," he said. "Besides, what do they have to lose? One more round of looting is probably all those boys in the bush have to look forward to."

The man leaned into Danny, dropping his voice so it did not carry to the other passengers.

"I've been all over Africa," he said. "And there's one way to judge if a country is in trouble. Is the brewery closed? I've been in the deepest bits of the Congo and they always had beer. That Primus may be shit, it may kill you if you drink two bottles, but they still make it. That country will be okay."

Danny looked at the man. He could not tell if he was being serious.

"How's the brewery in Freetown?" Danny asked.

The man let out a belly laugh.

"That brewery's been shut for two years, man. The RUF burnt it down. You're going to be drinking imported Heineken right up until they cut your hands off."

Danny looked out of the window as the man talked further. He monologued on Freetown's recent troubles and his own "business," which remained undefined and profitable but never quite profitable enough. He still did not give his name but revealed he was a Lebanese, a relic of the French Empire that had once ruled most of West Africa. Outside the window the helicopter danced about one hundred feet over the wave tops of the wide bay that separated Freetown from Lunghi. He could see a long chain of mountains that curled out into the sea like a reproachful finger. Freetown's ramshackle sprawl crawled along the shore, climbing the hills and straddling the gaps between the peaks. Below him he glimpsed little canoes dotted on the choppy waters, packed, like the helicopter, with people and baggage. The tiny craft were going to and from the airport by open sea. It looked terrifying, with the waves roiling high above the frail dugouts. But if the road was held by the RUF, he supposed there was no other way.

Then they were upon the city. For the second time that day Danny emerged blinking into sunlight and chaos. He looked for the Lebanese, hoping to at least get a name and maybe a business card, but the man was already gone. Danny grabbed for his luggage and tried to walk out of the crowd that had surged against the helicopter, but it only got deeper, a sea of faces pressing up against him, tugging at his shirt, trying to grab his bag.

"Mister, mister. Need a car?"

"Need a driver, mister?"

Danny kept walking. But he could make no progress. He stopped and put up his hands when suddenly someone grabbed his shoulder. He turned to see the Lebanese.

"Jesus. I turn my back for a few seconds and you are already surrounded by hostile natives. Freetown's gonna eat you alive, man."

Danny was being jostled one way and the other. Arms and hands that seemed unattached to faces or bodies were all over him. The Lebanese dragged him forward and Danny found himself in front of a tall African, thin and wiry with a very dark skin. He was leaning on a beaten-up blue car and wearing a tatty pair of faded jeans, his white shirt unbuttoned to the navel.

"Kam, my friend," the Lebanese called, "I have a client for you. He's a journalist from London. Take him to the Cape Sierra and get him a room. Look after him for a few days, would you?"

The tall man bent down and picked up his suitcase.

"I am Kam," he said. "I will be your driver."

"Kam will sort you out," the Lebanese said. "He's the best driver in Freetown." With that he was gone again.

Danny decided to go with the flow. He did not believe the Lebanese man or this new stranger, Kam, meant him any harm. He pushed any worries to one side and followed Kam into the car. He tugged at the door, which seemed stuck. Kam reached over and with a heave shoved it open. Kam shot him a relaxed and easy smile. For a country on the brink of extinction, Danny thought, everyone seems more than friendly.

"I take you to Cape Sierra now. Best hotel for journalists," Kam said. The car pulled out and Kam slammed dramatically into top gear, scattering a handful of people crowding around the gate to the helipad. With a grinding of gears and screech of tires, the car hit the streets of Freetown and swept Danny with it.

THE CAPE SIERRA HOTEL lay on a small island, reached only by two causeways at the very tip of Freetown. The island had once been the center of the country's tourism industry and huge hotels dotted its sides, curving around a perfect crescent moon of white sand. Nearly all of the hotels were decaying hulks, their windows long gone and their lobbies home to squatters. But the Cape Sierra was still alive. Kam hustled Danny inside and raged at the desk clerk until Danny was soon sitting in an air-conditioned suite. Kam watched him unpack and then told Danny he would see him the next morning at eight o'clock after breakfast. Kam left no room for disagreement and Danny did not offer any.

When the Senegalese was gone Danny felt a strong urge for company and a drink. He descended back to the lobby and followed a low hubbub of voices until he walked into a room he guessed was the hotel bar. It had a counter at one end from behind which a man dressed in a white uniform fished cold cans of beer out of an icebox. The room was brightly lit by neon lights and in one corner a television set was tuned to CNN. Clustered in groups around tables piled high with beer cans were a motley collection of men. They were mainly white and looked ex-military. Their hair was short and their thick bodies betrayed muscular pasts only slightly gone to seed with middle age. Security consultants, Danny thought. Mercenaries, really. It was men like these, recruited for a hefty fee, who had saved the government two years ago when the RUF had last tried to take over.

"Can I get a beer?" Danny said to the man at the icebox.

A can of Heineken appeared on the counter.

"Do you have anything local?" Danny asked.

The barman laughed.

"No, sir. The brewery is closed."

Danny wiped the can across his brow, feeling the chilled metal against his skin. He took a deep swig and looked around the bar. He noticed another group of people sitting around a table a few feet away. They were a mix of men and women and clearly not mercenaries. Aid workers, Danny supposed. They too had amassed impressive pyramids of drink cans. Conversation was loud and the laughter raucous. He drank in the exotic scene. He grinned to himself. This was like the *Star Wars* bar, he thought. The noise continued unabated.

Slowly, however, the room became aware of urgent words drifting out of the television set. One of the aid workers turned up the volume. CNN was halfway through a report on the Sierra Leone crisis. The noise in the bar dulled as a blond CNN correspondent appeared on-screen, standing in front of what looked like a government army checkpoint.

At that moment a can of beer sailed across the room and struck the TV. It splashed foamy liquid over the set and roars of laughter came from one of the tables of mercenaries. A huge man got up and took an exaggerated bow.

"Freddie, you are such a cunt." One of the other men laughed in a gruff voice straight from Lancashire.

"Such a prick is more like it," came another voice, female, this time its twang from America.

The woman's words echoed across the bar. Danny looked in the direction of the aid workers' table. A young woman sat there, her black hair pulled tightly back framing an oval face. She sat with one quizzical eyebrow raised and a smile on her lips. The mercenary was less amused. He began to walk over to the woman's table. Her four friends shifted uncomfortably. The man stood over six feet tall, with arms that bore an array of fading, inky tattoos. The woman, however, did not flinch.

"Leave it, Freddie," one of the mercenaries called over. But the man kept walking. He bore down on the table and the woman suddenly stood up. She stared him straight in the eye and began to speak.

"Before you ask me to 'say that again,' Freddie, I'll save you the trouble and spell it out to you," she said, her voice dripping with aggression and scorn. "I know all about you, Freddie. And if you think I haven't got some friends in the government who wouldn't terminate your little work contract at my say-so, then think again."

She paused for effect. To let the words sink in.

"Now why don't you sit back down, drink another beer and shut up like the good little child killer you are."

The man stood statue still. The woman spoke again.

"Go on. Fuck off," she said.

The man loomed over the woman, dwarfing her. But there wasn't a flicker of nerves about her. Freddie seemed to be weighing his options, rattled by the unexpected threat. His nostrils flared with anger, like some gigantic bull staring at a matador, at first puzzled and then afraid of the swirling red cloak.

Then from nowhere a man appeared in a pressed black jacket. A shiny badge on his lapel identified him as the bar manager. Deftly, and clearly after many years of practice, he took Freddie's elbow and steered him full circle.

"Mr. Freddie," he said. "Time for more drinks. On the house. No need for fighting, just drinking."

Freddie allowed himself to be led away but not before turning his head over his shoulder.

"Bitch," he muttered, and then stalked back to his table to a deafening round of laughs and insults.

The woman, meanwhile, looked back to her companions.

"More drinks?" she said as if nothing had happened. She walked to the bar.

Danny looked at her properly for the first time. She had olive skin and a button nose tucked below a pair of brown eyes. He felt he saw a faint flush in her cheeks, perhaps the only visible hint of what had just happened.

"You've got balls," he said, and instantly regretted it. Idiot.

"Excuse me?" she said, turning to him without amusement.

"Sorry. That came out wrong," Danny said. "That guy seemed like a real bastard. Who is he?"

"Everyone knows Freddie," she said. "Freddie the Fijian? He flies a helicopter gunship for the government. It's about the only reason the RUF isn't here yet and joining us for drinks in the hotel."

"Ah. I'm sorry. I only arrived today. I hadn't realized he was a local celebrity."

The woman's brow darkened.

"He's a murderer, just like the rest of those mercenaries. At the moment, we need them, but I don't have to like it and I can't stand their dumb behavior in bars. They act like British soccer hooligans."

Danny wondered if the woman had recognized his English accent. She ordered four beers and there was silence as the barman fished for them in the icebox. He looked at her. He could not help it, running his eyes over her face, straining not to let them go any lower. There was something instantly magnetic about her. She felt his gaze and looked at him.

"I'm Danny Kellerman," Danny said, bereft of anything better to say. "I work for *The Statesman*. It's a British newspaper."

She nodded.

"Ah, a journalist," she said. "You're fresh off the boat and come to look at our little war. You're just what we need. More spectators."

"I wouldn't put it quite like that," he said.

"How would you put it?"

But even as the question left her mouth she was scooping up the beers and starting to walk back to the table.

"Hang on," Danny said, thinking better of grabbing her elbow. "What's your name? I'm Danny Kellerman. You're . . . who? It's only polite to tell me your name once I have asked and I know you don't like rude behavior in bars. You just said so."

The woman stopped. She gave out a little laugh. Danny felt a light come on in his world.

"Dumb behavior. I said I don't like dumb behavior in bars. Rudeness is just fine with me." She turned again to go back to her friends but not before she looked back and said: "Maria. My name is Maria."

4

[2004]

DANNY STOOD ON Lumley Beach near the Cape Sierra and watched the sun sink toward the horizon. A few hundred yards away a cloud of white seagulls swarmed around fishermen dragging a net from the sea. He could hear their shouts mingling with the sharp cries of the gulls as they tried to steal the catch, ignoring the waving arms trying to keep them away.

He had paused in front of a collapsed mass of concrete walls. He had come here once with Maria during the war. Four long years ago. They had sought out this spot in the shadow of what had once been a beach bar but was now rubble and rusted steel. He was perversely pleased to see the ruin was as they had last seen it. There was no re-building this lovers' bed.

He stood here now like a stranger. Like everywhere else, he felt he had never been here before though his eyes spotted a familiar sight at every turn. What sort of trouble were you in, Maria? What happened to you? They were empty questions. His mind did not want to think of her last moments. The fear and the realization the robbers meant to kill her. He only hoped it had been swift. Instinctively he shied away from thinking about it. There was nothing to be gained from going down that path. He concentrated again on their time on Lumley Beach, lounging in the ruin of a shattered café, drinking bad French wine in the middle of a war zone and making love in the soft sand.

Suddenly he felt his mobile vibrate in his pocket. Its ring brought him back to his real life, as did the number flashing on its face. It was Rachel.

"It's good to hear from you," he said.

Suddenly he knew he was telling the truth. He felt a strange mixture of guilt and relief at her voice and he sat down on the sand, feeling the firmness beneath him, drawing a comfort from its solidity.

"Hey, you. It's lovely to hear your voice too," Rachel said. Her tone was soft as usual, but Danny sensed there was something harder behind it too. He knew he should have called her earlier.

"I was going to call you this evening," he lied.

"Good. I was hoping to hear from you soon," she said. "But I'm going out a bit later and wanted to speak to you before I left. How are things over there?"

"Fine," he said. Then he winced internally. "Fine" was a word that covered a multitude of sins. No one ever said things were fine when they actually were fine.

"Everything is fine," Danny repeated. He could not help himself.

"The country's changed, it's really changed a lot and it looks to be getting better. I had tea with a bona fide army general this morning. It was . . ."

His voice trailed off. It was hard to describe his encounter with Hinga and his sullen band of soldiers. He did not know how to deal with the implied threat to stop asking questions and to let the dead rest. Or at least to ignore their pleas.

"It was . . . interesting," he said halfheartedly.

"What about your friend? Did you find anything out about her?"

Danny knew this was Rachel's way of probing a little, trying to get a feel for what was really going on, expressing that she was worried and feeling threatened. Danny felt a brief flash of anger despite his efforts to control it. Maria was dead, for Christ's sake. She was not going to steal him away.

"I'm still finding my bearings. I've got a lot of work to do," he said as casually as he could.

Rachel was quiet for a moment and Danny could feel her summoning up her feelings back in their Highgate living room, fiddling with her hair. Here it comes. . . .

"I spoke to your dad this morning," she said finally. "He sounded terrible. He also said you two had had a fight the other day."

Ah, of course. It had to be about Dad. The disappointment in Rachel's voice was obvious and for a moment he felt guilty that he had told her an easy lie. There was no getting away from how much Rachel loved Harry. Like so many others she overlooked his politics, and his personal life, for the enjoyment of another gin and tonic and an absurd tale he'd probably made up the day before. "It's just Harry being Harry" was practically a catchphrase of Rachel's. Danny felt bad now. He'd led her on with his line about them having a good time, when instead they had embarked on yet another slanging match.

"He didn't even know you had gone to Sierra Leone, Danny. When were you going to tell him? This will only make his health worse."

"Sorry, sorry, I completely forgot," Danny said. He knew it sounded unconvincing. He also knew she didn't believe it. Why on earth would she?

"I wish you two would get along. I lost my dad and I know how much it can hurt to have regrets when they're gone."

Rachel's own father had passed away when she was a teenager, getting sick and dying within a brief, traumatic year with skin cancer. Rachel had poured herself into looking after her younger siblings, even as she had desperately mourned. Years later Harry would become a new father figure for Rachel, and Danny knew she meant well, but now wasn't the time. "Look, I've got to go. I'll call you tomorrow," he said, sounding more snippy than he intended.

"We need to talk, Danny," she said.

"Tomorrow. We'll talk tomorrow."

"Fine" came Rachel's reply, whispered down the line. Danny stung at her use of the dreaded word. "No, wait. I mean . . . ," Danny began. He thought of a thousand things he should say but they all seemed to logjam in his mouth and instead he had only silence. He started to mouth the word "sorry" but the dial tone was already droning in his ear.

THAT NIGHT he told Kam he wanted to dine at Alex's, a Lebanese restaurant almost opposite the Cape Sierra. It had been one of the few places to stay open all through the war. Every trouble spot in the world had somewhere like Alex's. A place where the expensive drink and fine foods kept flowing even in the darkest moments. As they pulled up he saw the place was half empty. It had always been full four years ago, but tonight only a handful of people clustered around the tables and a few lonely men sat at the bar. He turned to Kam and asked him to join him. The Senegalese shook his head.

"Are you seeing a girlfriend?" Danny asked. He knew Kam had a little network of local shebeens where he took his harem, splashing some dollars around to pose as the Big Man; places where a bit of foreign currency could make one seem like a king.

"No, Mr. Danny. I have been busy so much that I have been neglecting all of my ladies. Soon I shall be a single man again if I am not more respectful to them."

Danny let it slide that for Kam being single only meant being married but with no other women on the side.

"Join me, then."

"I have some jobs to do," he said, and then added, by way of explanation, "I have some driving to do for a client who it is better not to refuse."

"Gbamanja? Or some other ex-RUF?" Danny asked. He felt irritated. He knew the attractions of money. He knew the spiel about moving on from the past. But how could Kam work for those people? Kam tried to laugh.

"It is just a driving job. But, yes, it is for Minister Gbamanja. As I said, he is not a man who it is good to refuse."

Danny got out of the car and Kam drove away. Four years ago, in the middle of war, Kam had been unflappable, a master of his chaotic domain who despised the warmongers ruining the country. Now, at peace, there was a secretive side to him, a deference to those now in power. It seemed prosperity had brought a different set of survival skills.

He turned and walked into Alex's and sat at the bar. He looked around at the scattered guests, a mix of Africans, Lebanese, Indians and Western businessmen. There was a hum of conversation only interrupted by the flitting presence of a half dozen or so young women dressed in short skirts or figure-hugging trousers. Every five minutes one would approach the single men, or if they were feeling optimistic, they sidled up to a table. They were looking for business. But tonight the heat seemed to be getting to everyone. Each sally ended with the woman returning to the pack, like listless predators, to chatter and giggle, sipping at Cokes laden with ice.

Danny ordered a beer and some lamb chops and fought off the approach of one of the women with as much grace as he could muster. The meal arrived and he picked lazily at the meat. It was the beer he really craved. It cooled him down and created a comforting blankness he could sink into, unfeeling and unthinking. He had felt out of sorts all day, doubts nagging at his mind, and fear too. He could not work out if Hinga had been threatening him or merely angry. He was confused by Kam too. Now the beer gave him a sense of place again.

He ordered another drink—the last one, he told himself—and then noticed a man take the stool next to him. He was a tall white man, wearing the sort of cream-colored cotton suit that people associated with European tourists in the tropics. It was baggy on his lean frame and had clearly seen regular wear and tear. If this man was fresh off the boat, then it had been a long sea journey.

The beer may have made Danny stare too long as the man caught his eye. His face was surprisingly young and his sudden smile warm and friendly.

"New in town?" he asked.

The voice was not English, as Danny had expected. It was American, well spoken and polite, with the gentle burr of the Midwest hiding behind clipped East Coast vowels.

"No, not really," Danny said, and then thought better of it. "Well, actually, yes. I've been here before though. Four years ago. But a lot has changed."

The man's grin stretched wider and he laughed.

"It sure has. Sierra Leone's on the way back, you know."

Danny shook the man's proffered hand and he introduced himself as an American diplomat, Harvey Benson. He'd been here for two years, straight from a posting in the Central Asian republics. He called them the "Stans" in a way that Danny usually hated but with this man it was endearing, charming even. Harvey was clearly enthusiastic about the country in a way Danny began to find touching. He seemed to know all the main players, name-dropping meetings with President Kabbah into his spiel. More drinks were bought with an almost imperceptible wave of a hand toward the barman. A few other men and women dropped by and Harvey greeted them. But he stuck with Danny, unwaveringly returning to his conversation and using him as an audience for what felt like a sales pitch for Sierra Leone.

"Diamonds will make this country, Danny," Harvey was saying now. "They almost broke it during the war. But they can make it now. I believe that. The potential wealth is incredible. If we can just harness that into doing something good for the country, in rebuilding it, instead of lining the pockets of a few. Imagine it, a rich Sierra Leone. We could all take a lesson from that, couldn't we?"

Danny was nodding. He was feeling bleary eyed now. He realized that the thin line between drinking a lot and drinking too much had been crossed. Harvey mistook Danny's drunkenness for boredom.

"Sorry. I can't help going on about it. I know this is just a little corner of Africa, but I'm really taken with the place. The people are just so amazing, so full of life, and when you think of all the terrible things they have been through and still they just keep on going. Fantastic. Things really are happening here at last." He paused again, regarding Danny with a smile. Perhaps now he had recognized he was in the presence of a drunk.

"Anyway, look, I talk too much. What about you? We don't get many reporters these days. Your tribe seems to just follow the wars. We're a peace story now. That officially makes us boring, or didn't anyone tell you that?"

Harvey put on a face of mock concern.

"Hang on, you don't know something I don't, do you? Things aren't about to go bad?"

Harvey had the innocent easygoingness of an instant friend, and with Kam off doing God knows what, Danny felt he needed someone like that right now.

"Actually, I'm here because a friend of mine was killed," he said. "Maria Tirado. She was an aid worker. The press reports have all said it was a robbery but I wanted to make sure."

Harvey looked puzzled.

"Maria Tirado? My God, I am so sorry. That was terrible. We dealt with it at the embassy. It was a nightmare to have to tell her family. But this country is still poor. Robberies will always happen, especially up in diamond country."

Harvey put a hand on his shoulder and squeezed it slightly.

"I know that doesn't make it much easier."

Harvey did not appear to be in the least bit drunk, but Danny was starting to lose it. He shrugged off his grip. He wanted to rage at the American, tell him: It wasn't just a robbery. She was in trouble. She wrote me a letter. She wanted my help. He started to get up, but as he did so he slipped slightly on his stool. Harvey caught him by the elbow. Suddenly, all Danny wanted to do was go back to Ali's house.

"I think I had better go," Danny said, swaying on feet that felt strangely distant. "I've had at least one beer too many."

Harvey steadied him.

"I'm really sorry about your friend," he said, "but I am sure I can help you out while you are here. I know a lot of people in the government. Let me set up a few meetings. Show you around some of the real players. Your trip won't be wasted. I'll get you a story about Sierra Leone."

Danny nodded his thanks. Great, he thought. What favors did Harvey owe around town? Danny was about to be a source of currency for him too. Just like for Kam. He scrawled his mobile number on a napkin anyway and watched the messy handwriting emerge from the pen as if it were not his own. Harvey smiled indulgently, suppressing a chuckle.

"That beer is strong stuff, especially in this climate. When they reopened the brewery they upped the alcohol content," he said as Danny staggered toward the door.

"I'll be in touch."

Danny barely heard Harvey's last words. He stumbled out of Alex's and was dimly aware of a slightly built figure helping him into a cab. He sat in the rear and tilted his head backward, trying to ignore the swerving of the car as it darted through the streets and began to climb up to Hill Station. It pulled up outside Ali's villa and he stumbled out, handing over a fistful of Sierra Leonean currency to the driver. Danny walked into his bedroom and lay down, waiting for the room to stop spinning. He needed to ground himself. He looked over to the bedside table onto which he had put Maria's letter. Reading it gave him a sense of purpose and calm, like repeating a mantra. Or a prayer. It dispelled doubt about his actions. He reached out and then stopped cold.

Someone had moved it.

Or he thought they had.

Through his befuddled mind he stared at the wilted note of paper lying faceup on the desk and swore that he had laid it there folded up. He always folded it to hide its contents. But now its print was open and visible to the world. Was he being paranoid? Nothing else in the room seemed different. He got up, steadying himself against a wall, and walked out of the villa to where the gate sentry stood, smoking a cigarette, the lit nub glowing like a coal in the dark.

"Has anyone been here tonight?" he asked.

The sentry looked offended, as if Danny were questioning his job.

"No one here. No strangers. Just George."

"Are you sure?"

"Just George," he said, and then added, "And Kam. He came an hour ago to pick something up. But no strangers, boss."

Danny retreated back into the villa. He was being paranoid. He knew it. Hinga had freaked him out. This whole situation had freaked him out. He folded the letter and placed it in his wallet. He would not leave it lying around again. It would remain by his side, close to his body. He tried to get up, to get undressed at least. But it was a losing battle, a struggle against booze and exhaustion he could not win. He surrendered to sleep, closing his eyes on a world grown confused.

THE NEXT MORNING Kam was once again already there when Danny dazedly, and nursing a crushing headache, tumbled into Ali's kitchen. But this time Kam was not alone. Sitting at the table, cup frozen in mid-lift to his lips, was a well-built African man in a bright green military uniform. He was clean shaven, his hair cropped close to his skull and his face chiseled like an ebony statue. A peaked cap, with an elaborate silver badge on the front, was placed in front of him. The man rose and Danny noticed the blue UN logo sewn on to his right-hand shoulder.

A look of brief distress crossed Kam's face as he saw Danny's disheveled state, but he recovered himself.

"This is Major Oluwasegun. He is with the Nigerian contingent of UNSAMIL," he said to Danny.

Danny stared at him blankly. Why had Kam brought this man here? He braced himself to endure painful conversation about the ins and outs of the UN's mission in the new Sierra Leone. Kam sensed Danny's confusion.

"Major Oluwasegun is a friend of mine," Kam said. Here we go, thought Danny. Then what Kam said next hit him like a splash of cold water in the face.

"It was men from his unit who found Maria," he said.

Danny sat down. Whatever Kam had been doing last night, it had not just been running errands for Gbamanja. It had certainly been more useful than getting drunk and maudlin down at Alex's. He felt a pang of embarrassment and shame as the memory of his suspicions about Maria's letter being moved came flooding back. Ridiculous. Kam had come up with the goods. If anyone was working to find out the truth about what happened to Maria, it was Kam.

Danny blurted a good morning. Major Oluwasegun looked a little uncomfortable.

"Mr. Kellerman," he began, "I do not know that I can help. But Kam tells me that you and Miss Tirado were close friends and so I said I would meet you and tell you what my men found on that day."

"Please call me Danny," Danny said.

The major visibly stiffened.

"I mean no disrespect, Mr. Kellerman," he said, "but I am a soldier of the Nigerian Republic on active service and you are a civilian. Even meeting you is against regulations, but I gave my word to Kam that I would do it. So here I am."

"And I thank you," said Danny. He began to recognize the type.

Amid the chaos of Africa, especially in its armies, there were always men like Major Oluwasegun. Men who reacted to the bedlam by imposing order, to the corruption with morality, to the rule breaking with obedience. They stuck out like tall flowers in the grass, and like tall flowers, they usually got cut down.

"My men were stationed on the road between Freetown and Bo. One of my patrols was coming back to base when some villagers flagged them down. They said there had been an accident and some foreigners had been killed. They followed them back down the road and found a vehicle. It looked as if it had crashed, perhaps after the tires had been shot. It was difficult to tell."

"Why?" butted in Danny.

The major stopped and glanced again at Kam in annoyance. Oluwasegun was not used to being interrupted.

"It had been set on fire. My men then radioed back to base. I set out to meet them after informing my own commanding officer. When I found them, it was as they said. The vehicle was burnt and they found the victims in a clearing about fifty yards from the road. There was your friend, Miss Tirado, and her three companions. They had all been shot."

The major stopped and swallowed. Whatever image was in his head, of the bodies lying in the bush, bloodied and mangled, it was not a welcome one.

"May the Lord rest their souls," he said.

"What happened then?"

"It is not our job to investigate such criminal things. I made sure the local police were informed and I wrote up the incident in my daily report. It was a sad day. I have been in this country for one year, Mr. Kellerman, and I have seen many bad things. The Devil has been at work here for a long time and he keeps us busy every day. But I had not yet seen such a pointless thing as this. My area was meant to be a quiet one. For six months we had had no reports of such bandits and then this happened."

He paused for a long moment. His voice lost some of its military order. Danny noticed for the first time that he wore a large golden cross on a chain around his neck. The major was touching it as he began to talk again.

"I was not born a man of God, Mr. Kellerman, but I became one as a child," he began. He had grown up in Yoruba land, he said. It was a small place, just another dirt-poor village at the end of a muddy track in the bush. His father had been the local headman and he was his eldest son and so, unlike his many brothers and sisters, he had gone to school at the church of a local missionary. An American man. A good man.

"Father Weissmuller was from a city called Cincinnati," Oluwasegun said. "I imagine it is very different from my home village. But Father Weissmuller taught me that we all worship the same God. I believe very strongly in that God. He guides me in my life. But sometimes . . . I do not understand His purpose."

He looked pained.

"The men who killed those people—who killed your friend—were without God," he said. "When I heard that the army had killed them, I rejoiced. The Lord did not tolerate such evil to go unpunished."

Danny looked at the major.

"Major, did you know if Maria was in trouble of any kind? Had she angered anyone in Freetown, made any enemies?"

The major slowly shook his head.

"Miss Tirado lived for her work, her children's home. There were some who thought she should not be looking after such children, many of them were RUF, little killers. But no one would be hurt because of it."

There was a silence that seemed to last long minutes. Then Major Oluwasegun stood up to leave.

"I have told you what I know and I think that you will find out little more than this. From what I hear, Miss Tirado was a very good lady. She loved this country and did good works here. Her soul will be in heaven."

From the look Major Oluwasegun now shot Danny, he could tell that the major had a very firm opinion as to where Danny's soul was headed. It was not to keep Maria company. The major turned to Kam.

"I shall walk back to town," he announced. "The exercise will be good for me."

Kam showed the major out of the villa and returned to find Danny pouring himself a cup of coffee. Before he could berate Danny for his hungover appearance, Danny interjected first.

"Where did you find him?" he asked.

"Kam knows everyone. He is a strange man, the major. He seems to be so straight that he can hardly bend over. He wants people to think he even shits standing up." Kam laughed. "But I am not so sure."

Danny frowned. "What do you mean?"

Kam sat down on a chair and put his legs up on the table. He scratched his chin, as if thinking.

"The Nigerians in his command are not a good lot. This country has been ruled by whoever had the biggest guns, and those Nigerians have a lot of weapons. They have a lot of girls too; they deal a lot of drugs. They even smuggle people. You know, trafficking. Some of it people who want to go, some of them not so willing. Then we have the major. He comes in with all his pious talk. But Kam is not so sure."

Kam shrugged.

"If he doesn't know what his men are up to, then for sure he'll be going back to Lagos soon. Or he'll end up dead in a ditch."

Danny ran a hand through his hair. His head hurt afresh and it was not just the impact of the night before. He did not know where to look anymore. No one seemed straight.

"He doesn't seem to think there was anything unusual about what happened," Danny said.

Kam shrugged.

"He says he is a man who just reports what he sees."

"How do you know him?"

"Some of my girls know some of his men. The major tolerates me because he says he cares for my soul. He says he wants to save this poor Muslim from going to hell. But we are two sides of the same coin. I think I can save him if I can persuade him to have a drink. So far, it seems, neither of us has had any luck. But it would not surprise me if the major had a little fun on the side. No one can be that honest. Not in this country."

Danny didn't know what to think. If the major was merely acting the Christian straight man, then he was very good. He felt sure he had not been faking disgust at Danny's morning appearance. After all, the man was a teetotaler and Danny could feel the stale sweat of alcohol coming out of his own pores. He did not like the major, but he believed him.

He sat and thought. First Harvey Benson, now Major Oluwasegun. They both said the same thing. Maria was killed in a robbery: plain and simple. He looked at Kam and suspected that the Senegalese thought so too. On some level he could feel a weight beginning to lift off his shoulders. What if that letter was not as sinister as it looked? What if Maria's death was just an accident? Fuck it, he thought. He was still here to get a story.

"Take me around town, Kam. Let's take a look at the presidential palace. Speak to any friends you have over there," he said.

Kam looked pleased.

"If we see Major Oluwasegun on the way, we can wave at him from the car as we go past. That son of a bitch always thinks he's too good to drive with Kam," he said.

5

THE NEXT FEW DAYS passed in a lethargic haze, a fuzz of nothingness drowned in thick, wet heat. Ali remained up-country and his cousin George had no idea where he had gone or with whom he was doing business. He had little to say when Danny asked about Ali's possible return: "Maybe today. Maybe next week. Ali will call when he has finished."

In the meantime Kam promised to find more people to talk to about Maria's death, and in return Danny agreed to meet some of Sierra Leone's new elite: a merry-go-round of minor officials sipping tea over their desks and listening to them mouth their platitudes. All the while Kam hovered in the background, nodding enthusiastically. He was building up a lot of favors.

But for Danny the parade of barren offices, tattered desks and chipped china cups blurred into one. The men he met—and they were all men—seemed blinded by the light of peace. No one seemed to know anything about Maria's death. It was a terrible accident, they insisted, shaking their heads at the tragedy of it before reverting back to whatever speech Danny had interrupted.

But elsewhere Danny noticed real change. New businesses sprang up in the ruins of office blocks. Lodging houses opened in villas. European families sunbathed on Lumley Beach. Sierra Leone was awake after a long nightmare. It was hardly a boomtown, but it was a faltering step in the right direction.

Danny spent evenings alone in Ali's villa, draining his drinks cabinet for help in getting to sleep. Ali kept a spectacular collection of single malts, but Danny assiduously kept to the cheap stuff. He had not been back to Alex's since he had met Harvey, though the American had left several messages on his phone, wanting to meet for a sober lunch. Danny ignored them. He felt Freetown was sucking the energy out of him, though whether it was depression or just the climate, he could not tell.

When his mobile loudly rang, as he fixed himself yet another evening drink, he expected to see Harvey's number flash up for the third time that day. But it wasn't him. It was a call from Britain. For a moment he thought he would ignore it and when he heard the voice on the end of the line, he was filled with regret at having answered. It was his father.

"Hello, Daniel," he said.

Instantly, Danny's hackles raised like hair standing on end at the approach of a summer storm.

"Hi, Dad," he said brusquely. He let the air die between them. He felt childish, embarrassed almost, by this instant hostility. Yet he could not help it, could not drag himself out of this pattern. Or he was too tired to even try.

"How are you?" his father said with a weary resignation at sensing his son's tone.

"Fine," Danny replied.

"Are you all right?" his dad said, ignoring Danny's baiting. That was unlike him. "I called Rachel last night for a chat," he continued. "I think she's worried about you. She's scared about you gallivanting around God knows where in search of God knows what."

This was the universal way of fathers. Their sons' girlfriends worried. Their mothers did too. But fathers: never. They masked their concerns with the fears of surrogates. Lest they appeared to actually care.

"Honestly, Dad. I'm fine. It's good to be back here. I think I needed to get out of London, have a break," he said.

"I am not sure traipsing off to some hellhole in Africa is much of a break. I prefer a weekend in Malta. The natives are a damn sight friendlier," his father replied.

His father's tone was jokey now. The familiar old comic routine. It irritated Danny as much as Rachel loved it. But Danny could sense his father desperately did not want a fight and suddenly he didn't feel like one either.

"Seriously. Please give Rachel a call, would you? She's a smashing girl. You don't want to lose her."

"Don't give me relationship advice, Dad," Danny said. "You lost the right when you left Mum. Besides, you are being ridiculous. Me and Rachel are great. She's just a bit concerned about me being in this part of the world. But I've tried to tell her, the war's over. It's safe now."

His father was silent on the other end of the phone. It was a silence that said everything. Rachel and Harry were close. She would confide in him. They both knew that war and safety were not Rachel's fears.

"Just speak to her. It's not about me, it's about her," his father said.

"Look, I will call her," Danny said. "As soon as I put the phone down. But how are you? You been to the doctor's again?"

Harry also seemed to welcome the chance to change the subject.

"You know I hate doctors. They prod you and poke you and most of them don't speak English anymore. There's nothing wrong with me but old age and too much booze and I can't do much about either."

There was a silence again. Danny did not know how to fill it. If they weren't yelling at each other, they did not seem to have much to say. "Look, Daniel, I'll ring off now. Lots to do, that sort of thing. But be careful and come home soon. Rachel's missing you, you know."

Danny said his good-byes and hung up. His father was right. Calling Rachel would make him feel better, more alive. She would comfort him, as she always did. Just lift the phone.

Danny reached for his glass of whiskey instead and drained it in a gulp. It burned his throat and he grimaced before pouring himself another. The world was full of righteous things that remained undone.

HARVEY HAD NOT so much insisted on meeting as bullied Danny into it. After Danny had ignored his cell phone messages, the diplomat had appeared at Ali's villa one morning. He stood on the doorstep, in the same suit, with a slightly goofy grin on his face. Danny, had he been more of a suspicious type, might have felt he was being picked up on a date.

Harvey laughed at Danny's puzzled look as he opened the door. Danny couldn't even remember if he had told Harvey that he had been staying at Ali's place. He guessed he must have during that drunken night at Alex's.

"Danny. You've been ignoring me," Harvey cried, but without real offense. "But you know us Americans. We don't take no for an answer."

Harvey gestured behind him. A sleek black limo was parked outside, driven by a young Sierra Leonean in a smart gray uniform.

"Come on, join me for a late breakfast. I want to see if I can still help you with anything while you're here."

Danny said nothing. He was mostly trying to blink the tiredness out of his eyes and adjust his mind to Harvey's sudden appearance. But the American read his expression for genuine reluctance.

"Oh, come on," he said, with a hint of pleading in his voice. "It's not like I've got much to do here. It's not often we get journalists coming through, let alone someone from *The Statesman*. If you don't let me buy you breakfast, I'll start having trouble justifying my salary."

Danny laughed. Harvey looked relieved.

"Sure," Danny said. "No problem."

The car swept them down into Freetown and Kam followed in his Mercedes, struggling to keep up. Danny had expected they would end up in some swanky restaurant out near Lumley Beach or around the pool of the Cape Sierra, but the limo instead headed into the center of town to a warren of old streets lined with squat old stone buildings. It was a part of town that had not seen much in the way of fresh development but was not obviously battle-scarred either. The car pulled up outside a restaurant that was little more than a collection of battered plastic chairs around rickety wooden tables in a small room.

"I bet you've had enough of fine dining," Harvey said, and led them inside. It was hot and sticky but not unbearable. They sat down around one of the tables, and a portly middle-aged woman squealed in delight at seeing her customers.

"Mr. Harvey," she said, and squeezed his arm.

"Mama Fornah," Harvey replied with a grin. "How is business today?"

The woman rolled her eyes.

"Ah, not good, Mr. Harvey. You are my only customers."

Judging by the mountain of dirty dishes already stacked up in a sink in the kitchen, Danny doubted that was true, but Harvey seemed happy to play along.

"Then we'll have your full selection," he said, and Danny noticed him surreptitiously press a handful of dollar bills into the woman's hands. She tucked them away in a fold of her dress and bustled back into the kitchen, where the racket of pots and pans being clattered around soon drifted out.

"This is not what I expected," Danny said.

Harvey shrugged.

"I grew up in a little town in the middle of Missouri," he said. "It's corn country. Exactly what you'd expect from the Midwest. But if you ever wanted to find out what was going on you went down to the local diner. It was called Grandma's, even though it was run by a guy called José from Mexico. It's no different here. If you want to find out what the white people are thinking, you go to Alex's, but if you want to listen to the locals, then you come to Mama Fornah's."

Soon plastic plates full of food began appearing on their table. Piles of fried plantains, rice soused with sauces of curried goat and fatty chicken. It was heavy food and far from delicious. But it was comforting and Danny tucked in greedily. At last he discovered an appetite for something that was not poured from a bottle.

"It's got about the same calorie count as a Midwestern diet too," Harvey said.

Danny wondered why Harvey had brought him out to lunch. It was probably just the desire to do something, anything, to justify his position out here in West Africa. Harvey seemed like one of those Americans who dedicated themselves fully to whatever it was they had been assigned, generally without question and with a good nature. "So how's it been going?" Harvey asked. "I've still got a lot of people I would like you to meet."

Danny shook his head.

"I'm still looking into Maria Tirado's death," Danny replied.

Harvey frowned.

"I thought that was a wild-goose chase," he said.

There was something dismissive in Harvey's voice that triggered a response in Danny.

"Hardly," he snorted. Without thinking he reached into his pocket and pulled out Maria's letter. He put it on the table. Harvey looked confused.

"Maria wrote to me a month before she died. She said she was in some kind of trouble and wanted me to help. Unfortunately I only got the fucking thing after she was dead."

A stunned look came over the American's face. He picked up the letter and handled it carefully, like it might explode. His eyes widened as he read it like an amateur poker player getting dealt a full house.

"Jesus Christ," he breathed, and then looked at Danny. "I had no idea. No idea at all."

Danny felt strangely pleased to have shocked Harvey.

"Any ideas?" Danny asked.

Harvey shook his head.

"Look, this is serious. Maria Tirado was an American citizen and this letter is evidence in her death. This means we might have to re-open her case," he said. Harvey looked exasperated.

"I wish you'd come to me with this straightaway instead of traipsing around Freetown."

Danny reached over the table for the letter, but Harvey placed his hand over it. There was a hardness to his voice now, a steely resolve that was intolerant of argument, and caught Danny like a swift jab in the guts.

"Danny. Let me repeat myself. This letter is evidence in the death of an American citizen. An American citizen who was killed on my watch."

Now Danny suddenly felt he was on the defensive, losing control of the situation.

"That's all I have of her," he said. He sounded almost whining. Harvey looked at him for a long while.

"Look, I need this for a few days while I ask around. But I promise I'll let you have it back. It's your property still," he said.

Harvey had already folded the letter up and tucked it away in his jacket and he stood up. Danny sat there feeling suddenly lost. The letter was all he had had of Maria and now it was with someone else. He felt adrift and out of control. Harvey rested a hand on his shoulder.

"You have to trust me. I'll give it back. I know what it's like to lose someone. Believe me, I do."

With that, Harvey left, leaving Danny suddenly without the one thing that had brought him here in the first place. He got up to follow but he saw the American's limo already pulling out into traffic. Kam was waiting nearby and walked over. He saw that Danny had gone slightly pale.

"Fuck," Danny spat, angry at himself. How had that just happened? For a moment he toyed with the idea of asking Kam to follow Harvey, but then he caught himself.

"Let's go back to Ali's," he said, and he and Kam got back into the Mercedes. Suddenly Mama Fornah's food was sitting heavy in his stomach, as indigestible as mud.

Kam switched the radio on as they drove sluggishly through streets suddenly jammed with traffic and Danny stared out of the windows, stewing in his loss and stupidity. The music was loud and local and Kam absentmindedly tapped away at the steering wheel. Then, suddenly, he lurched the car down a side road.

"Man, traffic is heavy today," Kam said. "I go a different route."

They cut through a slum with Kam expertly weaving the car down seemingly impossible side streets until, unexpectedly, they shot out onto a stretch of highway clear of traffic. They sped along and it was only gradually, at first not really believing it, that he realized they were being followed. Two black SUVs kept pace with them about thirty yards behind, their windscreens blacked out. Danny spotted them in the side mirror and then looked over his shoulder. He must be imagining things, he thought.

"That's weird," he said. "But I think those two cars are tailing us."

He laughed nervously. Kam glanced into his mirror and the expression on his face said it all. It was like the blood was draining from his body. Danny checked back again. One of the SUVs had quickened its pace and begun to draw level with them. Kam kept a steady speed, staring straight ahead.

"Kam, what the fuck is this?" Danny said.

The SUV was level now and its side window wound down. A black face peered out. A young man, expressionless and wearing sunglasses that gave him the look of some mask-like beetle, waved at Kam to pull over.

"It's the police, I think. We had better stop," Kam said.

Danny stared at the man. The man stared back, jabbing with his finger to the side of the road. Danny made a decision.

"Fuck that, Kam. Keep driving."

Kam looked over, panic on his face.

"Mr. Danny. It's the police," he said, and began to slow.

Danny was panicking now. The man looked clinically calm, so devoid of feeling that he could think of nothing worse than stopping. He looked around. Ruined, shell-like factories lined the roadway, most of them abandoned or destroyed. This was not a good place to stop. It reeked of abandonment, of solitude and vulnerability. Kam kept slowing the car and the SUV pulled ahead of them now, even as the second vehicle drew closer from behind. Danny looked at Kam.

"Kam," he said. "Keep driving."

They slowed even more.

"Keep driving!" Danny screamed.

Kam glanced at him wild-eyed, his face an expression of indecision. Then something in the Senegalese took control. He slammed his foot down on the accelerator and swerved the car into the center of the road. They pulled ahead of the first SUV, which seemed to lurch to try to catch up. The second vehicle too speeded up, but Kam had put them ahead. They were hurtling down the road now and Kam was swearing furiously under his breath as he drove.

"This not good. Not good," he intoned, rocking back and forth. Kam's obvious fear spurred Danny's own and he looked behind them again. The two SUVs were right behind, swerving madly in and out of traffic, which had grown heavier again as they left the industrial area behind them and went back into a slum neighborhood.

Suddenly Kam screamed and slammed on the breaks. A cart and donkey had wandered out into the middle of the road, led by a man not used to seeing cars travel the road at such speeds. The Mercedes swerved and for a minute Danny had a vision of it tumbling onto its side. Another accidental death in Sierra Leone. But Kam kept it under control, furiously spinning the steering wheel and pumping the brakes to keep the tires from skidding. They spun once, slowing almost to a halt. And that was enough for their pursuers. One of the SUVs swept by them, turning sharply in and side-swiping the front of the car. There was a jolt and the sound of scraped metal. The second SUV screeched to a halt behind them, blocking them in. Both Danny and Kam flung open the car doors and tumbled out. Kam struggled to his feet and then went to the front of the car, his face falling at the sight of the damage. Danny looked around him, rapidly abandoning the idea of flight. They were surrounded by a maze of tin shacks as forbidding as any jungle. He felt safer out in the open. The SUVs both sat, engines buzzing like angry bees, with their doors shut. Then from one of them emerged the man who had waved them to stop. He got out, stretching one leg and then another, unfolding himself like some sort of insect. He was tall and muscular, wearing a tailor-cut black suit. His face was unsmiling as he leaned back against the bonnet of his car. Whatever he was, he was not police.

"Can I help you?" Danny asked. It was an almost comical thing to say, but nothing else had come to mind. The man looked Danny up and down, not even casting a glance at Kam. His face twitched slightly as if something were crawling across his skin.

"Information Minister Gbamanja wants to see you. He wants to know why you are here. Why are you poking around? You have not come to him for permission to be in this country."

Danny digested the information with shock. He had been asking too many of the wrong sort of questions and had pressed the same buttons in government that he had pressed with General Hinga. No one liked hearing Maria's name.

"I am sorry. I meant no offense. Perhaps I can come by and see him tomorrow." Out of the corner of his eye Danny noticed a small knot of people from the nearby shacks had started to gather. God knows what they thought of this scene. But he saw the man glance in their direction as well.

"You come now," the man said. He scrunched up his nose like he had smelled something unpleasant and opened a rear door of the SUV.

Danny could not make anything out in the interior, just blackness. The man nodded his head firmly.

"Get in," he said.

Danny didn't move. The only way he was getting in that car was at gunpoint. That open door was the end of the world, for all he knew. He looked at the man, his heart pounding. Danny held out his hands in apology. The crowd had grown to some three dozen people, prodding each other and laughing and pointing. It must have made a strange spectacle, this face-off between black and white in the middle of their slum.

"I have other meetings scheduled today. Important meetings with the UN and the British ambassador. They are expecting me," Danny said.

He let the implication of the lie sink in. I will be missed, he was saying. By men just as important as your boss.

"In fact, I am already late. Perhaps I can come to see Minister Gbamanja tomorrow?" Danny said.

The man rocked back and forth on his feet. For the first time emotion cracked his face, a mixture of frustration and anger. But he weighed his options. UN commanders and ambassadors could not be ignored. They were men who had their own power bases and agendas to pursue. Though, of course, he did not know Danny was lying through his teeth.

"You come now," the man said, but his voice was already deflated and his shoulders sagged.

Danny sensed he had won this battle. The relief flooded over him.

"I'll come tomorrow. To his office. In the afternoon. I shall look forward to meeting him," he said.

The man stepped forward and pointed a finger at him.

"You come tomorrow. Otherwise, we will come and find you. When you have no meetings."

Danny nodded and got back in Kam's car. He stared ahead, straining his ears to hear the noise of the SUVs leaving. At last he heard doors slam and tires crush gravel as they sped away. He felt suddenly sick and afraid he would vomit. How many poor bastards in Sierra Leone had got in vehicles like that and never got out? God knows what Gbamanja wanted. Kam got back in the car too, sliding into the driver's seat. They both sat in silence. Then Danny laughed to break the quiet. It was either that or cry.

"I guess we have another appointment for tomorrow," he said.

"You will go?" Kam asked in surprise.

"I'll go. But only when people know where I am going. I'll tell Harvey. I'll tell everyone. Do it openly on my terms. If Gbamanja wants to see me so badly, then I want to know why."

Kam looked mournfully out of the windscreen at where the metal hood had creased upward like a wave. He sighed.

"Don't worry. This is the new Sierra Leone and no one kills journalists anymore. Or at least not white ones. He just wants a bit of attention or to kick you out."

Kam started up the engine, which coughed and spluttered into life. They began the painfully slow drive back to the villa. Somehow Kam's final words did not make Danny feel any less afraid.

6

[2000]

CNN WAS THE SOUND track to the war. It was the theme music playing in the bars, the restaurants and the hotels. The poor had their radios, tuned to local stations or the BBC World Service. But for the wealthy and the foreign it was the blaring TV that was ever present. It was better to watch the unfolding horrors via a box in the corner than to venture onto the streets.

In a move that was to become as instinctual as brewing a coffee, Danny woke up on his first morning in the Cape Sierra, after the night he met Maria, and switched the TV on. CNN flickered across the screen. Freetown was the top story.

He bolted upright. Things had gone downhill overnight. A handful of UN troops, surrounded by RUF and out of contact for weeks, had fought their way south and arrived on Freetown's outskirts. A haggard-looking officer was being interviewed, his face streaked with dirt. Fearing an RUF attack, they had been stuck in their base in the north without food and water. Desperate and terrified, they had decided to flee.

They had made it to Freetown without loss. But they had brought fear to the city, infecting people like a virulent sickness. Villages were being abandoned as Zambian peasants packed up and headed for Freetown. The night was no longer safe in their huts. Baby-faced RUF killers were emerging from the bush, creeping closer to the city. Bodies dotted many of the roads now. Danny watched the TV in disbelief. He did not know what to feel. Outside his window the tatty hotel grounds lay under a bright, blue sky, arching over the deeper blue of the ocean. Birds flapped lazily in the palm trees. A hotel worker stood with a hose and washed down the concrete path leading to the pool. It all looked so normal.

He dialed London. They were frantic. Hennessey came on the phone, his voice racing: "The BBC are talking about British troops being put on high alert. We'll be wanting something big from you. Thank God we sent you when we did. We must be ahead of our rivals. Might even get you on the front page."

Danny's heart quickened like an addict given a sniff of his chosen drug. It was the journalist's rush. Chasing the high of a front-page byline.

"No problem. I'll get out and about, try and find some refugees and call in when I get back."

Down in the hotel restaurant the dining room was virtually empty. A table had been piled with slices of stale white bread, plates of jam and a handful of hard-boiled eggs. Danny helped himself and a waiter brought him a pot of bitter-tasting coffee. He said thank you and a woman eating alone nearby looked up at the sound of an English accent.

"Are you a journalist?" she asked. She rose from her table, dabbing her mouth with a handkerchief. "I was hoping I would be alone. But it looks like it's you and me. I'm Christine Hoyes from *The World*."

Christine Hoyes. Jesus. Danny knew her stories. She had trotted the globe for a decade after making her name in Bosnia. Her diaries from inside the siege of Sarajevo had even been made into a film. "I only got here this morning and I haven't had the chance to check things out," Hoyes said. "But I picked up a driver at the gate and was about to head off. Do you fancy coming along? I find it's always safer to do things in pairs in these situations. Don't you?"

Hoyes's tone was immediately conspiratorial and comradely. Danny did not know whether she knew this was his first time in such a "situation," but he happily took the offer of company.

"That's what I always find too." He smiled.

"Excellent," Hoyes exclaimed. "We'll be a little convoy. I'll see you downstairs."

Ten minutes later when Danny walked into the lobby, Hoyes was already there. Danny looked around for Kam and quickly spotted him. The lanky figure was wearing the same ragtag shirt as before and jangling his car keys in his hands.

"Things are bad, Mr. Danny," he said, crossing the room and not bothering to say hello. "I hear the radio this morning and they say the RUF is very close now. Many refugees coming."

Danny introduced him to Hoyes. He seemed oblivious to her fame though not her loose blouse. Hoyes blushed under his obvious gaze.

"Right. You can lead, Kam. Take us out of the city. Let's see how far we can go," she said.

Hoyes strode off, evidently expecting to be followed. Out of the city? They would be going in the exact opposite direction to the Zambians. Going into the countryside they had fled. This is really it, Danny thought. He felt exhilarated as a flush of adrenaline shot through his veins.

KAM BEGAN to talk as he drove. Like everyone else in Freetown, he had been up most of the night glued to the radio and he bore deep bags under his eyes. "I really think about leaving last night, Mr. Danny," he said. "But I have seen this before. This is a crazy country for people like me. For drivers like me, the worse it gets, the more money I make. I have to stay here. For my family in Senegal. My dollars will send my daughters to school in Dakar."

He shook his head and snorted a laugh.

"You know, the whole situation is good for me. Good! Can you believe that?"

Danny looked out at the streets. Shops were open and cars weaved their way through traffic and potholes. People crowded the pavements.

"How bad is it going to get, Kam?"

Kam paused for a moment and looked straight at Danny, seemingly steering the car through instinct not eyesight.

"All the people here know the RUF are coming. They want to get it over with."

His tone was harsh.

"It is like a virgin on her wedding night with a bad husband. She wants it done quickly. You English have words for it. How do you say it in your country?"

Kam adopted a faux British accent and a wicked grin.

"It's time for Freetown to lie down and think of England," he said. He laughed loudly, pleased at his own joke.

Outside, Freetown's streets passed by. Danny hung his hand out of the window and felt the warm air, uncooled by the speed they were traveling. A smell came into the car, of the acrid smoke from a thousand morning cooking fires. It was mixed with something else too, something riper from open sewers that ran down the sides of the roads. Danny watched the people outside. Most ignored him, but a few caught a glimpse of his face inside the car and stopped to stare, gazing at the white man looking back at them. He tried a few smiles but received only puzzlement in return.

AT THE HEART of downtown was a large roundabout in the center of which stood an ancient tree where auctions of human cargo had once been held. It was half dead now and surrounded by hawkers selling fruit, breads and other wares. Kam circled the roundabout slowly and Danny could see a cluster of high-rise buildings, most with windows streaked with ancient burn marks like mascara running down weeping faces. There appeared little left for the RUF to loot when they arrived. Apart from the people themselves.

They soon hit a long stretch of highway that skirted the coastal slums. It was the main road out of Freetown and for the first time they came across government army roadblocks. They were nothing more than a jumble of oil barrels and bricks thrown together. A few youths lounged around, cradling an assortment of weapons. Most wore green uniforms but others were dressed in nothing more than rags.

Soon UN checkpoints began to appear too. These were different. They were made of concrete breeze blocks and turned the road into chicanes, forcing vehicles to slow and swerve. They were manned by Indians who peered over the tops of their little mini-fortresses, each with a UN flag fluttering in the wind. Their blue helmets glistened in the sun, but the UN soldiers did not even stop the traffic. Kam did not hide his disgust.

"They could end this if they only fought," he said. "But they will only protect themselves. When the RUF come, they will kill the people right in front of these UN soldiers and they will do nothing."

Kam was right. The UN mandate was only for self-defense. If the RUF did not attack them, they would not intervene. That was how boys wielding AK-47s and rusty machetes had forced the UN's armored vehicles and tanks to flee. They had the will to kill. The UN did not.

About twelve miles outside Freetown, the first groups of refugees appeared, quickly swelling to a crowd. Kam slowed the car down. Hundreds of people were trudging down the road, young men, old men, mothers with babies. A few pushed wheelbarrows or hauled carts piled high with belongings. TV sets, clothes, even a fridge, were all being dragged down the road to Freetown.

Kam drove on, crawling slowly forward against the tide, which parted grudgingly in front of them. They soon arrived at a cluster of buildings, which a rusted sign announced was the town of Waterloo. It was less a town than a line of collapsed huts along the road. The ruins were old and overgrown. Whatever spasm of war that leveled them had happened years ago, not hours. That, at least, was good news. Danny could see a government roadblock ahead. It was a line of rope, tied with rags and strung between two barrels. About half a dozen soldiers manned it. Though the flood of people could have easily overwhelmed it, or even walked around it, they stopped obediently at the string. There was a low murmur of shouts and pleadings. As often as one soldier would push one person back, another would let them through, lowering the rope so they could step over and continue their walk to Freetown. Danny assumed each refugee left the roadblock a little lighter than when they arrived, relieved of a few grubby banknotes or some food.

Kam stopped the car and they got out into the crowd. Danny stopped and stared. All these people were being pursued by something awful; something that made Freetown's slums more attractive than their homes. He felt Hoyes stride by him, notebook already out. She walked up to the roadblock and began haranguing one of the soldiers.

Kam shook his head.

"I know that kind of woman," he said. "She will get us killed."

Danny did not reply. Instead he approached a young man dressed in a shabby suit that made him stand out from the other refugees. The man smiled politely. He was carrying a briefcase and looked more like a businessman than the farmers and their families who surrounded him.

"Excuse me, sir. Where have you come from?" Danny asked.

"I have come from Rogberi. It is about one hundred kilometers from here," he replied in excellent English.

The man waited attentively. He must have been on the road for days but he seemed happy to stop for Danny. Perhaps he was glad for some sort of recognition for his journey. Danny fished in his pocket for a notebook.

His name was Sulaiman Ramanu. He spelled out his last name carefully, checking that Danny got it right. He was a teacher and had been on foot for five days. His village had endured a week of fear; of gangs of youths spotted in the bush, of shots in the night. Then, six days ago, two farmers who had gone to their fields in the morning did not return in the evening. That had been enough. The village had fled en masse. Ramanu, like nearly everyone else, had relatives in Freetown, brothers and sisters and cousins scratching out lives in the slums. They would provide some form of refuge. The city streets would feel safer than the forests. For a while.

Other interviews followed the same pattern. The RUF were creeping through the bush to bypass the roads. Child soldiers with dead eyes would appear suddenly in the night, demanding money and meat. Usually that was enough to trigger the panic. When it was not, killing a few villagers did the job. For an hour Danny spoke to the refugees, his notebook filling with their stories. Finally he had had enough. He felt overwhelmed by the collective misery. He turned at a tap on his shoulder and looked into Hoyes's beaming face.

"This is amazing stuff," she said. "The soldiers at the checkpoint are freaking out. They say the RUF has been seen in the next village. That's just four kilometers away."

Hoyes seemed pleased at this. Danny looked again at the refugees' faces. Now what had appeared to him to be stoicism, or exhaustion, suddenly seemed to be just stone-cold fear. Danny looked down the road, over the heads of the refugees. The gray tarmac stretched out behind them in a heat haze.

"Mr. Danny . . . ," Kam began to say.

Danny looked down the road. For a moment he felt an urge to go down there, but he dismissed it. He was not here to play games with his life.

"Don't worry, Kam," he said. "I think we should be getting out of here."

Hoyes looked puzzled.

"Are you sure?" she said. "I think we should head up the road to the next village, see if we can see anything."

Danny shook his head. Then they all heard it: a single, far-off crack of a rifle shot splitting the thick air. For an instant the whole stream of people froze and glanced behind. Then they resumed their march. Up at the roadblock came a few panicked shouts from the soldiers. They dropped the rope and let everyone through.

Danny wanted to leave. Now.

"We're going," he said bluntly. He could see Hoyes think about it for a second, mulling her options. She looked up the road and Danny saw a brief look of longing cross her face. But she made her decision too.

"You're right," she said. "Best to play it safe."

WRITING THE REFUGEE story was simple enough work. Danny mined his notebook for the heartbreaking and the cruel, the sorrow and the fear, letting it pour through his keyboard. Hennessey had wanted everything. Rumors of a British military intervention were rife now in London. Sierra Leone was big news. Danny found himself feeding a monster with a voracious appetite for his words.

"Danny!" Hennessey growled happily down the line. "Fantastic job. It's a shame Hoyes is there too, but we're ahead of most of the competition for tomorrow. We'll run it big on the front."

Danny felt good, like a boxer surviving the first round. He was in the mix now, and ahead of the game. He wanted to track down Ramanu the teacher, and tell him what he had done. I am doing the right thing, he would say. I am telling the world about what is happening here. Your long walk was worth it.

But for now he would settle for a drink.

The Cape Sierra bar was full when Danny came downstairs and from the moment he walked in he knew the bar was different from the night before: louder, busier, more frenetic. Groups of men and women thronged the place as the international press corps began arriving in strength.

Then he saw her. Maria. He had not thought of her all day, but now in a single moment she filled his mind. She was sitting at the bar, apparently alone. God, she's beautiful, Danny thought. Her long dark hair, her brown skin, those deep eyes. He felt like a teenager getting ready to approach the good-looking girl at school. He realized he was standing aimlessly in the door of the bar. Sod it, he thought and walked over.

"Hello again," Danny said.

He held out his hand. "I'm still fresh off the boat. But I'm willing to learn about this place. Now, if you let me buy you a drink, I'll sit here and you can be teacher. Subject: what dumb foreign journalists should know about Sierra Leone."

Maria shook his hand. "Whiskey and soda," she said.

The barman, evidently through long familiarity with her tastes, had put the drink on the counter before Danny had even repeated her order.

"Come here often?" Danny laughed. Maria laughed too.

"You know, it's a big subject: the dumbness of foreign journalists. I am not sure where I should begin. Most of you just turn up for the crisis, walk in front of the cameras looking pretty. Say something ignorant about the locals. Then head to the next trouble spot."

"Then thank God I found you," Danny said. He would not rise to her bait. He would keep on smiling. "You can tell me what not to do before I start making mistakes. Anyway, I know I don't look that pretty and I have no camera."

She smiled; he sensed it was despite herself.

"You'd do all right on TV, Danny. So watch that it doesn't go to your head. Why don't you tell me about your first day in Freetown?"

"I left town. Headed up the road to Waterloo."

He told her about the refugees. The urge he felt to do justice to the polite teacher's story. Then the shot out in the bush and the panicky rush back to town, exorcised by the act of writing it all down and sending it back to London.

"You went to Waterloo?" Maria said when he finished. "On your first day? Jesus, Danny. That's right on the edge of government territory. In fact, by now it's probably over the edge. Are you trying to get yourself killed?"

Danny shrugged. Her words both scared and thrilled him. She gave a little snort of a laugh.

"You know, maybe you're not so fresh off the boat now."

He smiled triumphantly and ordered another round.

THE NEXT MORNING Kam met Danny early in the lobby. There had been an announcement on government radio. There was to be an anti-Sankoh rally in the national stadium. "Easy work," said Kam. "It will be the only story of the day. No need to go outside of Freetown again."

Kam's relief was obvious. They drove through streets that were now quiet. Shops were shuttered and the few pedestrians around were walking steadily in the same direction: toward the stadium on the outskirts of downtown. As they drove, more people appeared, gradually congealing on the pavements into a crowd. In among them were a few minivans, with loudspeakers attached to the roofs blaring out slogans. "Stand up to the RUF," they shouted. "Down with Sankoh!" Groups of young men carrying wooden sticks danced and chanted, jumping up and down in tight circles.

Despite the distraction of the scene, Danny couldn't stop thinking about Maria. They had talked for hours at the bar, long into the night. She was an aid worker with War Child International, a charity that rehabilitated child soldiers. It ran orphanages all over West Africa, including one just south of Freetown. She had been in Sierra Leone for five years already and even picked up Krio. She spoke of the country with passion tempered with a brutal realism. "I don't want to change the world," she kept saying. "I just want to change one corner of it. If I reach a few of the kids I look after, just a few, that will be enough for me."

Danny had told her of his famous father, of growing up in his shadow, of standing on the opposite side of an intractable ideological divide. To cap it all, he added, the old bastard ran off with one of his secretaries. She had laughed uproariously at that, snorting beer out of her nose and apologizing as she giggled. Then he had laughed at his father too. It had felt good to unload his anger. Such a release.

Her own family was very different. The Tirados were a huge clan from Puerto Rico. They had grown up poor and moved to Ohio, the heartland of America. She had been the star of the family's prospects, hard working and bright. Behind her successes lay an entire family's dreams, not just some kickback against a father figure.

She had left the bar eventually, grimacing at the lateness of the hour, and kissed him casually on the cheek as she went. "I was wrong about you, Danny. You're not another journalist asshole." She giggled. "I'll see you around." Her hand lingered on his arm and she was gone. It had taken him two hours to get to sleep.

The jolt of the car coming to a halt rudely hauled him back into reality as Kam pulled up outside the stadium. They had become jammed in the crowds five hundred yards from the main entrance.

"This is far enough," Kam said. "Let's get out and walk."

The crowd was so thick it carried them along like flotsam, forcing them into the stadium. Inside, people thinned out into a vast arena of low terraces surrounding a dusty rectangle of ground on which a soundstage had been erected. Danny saw a cluster of journalists. Teams from CNN, Sky, and the BBC mingled with reporters and photographers.

They waited in the stifling heat. The stadium kept out the sea breeze and was several degrees hotter than the streets outside. Yet the arena was ablaze with color and noise. Thousands of people lined the terraces and every one of them was singing and dancing. Chants began at one end of the crowd and spread down the tiers, merging and mingling with one another. Eventually several speakers took to the stage. All of them were portly-looking men who had forgone their politician's suits to share in the T-shirts and trousers look of the crowd. One by one they railed against Sankoh.

"Sankoh is here in Freetown in his big house!" one man shouted to a pantomime of boos. "He is preaching peace at the same time as his men are in the bush killing our brothers and sisters."

On and on it went. Each speaker would lambaste the RUF, warn of the dire events to come and then—mindful of the television cameras—appeal to the UN to help them. "We see you on our streets with your guns and your tanks, but you do nothing," one man shouted. "We appeal for your justice; we appeal for your help." The man's tone became hysterical. Few in the crowd, and none on the podium, could doubt what would happen to government officials when the RUF entered Freetown. Short sleeves or long? Chop, chop.

Suddenly Kam appeared next to Danny. His face was earnest and he spoke in a low tone.

"Mr. Danny," he said. "Some of the people have left the stadium and they are going to Sankoh's house. They say they are going to drag him here."

Kam sucked in his breath and made a tut-tutting sound.

"If they get to the house . . . there will be big trouble," he said.

Danny looked around. A BBC crew was hurriedly packing up. No doubt their own driver had given them the same tip. He felt a buzz of gratitude to Kam. With him around he could stay ahead of the game, make sense of the whirlwind of events.

"Right. Let's go," he said.

They fought their way through people still coming into the stadium and were soon driving down streets empty of traffic. They climbed out of downtown and into one of the wealthier suburbs on the slopes leading up to Hill Station. As they wound up the hill a few groups of people appeared again. But these people were different from the previous crowds. They were nearly all young men. They marched in groups, some clutching sticks or bits of concrete torn from derelict buildings. They stared sullenly at the passing car.

Finally they rounded a bend and ahead of them, perched on a low hill, Danny saw a white two-story house surrounded by a concrete wall. A crowd of several hundred people had gathered, unsure of what to do next. A lone white UN armored car was parked in front, its sky blue flag hanging listlessly in the air. An Indian soldier had his head poked out of its gun turret, like a nervous turtle peering from its shell. Kam swung the car around and left it facing back down the hill, away from Sankoh's house.

"In case we need to get out of here double quick," he said.

Danny got out and walked up the road. Kam followed a few steps behind, looking nervously around. There seemed to be no real order to the crowd, no leaders at all. Danny moved among them, slipping through their ranks to get a look at the house.

Two muscular young men in casual tracksuits stood outside a green metal gate. Each wore mirror shades and touted an automatic rifle. They appeared without emotion or fear; just cold and purposeful and

waiting for the crowd to make a move. For twenty minutes the march-
ers milled around like waves lapping on a beach, forward and backward, forward and backward, and each time the two guards stared back
as unmoving as stone. The situation could not hold. It was a length of
elastic being stretched that would soon snap. Suddenly the Indian UN
soldier had had enough. He ducked his head back into his armored car
and closed the hatch. The sound of the steel door being slammed shut
clanged through the crowd.

Then a small stone arced through the air, tossed from the back of the
crowd by some unknown hand emboldened by distance and numbers.
With a low crack it struck the concrete wall of the house behind one of
the guards. The guard turned to look at his comrade. For a moment it
seemed nothing would happen. Then a second stone emerged from the
crowd, thrown more wildly than the first. It sailed over the wall of the
house. Then a third and a fourth. All of a sudden the crowd was acting
as a single creature, bending down to grab anything that came to hand
and flinging it. Stones, sticks, gravel, tin cans, all tumbled through
the air. One of the guards was hit square in the face by a can of soda,
sending his glasses tumbling into the dirt. The crowd roared. The eyes
behind the sunglasses were exposed and they were ablaze with rage.
Putting up their hands to shield themselves, the guards opened the
gate and slipped inside. The hail of missiles intensified, many of them
being hurled over the wall, behind which could be heard a crescendo
of smashing glass. Sankoh's house was under siege.

Danny was elated and terrified. The crowd was out of control,
drunk on its own power. A few men ran forward and began hammer-
ing on the gates. Danny, instinctively, moved to follow them. He had
to see what they would do next. But Kam grabbed him from behind.
He struggled for a moment trying to shake off the Senegalese's strong
arms. Kam held him firm.

"We must get away from here," Kam said, pulling him backward. As he did so Danny heard the engine of the UN armored car rev into life. The vehicle lurched forward. It too was keen to leave. Missiles began to clatter against its thick metal skin, like the patter of a hard rain.

"We must go," Kam repeated. "No argument."

Danny let himself be dragged away. He could not resist Kam's insistence, but looked over his shoulder as he reached the car. The crowd was at a fever pitch now, banging on the gates and dancing in triumph. Then, as if in defiance of the rules of nature, the gates suddenly swung open of their own accord. The loud crack of rifle fire echoed from within the house.

In an instant the crowd broke, fleeing like a flock of startled sheep, first one way then another. As volley after volley of shots rang out, people poured down the hillside, tripping and falling over each other in the desire to get away. A few screamed in pain and Danny thought he saw one young man, barely older than a boy, flip into the air, twisting and turning like a puppet caught on the end of some tangled string. Young men were emerging from the gates, rifles held on their hips, firing wildly into the crowd. Through the chaos Kam's voice rose.

"Get in the car, Mr. Danny. Get in!"

Danny did as he was told and before he had closed the door it was moving forward. Kam sped down the hill, not slowing for curves. Danny felt it rise up on two wheels and he clutched his seat desperately.

"Jesus, Kam. Slow down!" Danny yelled. Kam ignored him. Safety was the Cape Sierra and Kam would get there as fast as he could, no matter what the screaming white man next to him might say.

LIKE EVERYONE ELSE in the Cape Sierra, Danny passed a terrified, sleepless night glued to CNN and listening to the radio. The news was grim. In the wake of the shootings the UN had retreated to barracks in Freetown. There were already rumors of RUF soldiers in the city, coming out of the jungle and setting up roadblocks in the slums. No one knew where Sankoh was. The only hope seemed to come from rumors of a British intervention force. But panic was setting in. When Kam came to his door in the first light of morning, he summed up the situation with a shrug.

"The foreigners are all leaving Freetown, Mr. Danny," he said.

They drove to the heliport and Danny instantly saw what Kam meant. There was a frenzy of activity. Three huge choppers sat on the tarmac and into each a long snake of people poured: aid workers, diplomats and businessmen. A throng of locals had also gathered, pressing against a chain-link fence surrounding the landing area and clamoring at the heliport gate. Often they had their hands raised in supplication, proffering random sheaths of paper—letters, documents and passports—like offerings to an unfriendly shrine. A handful of frightened Pakistani UN peacekeepers stood on the other side, occasionally spotting some lucky soul with the right passport—European or Canadian or American—and the gate inched open to let them through. Invariably whoever it was did not even look back as they ran, dragging whatever luggage they had, toward the choppers.

Danny walked up, followed by Kam. The crowd parted in front of him with looks of angry resentment.

"Mister, help me. I have lost my papers," came one voice. Then others, more urgently.

"Mister, mister . . ."

Danny had no passport, but his skin color was enough. The gate inched open and Danny squeezed through. It shut in Kam's face as he tried to follow.

"He's with me," Danny said.

The gate remained shut. It led to another world, and Kam's black skin forbade him entry. Outside the fence was Sierra Leone and what was about to happen there. Behind it was a ticket to the rest of the world.

The churning wind from the helicopters blew through Danny's hair as he walked toward the queues. One chopper lifted sluggishly into the air, straining against the bonds of the earth, before it dipped its nose and began to drift out over the sea. Danny watched it go and turned to see a second chopper load up.

He took out his notebook and walked through the crowd, talking with those leaving. They were teachers, diplomats, aid workers, missionaries and businessmen. The orders had gone out last night, long prepared by each country's embassy. After weeks of warnings to leave under their own steam, the violence at Sankoh's house had prompted mandatory evacuation orders. It was leave now or risk never leaving. That was a gamble few foreigners were willing to make.

Danny watched for an hour, occasionally jotting notes, and then he noticed a slim figure walking toward him. He jolted to his feet when he recognized her. It was Maria.

"Hey there," she said, as calm and collected as if meeting on a neighborhood stroll.

"Hi," Danny replied. She was wearing a white shirt, stained with sweat, and her hair hung in damp strands across her face. "Are you leaving?" he asked. "I thought you would be here for the long haul. I won't survive alone."

She looked at him with a pursed smile, half irritated and half—he hoped—flirtatious.

"No, Danny," she said. "I'm not leaving. I've just spent the morning at one of our orphanages, trying to secure the place if the worst comes to the worst. Then I gave a few of our staff a lift here. They've decided to wait out the crisis in Abidjan."

"But not you?"

"No. I have a lot of friends here. They'll look after me if it comes to it. Until then, someone has to make sure our kids are all right. Half of them lost relatives to the RUF, the other half were RUF. You have no idea how much all this is messing with their minds. They're terrified, and someone's got to keep a lid on that."

She sounded matter-of-fact, like an office manager discussing supply problems. Not like a young woman preparing to stay in a city under siege to look after a group of war-damaged orphans.

"What about you?" she asked.

"I'm staying. The Cape Sierra seems okay, and this is where the story is going to be."

He felt a pang of idiocy. He had just referred to their situation—to her personal risk—as a "story." It seemed a trivialization. But she did not seem to take offense.

"Ah, the good old Cape Sierra under siege." She laughed. "Do you know what happened last time?"

Danny shook his head.

"Well, when the RUF looted Freetown a year and a half ago, they got over the causeway and were heading to the Cape Sierra. They fancied killing a few foreigners. Anyway, they never made it all the way because the hacks had security specialists with them who were able to pick off a few from the rooftops. One reporter from the BBC ended up firing an AK-47 from his balcony."

"Jesus, that sounds like the Alamo," Danny said. His words were more jokey than he felt. Was this story really true?

Maria laughed.

"So how's your marksmanship, Danny? Do they teach you that at journalism school in London? I assume they don't give you lessons in how to shoot your way out of a good story."

There was a sudden shout behind them. Maria turned and saw someone waving at her from the helicopter pad. It was a tall white man, wearing a dark suit that stood out under the African sun. He looked like a bodyguard of some sort, all stiff-backed and unsmiling. Maria seemed to hesitate a moment on seeing him. The two gazed awkwardly at each other across the tarmac. Then she waved at him and he slowly raised a single hand in return. Danny shot her a questioning glance.

"Who's that?" he asked. But she just shrugged and ignored him.

"Oh well, gotta go," she said. Then she noticed Danny's unsettled expression. She put a hand on his arm and he felt her warmth.

"Relax," she said. "It will be fine." Danny watched her go. And as she did so—with the feel of her skin still caressing his arm—he believed her.

THE STREETS of Freetown were empty as dusk crept in. Danny had already filed his story on the evacuation, but there was something about it that bothered him. He knew the dynamic of news, he knew it was the foreigners—the whites—that his editors were interested in. But it had felt wrong that he should write about those who had left, not those who had remained to face the end. He went down to see Kam and told him he wanted to take a spin around town. He had suspected Kam would think him mad, but instead he started up the car without complaint.

"This is the calm before the storm." Kam had shrugged. "We should be all right." Danny ignored that judicious "should." They drove through a deserted city, its shops shuttered up. Of the Sierra Leone Army there was not even a hint. Nor of the UN. Roadblocks were abandoned and empty. In street after street there were only a few half-glimpsed figures darting from alley to alley: a city of ghosts. Yet behind doors and curtains and under tin roofs hundreds of thousands of peoples cowered and waited.

Kam tuned into a local radio station, translating the news reports for Danny.

"There's nothing going on. No one knows where Sankoh is. No one wants to find out either. Because when he comes out of hiding, that is when it will begin. That is when the killing starts."

In the center of town they drove down a street that was the home of the country's diamond industry. It was usually all colorful posters, Indian and Lebanese traders and the black miners who came from up-country to hand over their precious wares. The trade had dried up since the crisis began, but there had always been a few people willing to dodge the RUF. But not today. The street was deserted, the tower blocks dark, the lights and generators off.

Except one. Kam pointed upward.

"Someone's still here," he said.

Danny got him to stop the car and together they entered the building. It was a six-story block, mostly bare concrete with an out-of-work elevator. They trudged up the stairs to the top floor and saw a door from under which a light glowed. Danny walked toward it with Kam following. He pushed it open, stepping forward into unexpected light. A dark-skinned man was standing in the corner shuffling through papers. He turned slowly at the intrusion and Danny noticed his hand drift behind his back, reaching for something. Then the man looked puzzled for a second and his face lit up in recognition.

"Danny Kellerman of *The Statesman!*" he shouted. "Well, fuck me. You are still alive."

It was the Lebanese businessman from his first day in the country. The man strode forward and pumped his hand and then saw Kam.

"Kam! I knew you'd look after him well," he said. He threw an arm around Kam and laughed again. "I told you he was the best driver in Freetown."

The man sat down behind a desk and pulled something out of a drawer. It was a bottle of Johnnie Walker Black Label. He rapidly produced three tumblers of Scotch and handed them around.

"I'm Ali Alhoun," he said to Danny, by way of introduction at last. Then he added, "You know you shouldn't just open any old door in Freetown." He reached around behind his back again and produced a large black pistol. He laid it on his desk with a dull metallic clunk.

"These are shitty times," he said.

Danny felt the whiskey burn his throat.

"What is going to happen?" Danny asked.

Ali poured himself more whiskey into a glass that was still half full.

"What's going to happen?" he echoed. "I tell you what I didn't think was going to happen. Which is that a first-timer like you would still be here when practically every other white man has just left."

He snorted a deep, throaty laugh. "There's nothing like swimming in the deep end, is there?"

Danny raised his glass. The alcohol had given him an urge to match bravado with bravado.

"I wouldn't miss this for the world," Danny said.

Ali laughed again. Then he stood up suddenly. He tucked the gun into his belt and piled some papers into a black briefcase.

"Fuck this," he said, gesturing at the whiskey bottle. "Let's go to my villa and get proper drinks. Kam, I hope you don't mind if I borrow him for a few hours and show him some Lebanese hospitality."

Within minutes Danny was in Ali's black SUV careering through Freetown. Kam had seemed only too happy to have an excuse to head back to the Cape Sierra and safety. Now it was just Danny and Ali hurtling through town. Ali steered the car with one hand, expertly dodging potholes and grinning as he talked nonstop.

Sankoh was his obsession. There were sightings everywhere, he said. The Freetown rumor mill was in overdrive, churning out outlandish stories. He was in the mountains above town, he was back in the RUF's heartland, he was in league with the Nigerians. Ali confessed he believed none of them. "Where is that wily bastard?" he cried out. "There's nothing going to happen until we know that."

As they careened through the streets, the sun finally dipped below the ocean, bringing full darkness to the city. Normally it would set off a blaze of twinkling lights, of cars, of houses with generators for the rich areas and wood fires for the poor. But now twilight was replaced by a thick darkness. Only the headlights of Ali's SUV showed the way. Without touching the brakes Ali plunged the car toward an imposing-looking villa and Danny saw the shadows of a couple of guards scramble to open a wrought-iron gate just in time to dodge the vehicle. Then Ali killed the engine and coasted to a halt.

"Aren't you afraid of being a little conspicuous?" Danny asked as they walked up to the door, pointing to the villa's shining lights.

Ali shook his head.

"Anyone who is anyone knows this is the house of Ali. Doesn't matter if they are RUF, SLA, or who-the-fuck-cares, they know this is my house. If they don't know and come anyway, then we have ways of keeping them out."

Ali pushed open the door to the villa and Danny saw what he meant.

Inside was a large front living room, decked out in a Middle Eastern style with carpets and cushions arranged against all the walls. Lounging on them was an assortment of men and each held weapons that would have made a general blush. There were assault rifles, pistols and Uzis. In the center of the floor were large cartons of bullets, piled up in different calibers. Most of the boxes were half open, spilling their golden contents like sweets.

The men were Ali's relatives, part of an extended Alhoun clan that had gathered to wait out the crisis. The wives, sisters and daughters had all been sent out of the country several days ago. Ali introduced them to Danny in a wave of names and handshakes. They were, like Ali, a resolutely cheerful group, half of them drunk on the expensive wine bottles that Danny noticed also littered the room.

Ali pressed a glass of wine into Danny's hands. It was red and dark, looking for a moment like blood. Danny drained it. On top of the whiskey he could feel the alcohol massaging his mind to relax and unwind. He smiled, feeling a release of pent-up energy. He listened as Ali described his business interests, his diamond concessions all over the country, his shops, the huge Alhoun family back in Beirut and in America. He was worried now, he confessed, about the prospects of doing business in a Sierra Leone run by Sankoh. Those guys were mad and blood crazed even by West African standards. Somewhere there had to be a limit. But with the RUF . . . who knew? Ali's voice trailed off, and suddenly Danny found himself talking about Maria. He was not sure why he would tell Ali. But there he was, drunk in the middle of Freetown, talking about Maria like she was a playground crush.

"You've got it bad, my friend," Ali said. "That's great. Great for you, I mean. It's not my style. But for you, I think it's good."

He grabbed Danny by the hand.

"If you like her, you should go for it. Make her yours. Maybe you'll fail. Maybe she blows you out. But at least you tried."

Ali told him about a girlfriend he had in Abidjan, a local girl who he rented a flat for and paid a monthly "allowance."

"I like her. That's the stupidest thing. She's a bright girl. She uses the money I give her for college. Sometimes I let myself dream that she likes me, but I know deep down I'm just a meal ticket. . . ."

Ali stopped himself.

"Fuck it, Danny!" he cried. "Listen to my miserable talk. Who am I kidding? When it comes to it, I'll just settle down with some peasant girl from the Bekaa. With wide hips. Good child-bearing stock."

Ali shook Danny's shoulder.

"You ever fired a gun, Danny? Do you know how to shoot?" he asked. Danny paused. It was a strange thing to ask; an echo of Maria's comment that afternoon.

"Come on," Ali said. Ali dragged him half stumbling out into a dark, overgrown garden. He felt the vegetation all around him, crowded and dense. Ali held up a torch in one hand and with the other passed him a gun. It was an AK-47, just like those that government soldiers carried, except this one was not old or tattered. It was gleaming new and smelled of fresh oil. Danny felt the weight of it in his arms. He tried to mouth a protest but already Ali was behind him, pressing the stock of the gun into his shoulder and making sure he aimed into the sky.

"You just squeeze the trigger. Don't pull, squeeze, and keep it aimed high. We don't want to kill the neighbors."

Ali backed slowly away. Danny stood in the garden, holding the gun like it was a living thing. His finger curled around the trigger and he looked down its black barrel. At the end of it he could see stars twinkling in the night. Slowly, he squeezed.

The sound deafened him as the orange muzzle flash spat bullets into the darkness. A spray of sparks tore upward and Danny found himself flung onto the ground.

He was laughing, a high-pitched hysterical sound. He was drunk and guffawing with the AK-47 beside him, feeling the soft, clammy earth at his back. Ali, off to the side, laughed too as he took another swig from a bottle of wine and then flung it after the bullets.

"Come on then, Sankoh, you bastard," Ali yelled. "Where the fuck are you?"

From the night there was no reply. Just silence.

WHEN ALI DROPPED Danny back off at the Cape Sierra, his shoulder was bruised and sore from the kickback from the AK-47, and his head spun with the whiskey and wine. But he felt alive; stunningly alive. He knew he could not head up to his room.

He followed the low noise coming from the bar and walked into the now familiar place to find it mostly deserted. CNN was on in the corner and he stood blinkingly focused on the droning TV for several minutes until he noticed that someone sitting at the bar was staring at him. Maria.

She beckoned him over.

"Hey, you," she said. "I thought you might have left after all, leaving me all alone."

Danny fought desperately to make himself sober. He suspected, however, that the smell of wine on his breath was already obvious. But if Maria noticed, or cared, she did not let on. Danny saw a half-empty tumbler of whiskey in front of her.

"Don't worry," he said. "I'm still here. After what you said this afternoon, I was just taking some shooting lessons."

"I was telling the truth, you know," she said. "That gunfight with the journalists has become a legend in these parts. That was real hands-on war reporting."

"I was telling the truth too," he said. She looked at him, not sure if he was joking.

They ordered more drinks. There were only half a dozen other people around, a few journalists, including Hoyes, who waved at Danny but made no move to come over. Danny felt relieved. He wanted Maria to himself. He looked at her and his vision became steady. She was talking about the British warships she thought were just offshore. She seemed convinced the world would not let the RUF take Freetown apart again. He leaned into her—she did not edge away—and he found that their knees were touching. She was talking up the idea that the British army would come. Danny thought he could see a little fear in her eyes. Anyone who had spent as much time in Sierra Leone as she had must have learned not to put much faith in rescue. Trusting to the mercy of the future was a surefire way to get disappointed. Or dead.

"What if they don't come?" Danny asked.

"I don't want to think like that, Danny," she said. And then repeated, "I can't think like that."

He could feel her breath, sweetened by whiskey, on his face, and her eyes caught his, returning his stare. He had no idea what lay behind those dark pools. He put a hand to her face and pulled her into him. He felt—for the briefest of moments—a tiny bolt of resistance and then it gave way and their lips touched and their mouths melted into each other. After a few seconds she pulled away.

"You see," she said, leaving a hand pulling through his hair and resting her forehead on his, "you can always rely on the British."

They both laughed and looked about the bar like guilty children. Danny noticed a surprised look on Hoyes's face.

"Come on," he said. "Let's get out of here."

They went upstairs and Danny led her to his room. He opened the door and wordlessly they tore into each other before it had even shut behind them. It was frantic and animal, a release of tension and a forgetting of the moment. Sierra Leone and Freetown did not matter. The

RUF and Sankoh did not matter. The nightmares gathering at the edge of town were forgotten. Tomorrow was forgotten. The darkness was banished in the smell and feel of sex, where words were replaced by other sounds, where here and now was all that counted. There was nothing outside this moment and the two of them. Danny felt himself letting go, falling into her, a feeling that was echoed in her flesh and ending in an explosion of light and sound—like firing the guns at Ali's house—joyous and manic, briefly lighting up the surrounding darkness.

7

[2004]

DANNY FORCED HIMSELF to look away from Ali's drinks cabinet. It was still midafternoon and he craved the soft blurring alcohol
would bring him. His nerves were still buzzing from the car chase with
Gbamanja's men like someone had struck a gigantic church bell inside
his body. A car chase? It seemed insane.

He had a sudden urge to get out of the villa and try to claw back
some semblance of normality out on the streets. Get away from the
temptation to calm himself with a drink. He thought about phoning
Hennessey just to let him know he was planning to visit Gbamanja's
office tomorrow. The more people who knew, the better. It would be
safer that way. But, for reasons he could not quite put a finger on, he
did not want to want to hear a British accent; a voice speaking from
that other world that existed outside Sierra Leone. He decided he would
send an email instead. A few streets away from Ali's villa there was a
rickety line of shacks that served as a local market and one of the more

resourceful owners had rigged up an ancient computer to one of the few reliable telephone cables in Freetown. There was usually a queue but as he charged Westerners about ten times what he charged locals, Danny would have no trouble in moving to the head of the line.

It was just a few minutes' walk and it felt good to be away from everyone else. It was hot, of course, but for once Danny did not mind. It just felt good to be strolling down the streets, unafraid and unthinking for a moment. Just watching life roll by. And it was life. Pedestrians walked between the villas that were inhabited, security guards lounged at their posts. Vendors stood on the corners selling fruit and newspapers. Four years ago these streets had been full of fear. Once, people would have looked at him with curiosity or nervousness; white people usually meant a crisis or someone was needing help. But not so much now. He was a subject of mild interest or none at all. In fact, as he suppressed another wave of jitters, it seemed he was the only one walking these streets who had reason to fear. And even he was not so sure. He played the car chase incident back in his mind. After all, it was he who had insisted that Kam try to escape. The crash had happened, not because of the SUVs, but because Kam had swerved to avoid a donkey. He thought for a moment the whole thing could have been a misunderstanding that had spiraled out of control. Then he thought of the man's blank gaze and the terrible darkness within the SUV he had wanted Danny to enter. Doubt filled his mind again. It would be best to send that email.

He settled down at the console—surprised to find the makeshift Internet café empty—and typed out a note. He kept the tone casual but let Hennessey know who he was meeting and why. *It's just a precaution. Nothing to worry about,* he wrote. As he signed off, a small boy tugged at his shirt. He was carrying a bundle of Freetown newspapers and he thrust them at Danny. The smell of the street kid filled Danny's nostrils and the need written in the boy's eyes stared plaintively at him. Danny dug in his pocket and pulled out a few Sierra Leonean notes. He grabbed the top few newspapers and handed the boy the money. He was not going to wait for change but neither did the boy offer any. Instead he sauntered out of the café. Undoubtedly he had made his biggest sale of the day.

Danny walked back to the villa and brewed himself a coffee. He spread the newspapers out on the table and began to read them. Some were modestly professional in look, but most were just a handful of crudely photocopied sheets stapled together. Even during the worst parts of the war Freetown had produced dozens of such newspapers each week. Many lasted no longer than a single edition. They varied from attempts at serious news to gossip rags extolling the unlikely virtues of one politician against another. They were never short of entertaining. It was these that Danny read now. He had no desire for dry government news or pious announcements from the president's office. He wanted street gossip.

One column caught his eye. With surprise he realized he remembered it. It was penned by an anonymous writer called The Dog. He was an infamous columnist on the back page of *The Freetown Views,* one of the few papers that had been going for years. It was mostly scandal-mongering, written without bylines in a halfhearted attempt to protect its staff. Most of it was clearly false or exaggerated. Danny scanned the chaotic page of type and garish cartoons and then his eyes saw her name. Maria.

He stopped cold.

In the middle of the The Dog's column there was a brief story, just a single paragraph.

The Dog is growling. He cannot believe his own ears. News
is reaching the Kennel that sometimes a tragedy is not just a

tragedy. Did someone strike our Angel Maria down? Some-one fearing too much Information? But fear not, fellow citizens, The Dog is watching.

He put the paper down and called out to Kam. He was not alone. Someone else in Freetown knew Maria's death might not have been just an accident. Kam walked in from outside and Danny pushed the paper toward him. Kam read it twice and then pushed the newspaper back to Danny. The two men stared at each other, neither saying anything. Kam eventually broke the silence.

"Mr. Danny, this is too much," he said. "Can we not let this lie? Maybe Maria was killed, maybe she was not. Either way, she is still dead."

Danny looked at his old friend and Kam seemed suddenly craven and shrunken. He thought about that phrase The Dog had written: "too much Information" with that capitalized "I." Was that a hint at Gbamanja?

"Are you scared you might lose your job? Your well-paid work with Gbamanja," he hissed.

Kam was silent for a while. Then he looked Danny square in the eye.

"No, Mr. Danny. I am not scared. I have lived in this country for fifteen years and I have seen more bad things than you visitors can imagine. I have seen the war come and I have seen it end and Kam is still here."

Kam was speaking deliberately and firmly. It was not the speech of a defeated man, or a scared man. It was a little revelation as to how Kam had survived so long and finally prospered in this little stretch of West African hell on earth.

"But I think now you don't care about the living anymore. Look around you. People here are the ones who survived. There are enough dead. We don't need another outsider coming in and stirring it all up."

Kam paused.

"She's not coming back," he said.

Danny was silent now. But he held Kam's gaze and—though he feared he would not be able to speak—when the words finally came they were strong and clear.

"But I loved her, Kam," he said. "I loved her."

He pushed the newspaper toward Kam again.

"We need to speak to this guy. Do you know who The Dog is?"

Kam regarded him for a brief moment and then let out a short laugh. It was a sound of mirth that cleared the tension out of the room like fresh air after a window has been flung open. He picked the newspapers up and tucked them under his arm.

"Of course. Kam knows everybody," he declared.

BANKELO CONTEH SAT in darkness behind a thick cloud of cigarette smoke. He regarded Danny with eyes tinged with red that gave him the look of someone who had not slept in days. They were in the back room of a tiny tin shack in one of the slums just off the coast road. It was thrown together from planks and corrugated metal and looked like driftwood tossed up by a powerful tide; a collection of rubbish that had required just a hint of a human touch to assemble into a home. The only thing that disturbed the bare inside was a pile of newspapers on a rickety table and an ancient typewriter. Behind them sat Conteh.

"Fuck, Kam. Why did you bring him here?" he said.

Conteh's voice was not angry. There was a lightness behind it, something playful. He inhaled another lung full of smoke and blew it out through his nostrils in a billowing cloud like some nicotine-addicted dragon.

"We read your column today. The one about Maria Tirado. It seems you can help us with something," Kam said.

Conteh shook his head.

"I don't know anything," he said.

"Mr. Danny was a friend of Maria Tirado's. He knew her during the war. He has come here from London to see what happened to her," Kam said.

Conteh shook his head.

"I don't know anything," he repeated.

Danny interjected.

"You know something," he said. "Otherwise, why write what you did?"

Danny leaned forward and opened his mouth to speak again. Kam rested a hand on his arm.

"Bankelo, my friend," Kam said. "We are here for your help. Perhaps if you don't know anything you can tell us about someone who does. Someone must have told you something to make you write what you did."

Conteh regarded them both for a long time. His cigarette had burnt down to a glowing red coal and he used it to light another.

"Why should I help you, Kam? I don't know this man." He gestured at Danny.

"You knew Maria, though. This is not about Danny; it is about her."

Conteh let out a long sigh.

"Kam, I really don't know anything," he said. "What did I say in that piece? I said someone took her. They did. Some bastards shot her dead. I said nothing more than this."

"But why now, Bankelo? Why did you put this in print?" Danny said, and then repeated, "You were causing trouble. You seem to be trying to say something about Gbamanja. If you know nothing, then you know someone who gave you reason to say that."

Conteh looked again at Danny and seemed to be measuring him up. "Kam, why did you bring him here?" he said again, but this time he rose from his chair.

"Look," he said firmly. "There is someone who came to me. A woman who worked with Maria Tirado and who is very afraid. She tells me certain things and I decided to put them out there. I don't know if it is true. It is my job to pass along the gossip on the street. I don't even really know why she is so scared. After I spoke to her, I wrote that little piece. I was angry on her behalf. But now she is even more scared after the story came out. I regret what I did."

"Can we meet her?" Danny asked.

"That's not up to me. That's up to her."

A few minutes later Kam's Mercedes was weaving in between the shacks and heading deeper into the slums. It drove slowly down a muddy road lined by wooden homes, tacked together like everything else here with string and nails. Each was crowded with people, mostly dressed in rags, but here and there was a flash of color: a smartly dressed nurse in a white uniform, schoolchildren clutching a book like it was their only possession on earth. Women hauling buckets and sacks on their heads, walking proudly erect, aloof from the squalor, their backs as straight and stiff as any Victorian soldier.

A gaggle of children, playing in a yard, watched the Mercedes inch by, gears grinding crazily as Kam struggled to avoid an open sewer down the middle of the street. The kids easily kept pace with the vehicle.

"Mister! Mister! Give me something!" they shouted, their hands open in intense supplication. They followed the car like pilot fish, clinging to the sides, darting away and reappearing on the other side, reaching out, touching, probing and disappearing again. The old—stooped in front of shacks or walking listlessly down the road—looked with anger at the car. One old man, with only stumps for legs, spat in the dust as the car inched by, his mouth opening and closing in impotent rage.

Conteh gave Kam occasional instructions from the rear seat and soon Danny was utterly lost. The slum had no order. Its streets were winding and each lined with the same mess of houses. But Conteh knew the place like a lover's body, each bend and twist familiar. Eventually he tapped on Kam's shoulder and the car halted outside just another shack.

"Wait here," he said, and got out. Half a dozen children crowded around him tugging at his shirt. He said something Danny did not catch and they left, evaporating back into the slums. Conteh pulled aside a plastic sheet over the door of the shack and ducked inside.

They waited.

Suddenly Danny felt an urge to leave. He wanted out of this slum, out of this heat, out of this country with all its poverty and misery and to get back to London. He wanted to forget Maria; he wanted to forget he had ever been here. He could feel the slum crowding in on him, the tatty wooden walls encroaching on the car. There was a sharp tap on the window. Conteh's dark face nodded in the direction of the shack.

"Go in," he said.

Inside the shack the air was acrid and stale. Danny was blinded by the darkness and he felt Kam bump into his back as he blinked to get his eyes to adjust to the gloom. At first he thought it was empty apart from a pile of clothes on a mattress in the corner. Then he realized the pile was a woman.

"Sister," Conteh said. "This is Maria's friend." He pointed to Danny.

The woman rose and sat on the mattress. Her painfully thin arms were like jagged twigs on which her muscles were just an afterthought. She would not hold Danny's eyes and when she spoke her voice seemed to come from everywhere at once, filling the room in a parched whisper though her lips barely moved.

"I have some things of Mama Maria's. I am glad you have come here for them," she said.

She reached out a hand and Danny saw she was holding a small cardboard box. Danny took it. It was heavy.

"These are all the things that I have from her," she said. "The other one wanted them, but I told him there was nothing more."

Her voice seemed to come in an effort but as she released the box it seemed like a weight had lifted from her. Her shoulders, which had strained with the effort, relaxed.

She said nothing more and Conteh tapped him on the arm to suggest they should leave. Danny was confused.

"No, wait. How did you know Maria?" she said.

Conteh made to pull Danny away, but the woman raised a hand.

"I am Rose. Maria was my angel. She took me in during the war. I worked with her at the orphanage," she said. As she spoke she started to slowly rock backward and forward on the mattress.

"She give me back life. Now I give these things to you. She spoke of you with love, Mr. Danny. More than the other. When they traveled together I felt nothing between them," she said.

"The other who? Who else? Who else wanted these things?" he asked.

"Mr. Harvey," she replied.

Danny felt a rush of blood to his head. Harvey? He moved forward. But Rose started like a scared animal and shrank back onto the mattress. Conteh grabbed his elbow.

"Enough, I think," he said.

"Wait. Rose, what's going on here? Do you know something about Maria's death? What can you tell me?"

Rose was like a cornered creature. But she started to slowly speak. Danny bent down low so as to catch her voice.

"The RUF killed my family. They killed all of them, even the ones that were left living, they had killed inside. But Maria gave me back my life. She made me reborn after I told her my story. But I should never have told her. It was a curse I should have carried alone. Now it has killed her too. . . . It is all my fault." Her voice tapered away and Danny felt a tugging at his sleeve. Conteh wanted them out.

"But what about Gbamanja?" Danny blurted. Rose stiffened with a force that looked like her frail bones would snap.

"I wish he had killed us all in the bush," she said. "Take her things, Mr. Danny. I am glad that you have them, but that is all I will do. I have done enough," she said.

On the word "enough," she turned and faced the wall, showing them her back. Her shoulder blades stuck out from underneath her ragged dress like mountain peaks.

This time Conteh would not take no for an answer and Danny no longer had the strength to resist him. His mind was whirling with thoughts. They emerged back into sunlight. Danny leaned against the car and stared upward at the bright, blue sky. Conteh tried to explain.

"Rose lost her family in the war," Conteh said. "The RUF took them. Maria was all she had and now she's lost her too. She is mad with grief," he said. "She told me Maria was involved in something, some fight with some bad people. But she knows nothing more than that."

But Danny wasn't listening. He wasn't listening to news about Sierra Leone anymore. "Harvey" was the name that filled his mind with a sickly feeling he recognized as envy. Had they been lovers after him?

Had Maria fallen for that Midwestern charm: two American strangers meeting in a foreign land?

He looked at the box Rose had given him and lifted the lid. Inside was the pitiful collection of all he had left of Maria: a tattered driver's license, its faded picture grimy with time, a golden locket he remembered adorning her wrist, a broken watch; a clutch of dollars and coins. It must have been all Rose managed to gather.

He took the watch and held it to his face, hoping against hope to catch some hint of perfume, of sweat, of anything—some suggestion that she lingered, even for a fleeting moment. But there was nothing. He saw the hands were frozen at 3:48 p.m. beneath the cracked and broken face. It occurred to him in a moment of awful clarity that it was stuck at the time—the very moment—at which Maria had died. He felt a great heaving in his chest, like an earthquake crushing his ribs, and realized, almost with shock, that for the first time he was weeping over her death. Sobs crashed over him like waves and he was only dimly aware that Kam was holding him, clutching him in his arms, tightly, like a father would a son.

8

MARIA'S WATCH LAY on his bedside table, stranded amongst the clutter of everyday life: an alarm clock, a packet of sleeping pills, a half-empty glass of water. Danny picked it up and sat on the edge of his bed. He held it his hands. Maybe Harvey had bought it for her as some lover's gift. No. That was ridiculous. He couldn't imagine—wouldn't imagine—Maria with Harvey. As lovers? The diplomat was too eager and upfront for Maria. She'd have cut him off long before he made a move.

It was an unremarkable timepiece, thick and sturdy. Not cheap, but not expensive either. He stared at it. He could not remember it and because of that he felt he had failed her in some way. It was a common complaint of all his lovers that he never noticed the small things: the changes in hairstyle, the new shoes, the extra care with makeup. He always said they were not important. It was other stuff that mattered. Big stuff. But it was the small things that mattered now. Maria's watch was the only thing he had left. There was no big stuff to care about.

He stared at the dirt-caked face of the watch, looking at the moment it had stopped, trying to remember what he had been doing on the day she died, when he realized someone else was in the room with him. He looked up.

Ali Alhoun was standing there, a wolfish grin on his tanned face. Danny leaped up and flung his arms around the man. Ali clasped him back, thumping his back with his palm.

"It's great to see you, man," Ali said. "Sorry I've not been around, but I'm a busy man. Far too busy in this fucked-up place."

Danny stood back. Ali had not changed. His slight but lithe frame was every bit as smartly dressed as ever. His familiar Italian sunglasses were still pushed high up on his forehead, even though it was long past sunset. He didn't look a day older than when Danny had last seen him. His skin was unwrinkled and his familiar smile jogged a hundred memories. Danny drew warmth from his embrace, relief that one person seemed so unchanged from four years ago.

"How have you been?" Danny asked.

Ali shrugged.

"You know, some good, some bad. Never quite as profitable as one would like," he said, and then he gestured to the surroundings. "But we manage, Danny. We certainly manage."

Ali noticed the watch in Danny's hand and his face grew somber. He plucked it out of his palm. Kam must have filled him in on the day's events and what Danny was doing here. He examined the watch like he would a diamond, turning it around from every angle, and then he carefully handed it back to Danny.

"This is some fucked-up stuff," Ali said. "She was a fantastic woman, Danny. I can't imagine how you feel, but I can understand why you've come back."

The two men stared at each other in silence, Maria's death suddenly present in the room, asking its unanswered questions, filling the space between them. Ali broke the silence in the way that men do: by suggesting they grab a drink. They went into the living room and Ali scanned his collection of whiskeys, ignoring that some of the cheaper blends were almost empty. The victims of Danny's lonely nights in. He selected a Glenfiddich and poured out two large glasses, carefully slipping a single ice cube in each. He handed one to Danny and they clinked the glasses together. Ali took a deep swig.

"Kam says you had a run-in with Gbamanja's men," Ali said.

Danny nodded.

"I don't have a clue what's going on. But I do know that mentioning Maria's name around town has got him interested. And I know I'm not the only one who's making the link. The Dog's mentioned it too."

Ali rubbed his chin.

"Ack, The Dog will say anything to sell newspapers, man. But I, on the other hand, do know something. Gbamanja's name is coming up a lot up north and up in Bo. There is a rumor that he's going to be the new Minister of Mines. If he does, that will give him access to the diamond industry. It will make him an official Big Man."

Ali snorted in disgust.

"That fucker thinks he needs a payoff, I bet, to keep him out of the bush. To stop him going back to war. To make him a respectable fucking Mosquito."

"I'm going to his office tomorrow at the ministry," Danny said.

Ali put down his glass. He got up and started pacing around. He started to talk, grinding his fist into his palm, describing the situation up in Bo. It was where the Alhoun family's diamond interests had been for decades, leasing mining rights to the locals, skimming off the top, defending their clients from outside interference. Ali never pretended it was anything other than a protection racket. But now things were changing. A few other traders—another Lebanese and a couple of Indian families—had sold out cheaply to Sierra Leonean interests. Word was out on the street that Bo was not safe for foreigners anymore. That the new rules of Sierra Leone would put Africans first, not those who sent their money back to Beirut or Bombay.

"If you're meeting with Gbamanja tomorrow, perhaps you could snoop a bit for me?" Ali asked. "Just check him out. Mention the mining ministry rumors."

Danny shook his head.

"Ali, I can't. This is about Maria. Not diamonds. Not money. I just want to find out what happened to her."

Ali was silent. He walked over to the drinks cabinet and poured another stiff drink.

"It could really help me out," he said.

Danny shook his head. "I'm sorry."

"Ah, well. We each fight our own battles," Ali said, and laughed. "But I tell you, Danny, I've kicked some evil fuckers out of Bo before. I'll damn well do it again if I have to. No one messes with the Alhouns without taking some damage."

Danny did not doubt it. No family got rich in such a business in Sierra Leone without also getting dirty. But the conversation seemed to have sapped something in Ali. He put down his half-drunk glass.

"Tomorrow we'll have another drink, man. Like we used to. But tonight I'm bushed. It's been a hell of a week and I need sleep."

"It's good to see you, Ali," he said as the Lebanese closed the door behind him. Then Danny went back to his room and lay on his bed, turning the broken watch over in his hand.

He had no idea how long his mobile had been ringing when he finally noticed it. Possibly seconds, possibly minutes. He fumbled for the phone and looked at its display. It was Rachel. It was home calling.

Her voice sounded surprised that he had answered. He mumbled a hello.

"You've been ignoring my calls, Danny," she said, snapping out the words. Danny had never heard that level of anger in her voice before and his face stung like he had been slapped. For the first two years of their relationship they had barely fought at all, but then, as he felt himself growing distant from their life, disputes had cropped up. But they had always been Cold War affairs, ended with a thawing of tensions. This was hot war—sudden and brutal—and Danny had no idea how to react. He felt ill.

"You insensitive bastard," she said, sounding on the edge of tears.

"I haven't been ignoring you. I've been all over the place. Half the time I don't even get reception on this bloody phone," he protested. Then he realized that he was about to get caught in a lie.

"Then why the does the phone ring every time I try to call?" she said. "If you were out of reception it would just cut straight through to the voice mail. You are ignoring me."

Danny was silent.

"Don't lie to me, Danny. Everything else I can take, but not that," she said, and he could tell she was crying now. He felt an empty chasm open in his chest. He wished he could reach out to her across it.

"I'm sorry," he breathed. Then louder, "I'm sorry. It's just . . . it's just this place . . ."

He searched for the words. He was desperate to find the magic incantation that would stop the sobs on the other end of the line.

"Half the time I feel like I don't know what I'm doing here, that I want to come back and see you. . . ."

He had no idea what he wanted to say. His mind felt like the air outside: stifled, stuffy and confined; screaming for a way out of the heat but caught and unable to move. Like an insect trapped in amber.

"Then come home. Right now. You are coming back, aren't you?"

"Of course."

"Why not now?"

He paused. Not even for a moment did he really think he would leave soon. Not now. Not yet.

"I can't. I've got work to do. I'm here on a story, remember."

He did not hear it, but he knew those words had broken something in Rachel. Back in London something cracked open, releasing a torrent of emotion down the line.

"We have a life here in London, Danny. We've built a life together," she whispered furiously. There was a grim silence. Danny had no idea what she would say next. Then it came.

"She's dead, Danny."

The words cut him like a blade.

"You're in love with a dead girl." She paused for a response, but there was just more silence. "A dead girl," she repeated.

Her voice was rising as she said the word again. "Dead." It crashed against the inside of his skull, pounding behind his eyes, filling the void his mind had become. A third time. "Dead." He had to make her stop saying that.

"Rachel, stop it," he gasped. "Just fucking stop it."

But he heard her again. Dead, dead, dead. Or at least he thought he did. Though he could not tell if the sound had come from the phone or from an echo inside his own mind. He just heard Rachel's voice mouthing the word. Again and again until he screamed and the phone—as if by its own choice—hurtled through the air and smashed into the wall and broke into what seemed like a thousand little pieces.

THE CLERK at the Information Ministry regarded Danny with eyes that were half asleep. The minister was not in today, he had said, and then scrawled an address on a piece of paper. It was Gbamanja's home up in Hill Station and he had left instructions that Danny was to be redirected there. Kam, of course, already knew the way.

"Is this dangerous? Going to his house?" Danny asked. "I said I would come to his office. He's not here. So I think: Screw him."

Kam frowned.

"That's not a good idea, Mr. Danny. If you don't come, they will come looking. I must take you there, otherwise there is going to be more trouble."

He gestured to the front of his car, which—despite the best efforts of Freetown's busy panel beaters—still bore the scars of the car chase the day before.

"They did this to my car. Think of what they would do to you."

Danny felt nervous. A ministry meeting was one thing, but some house up in Hill Station, far from the busy streets of the city, was quite another. But Kam was insistent. Then Danny had an idea. He borrowed Kam's mobile and punched in Harvey's number. The American seemed delighted to hear Danny's voice.

"Danny!" he said. "How are you?"

"I have a problem. Perhaps you can help," Danny said.

"Anything. Just ask."

"Some of Minister Gbamanja's minders tangled with us yesterday. They wanted me to go with them. I said no, but I am going to his house this afternoon for a meeting. It's probably nothing, but I just wanted a few people to know where I am."

There was a brief pause on the other end of the phone as Harvey digested the information.

"Gbamanja? What does he want?"

"I don't know."

Again, a pause.

"You're being a little melodramatic, aren't you?" Harvey said. "I know Maria's letter must have freaked you out, but this isn't a country at war anymore."

"It's just a precaution. We all know what sort of man he is."

"Was. Danny. Was. They're all part of the same government now. But I'm glad you told me. Let me know how it goes."

Danny rang off. They had climbed high out of Freetown to the very top suburbs of Hill Station. Gbamanja's mansion sprawled over the summit of a hill. It was a three-story house originally built for some colonial officer. It was Victorian in style and constructed out of tough stone to reflect some misplaced vision of an English manor house. Gbamanja had rescued it from decay by putting fresh glass into the shot-out windows and repairing the woodwork, but the gardens had been left to fend for themselves. So instead of being surrounded by oak and lawns as it would have been in Surrey, the house was besieged by an angry riot of palms and tropical bushes.

The gateway was open and unguarded, but three young men lolled on the colonnaded porch that ran the length of the house's ground floor. They sat up as the car approached, moving swiftly into the road with a series of frantic gestures to stop. Each carried an assault rifle. Kam pulled to a halt. The men regarded the car with a cold curiosity, utterly in control. Danny thought, for a moment, of Sankoh's house in Freetown, four years ago, and the bloodshed similar-looking young men had inflicted on an unarmed crowd. He wondered if these men had been there that day. Or had they been out in the bush, butchering women and children? That was where Gbamanja had been at the time. General Mosquito had been one of the architects of the RUF advance on Freetown in 2000, earning more than his share of blood. Now he was a government minister. Danny felt a knot tighten in his stomach.

Kam wound down the window and put on a deferential grin.

"Danny Kellerman. He has a meeting with the boss."

One of the young men peered inside the car. He jerked back his head to indicate Kam should park in front of the house. He did so and Danny got out of the car. Kam stayed inside.

"I'll wait here," he said, his hands still gripping the wheel.

The same young man beckoned Danny to follow him. Inside was a maze of corridors, some freshly painted, and others still bare, with rotted wallpaper peeling off to expose the house's wooden bones. Danny followed the guard down a corridor. They passed other young men, all dressed in the same casual shirts and jeans, all carrying weapons. He glimpsed women hunched over pots or washing clothes. Finally, they emerged into a large living room at the rear of the house. Here, things were different. It was luxuriously appointed. Rugs had been laid over wooden floorboards and the back wall consisted almost entirely of glass looking out over what was once a garden but was now a forest. A plush leather sofa sat in the middle of the room opposite an enormous widescreen television, the biggest Danny had ever seen. He had friends back in London who would have salivated at the prospect of owning such a monster. The guard stopped at the entrance to the room and gestured Danny inside.

Sierra Leone's Minister of Information was waiting for him.

Gbamanja was a squat man with a potbelly rapidly acquired in the four years since the war had ended. He was wearing a white shirt unbuttoned almost to the waist, exposing a hairless chest crisscrossed with a jagged scar. He was standing by the TV fiddling with the remote control as the set blared out angry white noise. He saw Danny and switched the TV off with a grunt of frustration, and then flopped down on the couch. He lay there and looked Danny up and down like a piece of meat for sale.

There were to be no social niceties here. Danny was left standing in the middle of the room. Gbamanja appeared to be chewing something and he wrinkled his nose and spat onto the floor.

"Danny Kellerman, I am insulted. You come to this country from your newspaper and you ask questions of everyone and yet you do not come to me. You know I am Minister of Information and yet you do not come. This does not show respect."

Gbamanja's voice was deep but slow. His English was thickly accented and Danny struggled to understand it. He began to apologize. But Gbamanja snorted and held up his hand.

"You want information. I am Minister of Information. If I came to England and wanted to write an article, I would have to ask your government. Why do you think it is different here, just because this is Freetown?"

Danny did not even think of pointing out that this was not true.

"You have been meeting with people. Asking them things. Things about a terrible accident. Always you are asking them things about this and yet you never come to me. Why is this?"

"I am sorry, Minister," Danny said. "I meant no offense." Gbamanja cut him off with an angry wave of his fist.

"All you are interested in is one dead white woman. That is what you care about. You don't care about this country," he said.

His anger flared through his eyes. Danny noticed that tucked into his belt was a pistol with an elaborate ivory handle, delicately carved. Almost absentmindedly Gbamanja took out the gun and weighed it in his hand, all the time keeping his eyes firmly fixed on Danny, not looking at the gun at all.

"You have been sneaking around town, asking here, asking there. But all is gossip and lies. I say it again: You don't care about this country. You don't care about the peace that we have."

Gbamanja popped the clip out of his gun.

Danny felt cold sweat break out in his palms. It was like he had stumbled upon a hissing snake, its angry rattle shouting a warning. He wanted to back away. Danny swallowed and his throat felt like sandpaper.

"I assure you, Minister, I am also writing about the new Sierra Leone. The good things that are happening here," he said. He had to force the words out. He wanted out of this room now, out of this place with this creature of a man.

Gbamanja sat down. He reached into another pocket and took out a fistful of silver gun cartridges. Without even looking at his weapon, he slowly loaded one of them into the empty clip. Then another. And another.

Any thought Danny had had of confronting the minister was gone. He felt suddenly abandoned, even by Kam: the man who had brought him here, who had insisted that they come to Gbamanja's house. Gbamanja stood up, loaded the now full clip into his gun and tucked it back into his belt. He stretched his arms and sighed. Perhaps he sensed his message had got through. "You know we have much to tell you. The war is over. Me and my men fought for a long time and now we have our reward. We are men of peace now. We don't go around killing American women. But always people rush to blame us. Blame us because of our past," Gbamanja said.

He walked over to the window and looked out over the thick bush that now grew outside, clambering its way almost to the freshly set panes.

"I tell you, Mr. Kellerman. It's not just us who have created trouble here. You Europeans think that the UN has saved us. But you have never lived with the UN. Not like in this country. Here all the men in blue helmets are Nigerians. They are not of this country, but they treat it like one of their whores. They take what they want, they bring in drugs and bad women. Often the things that get blamed on us are carried out by them. Your friend was traveling in part of the country ruled, not by Sierra Leoneans, but by these invaders. These Nigerians who claim they help us, even as they rob and steal."

He turned to face Danny. He had pronounced the word "Nigerian" with utter contempt.

"Perhaps you should look elsewhere for why your friend was killed, Mr. Kellerman. Because for me this war is finished," he said, and then repeated, "It is finished."

He looked at Danny and his face split into a wide smile that flashed a mouth with half its teeth missing and hot breath that stank of decay.

"No more war," he said, and he laughed.

He gestured Danny to leave and as Danny turned around he saw that the young man was still there in the doorway, cradling his gun.

"Write your article about our struggles, Mr. Kellerman," Gbamanja said. "Write about our country, but on this other matter of your friend, you should let things go. What happened was very sad. I too feel for that poor woman. But this country has seen many deaths. We should not care so much about just one."

Danny mumbled a thank-you and walked out on unsteady feet. He could hear the young soldier padding softly behind him like a cat. He did not turn around and he kept his eyes focused on the doorway at the end of the corridor. It was open and he could see daylight outside. His heart was beating so loud he felt the man behind must hear it, must sense his terror. Finally he was there, emerging into light. Kam sat in his car and started the engine. Danny walked hesitantly forward, swaying slightly, the sunshine on his skin feeling like a rebirth.

IT WAS ONLY OVER lunch in a simple roadside restaurant that Danny felt able to talk about what Gbamanja had said. Kam was wolfing down a stew as Danny sipped at a Coke. His insides felt shaken and any solid food would not have stayed down. Kam stopped chewing as soon as Danny told him Gbamanja was afraid of his questions about Maria, but that he sought to blame Nigerians for it.

"Perhaps it is time to stop stirring up bad news," Kam said.

Danny sat back in his chair and shut his eyes, blotting out the light. He was still here. He had come through the terror of being alone with Gbamanja and emerged back in the world. He had stared a beast in the eyes and walked away unharmed. Maybe Kam was right. Accept this gift. Move on.

Just then they both heard a commotion in the street outside. A car horn blared amid a growing cacophony of shouts and yells. Danny got up and walked outside and could see a group of people gathered in the middle of the road. They were shouting and jostling each other over. He couldn't make out what they were saying, but one word stood out.

"*Ayampi! Ayampi!*" they said.

Danny could make out something on the ground now, between the forest of legs. It was a boy, perhaps ten or eleven years old, lying on his back and looking up at the angry people surrounding him. He was trying to back away, crawling on his elbows like a crab, but the mob prevented him from making an escape. He was dressed in a ragged shirt, too dirty to even tell what color it had originally been, and a pair of trousers that was more hole than cloth.

"*Ayampi! Ayampi!*" came the cries. And with one ugly kick, one of the adults planted his foot smack into the boy's face. His head jerked back and hit the road with a sickening thud. Danny winced and started forward.

"No!" came Kam's voice behind him. "He is *ayampi*. A thief. They have caught him stealing. Let them be. This has nothing to do with us."

Danny halted. The boy was crawling again. His eyes were wide-open and red with tears. It was the look of a wounded dog, animal-like and primeval, screaming out a simple message: *Pity me. Please stop.* The man who had kicked him was immune to the plea. He tore the boy's shirt off and threw it in the street. Then he slapped him across the face. Blood gushed out of the boy's nose and onto the road. The crowd was reaching a fever pitch now. Another man stepped forward and aimed a kick at him. It missed, but a woman, a girl, really, barely older than the boy himself, rained down a series of blows on his face. The boy turned over, hunched into a fetal position, curling his legs up into his belly, burying his head into his arms. Danny knew—they all knew, boy and crowd alike—that this was going to end only one way.

"Fuck this, Kam. Not while I'm watching," Danny said.

He ran forward and screamed at the top of his lungs. It was enough to make some in the crowd look up. They saw an enraged white man running toward them, yelling and waving his arms. The beating stopped and Danny pushed his way forward, shoving people out of the way. Suddenly it felt like he was all energy. The stifling heat was gone and nothing else mattered but that he would save this one boy.

He bent down to the boy, who looked up, eyes confused and pan-icked. His face was streaked with blood and mucus from his shattered nose. A sour stench of shit rose up from where he had soiled himself. Danny blanched and then reached down. As he lifted him up, Danny saw a burst bag of dried beans on the roadside. This was what the boy had stolen. It was for this he was about to die.

"Not today!" Danny yelled at the crowd of faces around him. They looked angry and confused, but the fight had gone from them. A few laughed, their mood turning from murder to amusement in the blink of an eye. The hysteria that had created the mob had been broken. A few stragglers began to walk away, muttering as they did so. One spat in his direction, but he barely noticed. He had taken the boy from them. Reclaimed him.

He saw Kam staring at him in disbelief.

"This is not the right thing to do," Kam said angrily. "He is a criminal. He stole from those people."

He could see Kam agreed with those laughing and pointing in the crowd. He could read it in his face. He thought Danny was just another white man going mad in the heat and the dust.

"We're taking him to the UN hospital, Kam."

Danny stripped off his shirt and wrapped it around the boy, soaking up the blood. Kam watched him, shaking his head, but Danny felt liberated. He thought of Gbamanja up in his mansion, trying to tune in his wide-screen TV and loading his gun. In Freetown the killers got a place in the government while the hungry boy got beaten to death. It was the same yesterday; it would be the same tomorrow. But just this one time, he had stopped it. Not today. Today this boy would live.

9

DEEP INSIDE THE U.S. embassy compound Danny sat opposite Harvey Benson and wondered exactly what sort of man he was. Part of him looked out of place here: that "American abroad" friendliness and eager-to-please puppyish attitude that always broke through when he began to talk about Sierra Leone's future. If Danny was in a good mood, it made him feel ashamed of his own cynicism. If he was in a bad mood, it made him angry at its naïveté.

Today, Danny was in a bad mood. Before, Harvey had just been a harmless diplomat. Perhaps a potentially useful source. Now he may have been a past lover of Maria. His friendliness made Danny feel ill. Harvey had invited him over in a rushed phone call. His usually unflappable voice tinged with a just a hint of . . . what? . . . He could barely imagine it was panic. But it was definitely something a little nervous.

"Come over. I have something for you. I really shouldn't be doing this," he had said.

Now Danny was sitting in a little garden at the rear of the embassy. One of the staff—a white man—had brought them coffee. They sat uneasily together. He had no idea what Harvey was thinking, but one thought was clear in his own mind. Harvey still had Maria's letter. And he wanted it back more than ever. He suspected Harvey's taking the letter had been more than just the action of a professional diplomat; it had also been the act of an ex-lover, stealing a totem off a rival. He looked at Harvey's bland features and an ugly question swaggered into his mind.

Did you fuck her, Harvey? he thought.

Harvey seemed to be gathering his thoughts. Or waiting for Danny to speak. But Danny let him hang, sipping his coffee without saying a word. Finally, Harvey took a deep breath.

"Look, Danny," he said. "This goes against a lot of what I am supposed to be doing here. I am supposed to be helping rebuild this place, not digging around into things better left alone. But I know what Maria meant to you, Danny."

Danny said nothing. Harvey regarded him through his pale, watery blue eyes. Then he continued.

"I knew Maria a little myself. So out of respect for that, and for what she felt for you, I am going to tell you something about her death that hasn't come out yet. Hopefully it never will."

Harvey leaned in.

"It wasn't just a robbery. She was targeted," Harvey said.

Danny felt like someone had punched him in the face. His skin flushed red and he struggled for breath. Harvey paused for a moment, as if steeling himself for something. He looked genuinely upset.

"Look," he said. "Maria was involved with some pretty bad people. It was the nature of her work at War Child. I'm guessing you saw that place yourself during the war. Some of those orphan kids are damaged, terribly damaged. No one here wants them. A lot of people want them dead, to be honest."

"What are you saying, Harvey?" said Danny, confused. Why would someone hurt Maria over the orphanage? he thought. Was it one of the kids who attacked her? That hardly seemed likely.

Harvey swigged back his coffee and stared up into the sky.

"What I'm saying is that no one wants those kids here in Sierra Leone, Danny. But that isn't true elsewhere in the world. There are a lot of people—well-meaning people, I am sure—who want children and can't have them. That creates . . ." Harvey struggled for the right word ". . . a market."

Danny stared open-mouthed. Harvey continued.

"God knows what she thought she was doing. I guess she just wanted to give her kids the best shot at life. But she knew some people who would arrange these things, take these kids abroad, the younger ones, the ones she thought still had a chance, and settle them overseas. People will pay a lot for an African child," Harvey said.

Then he added, "But it is a bad business. There are nasty people involved in it. There always is when there is a lot of money going around. We think she got out of her depth, made a few enemies. It's easy in a place like this when there are a lot of dollars concerned. That's why we think she died. . . ."

Harvey let his words trail off. Danny stood up. He waited for the world to stop swaying, walking in a tight circle, ending up behind Harvey. He could see the sweat forming on the diplomat's collar, staining his shirt at the neck.

"Are you seriously suggesting Maria was involved in child smuggling?" he said. "Because I would suggest that if you are, you should go fuck yourself."

Then he caught himself. A memory flooded back to him of a different time and place and a long drive into darkness. Maria, he knew all too well, had done something similar before. She had always kept secrets from him, hidden her dark side. But he did not want to remember that night. It had been a one-off that had led him to betray his profession's precious ethics and to keep secrets of his own. He did not believe she would have been so stupid again.

"Sit down, Danny," Harvey said coolly. "I think she was trying to do good. I guess she felt she knew her kids and she wanted to give them a chance. She thought life had not been fair on them. So she tried to put the balance right."

Danny looked at Harvey. Not fair? Those words sounded like Maria's own. Like Harvey was repeating something Maria had perhaps once told him.

"You said it was an accident. Why did you lie?"

Harvey turned his palms faceup and made a face.

"Jesus, Danny. People lie all the time. You know that. As I keep trying to tell you, I've got a job to do here. That job is making sure this country doesn't fall apart again. That means good press and international goodwill. Not child-smuggling scandals."

Harvey's voice had risen as he spoke. But he brought it back under control.

"The fact is that we have a problem in parts of this country. Criminal gangs from outside have come in from other countries. Guinea, Liberia, Nigeria. Maria was getting her kids out with the help of a Nigerian gang, one that had strong links to the Nigerian UN contingent here. They are bad people, Danny. They would not think twice about taking her out."

"Are you talking about Major Oluwasegun's men?" Danny asked.

Harvey sighed.

"We have no idea if Oluwasegun was involved. We know for sure his men were linked to the smuggling ring. We also know they were the first on the scene. But as for the major himself? He seems clean. . . ."

Harvey seemed almost to be giving up. But he started talking again. Firing up his resolve.

"We don't need the bad publicity from this getting out. Christ, this country doesn't need more bad news. Think about it, Danny. And think about Maria. Do you want her name dragged through the mud? We're better off leaving her memory intact."

Harvey reached under his chair and pulled out a brown manila envelope. He offered it to Danny.

"If Washington knew I was doing this, I would be in serious trouble. But I want you to read this. I want to show you that what I am telling you is true. This is our internal report into Maria's death. It is not nice reading. But it's proof of what I am saying," he said.

Danny took the envelope. He could feel some sort of file inside. "Why are you giving this to me?" Danny asked. "If you don't want me to write this story, why are you showing me this?"

"You've already got a story," Harvey said. "Write about Sierra Leone, write about its future, not its history. Put Maria in it if you like, but not like this. Put in her good deeds, not her mistakes. I am showing you this because I think you yourself need to know it. Then I am going to trust you not to use it. I'm trusting you to do the right thing."

Danny stood up. Trust. Danny did not know what to make of the word anymore. He glanced down at the blank envelope. Was Harvey trying to spin him? Or was he so desperate to avoid a PR calamity that this was his last chance to keep a lid on things?

"You have two days with that, then I want it back," Harvey said.

"You've still got my letter. The one Maria sent me."

Harvey reached into his pocket and pulled it out. Danny thought he saw a flicker of regret cross his face.

"Of course. We've taken a copy though. It backs up what we found. She was in trouble, Danny. She'd got involved in things way over her head."

Danny did not reply. He fought the urge to press the letter to his face, to feel its smell and touch. He folded it up and put it in his pocket.

Danny turned to go. He felt like his whole world had moved off its foundations. What Harvey was saying felt so outlandish and yet at the same time plausible. It ticked all the boxes. Maria had never given a shit about the niceties of life, had always been one to take the most direct route in a cause she thought was right and she had had no other cause like her work at War Child. She must have wanted his help in getting those kids out, or getting her out after things went wrong. He looked at Harvey, at his pale face, his clammy handshake. He tried to fight it, but the same old question rose in his mind despite himself.

Did you fuck her, Harvey?

He stopped as he was leaving.

"How well did you know her, Harvey?"

His tone was not subtle. But Harvey's expression merely softened in to sympathy. "I met her a few times. But everyone says what a wonderful person she was."

Danny tried to read something else into that face. But he found nothing. He turned and walked out, clutching the envelope in his hand, feeling the weight of the letter in his pocket. As he left he heard Harvey call him one more time.

"There are things in that report best left unread. Be careful."

But the diplomat's words fell on deaf ears.

ALI WAS FURIOUS. When Danny returned to the villa, he and Kam had been waiting to hear his news. As Kam blankly absorbed what Harvey had revealed, Ali refused to believe it.

"This is bullshit, man. Bullshit," he roared. "There is no away Maria would have been involved in that sort of crap. Child smuggling with Nigerian gangs? It is rubbish. No fucking way. Maria was a bunch of things, but stupid was never one of them."

Kam, though, said nothing. He let his silence speak his opinion. The manila envelope sat unopened between them on Ali's kitchen table. Sitting there like a brick of gold, being fought over by treasure hunters.

"Look, man. All I am saying is that this Harvey is up to something. None of this adds up. I bet he was screwing Maria. I just bet it."

"Fuck you," Danny said coldly. He snatched the folder off the table and walked out of the kitchen. Ali and Kam watched him go and then exchanged glances. The Senegalese looked at Ali.

"With respect, Mr. Ali," he said. "You can be stupid at times."

Ali did not reply.

Danny sat on his bed and looked at the folder. His mind replayed Harvey's warning to be careful reading it. To be spared all the details. He picked it up, slipped a finger under its creased top and neatly tore it open.

Inside was a thin, plastic-bound report. It bore the seal of the U.S. State Department and was stamped "confidential" in red ink. Slowly he began to read. The first section was an internal report from the Sierra Leone police. In halting English it described the first calls from Major Oluwasegun's UN unit reporting an accident, the police response, finding the bodies of Maria and her coworkers in the bush. Then came a second report. It was from the police again, but a different unit, a paramilitary unit. It described reports from villagers of bandits nearby and a police sweep of the area that had turned up an encampment about five miles from where Maria had died. The bandits had been attacked. Six had been killed and two captured. The two survivors—Emmanuel Sesay and Winston Fofanah—had been interrogated by police. Sesay had later died of a bullet wound sustained in the firefight and Fofanah was transferred to a jail in Bo. It was from these two that the story of the child smuggling had emerged. They had told police that they had been working for a group of Nigerians based in Bo, diamond dealers mainly, but who had the contacts for a sideline in supplying orphans to a Western market desperate for children. The UN units based in the area had allowed them to run their operations for a cut of the profits. They had also provided muscle and firepower against rivals. It was not clear how Maria had crossed them, but somehow she had angered the Nigerian gang. A group of local ex-RUF soldiers, languishing in some refugee camp, had been recruited to carry out an action. It was Nigerian UN soldiers who had helped arrange it, making sure the young boys were released from the camps. They had then simply been told to plan an ambush on a car of Westerners coming to Bo. They had not known who they were attacking or why. They had been surprised that there was just one white woman in the car but had killed everyone to make sure.

Danny turned the pages. After the police report came an official embassy document. It was marked "top secret" and written by Harvey. Evidently Harvey had been making the rounds in Freetown as word came in of Sesay's and Fofanah's allegations. He had harangued local officials, trying to see if what was being said was true. Most had stonewalled him. But not all. Unnamed people in the Interior Ministry, Harvey had written, had warned him off going much further, warned him in a way that indicated what was alleged was true. Then Danny's eyes saw a familiar name. It was Gbamanja who, eventually, had met with Harvey and assured him that whatever Maria had died for was no longer an issue. It was a scandal, yes, but it was being dealt with. The Nigerian gang had fled the country. The UN soldiers were harder to touch. In the end the reason for Maria's death had been about simply money. There had been an argument over price and the Nigerians had taken things too far. Maria had threatened to expose them if they weren't more reasonable. The Nigerians had responded to the threat.

Danny looked at Harvey's written conclusions.

"Little can be served by pursuing this incident. In attempting to place orphaned Sierra Leonean citizens with families in the U.S. and Europe, Tirado was breaking Sierra Leonean and U.S. law. It is hard to make the case for taking up this issue at a crucial time for the country's development and when we are seeking to cement Sierra Leone into our sphere of influence. I have received assurances from Gbamanja that this trade in children has been stopped. It seems best policy to accept that and move on."

Danny turned another page and there was the final chunk of the report. Maria's autopsy. He had already begun to read it, almost unthinkingly, before it was too late.

"Samples taken from the victim indicate that she was raped, perhaps by several different individuals, before death. Death occurred due to two shots to the head and one to the abdomen. Any of the wounds would have been fatal."

They raped her.

Danny bent over double and stumbled out of the door. He pushed past Ali and staggered into the bathroom. He collapsed onto the tiled floor by the toilet and vomited into the bowl. His insides were crawling up his throat, struggling to get out, and he felt hot tears streaming down his cheeks through closed eyes. His mind, terrified of conjuring up an image of Maria in her final moments, could only settle on Harvey. Harvey sitting in the garden and telling him to take this one on trust. Urging him not to read the report. You fucking bastard, he thought. Though the accusation, he knew, should have been directed at himself.

*　　*　　*

KAM AND ALI sat around the table by themselves. The report was between them, lying where Kam put it after he had fetched it from Danny's bedroom. They stared at it.

"He should not have read this, Mr. Ali," Kam said. He was drinking from a thick tumbler of whiskey and Ali poured him another shot.

"The poor fucker," Ali said.

"The dead are dead. Let them lie," said Kam. "This I say when Mr. Danny arrived. There is no point in going on with this. What good has happened? Nothing at all."

Ali swirled his own glass of spirits around.

"Tell me, Kam. This child-smuggling crap, do you think it's true?"

Kam shrugged.

"It makes sense. I have never been able to make out Major Olu-wasegun. But I know his men. They run with bad people from their own country. Why not kill a white woman who threatens them?" he conceded.

"Just because it makes sense does not mean it's true," Ali said.

They both stared at the report. It was the unspoken third guest at the table.

"Fuck it," Ali said, and picked it up. Kam made a move to stop him and then, as Ali shot him a glance, his hand fell back onto the table.

Ali read in silence for a long while. And then he looked up, his eyes thoughtful, his voice soft.

"There's something wrong here, Kam," he said.

He pushed the report forward. Kam looked at it. He was afraid Ali would be showing him the autopsy of Maria. He had no desire to see that. No desire at all. Best leave the dead where they are. Dead. But instead Ali was pointing down a list of names. They were the boys who had ambushed the car. All of them—except Winston Fofanah—were now dead. They were the boys recruited from the refugee camp for one final violent act. Kam read the list. Sesay, Fofanah, Sorie, Amara, Kragh . . . just names. But yet not just names. For names tell a story, and he saw what Ali was talking about.

"Those are all names from Kakumbia. All of them. Gbamanja is from Kakumbia, is he not?" Ali said.

Kam said nothing.

Ali continued, "There's stuff going on in Bo at the moment. Stuff that's bad for business. But I didn't imagine it was anything to do with this as well." He was silent again, looking at the list.

"Bad for business," Ali repeated.

10

MAJOR OLUWASEGUN was not a happy man. He stood by the side of the road and fumed to himself. They had taken three hours to come here to this accursed spot. This place of death.

"This is where we found the car," he said, pointing to a grassy verge and a tree whose trunk still bore the scars of being sideswiped by a crashing vehicle.

Danny stood there and looked at the spot. The drive up from Freetown had been tense and quiet. He had sat in the back of Kam's Mercedes, surrendering the front seat to the major, staring into the man's thick, muscular brown neck. The contents of the report had haunted him through the trip, as had Kam's suspicions about the major's real character. The major had again been wearing a golden crucifix around his neck and insisted on saying a prayer before they began. Danny had bowed his head in obedience to the request but it had made him sick to his stomach. Even if the major knew nothing of what his men were involved in, he was at least guilty by association. By ignorance.

But at the same time he had wanted to see where Maria had died and it was the major who could do this. God alone knew how Kam had bullied the major into accompanying them, but he appreciated the effort. There was no grave for Maria in Sierra Leone. Her body had been flown back to Ohio, but this spot was her last testament in Africa. It was here perhaps he could say good-bye.

He also needed to ask the major about the report. That morning Ali told him of his suspicions about the truth of the Nigerian link. Sierra Leone was a clannish society, Ali said. When you see Krio names you see Krio. When you see names from Kakumbia you see men from Kakumbia, not Nigerians. And Gbamanja too is from Kakumbia. What you don't see is a bunch of Nigerian smugglers who have disappeared as soon as they have arrived. Danny would have questions for the major now. But not yet. He would say his good-byes first.

So here they were. "This is the place," Oluwasegun said.

Standing in the thick heat of noon on a stretch of road that looked like any other. Except, of course, it was not. It was where Maria had died. Her life, that vast and glorious stretch of time and place from Puerto Rico to Ohio to Freetown, had ended here.

Danny looked at the scars on the tree and then back down the road. He could almost see her car approaching through the unchanging heat. It would have been a spot on the horizon at first, inching across the landscape, unclear through the heat haze of midafternoon. He remembered the time on the watch. It would have been after three p.m. that they struck. The attackers, waiting, perhaps nervous, perhaps drugged up beyond any emotion, would have prepared to fire. A signal would have been given as the car drove by. The first volley had taken out the car's tires, forcing it off the road and into the tree. Then they had swarmed over the vehicle, dragging its occupants out.

"Take me to the spot where the bodies were found," Danny said softly, and he followed Oluwasegun as he walked into the trees. He looked back at Kam, but the Senegalese was standing by his car. He would not enter such a place. Muslim, Christian, whatever. Such a spot was cursed. Kam had no desire to see it. Danny turned back and jogged a few yards to catch up with the major's disappearing broad back.

If there was a path, then Danny could not see it. Within ten yards he could not see the road anymore. After twenty he felt like he had been swallowed inside a green maw, surrounded by thick, humming life as warm and close as being inside a body. Then they broke into a small stretch of grass no more than twenty yards across. If Maria and her colleagues had been hoping this would be just a robbery, this was where those hopes had ended. Her three colleagues, it appeared, had been killed first with bursts from AK-47s. Maria was the only one raped, perhaps because she was foreign. Then three swift shots had ended it.

Danny sat on the earth, felt its firmness beneath him. This awful, unimaginable thing had happened here, he thought incredulously. In this place. His head swam. As he had been in London, working at a desk, making a phone call, thousands of miles away, at that exact time, this wonderful woman was being raped and murdered. He shut his eyes. The Sierra Leone bush was always full of noise, the buzz of insects, the ripple of wind or the cries of birds, but he could hear nothing. It was like a crypt.

He opened his eyes and looked at Oluwasegun, who was looking down on him.

"Major. I have some questions for you," he said. "I have seen a report into Maria's death. It says she was involved with child smuggling, getting orphans out to a better life in the West. The report says that a group of Nigerians in Bo were responsible for this. They and Maria had a falling-out. They arranged to have her killed. The report said that men from your unit were involved with this gang.

They helped arrange the men who carried out this crime. What do you know of this?"

The major took off his peaked hat and held it to his chest as he mopped his brow.

"I have been in many countries," he said eventually, his voice sounding weary. "And always it is the same: Blame the Nigerians. You would think there is no crime in Africa that is not committed by Nigerians."

The major shook his head and prepared to speak again. But at that moment a strange sound cut through the bush. It was a large vehicle coming to a halt, its powerful engine purring over like a lion. The major and Danny looked at each other and began to head back to the road. Then came the sound of raised voices and shouts. And suddenly they heard Kam yell in pain. The major moved toward the noise with a powerful stride that was almost as good as a sprint. Danny followed him, reassured now by the major's muscular frame, but afraid of what they might find. They heard Kam shout again. Then they broke into the open.

A white-painted UN armored personnel carrier sat in the middle of the road, its rear hatch open. A half dozen blue-helmeted soldiers stood in the road. Two of them had Kam's arms pinned back, thwarting his flapping attempts at breaking their hold. A trickle of blood was leaking from his mouth. They turned at the sound of rustling in the bush, a look of contempt on their faces. It turned to confusion when they saw the major. It was then that Danny noticed the insignia on their uniforms. The green and white flag of Nigeria.

"What is this? What is this?" the major shouted. He had not slowed at all and he marched right up to the two men holding Kam.

"Release this man," he yelled.

The two hesitated. They looked at another of their number. A slimly built man, with a pencil mustache. The men did not release Kam, though their grip lessened.

"What are you doing here, Major?" the mustached man said.

The major drew himself up to his full height.

"Colonel Suleiman. Have your men release this man. He is with me."

The man nodded and Kam violently shrugged off his captors and wiped the blood from his lip. He spat at their feet as he walked over to Danny.

"What is the meaning of this?" the major hissed.

Suleiman ignored the question. He jerked his head in Danny's direction.

"This is a crime scene. We are making sure that no one comes around looking for more trouble," he said.

"Is that so, Colonel?" the major said.

His voice was quiet and reasonable. Then he raised his arm and brought his right hand full force across the face of Suleiman. Danny heard a slap so loud he almost felt the shock wave. Suleiman staggered under the blow, his helmet popping from his head like a champagne cork. He went down on one knee clutching the side of his head and the major bent down to his ear. He hissed something in a language that Danny could not understand. Suleiman gestured at the rest of the men. Sullenly they clambered back into their armored car. With a belch of black smoke it trundled away, heading up the road to Bo. The major watched it go, his hands on his hips. Then he turned around.

"I offer you my humblest apologies. Especially to you, Kam. These men are brutes at times. That was unforgivable," he said.

Danny stared at him.

"Major. I'd like to ask you again. I have a report that says your men were involved in this. What do you know?"

The major shook his head.

"Mr. Kellerman. My men are not all saints. I know what my men do when my back is turned. I know they fornicate with women. I know they lie and they cheat and sometimes they steal. I know all these things and when I catch them I punish them. But they are not all sinners either. If they had organized such a thing as this I would know about it. And those men would be dead or in jail. But I have heard nothing."

"You think the report might be wrong," he said.

"I have heard nothing," he repeated. Then he looked around. "I have had enough of being here, Mr. Kellerman. Your friend is dead. She is with God and this is all that matters. If justice is needed here, then leave it to God," he said.

Then he turned and tramped back to the car.

DANNY SAT in his bedroom back at Ali's villa and took out Maria's letter. What, he wondered, would she have asked him to do if it had arrived in time? Would she have tried to get him to help with her plans to get her kids to a new home? Get him to publicize their plight with a well-timed newspaper story? Or was it all bullshit? That is what Ali and the major thought. He felt he was trapped in a hall of mirrors. He could not see the truth. He folded the note back up and heard the ring of a phone in the living room. He went to answer it.

He knew it would be Rachel and he felt an intense heaviness descend upon him. She would need him to say things he did not feel and she would not understand why. At this moment he felt like it was he who needed comfort, to have things explained to him. He picked up the receiver. He expected her to be upset or angry. But she just seemed tired and that was worse.

"I feel like we're losing each other, Danny," she said sadly. "And I can't do anything about it."

"Don't talk like that," he said with more conviction than he felt. He was still trying to bury the emotions of seeing where Maria had died. He could not bring himself to deal with this too right now, no matter how unfair it seemed. But Rachel did not give him the chance to say anything more.

"Look, forget about us for the moment. It's not why I called," she said. "I just wanted to tell you about your father. He had a bad turn the other day and ended up going to hospital. They kept him in overnight but the doctors seem to think he'll be okay. But he's not well, Danny. I think he's really sick."

Danny imagined his father for a moment. Huffing and puffing as he was forced into a hospital trip. He knew Harry would hate being there every bit as much as the doctors would hate having him, chasing the nurses and shouting at the staff.

"Is it serious?" he asked.

"He's old and he's never looked after himself. That makes hospital always serious, Danny," Rachel said. There was a trace of panic at the edge of her voice that he could not ignore. Danny knew she must be thinking of her own dad. He felt a brief flash of hostility but he knew he was angry only because she seemed to care more than he did and he knew she was the better person for it. He opened his mouth to try to soothe her, but at that moment he saw Harvey enter the room. Kam was trailing behind, looking flustered and waving his arms. Danny started in surprise at the American's sudden appearance.

"Just ring your dad. Please, Danny. He'd love to hear from you. I know it," Rachel's voice sounded again. Danny stumbled his reply.

"Yes, yes, of course. Look, someone's just come in who I need to speak to. I'll call you right back," he said, and he put the phone down.

Harvey reached over and put a hand on his shoulder.

"I'm assuming you read that report, Danny," he said. "I'm sorry you know what happened to her, but I need the report back."

Danny thought he could hear the slightest hint of reproach in Harvey's voice, a regret that he had been forced into revealing too much. Whatever his relationship with Maria, perhaps he had just been doing his job as a diplomat.

Danny went into his room and fished it out from under his bed and handed it over. He had photocopied it and was actually glad to get rid of the original. It would build a sort of wall between him and the events that it described.

"Thank you, Danny," Harvey said. They shook hands and Harvey's grip was firm and friendly. Danny watched Harvey leave and then listened as the phone rang. Rachel again probably.

He picked up the receiver, but it wasn't Rachel. It was a man jabbering expletives at him. Hennessey. Danny had been ignoring his calls too. "What the fuck?" Hennessey was screaming. "You've been fucking AWOL for days. On my expenses. What do you think you are doing?"

Danny had never heard Hennessey so irate. He had wanted to return the calls, but he needed to follow Maria's story and had little time for anything else. But he felt as far away from the truth as ever. In the pit of his stomach, Danny knew it was all over now. Maria, Freetown, Sierra Leone . . . all this was ending. No nearer the truth.

"I want you on the next flight home."

Danny mumbled a yes and put the phone down. It was done. He

looked up into Kam's eyes, which blinked darkly in the dim light of the kitchen. They were full of concern. But Danny felt unexpected relief crashing over him, like the moment a long-awaited blow lands. It was a coup de grace. Accept this, he thought to himself.

"I have to leave, Kam," he said. "I have to go back to London."

11

[2000]

DANNY AWOKE AS DAWN slipped in through the open curtains. He stretched an arm across the bed, reaching out for Maria. But she was gone. He awoke with a start. It was as if daylight had taken her, suddenly and mysteriously, leaving only the shape in the mattress where she had briefly slept and the smell of her sweat. He frowned and felt a moment of sadness. She had not even said good-bye. He pulled away the covers and stumbled into the bathroom. He caught a glimpse of himself in the mirror and was taken aback. His eyes were red and bloodshot but that was not what really caught his attention. It was the mottled bruising around his upper arm, the mark of his playing at be-ing a soldier at Ali's; blindly shooting bullets into the night. He winced at the memory. Sober, it seemed foolish and child-like. But there had also been undoubted power in that gun. A strange joy in firing it. He turned to get in the shower and caught a glimpse of his naked back and a long rake of scratches over his shoulder, fresh and red. She may have gone without a word, but she had left her mark. He had to see Maria again. Soon.

As he washed he became dimly aware of a low rumbling and groaning. At first he thought it was the mechanical complaints of the air-conditioning system. But it was growing louder and more complex. A roar of machinery that filled the air.

"What the fuck?" he breathed to himself as he walked over to the window.

He flung back the curtain and there was a sudden whir of rotor blades and an enormous helicopter swooped over the building. It was close enough that Danny could see the fair-skinned pilot looking down, his face masked by aviation goggles as he dipped away toward the ocean shore. This was no ordinary chopper. It was not painted UN white. It was combat green. Danny saw others too, far off in the distance, hovering in a long line, like predatory wasps.

"Jesus!" Danny whispered, and then he punched the air and began to laugh as a wave of relief and excitement crashed over him and he realized what had happened.

The British army had come. The RUF would not take Freetown again.

He flung on his clothes and grabbed his satellite phone and dialed London. They were manic at the news desk. The phone lines coming into Sierra Leone had been jammed and they had been trying to call him for an hour.

"Get the fuck out there!" Hennessey had yelled. "It's the biggest British military action since the Falklands, for fuck's sake!"

Danny ran downstairs. The hotel was already practically empty. Most of the other journalists were pounding the streets though it was only eight in the morning. He saw Kam, lounging on a sofa in the hotel lobby. The Senegalese raised an eyebrow at him and the two headed to the car.

"Let's go into town, Mr. Danny," Kam said. "We should see if they are taking over all of Freetown. Besides, I want to check on my flat."

They drove toward the causeway that led to Freetown proper through a stretch of the city that was transformed. British troops were everywhere. One of the derelict hotels near the Cape Sierra had been commandeered as a temporary base and heavyset soldiers weighed down with kit were moving into derelict rooms that had not seen guests since the 1980s. They were manning fresh roadblocks too. But the British barricades neither involved the menacing looks of the Sierra Leone Army's nor the ineffectualness of the UN's. Each car would be stopped, its driver politely interrogated.

When it came to Danny's turn, he smiled.

"It's good to see you," Danny said to the young soldier peering into the car. He jerked his head at Kam.

"Is he with you?" he said in a broad Scottish accent.

"He's my driver," Danny said. The soldier—who could not have been out of his teenage years—seemed to take a while to think about this. Then he whispered something into a radio.

"On your way, please," he said.

As they drove off, the Senegalese was beaming.

"These are real soldiers," he said, his joy obvious on every inch of his face. He was unaccustomed to something good happening in Freetown. The roadblocks came every five hundred yards, manned by the same hard, professional young men. Whatever happened now, they were safe here. As they drove over the causeway, the soldier there told them this was the last one.

"You should just know we've secured this area, but it's only patrols in the rest of Freetown," he said. "If you go past here you are in an area beyond the control of British forces."

As Danny and Kam drove into town they exchanged glances. Kam looked a little crestfallen.

"Why do they stop here at the causeway? It is ridiculous. They can kill anything that moves in this country. Why stop?"

Danny had no answer. But even though they saw no British troops in the rest of town, their effect was still obvious. A few hesitant people were chatting on street corners and waving at the occasional chopper that flew overhead. Danny decided to visit the British embassy. They passed through the center of town to where the British compound stood on a bluff above town. A pair of open-top British Land Rovers were parked in front of its closed steel gates. Each was mounted with a heavy machine gun, and burly-looking paratroopers stood around, smoking cigarettes. Danny told Kam to wait in the car and he walked over.

"All right, lads," he said.

One of the soldiers looked down at him. He seemed taken aback by this solitary Englishman wandering around by himself in what they must have been told was hostile territory.

Danny fished out a notebook.

"I'm from *The Statesman*. I just want to say I've never been so happy to see you guys. I thought we were in real trouble, but now you're here."

It was true but it was also flattery and it worked.

"This is what we've trained for," he said. "We signed up for action and action is what we've got. At long fucking last."

"How's your first day in a war zone?"

The soldier frowned.

"Not seen anything," he said. The sense of disappointment in his voice was palpable. He spoke of briefings before they landed of the hazards of West African fighting, of their mission and of the ferocity and atrocities of the RUF. Then they had landed, driven through an empty city, been hassled by legions of journalists and finally stationed here, looking after diplomats.

"But at least we're out in the city, not stuck back there on Lumley Beach," he said. This comment was chorused by grunts of agreement from the other soldiers around the Land Rovers. Danny was about to press further when he heard a crackle of noise over a radio. One of the other men shouted over. "Sarge. There's reports of a contact two miles from here. Request that we check it out."

The man behind the machine gun smiled.

"Right. Let's go," he barked. The two vehicles roared into life. The man looked over to Danny and winked. "Looks like we're going to war after all."

It was pure bravado. The boy soldiers of the RUF would not last three seconds if they came anywhere near these soldiers. The young Britons, only a few years older than their enemy, were less practiced in killing. But, in their own way, they were even more eager for the fight.

"WHAT EXACTLY did you expect them to be? Grateful?" Maria asked him, pointing a fork at him across a table at Alex's. With the arrival of the British army, the restaurant was not only open, it was almost full. "I mean, Danny, they don't have much to be grateful for."

Danny had spent the afternoon interviewing people at the amputees' refugee camp in downtown Freetown. He expected the people there to be relieved and pleased to see the British troops, but instead he found nothing but misery. Their stares and stilted answers to his questions shook his expectations. "Why have you come here?" their leader had said, his missing hands waving in the air like an accusation. "What have you brought us?" Danny had had no answer.

Now Maria was providing him with one. They were sitting at a table overlooking the sea, eating a platter of Lebanese food. It seemed oddly like a first date. But their conversation was hardly of flowers and favorite movies.

"They had their arms hacked off. They all get asked for long sleeves or short sleeves," Maria said. "They will never be grateful again."

"I thought they would have felt something. Perhaps just relief."

Maria shook her head.

"A little bit of attention and pity from some foreigner is not going to grow their arms back."

"Then why do you help? Why are you here?"

She put down her fork. She looked suddenly focused, driven almost. He had touched a nerve.

"My parents struggled for me, to make sure that I had things that they didn't. I know it's a cliché, but I feel I owe a debt to this world. I could have worked in government, formulated policy or whatever. But I want to see my debt being repaid. I want to feel it. For me that means I have to get on the business end of things. I know I don't change the world. But I do change some people's lives. I really do."

She paused for a moment. She was looking out beyond the light cast by the restaurant's tattered electric bulbs, out into the darkness of the rest of the city.

"There are people. Kids, actually. And I can look at them and say: I have changed this person's life. I have made it better. It may be a drop in the ocean, but for them it's their whole world."

Danny looked at her and he was lost to her; disappearing into those dark eyes, the heat of her passion and the starkness of her morality. She stood like a marble statue amid all the chaos. He feared he did not know her, perhaps could never truly get under that skin. But he felt pulled toward her regardless of the risk. They looked at each other. Danny held her gaze.

"Why are we sitting here when we could be in my hotel room?" he asked.

She laughed.

"I have no idea," she said, and got up to leave. Danny flung down a sheaf of banknotes on the table and followed her out.

The next morning Maria woke him before she left. She planted a soft kiss on his forehead, her breath warm and moist as the tropical air. He rolled over and smiled. She reached under the covers and he tensed briefly as she kissed him again.

"Take care of this for me. I'll be needing it again," she said. Then she was gone. Danny did not even try to get back to sleep.

HE KNEW it was dumb. But he could not help it. Sex with Maria was making Danny feel invulnerable. As he came down from his room to the familiar hubbub in the breakfast room, he knew today he would try to get out of Freetown. It was time to go up the road into the bush. To see how far he and Kam could go. He needed fresh copy for Hennessey back in London and he knew other reporters had already launched sallies out of town. Thinking about the idea, he did not feel afraid. He felt excited. Bold.

When he saw Kam in the lobby with the other drivers, Danny told him he wanted to venture out of Freetown, and he was relieved when Kam agreed. Kam was Danny's barometer of his actions. He had not forgotten it was Kam who had pulled him out of the crowd outside Sankoh's house just before the shooting began.

Ten minutes later Danny watched as Kam returned to the car carrying an armful of bread, cartons of cigarettes and little bottles of gin, vodka and whiskey.

"That will get us through most of the checkpoints," Kam said, and then laughed. "I hope that when we are coming back, they won't have drunk all the booze. That is when we hit trouble."

As they headed out of town, with the slums a thick line on the horizon behind them, the first few checkpoints were easy. They were Sierra Leone Army posts and it always ended with a carton of cigarettes and bread being handed over while the rope blocking the road was lowered. Eventually they made it again to the straggly ruins of Waterloo and the road beyond. Danny was, at last, on unexplored ground.

It was about five kilometers later that they hit the first militia checkpoint. It was just a flimsy bit of rope strung between two oil barrels. But as they slowed, ragged-looking figures emerged from the bush, cradling AK-47s and gesturing for them to stop. Danny felt a pang of panic. RUF?

Kam looked relaxed.

"Civil Defense Force," he said. "Government militia."

Kam wound down his window. One of the men, barely out of his teens, poked his head inside. He smelled of campfires and sweat. His unwashed hair hung in ragged braids. The barrel of his gun cracked against the car door.

"We are with the British. Journalists. Going up to the front," Kam said.

"Do you have anything for me?"

The man's tone was pleading. Kam reached beneath his seat and pulled out a tiny bottle of gin. The man craned his neck over to see where Kam had kept the bag. But Kam shuffled his feet to cover it. The man took the bottle and waved aggressively at the other gunmen by the rope.

"Pass!" he said.

It became an easy routine. Every couple of kilometers they would meet a similar checkpoint. Always bribes would be offered and they would get through. Until they reached the final roadblock. A handful of other cars were already parked there and Danny could see several journalists squatting underneath the ample arms of a banana tree. Among them was Hoyes.

"Hey, Caroline. What's up?"

Hoyes filled him in. This was as far as they could get. Beyond this was bandit country. The army were not letting anyone through, not for bread and booze. Hoyes had even tried money but was turned down.

Now they were waiting. The officer here thought that there was an RUF position just a kilometer or two away. They had called in for help. Once help arrived, they could try to proceed.

Danny joined them sitting in the shade. He wondered what that help would be. More ragtag soldiers or perhaps British troops. But it wasn't. A distant hum, barely noticeable at first, transformed itself into a helicopter gunship hovering above the trees. Danny looked up. It wasn't British. It was government. He thought of Freddie the Fijian from the bar. Was he at the controls? The man Maria had called a child killer. The gunship circled the checkpoint twice before heading off along the path of the road. It disappeared and silence returned to the bush. No one spoke. Then they heard a distant rattle of gunfire, coming in long-sustained bursts. Danny looked over at Hoyes. She was grinning like it was Christmas.

"Brilliant," she said. "This is brilliant."

After a quarter of an hour the gun blasts diminished to the occasional short burst and then the chopper appeared again, heading back in the direction of Freetown. The journalists scrambled into their cars, matching the activity of the government soldiers. From out of the bush an old flatbed truck emerged and a dozen soldiers clambered aboard, waving their rifles and shouting. It rumbled through the checkpoint, followed by a line of cars.

Danny ran back to find Kam already had the engine running. They drove slowly forward through the bush and then the convoy stopped. Danny saw Hoyes clambering out of her own car a hundred yards away. He shoved open the door and sprinted forward, running up the line of vehicles. Then he saw what they had come to see.

A group of shacks made up of rags and wood surrounded a low concrete building at the side of the road. It had been shot to pieces and sprays of fresh white bullet holes marked the building's walls and drifted across the tarmac in long, dotted zigzagging lines. Golden cartridges, which had fallen from the chopper, littered the ground, glinting in the sun like fresh hail. It had been a one-sided battle and the losers lay scattered on the ground. Two women lay by the road. One had had the top of her head neatly removed, where a bullet had sheared off part of her skull.

Danny walked carefully among the dead, not daring to come too close. They were mostly children, teenagers at most. None wore uniforms unless a constant theme of rags, torn shirts and strange little pieces of jewelry could be called a uniform. These were the feared RUF. The fallen weapons by their side, the garish ornaments strung around their neck, their gruesome reputation, none of it could hide the simple fact of their age. They were kids.

The government soldiers whooped and hollered amid the dead. One soldier had cut off a long, thin stick from the bush and he returned clutching it in one hand. He danced around one of the dead

RUF boys, shouting loudly and bringing the stick down in long, stinging arcs to whip the dead body. Danny looked over at Hoyes. She gave him a thumbs-up.

It's good copy, he thought. He knew she was thinking the same.

THE HELICOPTER SKIMMED low barely twenty feet above the treetops of the jungle. It reminded Danny of every Vietnam War movie he had ever seen. The thought made him excited. No other story he had ever done compared to sitting in the back of a helicopter, roaring over an African war zone.

Maria was shouting in his ear.

"We have to keep low like this," she yelled. "If we stay at this height we are too low for any missile to be fired at us and moving too fast for anyone with a gun to know we are coming before we have gone again."

He turned to her.

"It's also great fun," he said. She laughed.

He had not seen her in days. The trips up the road had become a sudden routine for every journalist in Freetown. Each time he, Kam and the others would push a little farther, a few more kilometers, as the Sierra Leone Army moved out of Freetown. Now it was possible to get forty kilometers out of the city before hitting the inevitable checkpoint that bribing could not get through. It had been fun for the first couple times, but now it felt frustrating. He knew there was a story beyond the final checkpoint but it was being denied them. At the same time he had been trying to see Maria but she had been working through the nights.

Then she had called with an offer he could not refuse. She was organizing a trip east to one of the few towns there in government hands. It was to Bo, on the edge of diamond country, and they would see a food distribution at a children's center. It was meant to be a trip for the U.S. press only, but Maria had scrambled an extra space. Danny had not hesitated. Maria seemed in her element too. She flirted with the other journalists, bending them around her little finger. He could see them falling for her, one by one, and all the time he thought: She is mine.

After a couple of hours the chopper rounded a final ridgeline and Bo lay before them. It was spread over low hills in the bend of a sluggish river that cut through scrubby bush. The chopper headed for a dusty football pitch, where it threw up a huge cloud of dust as it came down. A line of SUVs was waiting. Danny was amazed at how normal the town looked. Its streets were not potholed and its market was crowded. Lines of stores, owned by Indians or Lebanese, flanked the streets. Given that all around was country overrun with the RUF, it was an unexpected jolt of calm.

"Diamonds," said one American journalist, turning to look at Danny with a skeptical eye. "This place is surrounded by diamond fields. It means the RUF have a working relationship with the folks who live here. Keeping things peaceful means more money. The rest of the country is not so lucky."

The city had still attracted its fair share of the poor, the homeless and the hungry. Thousands of refugees thronged a camp just outside of town. A multiple array of aid agency flags fluttered from rows of white tents like some medieval tournament ground. Here and there the familiar white SUVs of the aid workers picked their way through crowds of Sierra Leoneans, listlessly walking or huddled in family groups around small fires. The diamond economy driving the town did not reach here. One could have a camp of starving refugees in the same place as a bustling market town: two different worlds in the same city.

The convoy pulled up outside a large tent from which flew a War

Child International flag. A crowd of people, all young women or old men, sat on the ground outside. They crouched in the dust, immune to the need for shade or water; silent and waiting. Maria got out and gathered the reporters around her. It was supposed to be a food distribution for families looking after young orphans. Maria painstakingly explained to the dozen or so journalists the work the charity was doing and how each family had to present its registration slip before getting rations of food. There had been no deliveries for fifteen days, she added. These people—she pointed behind her—are beginning to starve.

The engine whine of a lorry interrupted her. It was a white truck with a tarpaulin stretched over its back. It sounded old and sick, giving an oily cough as it bumped over the rocky path toward the crowd. It juddered to a halt. Boxes and boxes of corn meal were stacked inside. A slow murmur built up among the crowd.

Danny saw a look of panic cross Maria's face.

"Not like this, you fucking idiots," she breathed.

But she was too late. One of the men on the back of the truck cut open a box and hauled out a sack. He threw it to the ground. An old man in the crowd got slowly to his feet and walked forward. With difficulty he hauled the bag onto his shoulder and walked away. The crowd seemed to be waiting to see what would happen. No one stopped him. Maria turned to run forward and began to wave furiously at the men on the truck. But it was too late. As one, the crowd stood up and surged toward the vehicle. The men on the back looked surprised but rapidly started opening the other boxes as fast as they could. A forest of grasping hands sprang up with each bag that was hauled off. There were cries and shouts and fights starting to break out. Women and the old lost their precious handouts to men and the strong. There was no order, just violence and struggle. It was like watching ants attack their prey, gradually stripping the truck bare.

Danny saw Maria. She stood watching aghast, then she slowly sat on the ground. He walked over and rested a hand softly on her shoulder. She looked up. Dust grimed her cheeks, but there were no tears. Just anger. Anger mixed with despair.

"Like this, it's just letting the strong get stronger. It's pointless. They don't need the food. They'll just sell it in the town," she said. "These people are so . . ." Her voice trailed off into the afternoon heat. Danny could think of nothing that would console her. He looked up. The truck was empty now anyway.

DANNY WALKED DOWN the streets of Bo in stunned surprise. He had just seen the starving crowd ransack an aid truck and yet here were restaurants serving stews and curries. Here were electrical shops and a travel agent offering flights to Bombay. It was a working city. It was normal life, recognizable to anyone.

He gradually became aware of someone shouting his name.

"Kellerman! Danny Kellerman!"

He spun around and saw a Middle Eastern–looking man crossing the road toward him, wearing shades and a black T-shirt. Ali.

"What are you doing here, man?" he said, clasping Danny by the shoulder. "I show you how to shoot a rifle and you've become a mercenary already? Jesus, I've never seen anyone go native so quickly."

Danny was pleased to see him. He told him about the trip, about Maria and about the morning's near riot.

"Hey, I am glad things are working out for you with that American lady, Danny. She's the kind of woman who would give me a conscience. That's why I steer clear of that aid crowd. Keep with the nice Lebanese girls. They'll give you hell at home but they don't care what line of work you do."

"What are you doing here, Ali?" Danny asked.

Ali paused.

"Come on, Danny. You know better than that."

Then, as an afterthought, Ali said, "Look, I've got to see someone outside of town. You got an hour? I'll show you a diamond mine."

Danny glanced at his watch. It was too good an opportunity to pass up. Most of the country was off-limits. But here he could get a tour of diamond country, right behind RUF lines. He knew Maria would be furious if she ever found out. He was here on her trust. But Ali seemed so cocksure . . . and this would please the editors back home.

"Sure," he said.

Ali led him across the street to a blacked-out SUV. He sat in the front and glanced backward. Two Sierra Leonean men sat in the rear. They wore sunglasses and carried AK-47s. They were unmoving and unsmiling. Ali ignored them as they pulled away from the curb. Within minutes they were out of town driving down a road so potholed that they slowed to a virtual crawl. Within ten minutes they were stopped at a roadblock. Child soldiers seemed to materialize out of nowhere. There were half a dozen of them, varying in size from one boy who could not have been more than ten to a lanky teenager. Danny felt his palms become damp with sweat. They looked confused when Ali rolled down his window and leaned out. Without a word, they let them pass.

"Were they RUF?" Danny blurted.

Ali shrugged nonchalantly. "Who knows or cares? This is Bo. It's more important that they know who Ali Alhoun is than I know who they are."

They drove on until they came to a wide river. There Ali pulled the SUV off the road and down a barely visible dirt track through the bush. Finally they came to a rest by the river's edge. For about a mile all the vegetation was gone, leaving just bare white sand. It was pitted with holes, some just a few bucket scrapes and others in which a whole family could disappear. Each hole was being worked by bare-backed young men, scraping out water and earth.

"Weird, isn't it?" Ali said. "All those pretty stones around all those beautiful ladies' necks and this is where it begins. Some peasant breaking his back in a shithole like this."

Ali got out and told him he would be gone for a quarter of an hour. One guard would wait by the car, the other was going with him.

"Talk to whoever you want, but don't leave sight of this car," he said. With that he was gone, threading his way through the open pits, the armed man following him like a pet dog. Danny watched him go and then he was aware he was being watched himself. One of the miners had stopped work and looked him up and down. Danny walked over and haltingly began to ask him questions.

His name was Edugu Tanana. He had worked the mines for two decades and the rippling muscles across his back told the story of every hour. He proudly showed off a registration card with his picture and the stamp of the Sierra Leone mining ministry. Whether that really meant anything in this place, it was hard to say. But for Tanana it was his most treasured possession. He kept it wrapped in a plastic bag, tucked inside his trousers. Whatever legitimacy he got from his life, it was encapsulated in that little card. He worked from sunup until sundown. Seven days a week. That was the rhythm of his life. If he was lucky he would dig out a tiny rough diamond. Men like Ali bought them from him. Then it was back to digging.

Ali reemerged.

He was flushed in the face.

"Danny, come on," he said. Ali saw whom he was talking to.

"Hey, Tanana. Any luck?"

The man shook his head.

"You wouldn't lie to me, now?" said Ali. If there was a threat there, Danny could not spot it in his tone. Perhaps the words were enough.

Tanana just shook his head, smiling broadly.

"Come on, Danny. Let's get you back."

Danny glanced at his watch. He had been gone over an hour. Shit, he thought, but when he stumbled back through the door of the War Child compound, no one had realized he was late. There were other problems going on. Maria was frantically talking into a radio and the other journalists were lounging around the room. Most were catching up on the sleep they had missed with the morning's early start. Maria looked up and mouthed a hello. Soon she came off the radio and walked over.

"Now the fucking chopper is late. Apparently someone tried to shoot at it after it took off, so the pilots are a bit wary of coming back. I've convinced them otherwise. They'll be here in a couple of hours."

She looked harried. He put a hand to her hair, but she brushed it off.

"Not here," she said. Then she looked around at the room, its inhabitants either busy or asleep. A smile broke out on her face and she turned and walked into a back room.

He followed a moment later.

It was dark and she came at him like an animal, dragging him against a wall and pushing him to the dusty floor. She pushed a chair with her foot against the door and raked her nails under his shirt and across his chest. Her tongue filled his mouth and he could taste the dirt on her lips. His hands reached for her breasts as she plunged her fingers into his trousers.

"Don't make a sound," she whispered.

*   *   *

THAT NIGHT all the talk at the Cape Sierra bar was—as usual—of
Sankoh. As the trips out of Freetown were starting to get routine and
the RUF was being pushed back, Sankoh seemed a missing piece of
the puzzle. The RUF in many ways was Sankoh. Without him, they
would collapse. With him they would never go away. Kam's theory was
that he was in neighboring Liberia, being looked after by that country's
warlord-turned-president Charles Taylor. When asked his thoughts by
Hoyes, Danny decided to throw that one into the mix. Hoyes nodded.
Like she was some sort of expert.

"Interesting," she said. "I suppose that could be right."

Just then Hoyes jumped in the air as a tall man behind her put his
hands over her eyes.

"Hello, darling," he purred. She spun around and hugged the figure.

"Lenny," she said. "I was wondering when you would get here."

Lenny Ferenc. He was a legend among war correspondents, and
despite being in his late fifties, he still looked the part. He was tall and
his hair was a dark thatch above a lined face. His blue eyes looked far
younger, though. They were clear and bright and twinkled when he
cracked a joke. Danny had never seen him before, but he had heard
the stories. From Saigon to Baghdad, Ferenc was either the first man in
or the last man out. Now he only wrote for the big monthly American
magazines. He was also an old university friend of his father's. The two
had gone to Oxford together and Harry had a long-standing habit of
breathlessly recounting the latest of Ferenc's adventures.

He extended a hand to Danny and introduced himself.

"Ah, Danny Kellerman. You're Harry's boy!" he said, his voice a perfect study in the English gentleman. "I heard you were up in Bo today, scooping your rivals. Good man. That's the way to keep up the family tradition," he said.

Danny felt himself being charmed by the freely given compliment. Ferenc accepted a beer from the barman and launched into the story of his trip there, via Liberia, for reasons that never became clear. He soon had all their rapt attention and Hoyes's in particular. It was a bravura performance. Hoyes offered him another drink, but Ferenc shook his head.

"Thank you, but no, my darling," he said, rising from his stool. "It's been a fuck of a day. I'm just glad to be here. I haven't missed a war yet and I thought I might be left out of this one. I should imagine I've got some catching up to do."

Danny saw Hoyes watch him go. He suspected that there must have once been something between the two of them. Though if all the stories were true, then she would have been far from alone in that respect. As Ferenc left he saw the smile drop from Hoyes's face.

"What's the matter?" he said. Hoyes looked at him.

"Having Lenny here raises the stakes for all of us," she said. "That 'just arrived' thing is an act. He'll have something planned already. If I know Lenny, and believe me I do, it will be something not far short of suicidal."

Now that Ferenc was gone, the huddle of journalists fell quiet. It wasn't just that Ferenc had removed himself from the room, it was what he'd left behind. Each day was simply another gamble. Weighing the risk against the gain in chasing a story. How far would Ferenc push things? It was the unspoken question that sucked up all the air in the room.

Hoyes knocked back her drink and got up.

"Sorry, chaps. I've lost the mood for this," she said. "We're all going to start needing better nights' sleep now."

*   *   *

DANNY LOOKED DOWN at the keys in his hand and then at the door of the villa in front of him. It was perfect.

"Thank you, Ali," he breathed.

The Lebanese had shown up at the bar the night before and asked about Maria. Danny was unable to shut up, gushing about how she made him feel.

"She's the one. She really might be the one," he heard himself say. Ali laughed and slapped his thigh.

"Really? How do you know so soon, my friend? You've been here a few weeks and already you've found the woman of your dreams. You must be a lucky man. Or perhaps one who does not quite know who he is dealing with."

"What do you know about Maria?" Danny asked curtly. He was offended to have Ali pour such cold water on his feelings. But Ali was still smiling broadly.

"Nothing, Danny. Nothing at all. I am just saying that sometimes in a place like this not everyone is what they seem. Perhaps it is best to be a little cautious." Ali paused and then reached into his pocket. "But until then, who am I to stand in the way of the only lucky man in Freetown?"

Then he tossed Danny a set of keys.

"My family has a villa down the coast," he said. "It's safe now. It's at the end of the peninsula. Take her there for a weekend."

He phoned Maria the next minute, slurring the invitation into the phone. She complained about her work, but it didn't take much to make her relent. She would come down later the next afternoon. Kam would pick her up.

Now here Danny was. The villa stood directly on a rocky cliff above a curve of white sand. It looked like a slice of heaven, far from the war, far from London. He unlocked the gate and walked inside. The place had a stale and musty smell and obviously had not been used in months. The fridge was gently humming with power. He opened it and was amazed to see carefully prepared dishes of hummus, bread and other Lebanese foods. There was chilled wine and beer. He reached in and took a can, popping its tab as he walked down some stone stairs and onto the beach.

By Sierra Leone standards the weather was cool and the little bay seemed to catch whatever sea breeze there was. He walked down the beach, reveling in the sound of the waves. He stripped off his shirt and jumped in, laughing to himself. Just offshore he could see a group of fishing canoes with men flinging their nets into the water. You would never know there was a war going on. He thought of the last few weeks and could barely believe it. He thought of the dead RUF kids he had seen on the road and the amputees' refugee camp. He scrubbed his shoulders in the sea, feeling there was an itch just beneath his skin that he could not reach. It all seemed like a faraway country.

He returned to the villa, exhausted and soaking wet. He stretched out on a hammock at the back of the house. It was nearly noon and the heat of the day was gathering strength. He was asleep within minutes, drifting in and out of dreams, unsure of where he was but feeling safe, for the first time since he had left England.

A kiss on his forehead woke him and he stared up into her eyes.

"Hello," Maria said.

She clambered into the hammock, which swung crazily, nearly toppling them out. Eventually she crawled in, laying her head against his chest, and they waited for the hammock to steady itself.

"Oh, well," she said. "I guess that answers my question."

"What?"

"I was planning to see if it was possible to have sex in a hammock. I'm pretty sure we'd break our necks."

They talked the afternoon away. He asked her about her family and where she was from. She described her childhood as the only Hispanic among the corn-fed blondes of a small town, miles from anywhere. Not that she hadn't loved it. She was grateful for the chances America had given her.

"I know that sounds like a cliché," she said, tapping him in the chest to make sure he didn't dare question her. "But it is true. I love my country, Danny. I really do. It gave my family everything. Kids like me, when we leave college we have debts other than just money."

Danny opened up too. He talked of how journalism had always been what he'd wanted to do since he was a little kid. Of how chasing a story could feel a little like chasing a drug, getting high, moving on to the next one. Of how covering a war had seemed like the ultimate hit.

"And what do you think now?" she asked. "Is it what you expected?"

Danny shook his head.

"I don't understand this place," he said. "I don't know how people can do the things they have done to each other. I feel there's nothing that can be done to make this better. I don't think we're telling that story. The other journalists here, they do it for ego. They do it for their own careers. They use this place like a game."

She hoisted herself on one elbow and looked right at him, her hands caressing his chest.

"That's why I like you, Danny Kellerman. You're thinking about the place you're writing about. It's changing you, not you changing it to fit a headline."

Danny stared off at the waves rolling in from the sea. It was the only sound in the world apart from their voices and yet he felt he should talk in a whisper.

"There's one road out of Freetown," he said. "Every day some of us go up that road. Every day we go a little farther, go to the next road-block, the next village. Just to get another story in the paper, just to say we've been somewhere else. It's the most dangerous place to go looking for a story, but it's also the easiest."

He looked at her.

"What happens after?" he said suddenly. He felt her flinch slightly.

"After what?" she said, buying time.

"This," he said. "This won't go on forever."

"No, Danny. Your job here won't go on forever. Mine will. Wars are just distractions. They get in the way of looking after my kids. But they are short-term visitors; they don't stay forever. Just like journalists."

Danny shook his head.

"When the war is over, leave with me. We can make it work."

She stared at him and he sought frantically to read her expression. But he could not. He just sank into those eyes, not knowing what thoughts lay behind them. Not knowing her. He felt a trace of anger mixed with his love.

"I can't leave," she said. "There are reasons for it that I can't tell you. You have to trust me that I just can't get up and go like that."

He made to speak, to ask her what it was keeping her here, why she could not give them a chance. She pulled herself up to him and hushed him with a kiss.

"Sshhhh," she said, and kissed him again. "Here and now is good for tonight. Let's not think about anything. Just here and now."

*   *   *

KAM PUT HIS FOOT on the accelerator and the little Renault hurtled down the road. He was in an exuberant mood. In the back was Lenny Ferenc. Even Kam had heard of the great man and Kam was a sucker for celebrity. It had made the other drivers jealous that morning and only partly because Ferenc was offering double the rate of other journalists. Not that Kam would ever leave Danny, but he had promised Ferenc that he could come along with them that morning up the road out of Freetown. And Danny had also been happy enough with the idea. He had a soft spot for celebrity too.

They were late starting. Ferenc had descended from his room at the Cape Sierra looking by far the worse for wear. Danny was amused that Hoyes was also a no-show. He suspected the two events were probably linked. It was not at all beyond Ferenc to scupper a rival with a one-two punch of boozing and seduction. Ferenc gave Danny a guilty smile.

"Sorry I'm late, Danny. I feel even worse than after a night out drinking with your father." Danny had laughed at that, but now as they sped through the familiar roadblocks it seemed less funny. Other journalists had gone ahead of them. Bribes of alcohol had already been handed out. After an hour of driving, they met their first drunk. It was a young militiaman whose wild eyes lolled back in his head. Kam thrust a pack of cigarettes in his hand. The gunman dropped them and scrambled to pick them up as they drove off. Danny exchanged a look with Kam that said it all: Kam did not like the way the day was beginning. That was enough to set Danny's own nerves on edge.

But if Ferenc noticed the danger, he gave no hint of it. He sat in the backseat and observed the passing scenery, drinking from a bottle of Coke.

"This place doesn't change," he said. "I was here two years ago and ten years ago and a few times in between. It's still the same roadblocks and the same crazy bastards manning them."

They drove on. The roadblocks became more spaced out. Soon they were about thirty kilometers beyond the spot where Danny had seen Freddie's chopper shoot up an RUF camp. They came to a long iron bridge that crossed a wide, winding river. At its near side stood a cluster of UN armored vehicles.

"Jesus," Danny said. "The UN are getting brave these days. These guys are a long way up-country."

Ferenc got out and ambled over to them. Danny followed. They were Jordanians and they looked like hard men, muscled and suspicious. One of them, atop a jeep, swiveled a mounted machine gun in their direction. Danny stopped in his tracks, but Ferenc didn't break stride.

Ferenc shouted something in Arabic. The man behind the gun looked surprised and then laughed. He was evidently the commanding officer and Ferenc made straight for him, holding out his hand. The man didn't have a choice but to shake it. Soon they were laughing and joking and Ferenc waved Danny over.

"This man says he does not know if it is safe over the river," Ferenc said. "He says they came here last night, heard gunfire just before dawn on the far bank but nothing since. He says we would be crazy men to go farther."

The Jordanian nodded solemnly.

"Well. We are crazy men and we do go farther," Ferenc said, and clapped the man on the back. Soon they were on the road again.

"What did you say to them, Lenny? You cracked a joke. In Arabic?"

Lenny laughed.

"Something I picked up in the West Bank. I said, 'Onward to Jerusalem, crush the Zionist entity.' It works with Arabs wherever you see them. Of course, if they knew my father was a Jew from Budapest who lives in Tel Aviv, they would feel differently."

Danny laughed out loud. His "Lenny story" was already in the bag and somehow that felt more important than anything he would write for the paper that day.

The trip eventually came to a shuddering halt at a Sierra Leone Army checkpoint. Other journalists had been waiting in vain for several hours. Some were already heading back to Freetown. This would be as far as anyone would go today. Ferenc disappeared in the direction of the commanding officer, but it became clear that even his charms were not going to work.

Soon they were the only journalists left. They crouched under the shade of a tree and the minutes ticked by. Danny was getting worried. He was mindful of how more drunk some of the militiamen would get as they took boozy hits off the journalists heading back. Danny looked at Ferenc dozing in the shade. He did not seem to have a care in the world.

Suddenly, a truck came into view down the road. It was lurching from side to side, like a drunk at closing time. As it got closer Danny could see the tarpaulin across its back was shredded with bullet holes and flapping in the wind. Ferenc was up and starting toward it as it neared the roadblock. Danny forced himself to follow. The truck pulled to a halt. Danny could see fear and panic on the face of its driver and saw that its windscreen was a frosting of white bull's-eyes. He could also hear screams and groans coming from the back. Danny edged around.

It was a horrible sight. The truck was piled with dead and injured. About a dozen young men lay there, some unmoving, others groaning and writhing. A few had halfhearted bandages wrapped around bleeding limbs. One man stared vacantly ahead, clutching his shoulder from which dark blood oozed between his fingers.

Ferenc was furiously taking notes and grilling the driver. Then a crack came from the bush, followed by a sharp bang, somewhere behind them. Ferenc looked up and saw Danny.

"That was a mortar, old chap," Ferenc said.

The truck roared into life again even as a few soldiers were attempting to unload the wounded. It jerked forward, flinging some off the back and onto the hard tarmac. One man, his legs shattered by bullets, hit the ground with a sickening crunch. He flipped and twisted like a fish plucked out of water. Danny felt a dark wave of panic crash over him. All around him government troops were running and starting to flee. Their commanding officer emerged from the tent and screamed orders at them, but they seemed to have little effect.

"Lenny! Come on!" Danny screamed, and he started back to the car. He got in. But Ferenc had not followed them. He stood, statue still, in the sea of panicking soldiers, a few of whom had begun to fire wildly down the road, shooting blindly into the jungle.

"Lenny!" yelled Danny, leaning out of the car.

Ferenc ignored him, then slowly strolled to the car.

"Things are just starting to pick up a bit," he said regretfully, as if talking about ducking out of a bar early. Reluctantly he got in. Kam turned the car back down the road and Ferenc silently sat in the back, glancing occasionally over his shoulder and reviewing his notes. Danny's heart finally began to beat at a normal pace. He looked at Kam. Kam looked back at him. They said it without words.

Lenny Ferenc was insane.

12

[2004]

LONDON GREETED HIM as it always seemed to when he was returning from abroad: with a cold, gray embrace. The train from Heathrow was half empty as it sliced through the suburbs and Danny saw the same grimy projects and people trudging through the rain.

He soon joined them, walking back to his Highgate flat, dragging his suitcase behind. It felt jarring to be back. Just twenty-four hours ago he had been in Freetown. Now here he was back in another world and another life, neither of which he felt part of anymore. He fiddled with his keys and opened the door to his flat. He did not bother calling out Rachel's name. The place somehow felt empty when he walked in and he knew she was not at home. She must have been staying late at work. Or, more likely, she was delaying coming home, trying to work out what to say and how she felt. He did not blame her. He padded slowly around the flat. The place appeared unfamiliar to him. He looked at last summer's holiday pictures of himself and Rachel together on the fridge. They seemed happy, that young and smiling couple somewhere in France. He remembered the cottage they had rented, tucked away down a leafy road in the Loire Valley. It was a short walk to the nearest village with its tightly wound cobbled streets and single café. They drank wine there every night, ignoring the stares of strangers and giggling at their stumbled attempts to speak French. Rachel loved that holiday, but even then, he thought now, he had felt empty inside. A cottage in France seemed cliché for a London couple. It seemed too easy. Too ordinary.

He turned away from the photograph and looked at a pile of unwashed mugs in the sink. He could see the faint imprints of her lipstick on each one, kisses good morning that he had missed. Then he went upstairs to their bedroom. Her clothes were folded neatly on a chair. He inhaled the scent of her from the room. It smelled sweet and good. But, as with Maria, he couldn't quite get it right, couldn't bring it back from his mind as it once was. He felt suddenly exhausted. He lay down on the bed and was asleep in seconds.

He woke up to the brush of lips across his own and felt a tress of hair caress his cheek. He opened his eyes. Rachel was sitting on the edge of the bed looking down at him. It was already dark and he had no idea what time it was. He tried to struggle upward but she pressed him down with a gentle push of her palm.

"Hey," she said. He flung his arms around her, burying his face in her neck, inhaling her. It felt good. She returned his grasp.

"I'm sorry," he said. "I know I've been out of the loop while I've been away. But it's done. I was chasing something I couldn't pin down. I don't even really know what it was, but I think it's over now."

She broke gently away from his grasp. She looked sad.

"Danny, you've been out of the loop for a lot longer than just the past few weeks," she said. "It's been a long time since I thought you were really here with me."

He felt a slight twinge of panic.

"Don't be ridiculous . . . ," he began, and then caught himself. Now was not the time to argue. That was not what she wanted to hear.

"I'm sorry," he said, and he slumped back down. "We should have this chat when we're both up to it."

Rachel nodded. She ran a hand down his chest.

"Try to sleep. I'll join you after I've sorted out a bit of work."

Danny wanted to stay awake for her, but it was a losing battle. He felt drained and he surrendered himself back to sleep. He never felt her enter the room two hours later. Never saw her as she stood, motionless, staring at this man in her bed. This lover who now seemed a stranger, obsessed with some cause she feared and could not understand. He never saw her fight against the tears as she took off her clothes and got in beside him. He never felt her light kiss at the nape of his neck as she switched off the lights. But the ignorance went both ways. Hours later, as morning sunlight streamed through the windows, Danny awoke with a start. He turned and looked over at her still-sleeping figure. She would never know that he had been finally, at long last, dreaming of Maria. Not her.

HENNESSEY HAD CALMED down slightly by the time Danny turned up in his office the next morning. But the news editor was still, by anyone's standards, furious.

"You let me down," he said. "I let you sell me this story. Then you disappear off the radar and chase after some story you now think might not be true. Do you mind telling me what exactly you have been doing? I'm certainly going to be very interested to read your expense claims."

Danny had few answers. He should have felt worse than he did. He had given it a shot, which was better than not trying at all. He would take whatever price Hennessey had in mind.

"I fucked up," he said. "I know it. But I've actually done a lot of work. I can get a good piece out of this still. Perhaps not for the magazine, but for the foreign pages, easily. We can do a nice two-page spread. The new Sierra Leone. It won't be a waste of our time."

Hennessey lit a cigarette and pointedly did not offer one to Danny.

"You're still in shit," he said. "But for the moment, get out of my sight and get me that piece by the end of next week. Let's see if we can rescue something from all this."

Danny walked out of Hennessey's office and let out a sigh of relief. He knew he must have been the subject of weeks of office gossip. The man who went missing in Sierra Leone. A journalistic Colonel Kurtz. He walked straight out onto the street. He suddenly felt like he was having a panic attack and couldn't catch his breath. He had been lucky. He still had his job. He decided to visit his mother. It would help him reconnect back to London life

Since her divorce she had moved to a little semi-detached house in the far north of London. It always seemed to Danny to be a huge step down from their grand old Oxford home. Four bedrooms had been replaced by two, Victorian brick swapped for 1960s concrete and the spires of Oxford exchanged for Barnet High Street. The fact that his mother never seemed to recognize her changed circumstances only depressed him more about their split.

She was, of course, delighted to see him. Her face cracked into a broad smile as she opened the door.

Danny relaxed as she fixed him up a cup of tea. She looked well, he thought. She was only in her mid-fifties and she still looked a fine woman, her face delicately carved. A great beauty in her day, his father had often crowed, not realizing there was a sting in the tail of that compliment.

"You're looking very well, Mum," he said, and was pleased his mother's cheeks flushed. It felt good to make someone happy.

"Rachel said you were in Africa for work. What was that about?" she asked, quickly changing the subject. She had never been able to take a compliment.

"Oh, just a story. It didn't go too well, actually, but I'll sort it out."

His mother looked worried.

"Is everything all right, darling?" she asked.

For the briefest of moments he thought about telling her everything. Of how he felt his whole life was going down the tube. Rachel, career, all of it swirling away from him as he lacked even the energy to try to hold on. But the feeling passed quickly.

"Don't worry. But what about you?" he asked.

His mother frowned.

"I'm worried about your father," she said.

This was typical. The man had divorced her, run off with some young blonde, left her alone in the depths of Barnet, for God's sake, and here she was, worrying about him.

"He's really not well. He needs to slow down at his age."

Danny mentally cracked a cruel joke about all the sex he was likely having with his younger second wife.

But he said, "I don't want to talk about him, Mum. How are you? Are you getting out much? You know, meeting anyone else?"

His mum looked genuinely surprised as she digested what he was asking. Then she laughed and put her hand over her mouth.

"Oh good God, no," she said. "You know your father was really the only one for me." Danny did know that. He could see it in her face. He just could not understand it. How had this kind and loving soul who had been so abandoned still care for that man?

"You should see him, you know. Go and see him this weekend," she said, her face brightening.

"I will," he lied. It seemed the nicest thing to say.

IN THE END though there was no need to lie. Danny was sitting at his desk on Friday afternoon when the call from Rachel came. Thoughts of visiting his dad had already been forgotten amid the hurried writing of a story that he hoped would rescue—no, salvage—something of his reputation with Hennessey.

He picked it up and could hear her sniffing on the other end of the phone and mumbling a stream of anxious words. Oh God, he thought. I can't deal with this. What had he done now?

"What is it?" he snapped. "I can't hear a word you're saying."

The sudden violence in his manner caused Rachel to stop talking. He felt the ice in her silence and then he heard her voice. Clear and distinct.

"He's dead, Danny," she sobbed. "Your father's dead."

And she put the phone down. Danny sat with the receiver in his hand for a long time, the buzz of the dial tone going unheard. Then he got up and calmly switched his computer off. The story on the screen disappeared. It was with only fleeting regret that he realized he had not bothered to save it.

DANNY STOOD at his father's grave and tried to feel something.
Anything.

He had borne the coffin with the other pallbearers, feeling the weight of the old man on his shoulders. It had seemed improbably heavy. He could still scarcely believe it; the phone call from Rachel, his own call to his mother. The strangled, awful cry she had made and his own panic at that. It was her reaction that had really brought his dad's death home for him. Could she really have been holding out hope for him? He had rushed to her house, found her staring into space, tears wetting her blouse, and awkwardly he held her, wanting to tell her what a bastard the old man had been but biting his tongue, knowing that was the last thing she wanted to hear.

Then the phone calls came in. From colleagues and, eventually, from Hennessey. Commiserations and sympathy all round. This wasn't just to be a family funeral. This was to be a Fleet Street wake. He had dreaded the prospect.

Now here he stood, at the lip of the grave, casting his own clod of earth downward, hearing the forlorn thump of it hit the wood, knocking on a door that was forever shut. The last time he saw his father had been a drunken row in a restaurant. It wasn't much to show off about. He glanced up at the gray sky, blank and formless, not even betraying a hint of the sun. A slow drizzle had been falling all day and now it began to quicken, forcing the mourners to huddle together and the priest to speed up his funerary rites.

"Ashes to ashes, dust to dust . . ."

Danny felt removed from it. Disembodied. As if he were taking part in a film and any minute the director would shout, "Cut." His father would rise from the grave and they could begin again.

Rachel was at his side now, slipping her arm through his. He squeezed her wrist and she smiled thinly through eyes wet with tears. He looked over at his mother. This had destroyed her far more than the divorce. She was pale and ashen. A crumpled woman, staring into the earth, beseeching for this ordeal to end. When he put his arm around her she felt as light and fragile as air, a mere ghost. He felt if he held her too tightly she might break.

Then it was over. The mourners drifted off, one by one. Danny and Rachel stood on either side of his mother and helped her trudge through the graveyard in the direction of their old home. The place where Danny had grown up and where his father's wake was being held.

It was a crowded affair, but Danny hovered at its edges. He did not know what to say to Rachel. She had probed him for his feelings but he was unable to express them, as if some sort of dam had built up in his mind and she couldn't get through it. Yet Danny was worried there wasn't that much being held back behind the wall; just emptiness. When they talked about the practical side of things—the whos, whats and wheres of the funeral—it was better. They worked things out, engaged in a common task. But whenever she wanted to talk about his feelings, he brushed her off. Now at the wake she drifted away from him and mingled with an assorted band of cousins and friends.

People gathered in the spacious lounge. He positioned himself to one side, content to let the party flow without him. But it was not easy. A succession of people shook his hand and offered condolences. Editors and columnists, foreign correspondents and old friends, all with a kind word and an anecdote about "old Harry."

"He was a fine man."

"Never a dull moment."

As the platitudes came and went he felt a growing anger. Everyone else seemed so upset, so full of fond memories, so deep in praise of the old man. He felt excluded as usual from his father's life. Deep down he knew he was being selfish, still reacting to the craziness of the last few weeks and Maria's death. But he could not stop the heat rising within him. He found himself zoning out as people talked to him, their words becoming a distorted noise as if his head were deep underwater. He was aware Rachel was next to him now, peering at him, but he could not see her. He was focused only on a sight he had never expected to witness. His mother was seated on the couch deep in conversation with a striking young blonde. It was his father's mistress—his second wife—and the two women were holding each other, talking and crying. His mother bent her head down and the younger woman stroked her hair, blinking back her own tears.

"What the fuck is she doing with her?" Danny hissed at Rachel. A few people heard his words and their heads swiveled around. Rachel jerked his arm. He had been too loud.

"Danny! Sshhhh!" she said.

He turned on her. The sight of his mother and his father's second wife sharing their grief appalled him.

"This is fucked up. What is that bitch doing here anyway?" Half the room must have heard. His mother looked up too.

"That's enough!" Rachel said, and yanked him by the elbow. A score of faces turned to watch as she pulled him into the drizzly rain outside.

"What has got into you?" she exploded.

He was taken aback. Was he the only one who could see this was wrong?

"That woman has no right to . . . ," he began. But Rachel stopped him.

"Fuck off, Danny," she said. "Just fuck off. This day isn't just about you."

Her words stung him into silence. He realized the suppressed emotions had been within her, not him. And the dam was now breached.

"You think everything's about you, don't you? You've been ignoring your life and everybody in it. Well, other people have feelings, Danny. Other people loved your dad."

She looked at him, her mouth opening and shutting as the words flowed out. "I really, really loved him, Danny. And now he's gone. And I'm not the only one to feel that way. This day is for us too. So, if you don't feel like being here, then just fuck off and leave. The rest of us have things to do."

She spun on her heel, leaving him standing in the rain. Then she stopped and looked back.

"I've wanted to get you back for months, Danny. But you're just not here anymore. I don't want to share my life with a ghost. I need more than that. I deserve more than that."

She went back in and Danny sat down on a wall. He needed to get back in control of things. He stared up at the sky and felt drops of rain on his face. God, just let this day be over with. He closed his eyes and when he opened them he saw Hennessey standing in front of him.

"Danny," he said. "This is a terrible day." He sat down beside him.

"Thanks," Danny said. "I don't think I'm handling this too well."

Hennessey must have noticed the "scene" inside. He looked worried and thoughtful.

"Look," he said. "Take a couple of weeks off. You need it. Come back after that and we'll see where we are. Call it stress leave or something."

Danny nodded.

"Thanks," he breathed, and managed a thin smile. He supposed Hennessey was trying to be kind, trying to help. But it sounded like a death sentence on his career.

FOR THE NEXT hour Danny walked around Oxford, ignoring the puzzled stares as he strolled down the soaking, suburban streets. He went through parks and down roads lined with familiar childhood sights. This was where he remembered growing up, chasing girls, starting a school newspaper. He had loved his dad then, he thought. It was only as an adult, proud possessor of his own neuroses, that things had soured. The walk centered him and he returned to the house calmer, with a sense Rachel had saved him from a much worse public disaster. He wanted to thank her, tell her that she was right. He had been a fool. But as he walked through the door he saw the wake was over. Rachel had already left and his mother was busying herself with the dishes. His father's second wife was helping her, standing at her side, drying. They were working in silence. He did not disturb them.

He caught a train alone back to London and walked home. It was only when he walked into a half-empty flat that he began to realize what had actually happened; what Rachel had actually been saying. Most of her clothes were already gone. Her bathroom stuff was gone. The pictures on the fridge were gone. In a growing panic he punched her number into his phone, but her mobile was switched off. He slumped onto his couch and now, at last, tears began to come.

She had left him.

DANNY FELT HE WAS losing his mind. It was three days before Rachel switched her phone back on and when she finally answered his call, her voice had a steely resolve.

"I couldn't take it anymore, Danny," she said. "I know I've done this at the worst possible time. I'm sorry for that. I truly am, but I had no choice."

"You left me at my father's funeral." He laughed roughly, half trying to make a joke, half sounding bitter. "It's hard to think of a worse time to dump someone."

Rachel was not in the mood for gallows humor.

"I know, Danny. I don't feel proud of that. But maybe that was what

I needed to push me into it. God knows, I needed something to get me out."

Rachel had come to this decision without him and there was no changing her mind.

"Look, Danny. I'm not going to do the whole 'let's be friends' speech here even though that is how I feel. I do want us to be friends. But I don't want to talk to you for a while. I need a break," she said, and then added, "You need a break too. You've got some time off. You've got to start looking after yourself a bit."

Danny decided to take a different tack.

"And if I do?"

There was a pause on the other end of the line. He repeated himself.

"If I get my act together, is there a chance for us to work things out?"

"I don't know, Danny," she said. She put the phone down.

That was four days ago now and there had been no word from her. Whatever intentions he had of pulling himself together did not last in the face of her silence. He started drinking in his flat, not trusting himself in the company of friends. He ignored calls on his phone, wanting only for the name Rachel to appear on his mobile. It never did and so he never answered. He lost his appetite, sending out for takeaway food that arrived and went uneaten. He knew he wanted her back, but had no clue how to do it.

And always, in the back of his mind, there was another woman: Maria. It was her he really wanted back, even more distant and impossible than Rachel. It was Maria that his thoughts turned to as he lay in bed at night, trying to drink himself into sleep. He thought only that she had still been thinking of him in her last weeks, enough to turn to him when she was in trouble. He had sought to answer her call, but he was too late.

He should not have left. He repeated it like a mantra. He should not have left. It was the one thing, aside from booze and pills, that could soothe him into sleep. The sweet, soft certainty of regret.

It was his mother who tried to snap him out of it. She had come around unexpectedly. The look on her face when she saw him, unshaven, still undressed despite the fact it was noon, was enough to make him feel ashamed. She looked afraid as she hustled him into the living room and began to tidy things up.

She had spoken to Rachel.

"Look, love," she said. "I think she'll come around. All this is just you reacting to your father's death. She'll see that."

But Danny knew better. There was another death in the room that she knew nothing about. A woman's shade that haunted him more than his father's ghost.

"Do you want to talk about anything?" she asked, handing him a steaming mug of tea. He sipped it. It was too sweet but it tasted good.

"Yeah," he said. "At the funeral. You were talking with her. With Janice. Why? Why wouldn't you just want to wring her neck?"

She was silent and pensive. At last she spoke.

"You know, Danny. At first I wanted to. I mean, believe me, over the past few years there have been a lot of times when I wanted her dead. She took everything from me. But when I saw her at the funeral, I realized something. You know what?"

Danny shook his head.

"Harry widowed us both. She was the only one who knew how I felt. Exactly how I felt. You certainly didn't."

Danny let the accusation hang in the air.

"I'm sorry, Mum. I really am," he said. She smiled, got up and kissed him on the top his head. He sank for a moment into the feeling. Mothers always forgave sons. It felt like a rock in a world that had been cracking up for too long.

DANNY STARED at the ringing phone. It was not Rachel's number. It was coming from Sierra Leone, from halfway across the planet, reaching out to him here in his London flat. He could just ignore it, throw it away. Cut off that part of his life and the world. But he took the call.

It was Ali, sounding excited.

"Danny! Is that you?" he said. "I've got news for you."

Danny sat down heavily. He could already feel himself being sucked back into the Sierra Leone bush. He could almost feel the heat on his skin.

"Ali. It's good to hear from you. How are you?" he stumbled.

Ali laughed down the line.

"Oh, you know. Some good, some not so good. Which is why I am calling you. Because of the not so good."

"What is it, Ali?"

He could picture the Lebanese on the other end of the phone, probably with a whiskey in his hand, trying to find the right words.

"I have the kid, Danny. Or I will have him soon. You've got to come back. Get on the next flight."

Danny looked around his flat. It seemed empty and gray.

"Hang on, Ali. What kid? What are you talking about?"

Ali began to talk excitedly on the phone and Danny had to ask him to slow down and start at the beginning. He could hear Ali take a lengthy gulp of something. I knew it, Danny thought.

[198]

"The report that Harvey gave you mentioned one survivor from the gang who ambushed Maria. Just one. That report says the kid spun the cops some tale about Nigerians and child smuggling. His name is . . . hang on . . . what the fuck . . . Kam? The kid's last name?"

He heard the muffled sound of Kam in the background and Ali laughed.

"Sure, right. Winston Fofanah. Fuck. I was born here, raised here and live here and I still can't get my tongue around these names. Anyway, little Winston Fofanah ended up in jail. Up in Bo. And now I have got him."

Danny was stunned.

"What do you mean, Ali?" he asked.

"Look, don't ask many questions of Ali. You know who I am, Danny. You know the sort of world I move in. I am being fucked over in Bo. I have a feeling that what happened to Maria was linked somehow. I need to know if I am going against Nigerians, Gbamanja or God knows what. This little boy might just know the answer to that. So I bought him."

"What?" Danny blurted. Ali laughed, as nonchalantly as if talking about a new car.

"I wanted him. I bought him. Everything is for sale, Danny. And this kid did not come cheap. But if you have the money you can buy someone out of jail. It's not rocket science, Danny. It's money science. I have some people bringing him to me in the next few days. They are coming down from Bo. I need you to bring me back your copy of that report. I want to check his story, and I suspect you do too. He may have the answers to both our problems, Danny."

Danny could hear himself breathe. He was at a crossroads, and he knew life as he knew it would never be the same.

"That story about Maria smuggling kids out of Sierra Leone with

Nigerians is fucking bullshit, Danny. You know it. I know it. Straight fucking bullshit. The kid's from Kakumbia. He's RUF. Gbamanja's boy. There's something else going on. For Christ's sake, Danny. This kid was there. He was there when Maria got killed."

Danny felt a stab in his stomach. If he had a choice any longer, he wasn't really aware of it. This was now the clear purpose of his life. Not Rachel, not his family, not his job. This. He had left Maria once and he would not do so again.

Danny felt a weight lift above him. The room seemed brighter.

"All right, Ali. I'll be there," he said, and then ended the call.

Danny wondered if this was what nervous breakdowns felt like. So normal. So seemingly logical. He picked up the phone and dialed his travel agent and told them to book him on the next possible flight.

"Will that be for the newspaper's account?" the woman asked.

"It's a personal trip," he said.

"And would you like us to arrange a guide to meet you in Freetown?" she added.

"No, I'll be fine," Danny said.

Kam would be waiting for him.

13

THE SEA OFF Lumley Beach was just dirt and silt, all trapped in a matrix of warm water that felt like it stuck to your skin. There were meant to be sharks in these West African seas, huge beasts that kept the locals out of the waves. But Danny could not imagine it. He could not believe anything actually lived in this stuff.

But it felt good to be back in Sierra Leone.

Danny tried a few quick strokes, struggling against breakers that rolled in like ripples of treacle. But the salty water forced its way down his throat, and he came up gasping for air and eventually just gave up and floated on his back.

Kam was sitting on the rocks above the beach. He had met him at the airport and Danny insisted he go for a swim before visiting Ali's house. He wanted to scrape some of the grime of the flight from London off his skin. Perhaps he wanted to shake the feeling of England off as well. There was no better place to do this than Lumley Beach and he had shed his clothes, like removing a skin, into a little pile on the white sand and plunged in.

Now he looked to shore and he could see a boy walking down the strand, keeping his feet on the dividing line between sand and surf. He was tiny, still a child and dressed only in ragged shorts of a color that had long ago been replaced by the mottled gray of dirt and sweat. The boy spotted him in the sea and stopped. He stared at Danny, until it was Danny who looked away. Then he walked over to Danny's clothes and crouched down. Danny swam for shore and the boy, sitting on his haunches, watched him come.

Danny emerged, dripping from the surf. He saw Kam had noticed the child now. He remembered Kam's unforgiving attitude toward young thieves and he raised a hand in the direction of the Senegalese, assuring him all was okay. Kam sat back down but kept staring at the boy. Danny had no such worries. There was something about the boy's placid demeanor, utterly calm, waiting for Danny. He did not think this child would rob him.

Danny walked forward. The boy did not move. He was even tinier than he had first seemed. He could not be more than eight years old.

Danny plucked his trousers from the pile of clothes and pulled them on.

"Hello," he said. The boy just stared back.

"What's your name?"

Still there was no answer.

Danny crouched down. The boy's face was grimy, his nose was dripping snot and his lips were rimmed with sores. One of his eyes was red and weeping. It must have hurt like hell. Danny doubted he could see out of it.

"You don't talk?" Danny said.

The boy rubbed his eye.

"Who are you, white man?" he asked. His voice was thickly accented.

Danny was unnerved. He did not know how to answer such a bizarre question.

"Who are you?" he said again, and the child pinched the skin on Danny's arm, like a doctor examining a specimen. His touch was cold and clammy.

The boy regarded him, placid and unmoving. Then a shower of pebbles disturbed them both. Kam had given in to his instincts and was scrambling down the face of the cliff. The boy looked at Danny one more time with that damaged, unseeing eye and then broke, sprinting down the beach. Kam arrived breathless and hurled a rock after him.

"Mr. Danny, you should not talk to kids like that. They have knives, all sorts. They will rob from you," he said.

Danny was not angry or fearful. He was unnerved. The boy had seemed weirdly calm. Perhaps he was high, which would explain much of his appearance. But his question—"Who are you, white man?"—had spooked Danny. The kid was just a little dot now, still scampering down the beach. Who am I? I have no fucking idea, Danny thought in silent reply.

ALI HAILED HIM with a bear hug and poured him a generous tumbler of Scotch. Danny sank into a cushioned chair and the liquor immediately began to rouse him and waken his insides.

"I knew you would come back, Danny," Ali said, pouring him another. "You can't stay away from this place now."

Danny sat back and watched Ali. He was at his most frantic and his most alive. Danny handed him the copy of Harvey's report. It was a mass of paper, but Ali pored over it now, reading the police reports and the account that Winston Fofanah had given of the Nigerian smuggling ring. He read Harvey's recommendations, of the need to keep things quiet and move on. When he came to Maria's autopsy he stopped and quietly turned over the sheets. He had no desire to read such a thing. Nor did he have a need. Danny felt he knew which feeling was most important.

"Just as I thought after the first time I read this. That Harvey is full of bullshit," he said. "You know how I know?"

Danny shrugged. He did not want to hear about Harvey.

"Whatever Maria was doing, whatever the fuck she was involved in up there, Harvey was right alongside her. He was up to his neck in this shit too. He's not just protecting Maria's memory, like he told you. He's saving his own backside."

"What?" Danny breathed. "What are you talking about?"

"Look, there's only one hotel in Bo. It's where things happen. If you want to do business, you stay there. Hell, it's where I stay. I know the manager, a sly old Sikh bastard. He keeps a careful log of people passing through. Of course, no one uses their real name. But he keeps a log nonetheless. I slip him some money and he lets me take a peek. Two names keep popping up over the last year. Two white names. Harry Johnson and Mary Hernandez. Always they appear together, staying in the same room. I ask him what they look like. He describes them. Says they don't come anymore."

He let the sentence die in the air.

"Maria and Harvey?"

"Must be."

Danny was confused. Why were Maria and Harvey going up to Bo together? He felt a surge of envy. That lying bastard had been sleeping with her. That fucker. But it didn't explain what they were doing.

"What about the child smuggling? Perhaps that was what she was doing there."

Ali slammed his whiskey down.

"You know I think that Nigerian stuff is crap. This is about Bo. This is about why none of my diamond contacts will speak to me anymore. This is about how everyone—everyone!—that Ali Alhoun used to know is too shit scared to even have a drink with me. This is about the rumors that anyone who pokes around in Bo either skips town or ends up dead. This is about how people up there think a white woman is already dead for this."

Ali paused for breath before one final pronouncement.

"This is about not letting any fucker push you around."

And this is about you, Ali, Danny thought.

Ali didn't look at Danny throughout his little speech. He had been staring out the window, addressing his words to a world that was not listening. He was talking about his life here, his decades of striving, of surviving against the odds and carving out riches here for himself and his clan. All that was being taken from him as the country settled into peace again. Ali was quiet now, looking for an answer in the night.

"Where's the child you bought? Where's Winston Fofanah?"

Ali looked at him and smiled a thin smile.

"He'll be here soon. I have people bringing him tonight."

He paused.

"You know that report does not say what happened when they killed her. It does not say who did it. Who fired the guns. Our kid was there. . . ." He did not need to state the obvious: what Danny had been thinking of since Ali had first called him about the boy.

"He may have killed her, Danny," Ali said.

He may have raped her too, Danny thought. It barely seemed real to him, this idea of coming face-to-face with someone who had been there. And he was a child, just fifteen years old. He'd probably been RUF for as long as he could remember. Killing Maria would have been nothing for him, just another brutality among countless others.

"Danny," Ali said. "When all this is done . . . when it's played out . . . you can just say the word and I'll have things taken care of with this bastard."

Ali's face was implacable. Danny shrank away from the idea, shaking his head furiously. He knew Ali meant what he said. He would kill him if Danny said the word.

"No, Ali. No," Danny said.

But the thought was there. He got up and walked into the kitchen. He leaned over the sink and turned on the taps, dousing his face with tepid water. His heart was racing in his chest. He had no idea what was being delivered to the villa that night. A child. A killer. A victim. A monster. And he held its life in his grasp. He could have vengeance, if that's what he wanted. He splashed more water on his face, desperate to cool off. He gripped the sink and tried to steady himself, to fight off a wave of panic. Ali followed him in, his face a picture of worry.

"Hey, chill out, man," he said. "I was just giving you the choice. I'll handle everything."

He was going to speak again when a shout from one of the gate guards cut him off. Ali's purchase had arrived.

The men who brought Winston Fofanah into Ali's villa were laughing and jovial. There were three of them and they walked through the door as if arriving for a party. They wore casual clothes and chunky jewelry. Ali hugged each one in turn and they slapped him on the back. But it was not those men that Danny was looking at. It was the tiny figure with them.

Winston Fofanah.

Danny knew he was fifteen but he seemed even younger. He was as thin as a stick and dressed in gray, torn clothes. No doubt the same clothes he had been wearing in jail. Probably the same clothes he had been wearing since Maria died. His hands were tied tightly behind his back, forcing his arms almost out of sight and jutting his chest forward, so that his ribs stuck out even more than they would have anyway. His face was grimy. But he stared ahead, his eyes not even moving from left to right to look at his surroundings.

Ali stared him in the face. He grasped the boy's chin with his hand, examining like he would if he were buying a horse. The child neither flinched nor blinked. Whatever he was looking at in the distance, no one else in the room could ever see.

"He talks, yes?" Ali asked. One of the men laughed and nodded. "He will," he said.

Ali stood up and walked the men out. Danny suddenly realized he was alone with Winston. He shrank back into his chair. The child did not even acknowledge him. He's already dead, Danny thought. He's been dead for years. Dead since they first took him. Danny looked at him with horror and wanted to leave the room and run far away from here. He began to stand up but Ali came back in. He was with Kam, who was carrying a bowl of maize porridge. The Senegalese looked at the boy with disgust and edged around the corners of the room.

"Feed him, Kam. I bet those fuckers that brought him haven't even thought to do that since Bo," Ali said.

Kam shot Ali a glance of pure anger. He hated being here, having to do what Ali was asking. Kam's view of such children was Darwinian: Wipe them out or they will turn on you. Breathing heavily Kam approached the child. He scooped up a spoonful of the porridge and held it in front of the boy. For a moment Winston did nothing, but then he greedily slurped the food into his mouth. He was starving.

Ali crouched in front of him again.

"You know why you are here?" he asked. Winston did not move a muscle or show that he had heard a word. Ali was silent for a moment, rethinking his strategy, and then began to speak again.

"You are here, Winston, because I value you. I value you enough to buy you. That's because I think you know things. You have information I want."

He paused and looked at the boy again.

"If you don't give me that information, then you have no value to me. You will be worthless. Do you understand what I will do? I will throw you away."

The implication was clear. For the first time the boy's eyes focused on the people in the room with him. They darted from side to side and his nostrils flared as he began to breathe quickly. He spoke. His voice was thick and slow, barely intelligible.

"What you want from me?" he asked.

Ali smiled. An understanding had been reached. He began to ask questions and sullenly, but willingly, Winston answered. Sometimes in English and sometimes, with Kam's reluctant help, in Krio. He never spoke more than a sentence or two at a time. He did not know anything about any Nigerians. "Men come. RUF men. My bush brothers. They take me from the camp where I am. They take others. They say, wait here. This spot. Wait for blue car. White people."

And that was that. They had done their job: killing. Then they themselves had been attacked, shot and caught. He knew nothing of any child smuggling. Or Nigerians.

That in itself did not show there were no Nigerians involved, but it did show Harvey had lied. "Fofanah? That's a Kakumbia name?" Ali asked. Silence. "You from Kakumbia?"

Winston nodded.

"Gbamanja is a Kakumbia."

Winston visibly stiffened at the mention of the name.

"Mosquito is my general. I fight for him."

"And now? When did you see him last?"

For the only time, Winston's face seemed to show some emotion. His mouth fell.

"Not since I went to the camp. Not since two year."

"Then who got you out?"

"My boss. My commander. Kafume."

Kam turned to Ali.

"That's another Kakumbia name."

Ali sat back in a chair. He was exhausted.

"Put him downstairs in the cellar, Kam. Give him food, give him water. But keep his arms tied."

The boy followed Kam out of the door like a beaten dog. When he was gone the room seemed a lighter place, as if Winston had been drawing in shadows from the bush. Danny and Ali sat in silence until Ali spoke.

"I've got to go back to Bo. There's no Nigerians to be afraid of there. Just the usual Sierra Leonean bastards. We need to find this Kafume character. You coming?"

Danny did not reply immediately. His thoughts were not on Maria's death. They were on her life. They were on wondering who she really was.

"I want to see Harvey first," he said.

HARVEY COULD NOT disguise his surprise at seeing Danny walk into his office the next morning. A flicker of shock crossed his face before his expression formed into irritation.

"I didn't expect to see you back here again," he said. His voice was studied and calm.

"What can I do for you?"

Danny shrugged.

"It's the same old story, I'm afraid. I'm still digging into Maria Tirado's death."

Harvey shook his head.

"Danny. I've tried to help. I shouldn't have given you that report. It was confidential, but you seemed to need to hear the truth so I broke a few rules. . . . I thought that would be enough."

"You left something out," Danny snapped.

Harvey did not flinch at the change in Danny's tone.

"What was that?" he said.

"You and Maria."

Harvey's face was a mask. The only sound between them was the drumming of Harvey's fingers on his desk. Danny felt envy well up inside him. How could she have even looked twice at this man, at this dressed-up diplomat in his white suit? But there was something hard under Harvey's watery eyes. When that familiar smile dropped, it exposed some bedrock underneath.

"You don't know what you're talking about, Mr. Kellerman," Harvey said quietly. "Whatever was between me and Maria is not relevant. The facts remain the same."

"You were traveling to Bo with her. You were helping her do whatever it was she was doing. . . ."

His voice became anguished.

"You were sleeping with her, Harvey. You were fucking her. You stayed in the same damn hotel room."

Harvey stood up and walked over to the door. He held it open.

"I've done all I can do for you," he said. There was to be no offer of a tour around Freetown this time. No spiel about the birth of a new nation and age of opportunity. Danny walked out but as he did so, Harvey leaned in close.

"Go back home, Mr. Kellerman. Go home," he said.

The anger in that voice was unmistakeable. He was right. Harvey and Maria had been together. But she had not turned to him when her moment of need came. She had come to Danny. Harvey and he were not rivals for her love. Danny had won that war when Maria wrote him the letter. Perhaps that was why Harvey wanted him gone. She had chosen Danny.

WHEN DANNY GOT back to Ali's villa it was clear he had learned nothing new from Winston. They had fed the boy again and put him in some ill-fitting fresh clothes. But the same story emerged. Winston was completely oblivious to what he had done, unable to comprehend the morality of it. His only loyalty was to his "bush brothers." To those who had done what he had done. Knew what he knew.

It was all he had.

"We leave for Bo tomorrow," Ali said as Danny returned.

"And Winston?"

Ali shrugged.

"Don't kill him, Ali," Danny said.

"Come on, Danny," Ali said. "Who do you think I am?"

That phrase in itself was confirmation enough. He knew who Ali was. He was his friend. He loved him. But he would kill Winston like stamping on a cockroach. Danny didn't know why he cared so much. That little monster had killed Maria, or helped. But he would not submit to this.

"He may still know something about what Maria and Harvey were doing up there."

Ali shook his head.

"He knows nothing. Or he's too fucked up to understand. He didn't even know it was Maria he was killing. Just some white woman in a car."

Danny winced. Just some white woman in a car. His Maria, butchered like some animal at market. For a moment he thought of Ali putting a bullet into Winston's brain. Down in the cellar. A swift bang, the sound trapped by the thick walls and the dark earth. It felt hot and good.

He walked out and stood on the front porch of the villa. Ali followed him, but the two men stood in silence. Freetown was below them, laid out as if a child had pushed over a box of toy bricks, all confusion and mess. Danny tried to visualize his flat back in London, his old life with Rachel. His father. But those memories were like they belonged to some other man. He could not think beyond here and now. He could not look back and yet could barely see what was lying ahead.

A blast from a car horn made him jump. Kam was down below in his Mercedes. There was someone else in the back of the car with him. He recognized the long dreadlocked hair of Bankelo Conteh. The Dog who had led them to Maria's colleague, the old woman who had kept her possessions until she could give them to Danny. Kam waved him down. When he got there Conteh acknowledged him with a nod.

"Get in. Rose wants to see you," he said bluntly, with a touch of resentment. He looked at Ali too and a frown crossed his face.

Ali spoke before he could say anything else.

"Danny's business is my business," he said. It was a statement that would brook no discussion. Ali was coming too.

*   *   *

IT AMAZED DANNY that Kam could retrace his steps to Rose's squalid hut without any direction from Conteh. But Kam had the memory of a bloodhound when it came to Freetown's slums. What seemed to Danny like just another stretch of ramshackle tin-roofed huts was to Kam a whole neighborhood, with its own stories and characters. He drove down the rutted paths and stopped outside the home. Conteh pushed aside the plastic sheet that made for a door and coughed once.

Danny blinked against the gloom and saw that Rose had been waiting for him. She looked even thinner than a few weeks ago. For the first time, Danny realized what should have been obvious. She was dying. She was wasting away, fading out until soon there would be nothing left, crumbling into dust. She was sitting behind a table, her hands clasped in what he took to be prayer, and she was rocking slowly backward and forward. She opened her eyes.

"Sister," Danny said, and he walked slowly forward and sat at her feet.

"Sister," he repeated, "I am here again."

She reached out a hand and ran her fingers down his face. Her touch felt leathery and her hands probed his features as if she were a blind woman. But he looked into her eyes and knew that she saw him clearly.

"I should have told you, when you came the first time. I was afraid, so I kept my silence. But now I hear things. Things that people say about Maria and I know them to be wrong."

Her voice was firmer than when they had met before, as if her spirit was growing in strength as her body began to give up.

"I know, sister," Danny said. "Many people are telling lies about Maria. They are saying she was smuggling orphans. That she had fallen in with bad men from Nigeria."

Rose put down her hand.

"They are lies," she said. "Maria told me that she was going to write to you. To ask for your help."

Danny nodded.

"That is why I came here," he said, and he took out Maria's letter. He put it in front of her. She picked it up and held it to her face. She inhaled deeply. Of course, he thought. She cannot read. But the smile breaking out across her face said that she could sense Maria somewhere.

"She knew you would come. But it was all too late."

Then she looked at him.

"Maria was a collector of stories," she said. "In my village before the war we had an old woman who would collect our stories and in that way honor those who had gone before. Maria was doing this for us now. She was collecting stories from during the war. She was trying to honor the dead."

Danny digested the information. He was confused. But Ali knew what she meant. Danny heard him swear under his breath.

"Evidence," he said. "War crimes evidence."

Danny looked at Rose again. "What sort of stories?" he asked.

"Maria did not want the country to forget. She did not want the men who brought us such misery to get rich. She saw them becoming fat as pigs, feeding on the diamond mines. She thought this wrong. So she began to collect stories, writing them down and putting them in a little blue file. Her bible, she called it. That file was her truth and testament. She kept it safe and carried it with her like I carry this holy book."

Rose picked up a book of prayers from the table in front of her.

"She and the other one would travel together. She and Harvey would collect the stories and she later would write them down in her file. I think it was that file that made people angry with her. They kill her. I think now Maria should not have collected those stories. She should have let the dead be dead. Let bad men become fat and rich. . . ."

She heaved a huge sob of bitterness. It was such a violent sound from such a frail body that Danny winced.

"You see, when I came to Freetown, I had nothing but my own story. I told her my story and from that day she changed."

Rose was staring off into a long-gone distance. Her eyes seeing her own past, some forgotten village hut, some life of fields and farms.

"I once had six children," she said. "I lived in a village in the north, in the district of the Kakumbia. We are quiet people and we want only to be left alone. One day the RUF came. We gave them food. But they came again and each day we had less to give. Until one day we had nothing. That day they came and their Big Man was among them. He shouted and he screamed, but we had nothing. He said we would have to give them something. So they came into my home and took my children outside. They said, 'Mama, you have five children too many. Choose one and we will take the rest.' I begged them. But they would not give in. I thought they meant to kidnap my children, to take them away, and so I chose my youngest. He was the smallest. He could not have lasted with them. I chose him to stay with me, but I had not understood. They took us outside and they tied up my others. And they gave my youngest a machete. . . ."

Danny felt sick. He knew what was coming. Rose seemed almost in a trance. Her voice was a low drone and he strained to hear it.

"He tried to fight, but they made him. They showed him how with my eldest boy. They cut him down and they made him do the rest. Or they told him they make him kill me. . . ."

Her voice was breaking now.

"He was so brave. My little boy. But after that we could not stay and he could not stay. They took him away, made him one of theirs, and my husband, when he came home, he beat me and forced me out in shame. It was Maria who found me. She gave me work, she gave me new life."

"The Big Man, Rose? Who was the Big Man that was with those who killed your family?"

Danny felt he knew the answer. Pieces were starting to fall into place.

"Gbamanja," she said. "General Mosquito."

It was enough. He knew what Maria had been doing. She had heard Rose's story and had not been able to take it anymore. She had been digging around in the pasts of all those new men coming to power, Gbamanja among them. He could almost feel her rage at Gbamanja's rise to power. Her indignation at the idea that the man who had butchered her friend's family would be a minister in government. A minister now with eyes on the country's richest diamond mines. It would have been personal for her. She could not have stood by. She had been collecting evidence, storing it in that blue file. Waiting for the moment to use it and bring Gbamanja down.

He put his head in his hands. Had she roped Harvey into this? Seduced the gullible fool into following her? He must have been scared off, and abandoned her in her moment of need. That was why he had come up with that bullshit story about her smuggling children out of the country. Harvey had chosen to preserve himself rather than carry on her work. Danny felt a red rose of anger explode in his mind but it quickly subsided. Harvey had perhaps risked his career to help Maria. Then he wasn't up to the final task and he let her down.

He felt Rose's hand on his shoulder.

"That monster Gbamanja took my child with him. He made him kill his brothers and then he took my little Winston away."

Danny felt like someone had kicked him in the guts. Winston? He got up, but it was Ali who reacted first. He grabbed Danny by the shoulders and thrust him out of the room.

"We have to go," he hissed. Danny shook him off, but Ali clamped a hand over his mouth.

"We have to go," he repeated. There was a layer of stone underneath his words, absolutely immovable and unforgiving. Danny let himself be bundled into the car, but they both knew the truth. Rose's lost son had helped kill Maria. Rose's lost son was lying in the dark in Ali's cellar.

14

IT WAS ONLY BACK at the villa that they finally spoke. "We have her child. We have to let him go. Give him back to her," Danny said.

"Rose is the reason Maria started making that file. What happened to her family made her start collecting evidence against men like Gbamanja. We can put some of that right."

Ali snorted a laugh as he paced around his front room.

"And look what happened to her, Danny. She's dead."

It was a grim statement. Just a simple truth: cause and effect.

"We have to give Winston back," Danny repeated pleadingly.

Ali pointed a finger at Danny.

"No, Danny. *We* don't have her child. *I* do. Me. I paid for him. We don't know what is in Maria's file. Stuff on Gbamanja, stuff on everyone. Powerful stuff. Little Winston is a link to all of that. He's a bargaining chip. We can't just let him go."

Danny had known Ali would react like this. He was shaped by this country, formed by the things he had done and the things he was willing to do.

"It's about leverage. It's about playing our hand right."

"Fuck that, Ali," Danny cried. "It's about having that poor woman's kid. It's about doing what's right and wrong."

That was enough to set Ali off. He threw up his hands in the air and let out a primal yell. Danny blanched as Ali thrust his face into his own.

"Right and wrong? You can't afford to have right and wrong here. You know what that kid did. He butchered his whole family. God knows how many others he's killed. Danny, for fuck's sake, he killed Maria. There's nothing right or wrong about any of this. Right or wrong is irrelevant. It's about coming out alive."

Danny forced himself to speak. He would not bow before Ali's rage.

"Bullshit. It's not just about living for you. It's also about you coming out on top."

"What?"

"You could walk away, Ali. Stay out of Bo. Cash it all in. But you can't. You don't just stay alive, Ali. You stay ahead of the rest. You have to win and you'll do anything to do that."

Ali was silent. Then he laughed.

"You know," he said softly, "you've got me right. I remember when I first met you on that chopper flight from Lunghi. You looked like a tourist. Now, Danny Kellerman, I am proud to say you look a bit like a local. You've got a bit of Freetown blood in you now."

Danny almost hated Ali at that moment. And Ali was wrong. For a moment Danny had wanted Winston dead but it had passed. Now that he knew who Winston was, he felt nothing but pity. He could not let Ali use him.

"We can't take him to Bo," he said. "We must let him go."

"Don't say 'must' to me, Danny," Ali replied. "You haven't earned the right. Everyone's expendable in the end. You, me and certainly Winston."

Danny knew the truth of what Ali was saying, but he also could tell something had changed in the Lebanese. He was looking around him at the endless pictures and photographs on the walls, of family, friends and homes.

"Look," he said, "I have someone here, a cousin, Hamid. We leave him there while we are in Bo. Perhaps this kid is no more use to us. If we find that out, we release him."

Danny smiled. "Thank you, Ali."

"But, I swear, if he is any leverage at all, if we can use him in any way, I'll do it. If it will help me, I'll hand him over for Gbamanja's men to kill before I give him to his mother," Ali said. "You have a weakness in you, Danny. It's a problem."

Ali wanted to take Winston away now. He made a few phone calls, shouting and haranguing someone in Arabic. Danny went down into the villa's basement to get the child. Winston was being kept in a dark room, little more than a large cupboard. He was still bound by the hands and had pissed in his new trousers. Danny doubted it was from fear—he could not imagine this void of a person ever being afraid—it was more likely from habit. But Danny felt ashamed nonetheless. He was part of this. He was helping keep this boy captive, trading him in a game of musical chairs. Danny guided Winston out, waiting while he blinked furiously in the light. Then he led him upstairs and into Ali's waiting SUV.

"It's not far," Ali said. "Hamid has a farm, about ten kilometers out of town. We'll leave him there and tomorrow we head to Bo. We'll find out if Gbamanja is really behind this shit."

Ali turned around and looked at Winston in the backseat. He reached over, checked the ties that bound his hands and tightened them. Winston did not even react, though Danny could see the bonds were almost cutting into his flesh.

Then they drove, heading through Freetown by night once again, its streets dotted with traffic and neon lights. Wordlessly, Danny was caught up in his own mind games, confused and conflicted. Ali plotting and planning, and Winston . . . Winston's eyes stared straight ahead. Perhaps he was thinking of that day when the RUF had come to his village. How that had led him here, trussed up like a piece of meat, the blood of many others on his hands.

About five kilometers outside of Freetown they caught a sight that had once been so familiar that Danny did not give it a second thought. Shadowy figures at the side of the road, a line of rocks pulled across the tarmac and a scattering of vehicles in the gloom. It was a roadblock.

But this was not 2000. There were not meant to be roadblocks in Sierra Leone anymore. He felt Ali slow the car down as two figures emerged from the dark, one on each side of the vehicle.

"What the fuck is this?" Ali said. One of the men shone a torchlight into the car and they caught a glimpse of his uniform in the headlights. He wore a United Nations logo on his shoulder. He was Nigerian. He began to walk around the driver's side of the vehicle. Ali slipped his hand down onto the gear stick, slipping the car into reverse while keeping his foot on the brake pedal. Danny could not believe this was happening. The other soldier was walking up his side of the car. He saw the face, unsmiling and serious.

The soldier on Danny's side caught Winston's face in his torch beam and let out a yell.

"He's here!"

Ali took his foot off the pedal.

The SUV lurched backward and Ali twisted the steering wheel around. The car careered to one side and spun. It was facing back down the road now, away from the roadblock. There were shouts all around them and a dozen soldiers, shouldering their weapons, were running out of the darkness. But the road behind them was not empty anymore. Another SUV had pulled up behind them. Ali hesitated. There was no way out except to try to ram it, but it was too late.

Almost simultaneously the car doors were yanked open and hands reached inside. Danny kicked and screamed, but he was torn from the car. A powerful blow to the back of his knee sent him sprawling to the ground. His mouth filled with dirt and grit as he lay on his stomach; he glanced to one side and saw Ali likewise pressed against the road. His eyes were glaring, angry and yet powerless.

The soldiers were shouting and talking in an unrecognizable language. He could hear the sound of weapons clattering around. Someone leaned down and stroked a gun barrel across his cheek, slowly and deliberately. He could almost taste the bitter iron. He shut his eyes tightly, fearing he would soon hear the sound of a gun being cocked. But it never came. Instead the knee pressing painfully between his shoulder blades slowly released him. He continued to lie on the ground, not daring to turn around. Then a voice, both rich and familiar, told him to stand up.

Major Oluwasegun loomed out of the darkness.

"I am sorry for my men's use of force," he said slowly, "but you deserve little more."

The major walked forward and signaled the men pinning Ali to the ground to let him go. Ali shook them off and got up as they backed away, keeping their rifles trained on him.

"I expect this sort of thing from men like Mr. Ali Alhoun. But somehow not from you, Mr. Kellerman. Yet here you are with a kidnapped child tied up in the back of the car."

"That kid is a killer," Ali spat.

The major grunted at him to be silent.

"I know exactly who he is," he said. "And that is why I am taking him from you." Danny looked behind him and saw that the Nigerians had already taken Winston out of the car. They treated him carefully, as if afraid. They checked his bonds but they did not loosen them.

The major did not take his eyes off Danny. Danny looked into his face and thought he saw something unexpected there. Pity? Disappointment?

"Why are you doing this, Major? What do you want with him?"

The major was silent.

"Did your men have something to do with this? Did they help kill Maria?"

It was the mention of Maria's name that prompted the major to speak. He shook his head.

"You are always thinking of her, Mr. Kellerman. But there are other things going on in this world. I have no interest in the men who took her from you. God will see to them. But I do have an interest in this boy."

He motioned toward Winston, who stood statue still in the grasp of two Nigerian soldiers. Oluwasegun took off his peaked cap and wiped a hand across his dark brow, dripping with sweat.

"I am a good man, Mr. Kellerman. I cannot say the same for my men. They rob, they steal, they consort with women. But I know two things. Firstly, they had nothing to do with the death of Maria. If others say they have, then they are lying. Nigerians are an easy scapegoat for other guilty men all over Africa. Secondly, my men will always obey me, and tonight I have ordered them to take this child from you. Because tonight I am doing God's work. In Sierra Leone I have needed my God. I have come across things here that are unnatural in His eyes. Children have killed their mothers. Parents have sold their children. The rich grow fat as their own people starve."

He paused for a moment, looking up into the stars before returning with a sigh to stare at Danny. He was building up to something. Danny could see the pressure rising up in his frame like a kettle coming to boil, rising up and up and nearing the surface. He looked at Danny.

"I still believe in that God I met at my parish school. He is all I have and sometimes God gives you a chance to make a broken thing right. This is that time. The boy you have is missing a mother. He is not a thing to be traded. No matter what he has done."

He turned to face Ali.

"Rose Fofanah shares my church. Maria's Rose is my friend. I pray with Rose; I read the Bible with Rose. I have known her pain for a long time and carried her burden as if it were my own. When one of my men—a man who knows many things that go on in Sierra Leone—told me that a boy in Bo had been sold to Ali and was being brought to Freetown, I recognized the name of that child. I realized the Lord has given me this opportunity to help my friend. That boy Winston is not yours to own. He is going back to his mother."

Ali saw his property slipping from his grasp.

"You're lying!" he shouted. "You're involved with this somehow."

The major shook his head and signaled to one of his men.

"No, Ali. I am giving a child back to his mother. That is all."

The soldier walked to the SUV parked behind Ali's car and opened the door. In the dim illumination of the inside light they could see that a frail figure was inside. The soldier extended a hand and an old woman walked out. It was Rose. She walked forward toward where Winston was being held. Her cheeks were draped with tears, but her face wore an expression of such joy that it seemed aglow.

"Sister, is this . . . ," Oluwasegun began, but the question was irrelevant. Her expression alone answered. She ran to Winston and collapsed around him, weeping, her hands clawing at his body.

The boy stood there immovable. And Danny thought for a moment of his own mother. Of her infinite forgiveness for his missteps. Few mothers would ever face Rose's task, but she had not hesitated to forgive. In her joyous cries, tearing an opening in the night and drowning out the sounds of the bush, there was redemption, a renewed acceptance and the chance to come back to a mother's love.

Danny turned his eyes away. He felt he had no part in this drama but that of a villain. He looked at Ali and saw that he was staring at the ground, lost in his own thoughts. Emotions he suspected that matched his own.

The major gestured for them to go. It was a release they both took gladly.

15

LENNY FERENC WAS the only person in Freetown not pleased Sankoh had been caught. Two days after the story broke, he was fuming at the news.

"I've never missed a war in my life and I'm not starting now. Those RUF bastards had better not give up the ghost just because their leader's been caught," he said over breakfast in the Cape Sierra.

It was a cheerless full stop to what had been a remarkable few days in Freetown. Sankoh—a demon who haunted the thoughts of millions of people—had been caught, not in some secret base, but cowering in a cellar, a few hundred yards away from the ruins of his old home. An early-morning newspaper vendor had spotted him coming out of his hiding place to take a piss. The army swooped in and took him away.

Copies of a hurriedly taken photograph capturing the moment were now appearing everywhere. It was surreal. Sankoh's beard was long and unkempt. He was fat and out of shape, his flesh flabby and limp. He

sat in the backseat of a car in a frame crowded with other faces leaning into the shot. They were grinning and one was aiming a punch at
Sankoh's bruised face. Sankoh himself seemed confused. He looked
into the camera, half posing. He could have been a victim, not the war
criminal.

Ferenc pushed his plate of toast and eggs away angrily.

"The RUF can't just give up," he muttered. Danny had no reply.

But Ferenc had little choice in the matter. The RUF would either
fight or melt away. If it was the latter, then they would be going home
soon. It was a prospect Danny himself was facing. Since Sankoh's capture Hennessey had changed his attitude to the story. Interest was starting to die and it was becoming harder to get a story in the newspaper.
Other journalists were taking huge risks, charging up-country to get
ahead of the government army and be the first into the old RUF heartland. That was how careers were made, but it was also how people
died.

Then there was Maria. The end of the war would mean the end
of them too. It was like a physical pain. Danny wanted more, but he
hadn't the slightest idea how to make it happen.

The evening of Sankoh's capture she had come to find him, clutching a bottle of French red wine and two glasses.

"I've been saving this," she said. "Today we celebrate."

They walked down Lumley Beach. It was easy to find a secluded
spot amid the ruins of the beach bars that dotted the shoreline. It was
approaching dusk and they had no fear of being disturbed. It was like
a huge cloud had lifted over the city. There was no war, just wine and
each other. They settled down in the shade of a ruin and opened the
bottle. It was warm but the wine was good and they both savored the
taste.

"To Sankoh! May he meet his just rewards," Maria said. They

clinked glasses and settled into the hugging sand. Soon it was dark but they felt safe in each other's arms, watching the stars emerge one by one, hearing the distant hum of generators stirring the night air. They made love and afterward lay half naked, their clothes spread around like flotsam. Danny tried to talk to her again, to press her on what was keeping her here. Why could she not leave with him? But she hushed him once more. He felt a rush of frustration. She would not let him in. She would not let him know her. But the emotion passed and again he surrendered to the moment itself, letting himself silently hold her. Not thinking of the end.

GOD ALONE KNEW where Ferenc had got a cricket ball, but now he was whizzing it straight at Danny's head. Danny ducked and swung with the bat that Ferenc had paid a local carpenter to carve out of a canoe paddle. He sent the ball looping back over Ferenc's head. The older man laughed and crouched over his knees.

"You lucky bastard!" he said.

It had been like this for a week. The Sierra Leone government was pushing hard out of Freetown, but trips into the bush had seemed to get more risky. No one knew where the front line was anymore and there was always a danger of unknowingly pushing that little bit too far. Even Ferenc didn't fancy making a habit of going down the road every day. Certainly not when the news desk back home was disinterested.

So, under Ferenc's cajoling, many of the press corps had started playing cricket each afternoon. Ferenc had produced his ball and his bat and a group of British journalists, including a few bemused Americans and Europeans, swatted the ball around a stretch of wasteland near Lumley Beach. They always attracted a crowd of locals, watching these crazy white men perform their odd ritual.

Danny saw Ferenc measuring out his run-up. It may have been a game, but the wily bastard still flung that thing pretty hard. Just as he began to run, Danny saw Kam waving at him from the sidelines. He had asked him to pick him up here to go and visit Maria's orphanage. He put up his hand to stop Ferenc mid-run.

"Ah, I'm afraid that means you're out then, Danny, my boy. Any interruptions of cricket for something so insubstantial as work are grounds for instant dismissal."

Danny left the pitch and got in Kam's car. He had not seen Maria since their night on Lumley Beach and the urge to see her was irresistible. She had warned him she was going to be working hard, staying out at War Child's orphanage down the peninsula. A new trickle of ex-RUF kids were starting to arrive at the charity, prompted by Sankoh's surrender and the advance of the army. A few had been captured, but most had just surrendered, finding a sympathetic priest or relative to take them in. They were all young. If any of the kids looked remotely old enough to be threatening they were usually lynched on the spot.

Kam drove him to the orphanage and Danny wondered what he would find there. Her work there was at the core of Maria's being. If he saw it, perhaps it would help him understand her more; provide pieces to solve her puzzle. It was a sprawling complex of buildings set at the end of a dirt road. It was hidden from view with only a scruffy and discreet sign at the side of the road betraying its existence. At first glance it looked like any village school in Sierra Leone, just a series of low buildings with glassless windows and a tattered tin roof. Children of various ages milled around, looked after by adults wearing white and black uniforms. Childish murals covered the walls, as they did at so many schools. They looked normal enough, but perhaps a psychotherapist would have detected something unnerving. The stick-like limbs and blank expressions, each figure by itself, not touching any other. Isolated and alone. Emotionless.

As the car pulled up, the kids instinctively moved closer to the adults. One man walked aggressively over, his hands on his hips. This was a place that clearly saw uninvited guests as usually bringers of bad news.

"Can I help you, sir?" the man said.

Danny smiled at him.

"I'm looking for Maria Tirado. I'm a friend. Is she here?"

The man looked him up and down. He did not say anything and then he gestured for Danny to follow. They went inside what seemed to be an administration building. It was an office full of books and old gray filing cabinets, stacked almost to the ceiling. Maria stood in the middle of it, staring up at some high shelves. "Maria. This man says he knows you," the man said. She turned around.

"It's okay, Michael," she said. She walked forward and for a moment he was afraid she would tell him to go.

"What are you doing here?" she said, and stroked his arm.

"I just wanted to see how you were," Danny said, and he bent down and kissed her.

She resumed whatever filing she had been doing.

"Crazy. This place is already full to bursting and we have to find room for thirty more kids this week alone. We need more space but we're always on the bottom of everybody's list, especially the government's."

She sat down in a chair and wiped the sweat from her brow, twirling a strand of her long black hair around her finger. It was a gesture that Danny had come to adore. God, he wanted her, he thought. Even here, even now, he wanted her so bad it hurt.

"I know what'll happen," Maria continued. "With Sankoh gone, the government will bend over backward to make nice with the RUF bigwigs. They'll work out who wants to play ball and they'll get big cars and a villa in Hill Station. But these kids? No one will care."

"You care," Danny said. She looked tired.

"Yeah. I care. That's the fucking problem."

She brightened for a moment.

"Hey, let me show you around."

They walked out into the orphanage's playground. It was a dusty square of packed dirt with a few tires forlornly piled in the center and a rusty swing. It was surrounded by buildings that served as classrooms. Behind them were about a dozen shacks that were meant to house ten children each. Now each one had at least a score of kids inside, probably more. Danny peered into one and waited for his eyes to adjust. It was dark and musty and the walls were lined with wooden bunks, laid down with straw. Kids lay listlessly everywhere, lying on the beds, huddled in corners. They did not speak and did not play. Suddenly Danny realized why this place could never be mistaken for a normal school. There was no noise here. The usual sounds of children, of laughter, of shouting, of play, were absent. There were just empty eyes, blinking back like creatures in a zoo.

He pulled himself back into daylight.

"Are they all RUF?" he asked

"Not all of them. There've been child soldiers on all sides," Maria replied. "But you don't really mean that, do you? What you mean is, are they all killers? I don't have the answer to that, Danny. Possibly, maybe, even probably. But there's one thing they all have in common."

"What's that?"

She laughed. "They're still just children, Danny. All of them. That's always the first thing people forget."

Danny looked at the kids again. Suddenly the small figures seemed less threatening, less malevolent. Just damaged, and not beyond repair.

They heard the sound of footsteps crunching across the gravel. Danny turned to see the other staff member, Michael, walking toward them. He whispered something in Maria's ear and her face darkened.

"I've got a phone call," she said, and she turned to walk briskly back to the office. Danny looked once more into the hut. Some of the kids were bunched together now, talking in low murmuring tones and glancing at the strange white man in their doorway. He tried a wave, but they ignored him. He turned back to Maria, but she was already gone.

He found her five minutes later, standing at her desk, and he knew something bad had happened. Her mouth was pinched in concentration and she was twirling a pen between her fingers, like a nervous tick.

"What's happened?"

She shook her head at him.

"You don't want to hear it. It's not your business."

He moved toward her, but she just flopped down into her chair and held her head in her hands, her shoulders tensed in anger.

"That was our international office on the phone . . . ," she began, and then she looked up and snapped, "The fuckers. The absolute fuckers . . ."

He knelt down and wrapped his arms around her. He felt the resistance of her tightly wound body but he held on and slowly, piece by tiny piece, as if she were falling, she sank into him. He savored the feeling. She needed his love.

"There is an RUF commander out in the bush, not far from here," she said. "He was one of Sankoh's closest bastards. But he's isolated and afraid. He knows the government is after him and he's got nothing left to bargain with."

Danny waited for her to gather her thoughts and continue.

"But he's got something that we want," she said. "He's still got his kids. About half of his unit are child soldiers. He contacted our office on his radio. He wants to hand them over to War Child. I think he figures a bit of charity now will do him good in the future. It's the only investment he's got."

"Then what's the problem?" Danny asked.

"My office says it's too dangerous. They don't trust him and they know the army wants him dead. If he doesn't hand them over tonight, he'll run for it. I wanted to meet him out in the bush, bring his kids back here. But my office has said no. They think it's too risky."

"What do you think?"

"I think I'm all those kids have got. My bosses have vetoed it. My staff here are too afraid. I am all there is."

"No, you're not. I'll go with you."

The words were out of Danny's mouth before he knew what he was saying, before he had begun to imagine the possible consequences. Maria looked up and pulled herself away from his arms.

"Why?" she asked.

She knew why he wanted to come. Her eyes told him that. But they also told him that the Maria he knew was back, invulnerable and in control. She was wondering what use he would be in the bush with the RUF. He felt anger again at her renewed distance. He knew he could not simply go with her because they were lovers. He would have to be more useful to her than that.

"It's a story, Maria. Let me write the story. Then, when your bosses find out what you've done, you'll be protected. The media can do that. If I write the story of your rescue mission, it will bring in more positive press for War Child than a hundred fund-raising campaigns."

He wanted this as a journalist, but he also wanted to protect the woman he loved.

"Let me help you," he said.

She thought for a while and then put a finger to his lips.

"Go back to your hotel. If I decide you're right, then I'll call you," she said.

He nodded. That was enough.

HER CALL CAME just as sunlight faded from the sky. He picked up the receiver.

"Hi," she said.

"Hi."

"I've thought about it, Danny. This RUF guy just wants some leverage and an act of charity is all he's got left. That means you'll be good for him as well as covering my ass. We can use the power of the press on this one for everyone's sake. So if you are up for it, I'll be around in an hour to pick you up."

Danny savored the moment. She needed him.

"I'm in," he said quietly.

"Good" came the simple reply. Then she put the phone down.

He felt a surge of energy. His skin tingled and the anticipation made his breath faster, like before sex. The feeling lasted until he went downstairs into the lobby and told Kam.

"You are mad, Mr. Danny," Kam said with such shock that Danny's excitement popped like a balloon.

"You would go and meet with some RUF crazy man hiding out in the bush. This is madness. I would not do this. Not ever. And why is she doing this? Just to save some RUF? There must be something else to this. Nothing in this place is what it seems. Perhaps she is not either."

Danny struggled to regain some of his composure. What was Kam saying about Maria?

"Kam," he said. "Maria has everything in control. She knows what she's doing. And they are just kids. Just some fucked-up kids that she can help."

Kam slapped his forehead in frustration.

"Madness!" he said. "She sees children in those killers, but those children are RUF. Sankoh is over. The rest of them should all follow. We should be killing them. Not saving them."

Kam put his hand on Danny's arm.

"I ask you not to do this," he said. For a moment a cynical thought crossed Danny's mind. He knew he was Kam's meal ticket in Freetown; the rich white man who paid him dollars every day. But he looked at the Senegalese and felt a pang of shame for having the thought. There was nothing but the concern of a friend in his face.

"I'm going, Kam," he said. Kam snorted through his mouth.

"I will not stay for this. I will come tomorrow but I do not know if you will be here."

So Danny waited for Maria alone.

She arrived exactly on time, her small frame perched behind the steering wheel of a huge white pickup truck plastered with the War Child logo. She was wearing a white T-shirt and cargo pants, as casual as meeting for a beer. She honked the horn and waved. Trying to dispel the doubts that had started to gather at the corners of his mind, Danny climbed in beside her.

"Ready?" She grinned.

"Definitely," he replied. They drove quickly through the city and out past the final slums of Freetown. Suddenly it was just blackness. Maria slowed the truck down and eventually she saw a narrow dirt track disappearing into a field of long-neglected maize. She turned slowly down the path.

"There will be roadblocks if we stay on the road," she said. "Government ones. We don't want to run into them. Not at night and certainly not when we are trying to meet the RUF."

Off the road, and swallowed by night, Danny felt a punch of real fear. But it was still matched blow for blow by excitement. He looked over at Maria as she guided the pickup through rut after rut until it seesawed like a boat at sea. He reached over and grasped her hand. He had never felt so close to her. But her gaze did not shift from the road ahead. She kept the truck plowing forward.

The bush was eerie. Danny wound the window down and peered out. He could hear nothing but the grunt and growl of the engine as it struggled over a jagged trail of potholes. Occasionally, caught in the flash of their headlights, he could see eyes looking back at him. Rats? Baboons? Perhaps even men? He could see nothing but brief flashes of color and then they were gone. Vanished. As unknowable as the bush itself.

They drove for several hours, speaking barely a word and passing neither village nor farm. Then, as the path dipped into a small valley and crossed a rocky creek, the car stuttered to a halt. Its engine died.

"Shit!" Maria said. Danny looked at her as she quickly clambered out of the pickup.

"What is it?"

She did not reply and he could no longer see her. Without the headlights, the darkness crowded into the SUV. He felt his heart jump inside his chest. Suddenly the thinness of the thread by which his life hung became clear. One single failure, some tiny broken bolt or nut, had stranded them. Miles from a road and on the way to meet an RUF commander.

"What is it?" he repeated.

A dim glow appeared from the front of the vehicle. Danny opened his door and climbed out. His feet squelched into mud. He edged around to the front, spreading himself against the reassuring metal of the pickup. Then he saw her. She had a pen torch clamped in her mouth. She glanced up and saw the look on his face and the paleness tugging at his cheeks.

"Hey," she said, "it's fine. Just a loose connection. It must have jangled free. I need you to go back and get the repair kit."

She fished into her trouser pocket and handed him a second tiny torch. Then she smiled, like she did first thing in the morning when he was just opening his eyes. He edged back into the car.

Holding the light in front of him Danny searched under the driver's seat, unsure exactly of what he was looking for but unwilling to admit it. He opened the glove compartment. It was empty except for a small brown leather bag. He took it out. It was strangely heavy and seemed to be full. He popped open the clasp and shone the torch in.

The bag was full of cash.

Lots of cash.

He stared at the wads of carefully packed twenty-dollar bills crammed into the bag. Danny had no idea how much was in there. Five thousand dollars? Ten thousand? Twenty? He could not tell. He shivered in the hot night air. What the fuck was going on?

"Are you all right?" came Maria's voice from the front of the car. He could find no words.

The silence was enough for her. He saw the light of her torch freeze. Perhaps it had just struck her. She had made a mistake in sending him back to get the repair kit in the car: a car in which she had stashed such a huge sum. Slowly, she walked back. Her face was calm and unmoved. She did not flinch when she saw the open bag in his lap.

"What the fuck is this?" he breathed.

She reached over and gently prized it out of his grasp, snapping the bag shut again. Casually she tossed it under the passenger seat.

"It's payment," she said simply. Danny looked confused.

"This RUF bastard won't give up those kids for free. He wants payment for them. Just a thousand a head. Christ, it's a fucking bargain. We spend more on phone bills every six months."

Oh Jesus, Danny thought. They were not just rescuing these kids. They were buying them. Their commander, whoever the fuck he was, was not coming in from the cold. He was raising funds with the only commodity he had left: his own soldiers.

"This is wrong, Maria," Danny said. "We can't do this."

She got into the pickup and sat down beside him.

"Look at me," she said. He did, and her eyes bored into his.

"The commander wants to give them over. But he won't do it for free. It's wrong. I know that. But it's how the world works. I'm not going to leave those kids to be killed by the government, just because of some principles. I'd rather just spend the cash."

She trapped him in her gaze. Danny was certain she did not even blink.

"This way, we all win. The commander gets his cash, you get your story. War Child gets to look heroic, and I get my kids. No one gets hurt. It's just money, Danny."

"But it's wrong, Maria," he said. He knew her logic and perhaps it would work. But this was not what he was here for. He was in over his head. She leaned over and kissed him on the lips, holding his cheeks in her hands.

"Trust me," she said. That was it. For her, the matter was closed. She was shutting him out yet again. She stepped back into the darkness.

"And find me that repair kit. I'm pretty sure being late is not a good idea."

Danny knew he no longer had any choice. Trusting her was his only option now. In silence, he obeyed her request. But in the back of his mind one question loomed: Where did an aid worker find all that money?

MARIA DID NOT take long to get the pickup moving again. She sat down in the driver's seat as if nothing had just happened. They drove on for another half an hour until again the truck juddered to a halt. For a moment Danny thought they had broken down again, but Maria said nothing. She just wound down the window, kept the engine idling and flicked on the headlights. They were in a small clearing on the banks of a winding stream. The bush gathered in on them from about fifty feet away but the ground in front was clear. Danny thought he could even make out the remains of a fire, a blackened crater, just a few feet away.

"We're here," Maria said.

They waited for what seemed like an eternity but it could not have been more than fifteen minutes. Maria leaned against Danny's shoulder, her hair flowing down his arm and teasing his skin. Her presence was enough for him, even here, in this lost spot, awaiting the unknown. Maria glanced at her watch and knocked it to make sure the hands were still moving.

Then a single snap echoed from the jungle. They were here too.

One by one they appeared like ghosts. Shapes that coalesced out of the blackness, seeming to break free from the leafy bush and take human form. Slowly they edged forward into the milky pool of light of the headlights, where they revealed themselves, not as spirits, but as boys. Ragged boys, draped with strange charms: a doll, a bundle of flowers, a string of old coins. They shouldered AK-47s, but the weapons looked outlandishly large in their hands. Their eyes were sunken and hollow and one by one they entered the circle of light and squatted down on the ground.

Danny caught a whiff of their stench. It was a sour smell of weeks without bathing and living rough. He instinctively shrank back but there was nowhere to go. Maria walked toward the closest of the boys. She crouched down to look at him. Then an adult voice called from the bush.

"They are not cattle to be inspected. These are my men."

It was a firm voice with a tone that rose and fell in unpredictable ways, pronouncing each syllable distinctly but differently.

Out of the shadows stepped a man. His uniform was clean and on his head he wore a red military beret, turned at an inch-perfect angle like those of the British commandos back in Freetown. A black pistol was in a holster at his side. He walked forward, sizing up Maria and Danny with a toothy smile. Maria said nothing.

"You are Tirado?" the man said, stopping his walk just a few feet from where she stood her ground. "You are from this War Child?"

Danny wanted to shrink away into the ground, disappear like rain. Or at least flee back into the night. But he stood stock-still. The man looked over Maria's shoulder at Danny and Danny looked into his eyes for the first time. They were rimmed with red and darted to and fro. Danny realized he must be high. He had heard that many RUF soldiers went into battle fueled by jungle cocaine, cooked up in primitive labs. It made the killing easier.

"Who are you?" the man asked.

"I'm a friend. I'm with her," Danny stumbled.

The man threw back his head and laughed.

"Ah-ha. An Englishman!" he said. "My God. Suddenly we have many of your kind in Sierra Leone. They are seeming to be everywhere."

Danny did not dare utter another word. He could not tell if the man was threatening him or not.

"Are you from London?" he asked, his tone suddenly conversational. "I have never been there. My lot was to go to America instead."

Neither Danny nor Maria spoke and the boys around them moved not a muscle. But their commander began to pace up and down, his hands folded behind his back.

"I spent a year at a college in New York. Fordham University."

He looked at his audience.

"Ah. I think you are surprised at that. We are meeting like this and yet I too have seen some of the world."

Now an edge of anger came into his voice, taking offense at their silence or some drug-imagined slight.

"Yes, I am an educated man. And yet I am reduced to this? To skulking in the jungle like some rat."

His voice was rising and his hand had dropped to his holster, fiddling with it like an itch. Danny felt the man's mind was dancing madly on the edge of some unseen precipice, his moods teetering from sentence to sentence. Then he heard Maria's voice cut through the night air like ice.

"We have money, Commander. Let's seal our deal."

The man smiled again, pulling back from whatever edge he had been toppling over.

"How very American," he said. "All about business."

He stamped his feet into the dirt and with a dismissive flick of his hands he barked something in Krio. It was as if a spell had been broken over the boys. They went from living statues to trudging to the back of the truck. As they moved, each one carefully laid down his rifle as gently as if it were a newborn baby. Or a ticking bomb. One by one they climbed in the back, like cargo or animals to market.

Maria nodded and retrieved the bag of cash. She put it at the commander's feet.

"One thousand a boy. And there are ten boys," she said.

The commander bent down and squatted in front of the bag. He opened it and looked at the cash, his eyes widened in awe. We got away with it, Danny thought. We are going to do this. And I'm going to write about it. He felt his nerve endings jangling but seemed unable to move. Indeed each person seemed stuck, caught in the moment.

Maria broke the silence.

"We're good," she said, seemingly half a farewell, half a prayer, and she turned. That was when the commander stood up and Danny knew that this was not over.

"You know, Miss Tirado. I think perhaps I have been too generous with you."

Danny looked at Maria. He could see a flash of fear twitch at the side of her mouth. She kept on walking to the pickup. Danny began to follow her.

"Wait," the commander said. They stopped now.

"We have a deal," Maria said.

"No, American. This price is too cheap. Not enough for ten boys. Alfred, come here."

One of the boys clambered down from the pickup. He shuffled over to the commander and stood beside him.

"Perhaps this money only buys nine?" the commander suggested in a calm voice. "Yes, that might seem fairer. Or maybe even just eight?"

He commanded another of the children to get down. The boy obeyed as instantly as the first. Danny heard Maria stifle a sob. Her jaw was clenched so tightly that her lips had disappeared into a thin line.

"Seven? Nyema! Get down, boy!" ordered the commander. Danny knew what Maria was thinking. She was losing them. One by one. Eventually she would lose them all.

"Enough!" she screamed. "This is enough."

She ran to the commander, whose face contorted into an ugly mass of rage. Seeing him up close, something seemed to click in Maria's mind, a primal sense of extreme danger. She was breathing heavily but her voice was steady as she laid a hand on the commander's arm.

"Let me have seven, then," she said.

For a moment it seemed to have worked. Which was why Danny never saw that the commander had his gun in his hand. He never saw him pull back his arm in readiness for the strike. He just saw a blur and heard an ugly thwack. Then Maria was down to her knees, groggily shaking her head. The commander walked away ten feet. Then he turned around.

He slowly leveled the pistol at her head.

For Danny the world hung in balance. He saw a thin trickle of blood drip down from Maria's jet-black hair. He saw the beads of sweat on the commander's forehead. And he felt his own feet move forward. Then he heard his own voice.

"No! We can get you more!"

Danny stepped in between the commander and Maria. As he felt fear that the pistol was now leveled at his chest, he felt bliss that she was no longer in the direct line of fire.

"More what?" the commander said.

Now Danny was speaking fast.

"More money. Dollars. Lots more dollars. If you kill us, then how will you get more? Who will pay? But if you let us go, then we can do this again. We'll pay a better price. One thousand a head is too cheap. We can pay more. Much more."

"Danny," Maria whispered behind him, but he ignored her and concentrated on the commander's face, searching his flared eyes for any sign of reason. For a moment the commander was blank, devoid of thought, and then, as if being reminded of something, he jolted back to life with another thundering laugh.

"Of course. Of course," he said. He slipped the pistol back into his holster and barged past Danny to Maria. Grabbing her by the elbow he hauled her to her feet.

"You see, American. Your friend is wise. He knows how to cut a deal," he chided as if talking to a naughty child.

"I think this price is worth five of my boys," he said. He ordered two more off the pickup. But five remained.

"Is this fair?" he asked, reaching out and wiping some of the blood off Maria's cheek. He examined it on the end of his finger before he repeated, "Is this fair?"

For a single moment she hesitated, her eyes locked on the five lost boys. The five who would pick up their weapons again. The five who would walk back into the bush. Then her mind fixed on the five she still had.

"That's fair," she whispered.

DANNY DROVE BACK, guiding the pickup down the rutted path as Maria dozed in the seat next to him. He stared straight ahead, hands clamped tightly to the steering wheel. He had his story, he thought. Buying back child soldiers from their psychotic leader with wads of cash from sources unknown. But even now he knew he could not tell the whole truth. It was his journalist's duty, but he had a higher loyalty. Revealing the truth would destroy Maria and he could no more do that than he could destroy himself. He would keep her secrets. He glanced up into the rearview mirror. In the back of the truck the five boys wordlessly sat; anonymous child-like shades staring. But Danny did not think of them. Or the terror he had felt in stepping in front of that gun. Nor even the half-true story he would write. He just knew one thing: He had saved her. He had preserved Maria's life. She belonged to him.

16

ALI'S CAR SPED out of Freetown toward Bo. He was driving furiously, swinging the vehicle around corners and speeding down the straights. The events of the night before went unmentioned. It was like a guilty secret he and Danny shared, each full of regret at their actions, shamed by the major's compassion in reuniting Winston and Rose.

Next to Ali sat George, Ali's cousin. He was slumped in the front seat and stared out at the passing bush through darkened shades. Kam had declined to come and that had unnerved Danny because he felt Kam was the lucky charm that kept him alive. Before they had left that morning Ali had gone into a backroom and handed Danny a gray metal revolver.

"Ali, what am I meant to do with this?" he asked, holding the gun between two fingers like a piece of roadkill.

This was ridiculous, he thought. Did they think they were in an action movie? He looked at the gun and it seemed like a children's toy. He tried to give it back, but Ali had refused.

"We're not fucking around. This is no game," Ali said. "If I find out who's taking over in Bo, then you find out who killed Maria for digging around up there. We can solve both our problems at once. But it's a serious business."

Danny was not laughing now. The gun was unloaded for the drive—Danny had insisted on that—and he took it out from the back of his jeans, where he had tucked it and weighed it in his palm. It was far heavier than it looked. Yet it fit snugly into his palm, naturally almost. The feeling triggered memories of being a boy and holding toy guns, of how they felt in his hands and the mysterious thrill of playing with them.

He looked out of the window and could not believe they had traveled so far so fast. During the war Sierra Leone had seemed a vast country. With every few miles of road fought over or infested with roadblocks, distances had become inflated. Up-country towns had seemed impossibly remote. But now they hurtled down a new asphalt highway, past thick verdant bush, clusters of farms and little towns. Most of the buildings were ruins still, but there were signs of growth everywhere. New roadside stalls set up, scores of minibuses packed with people like human sardines, careering along the highway. Trucks filled with cement and crops, belching out black smoke from their exhausts.

It was just simple life. If Harvey had ever really wanted to impress Danny with the new Sierra Leone, this is where he should have taken him. He wondered what Maria had thought traveling north on her trips. Had she seen rebirth? Or had her anger—her cause—blinded her so she could only see the blood and carnage of the past? She had lived through it after all. But then again, so had everyone in this country. Was it just Maria who could not make peace?

* * *

THEY ARRIVED IN Bo at nightfall and Danny could see the town had not changed much since his last visit. Bo had never really physically suffered from the war. It had been born a hardscrabble place of rough trade and diamonds and that is probably how it would always be. Ali steered the SUV slowly down its streets and toward the Hotel Leone. It was the hotel where all business was done in Bo. It was where Harvey and Maria had stayed under their pseudonyms.

The hotel was a two-story place on the main street. It had once had some sort of faded colonial glory. Wrought-iron railings lined a veranda, and peeling white paint scrolled off its walls like a tree shedding bark. They parked in front and walked in. They stood behind Ali as he walked to the counter. As Ali spoke and ordered a single room, a face peered out of the back office. It was an Indian man, wearing a Sikh's turban. The man registered a slight look of surprise at Ali, who merely nodded briefly in his direction. Then they went upstairs.

"Right," Ali said. "We need to make sure that we are seen. Nothing spectacular. Just enough so people know I am here. When word gets around Ali Alhoun has come back to Bo, then people will come and find us. That's how it works."

Ali unzipped a backpack and took out a carton of bullets. He counted out six golden cartridges and handed them to Danny. They clinked dully in his hand.

"You, my friend, they will think you are a bodyguard. So you need to be able to fulfil that part. Put these in your gun. Don't worry, you aren't going to need it, but there's no need to bluff with an empty gun. There's no point in a gun without bullets."

Danny was at a loss. He had no clue how to load his pistol. Ali took the gun from him and inserted the cartridges one by one. He spun the chamber and looked down the barrel. Then he flipped it shut with a flick of his wrist and handed it back to him. Danny tucked it into his waist.

George laughed.

"No, my friend," he said, gesturing at him. "Tuck it in your back, not your front. That way if it goes off by accident, you won't shoot off your cock."

That did not do much to alleviate the hollow ache that Danny felt in his stomach. How had he got here? He was a journalist, for God's sake, and here he was, in some rank hotel in the middle of Sierra Leone, armed to the teeth with a Lebanese diamond dealer and about to start some trouble. Ali sensed his unease. "Look, relax, man," he said. "You are on my turf. I didn't last this long here by wandering around shooting at things, or getting shot at myself. I'm taking precautions, that's all. We're going to go downstairs. We'll have a drink at the bar, make sure we're noticed, and then we'll come back here and wait. Eventually, we'll have a nice long chat with whoever comes looking for us. We'll ask them a few questions and get the answers to both our problems. Then we go home. The guns are just for show, to make sure it remains just a chat."

He squeezed Danny's shoulder and looked at George.

"You guys ready?" he asked.

George shrugged and Danny nodded. To his amazement, he was ready. He tucked the gun in his belt—snug against his back—and they walked downstairs to the bar.

THEY WAITED TWO DAYS before the knock on the door came. During that time they never left the room. Ali had brought a backgammon board and he and George played obsessively. Danny could not get interested. He sat in the stifling heat, sweating and nervous, eyeing the street below and watching the dance of everyday life. He watched the diamond miners with their taut muscles honed over years of hard labor, and the peasant women from the fields carrying sacks and buckets on their heads laden with fruit and goods for market. The Lebanese and the Indians who strolled the pavements or sat in the front of their shops. The rickety taxis plying the streets, some in such states of disrepair that it was hard to believe they could travel to the end of the road, let alone down unforgiving jungle tracks. And, every so often, other vehicles, signs of the outside world, would drive by. There were aid workers' white Toyotas, black sedans, and smoky-windowed SUVs. The local men of power. The ex-RUF, the police and the diamond dealers, moving among the rest like sharks through schools of fish.

On breaks from backgammon Ali would try to fix the lone fan that sat in the room. It was a fruitless task and in the end they had to just endure the heat. As he toyed yet again with the fan's motor, cursing and swearing, Ali would rail against Sierra Leone.

"These people have no civilization. No rules. In Lebanon we have been civilized for thousands of years. You go to my country and you see the buildings of the Greeks and Romans and they are still standing better than anything in this fucking place. You know what this place needs? You British back again. Recolonize this fucking country and put it in order."

It was an argument Danny chose to ignore. Ali was venting. His real concern was the loss of his business interests. It was a point he always returned to, no matter what the subject of conversation. Danny and George had taken to exchanging knowing glances when it happened.

"I've been here in Bo for twenty years," Ali would say, "and the bastards think they can edge me out. They think they can stop my miners selling their diamonds to me. Just so some miserable RUF bandit can have it all to himself. Well, fuck that," he said. "Fuck that."

At that moment, there was a rap on the door.

George and Danny froze, but Ali did not skip a beat. He raised his finger to his lips to hush the other two. He waved them to stand at the rear of the room, away from the door.

The knock came again, more urgently this time. To Danny the door suddenly looked impossibly flimsy made of wood as thin as paper. His heart pounded and he felt the edge of his vision start to cloud over. He looked over at George, but Ali's cousin was cool and standing perfectly still. There wasn't even a bead of sweat on his forehead.

Ali patted his back to make sure his pistol was slipped into the back of his belt. He pulled his shades down over his eyes and edged to the side of the door as he opened it.

Five men stood there, one in front and four behind. They were young, not out of their teens, though the one in front seemed a few years older. He was the only one in uniform, a dusty blue jacket that marked him out as Sierra Leone police. He craned his head into the room, taking a look at the three men inside. He entered the room while the other four waited in the corridor. All of them carried rifles.

"You Ali Alhoun?" the man asked. His voice was thick, straight out of the bush, struggling with English words.

Ali did not reply. The man repeated his question, looking at George and Danny. He asked a third time.

"You know I am. What do you want?"

The man stood to one side and motioned for them to leave.

"We have car. You come with us to the police station. You not wanted in Bo, Mr. Ali Alhoun," he said.

Ali was as cool as ice. He walked forward and reached behind his back. He took his gun out and laid it carefully on the table. As arranged, that was the sign for Danny and George to put their hands behind their own backs. They did not need to show their own weapons, but the implication was clear enough. The man did not miss it. The four men outside shifted nervously and one started whispering to his comrades.

Ali removed his sunglasses. His gaze did not move from the policeman.

"I think we would rather stay here," he said.

The man looked at Ali and whatever he saw, he didn't like. He glanced back at his own men, standing outside.

"I am police. You should not be in Bo, Mr. Ali. You must come," he said.

But his tone said it all. It was defeated and whining. He was not about to start shooting here. He was not prepared for violence. And he knew that something in Ali's eyes was saying exactly the opposite.

Danny watched the face-off, fighting the nausea in his stomach. God, please just go, he prayed to the men at the door. Get the fuck out of this room. Get the fuck out. He could feel sweat pouring down his back, dripping like a tap. His arm wanted to shake but he kept it in position, hovering over the pistol in his belt, which felt so heavy, like it was pulling him backward. Go. Fucking go, he pleaded.

And the men did.

"We see you later, Mr. Ali," the policeman said, and walked out of the room. Ali kicked the door shut.

"Stay where you are," Ali said, and then he crept to the window and looked out. After a minute, he laughed.

"They've gone," he said. Then he smiled. "I told you someone would notice us."

Danny felt the world judder beneath his feet. He pulled his pistol out of his belt and put it on the table, and then he ran to the bathroom and threw up into the toilet. He emptied his guts until it stung the back of his throat, and as his mind again became aware of the world outside, he could hear Ali laughing.

"Jesus, Danny. You're not much of a mercenary," he said. And Ali laughed again.

*   *   *

IT HAD BEEN RAINING all day in Bo. Not the English drizzle that Danny was used to, but real African rain. It beat out of the sky like a river, churning up the streets outside the Hotel Leone into a torrent of thick red mud. In the face of the downpour the streets had been rapidly deserted, even by the stray dogs that roamed around the rubbish piles. Every living thing had sought shelter.

Yet Ali had gone outside in the deluge. It had been two days since the policeman and his followers had come around. Two days of nothing but rice and leathery chicken from the hotel's kitchen. Two days of lethargy, heat and waiting. Now it had all seemed to build up to this rainstorm bursting over the town and in the middle of the rain, Ali had got a phone call. He then announced he was going out. He would be back in an hour. George had looked briefly concerned and then shrugged. He seemed to trust Ali no matter what he did. That had been two hours ago and still Ali had not come back; still, the rain beat down outside.

If the rain had been less noisy, Danny would have been annoyed by George's snoring. He had collapsed into a chair, his head hanging down and huge guttural sounds were emerging from his half-open mouth. But Danny ignored it and kept staring into the storm outside. It was still midafternoon but the thickness of the clouds had created a weird half-light in the town, as if day were turning into night. Then he saw a figure running from doorway to doorway, dodging through what shelter there was. It was Ali.

Danny shook George by the shoulder.

"I just saw him," he said.

George looked unimpressed. He had never expected anything else. The possibility of something going wrong had clearly not occurred to him.

"Ali's always all right," he said. "Ever since I was a kid I've seen him work. Here or in Beirut, wherever. It's always the same and he always comes out okay. I know he looks a bit crazy at times, but he doesn't take much in the way of risks. We did not become rich by being fools."

"Then why is he here?"

"He needs to know who's behind this. When he finds out who it is for sure, he'll be able to fight back and protect his interests. Protect our family's interests."

Danny tried to feel reassured. George certainly was the picture of calm. He even settled back in his chair, eyes shutting again as Danny waited at the door, looking at it like a faithful dog waiting for its master to come home.

Ali walked in as breezily as if he were just coming back from buying the newspapers. He was soaked through and he took off his shirt and flung it to the floor.

"God, it's like the Flood out there."

George opened one eye.

"Well?"

"Little Winston's boss is the new man in town. Kafume. The one who came and got that little gang out of the refugee camp."

"And Gbamanja?"

"It smells like a link. I can't be sure. If it is back to Gbamanja, then we've got big trouble. If it's just this new small fry trying to make waves, then I can take the fucker out. He'll be sorry he messed with Ali Alhoun, I swear it. We're meeting him tomorrow. He's going to try to make a deal. He's going to make an offer for us to clear out. I'm interested to hear what he has to say."

Danny looked at Ali and George, chatting conspiratorially together, and felt sidelined. He walked up to Ali.

"What about Maria? Was only Kafume behind that? Or Gbamanja too?"

Ali stopped smiling.

"My bet is that Kafume is Gbamanja's man. If Gbamanja is taking over here and this is where Maria was sneaking around, asking questions about him, collecting all the answers, then I don't think you need much more evidence to work out what happened. He would have taken her out. Snuffed her out like a candle."

"Did you just meet him?" Danny asked Ali.

"No. Our friend the policeman. He had a message for me. Just a time and a place."

"What if it's a trap? Why not just kill us and have done with it?"

Ali shook his head.

"No, my friend. You don't understand the mentality. They want an easy life now. They want riches. They would rather buy me out than risk that sort of thing. I bet Maria got herself killed because they couldn't buy her. Couldn't threaten her. They had no choice. With me, it is different. They know they can buy Ali."

He laughed.

"In fact, I've always wanted to know my price. I suspect it might be quite high."

ALI'S PHONE RANG. He barked a hello. Immediately his face fell and his brow furrowed. He glanced at George and mumbled something in Arabic into the phone. Then he walked into the bathroom and closed the door. Danny could hear the muffled shouts from inside and when he came out again he was grimacing.

"Fuck," he said. "That uptight Nigerian has really screwed things up."

"What?" Danny asked.

"That was my cousin Hamid. The one who was going to look after Winston. He's a well-connected boy, my Hamid, and his people are telling him something serious went down in one of the slums last night. A full-on police raid. No fooling around. They picked up a wanted prisoner, someone who had escaped from jail up in Bo. Someone who would have been fine with us, but whom the Nigerian army apparently can't protect," he said.

Danny felt like a light had gone out. Winston had been picked up by the police.

"Is he alive? Rose?"

Ali shrugged.

"They just took the boy. He was alive when they did. God knows if he is now," he said.

Danny thought of Rose's face when she had seen her son. Her look had said it all. She had never blamed him. She was given just a short time and then had lost him again.

"I want to know how they knew where he was. Freetown cops aren't known for great detective work. Christ, they normally don't even give a fuck about runaway prisoners," Ali said.

"You know what I think," George said, looking at Ali, avoiding Danny. "You know he's never been the same since he started doing jobs for Gbamanja."

Danny started in surprise.

"Kam?" he blurted out. "Hang on a minute."

But George didn't give him a chance to speak, to defend his friend. He continued to address Ali. This was family business.

"You shouldn't have let him serve two masters," he said. "This family is going through shit at the moment and we need to keep things between us. Having him around still, driving that fucking car, doing jobs for Gbamanja while all this is going down. It is too much."

Ali shrugged.

"Perhaps you're right," he said, and then he swore again. "I've known Kam for years. He wouldn't sell us out. He wouldn't."

Danny looked at Ali. He could read the doubt etched in his face. He could feel it in his own mind too.

"This is where good deeds get you," Ali said matter-of-factly, without reproach. "We could have used that boy as leverage. But the major wants to do a good thing. Now he's probably dead anyway and we have nothing."

Danny had no reply. He felt alone, in a bandit town, in a country far away from home, with two men who owed him nothing. What was his value in a place where sell-outs came and went with each new day? He opened his mouth to defend Kam, but the words would not come. He bowed his head and sat on his bed, looking at the gray metal of the gun on the bedside table. I am simply here, he thought. Just keep moving, like a shark far out at sea. It was stopping still that would kill you.

LOOKING BACK, it seemed inevitable that the meeting in the diamond fields would end the way it did. But it did not feel that way at the time. It felt like there were choices. Only later, much later, did Danny realize that by the time he got out of Ali's SUV on a deserted stretch of riverbank, he had already left his old life far, far behind. He had severed the ties that bound him, unmoored and floating downriver toward the edge of the falls.

Ali had steered the SUV down a dirt track. They were about thirty minutes outside Bo, heading for a mined-out stretch of the diamond fields. When they got there they entered a barren wasteland of pock-marked sand dunes. Another vehicle was already there, a battered old Mercedes. Inside were two men. Ali stopped the SUV.

There was silence for a moment. Danny felt he was in a dream, watching himself from above. He saw the three of them get out of the car, rest their hands on their pistols for assurance and then steadily walk forward, edging around the large, sandy holes that dotted the ground. The two men in the Mercedes did likewise. One was a tall, thin man and the other was the policeman, still wearing his blue jacket and cradling an assault rifle.

Ali walked ahead of George and Danny, whom he had told to hang back.

The tall man was wearing a suit. It fit him perfectly but he looked uncomfortable in it. Perhaps it was the man's shaggy haircut or his unclipped fingernails. He did not seem worried though. He seemed confident and in his element. The policeman stood at his side like a human shadow.

"So you are Ali Alhoun?" he said. His English was not perfect but it was better than the policeman's.

"I am and I'm wondering who you think you are if you reckon you can keep me out of Bo. I've been working here for years while you were out killing women and old men. So that's my question to you. Who the fuck are you?"

"I am Kafume," the man said. "You know this. You have heard who I am. You have had a good time here in Bo, Mr. Ali Alhoun. But times have changed now. It is time for others to come in. People who are from Sierra Leone, not Lebanon. Africans, not Arabs. That is why we are taking over. You should feel happy for your past successes and thank your God that they have made you rich."

Ali took a step further.

"Make me an offer," he said.

"Why?"

"Because I'm not leaving," Ali said.

Kafume did not back off. He too took a step forward. The policeman followed him.

"This could be a dangerous country for you," he said.

Ali laughed.

"I've been here longer than you've been alive, boy. I'll be here after you're dead."

The man's nostrils flared at the word "boy" dripping with colonial contempt.

"I think you do not understand, Mr. Alhoun," he said. He pronounced "Mister" the way Ali had said "boy," turning the tables on the honorific, rendering it a word of disgust.

"Your time is done here. We fought for our country. We have brought this place back to Africa. Out of the hands of foreigners like you. This is not for debating and talk."

Ali did not flinch. He stood rock solid, his hands on his hips, and spoke again.

"Do I look like I am moving?" he said. "If you want me to move, then you make me an offer to get out. Ali Alhoun leaves nowhere for free."

Ali's voice—so calm, so firm—had the desired effect. Kafume pulled a small bag out of his pocket. It was brown leather with a tight drawstring. He opened it and a drizzle of gray stones poured onto his palm. Uncut diamonds. Danny had no idea how much they were worth, but Danny was aware that George was shifting his feet from side to side. That must be a fortune, Danny thought.

"This is your price," Kafume said. "See it as a token of respect for your past work. Take this and go."

"Not enough," Ali said.

Kafume was unmoved.

"This is not a negotiation. This is what we offer you to leave Bo."

There was silence and then Kafume poured the stones back into the bag.

"Then I shall withdraw this offer," he said.

"Wait."

Ali reached out and stayed his hand. He leaned in close to Kafume's face.

"Tell me who makes this offer. It's not you, Kafume. You're right. I do know you. You're worth shit. You could not get stones like that together if I gave you a year. Tell me who you are with. Tell me who stands behind you."

Kafume paused. Ali stared at him. It felt like a world was in balance. Danny felt George shift again and saw his hand was reaching around behind his back. He saw the policeman looking at him nervously. The words between Ali and Kafume were faint, but they could all feel the emotion thickening the air.

Kafume grunted.

"I fought in the bush for years for this day. I fought with my chief, General Mosquito. I am his man. I am his brother. If you stay, it is Gbamanja who will see that you leave, not me."

For Ali a spell had been broken. The mention of Gbamanja's name was enough. He was a deal maker and he had just settled his account. He was cashing out and coming out on top.

"Then tell your chief that you have a deal," he said, and he plucked the bag from Kafume's hands. He turned to walk away. He nodded to George and Danny to follow him. George began to back toward the car.

Kafume nodded. "Good. Too many people have already died over this. It is enough."

Danny stayed rooted to the spot.

Too many people had died?

"What about Maria?" Danny hissed as Ali walked by him. He saw a flicker of recognition in Kafume's face.

"We leave now, Danny," Ali said casually, but Danny did not move. Danny was not listening.

It hit him. It hit him with all the force in the world. He was standing here with the man who had ordered his old RUF comrades to ambush the white woman's car. To kill her, to remove her, to take her precious blue file. To stop her questions and her interviews. To silence the past so the dead could not speak out against his boss, Minister Gbamanja. General Mosquito. To rape her as a warning.

He felt he was standing above a great swallowing hole, like the mine pits in front of him. All he had to do was step forward and he would be finally falling.

"Danny, what the . . . ?" was all Ali could muster as Danny walked forward, his hand swinging out from behind his back, thumb cocking back his pistol's hammer and pointing it directly at Kafume's face.

"What happened to Maria Tirado?" he said.

The next moment happened in a blur. Kafume stood rooted to the spot, looking down the barrel of Danny's gun with a perplexed expression, almost an amused one. Danny was dimly aware of Ali swearing loudly behind him. But the policeman was springing into action. He raised his rifle, screaming at Danny. Danny looked at the policeman, looked at the gun rising to the level of his chest, and saw the man's finger begin to pull back, whitening at the knuckle. He knew the man was going to fire.

Then he felt a breath of flame tear past his ear and an explosive crack of sound. He waited to feel pain, but it never came. He was not hit. The policeman was.

Ali had shot him.

Slowly the policeman doubled up and collapsed to the ground, clutching his belly. He toppled on one side and writhed like a wounded snake. Ali loomed behind Danny, pistol held in both hands, walking quickly forward.

Kafume spun around, saw his man fall and made a grab for Danny's gun. Danny stepped back out of reach and instinctively swung its barrel hard across Kafume's face. He felt it connect with his skull, just behind his ear, tearing open the skin. A spray of blood spurted out of Kafume's temple and splashed across Danny's face. It felt hot and warm. Kafume sank to his knees, groaning. Then there were two more explosive cracks and Danny crouched down too. He looked up to see Ali, standing over the juddering body of the policeman, a wisp of gray smoke twirling from his gun. A sickly rasp emerged from the policeman's open mouth, gasping like a beached fish. There was another shot and the man stopped moving.

There was silence.

"What the fuck did you just do, Danny?" Ali said.

But Danny was gone. He did not care about Ali's deal, or about the dead man, or the blood sprayed on his cheek. He just cared about the creature at his feet. Kafume. He lifted the pistol and put it to Kafume's face. With his other hand he hauled him up on his knees.

His voice barely rose above a whisper.

"You tell me the truth. What happened to Maria Tirado?"

Kafume spat on the ground and clutched at his bleeding head. Danny noticed that a slick of blood had stained the man's pressed white shirt, giving him a scarlet collar.

"Fuck that white bitch," he spat. Danny thought he should feel hot or out of control. But that was the wonder of it. He felt deliberate, he felt powerful, determined. Time lengthened like each second was an age. He had all the time in the world to get what he wanted.

"I should be asking you if you want short sleeves or long," Danny said.

Kafume looked at Danny as he said the words. He looked into Danny's eyes and he whimpered something unintelligible.

"But I don't have a machete. I only have a gun. So do you want a bullet in your arm or your leg?"

Kafume did not answer. Somewhere in his mind, from his own bloodied past, he remembered that no victim ever answered such questions.

Danny pointed the pistol at Kafume's thigh and fired. The bullet ripped into the flesh, splintering the bone. Kafume jerked onto the ground, howling in agony. Danny, splashed with gore, dragged him up by the neck until he was still, hanging there like the prize catch of a fisherman. Blood dripped onto the sand. Ali stood back.

"Danny, Danny . . . ," Ali whispered. But he did not move.

"Who wanted her dead?"

"Mosquito," Kafume spluttered. Now the words flowed out.

"She was going to make it difficult here. She was collecting information on us all. On what happened during the war. She would not listen. She would not stop."

Kafume was sobbing now.

"We offered her money. But she wanted nothing. Gbamanja did not want to kill her. But she forced our hand. He knew he had to have her put down. He said she had to die."

Danny knew. At least he knew. He cocked the pistol back again.

"Arm or leg?"

Now Kafume was screaming an inhuman sound. A cry that filled

Danny's ears. And his mind suddenly surfaced into the world again, swimming into air and gasping for breath. Danny could feel blood slicked all over his body and it sickened him. He could smell the iron in it, crude metallic and brutal. He dropped Kafume onto the ground and staggered back. Kafume lay weeping, clutching his leg. Danny felt Ali behind him, coming forward.

"Danny, Danny," he said gently, and Danny backed into his arms. He felt Ali gently prize the gun away from his grip, undoing the fingers one by one. "George. Get him out of here," he said.

Ali looked at Kafume on the ground and pointed his pistol at the back of Kafume's bowed head.

"Fuck," he said, and then lifted his head to the heavens as he screamed as loud as his lungs could manage. "Fuck!"

George looked at Danny like he had seen a ghost. He held him up as they limped back toward Ali's SUV. Danny had slumped against his side, staring at the blood from Kafume that had sprayed over his clothes. What had he just done?

George stood him up against the side of the vehicle and peered into his face. His hands ran up and down Danny's body.

"Are you injured?" he asked. "Does it hurt anywhere?"

Danny just looked blankly ahead of him. He felt he had crossed a wide Rubicon, to a foreign country from which there was no turning back but about which he knew nothing. He saw the world a darker place, like a faded photograph, all grays and blurred at the edges. George's face swam into focus.

"I'm all right, George," Danny said weakly. George tossed him a towel from the back of the SUV.

"You look like shit," he said. "Wipe yourself down."

"Where's Ali?"

George did not reply. Instead the answer came blown in on a soft wind off the diamond field. It was a series of terrible screams, punctuated by brief silences. Primal sounds that a wounded animal caught in a trap might make. It was pure pain and fear and a desire to cling on to life. The color drained out of George's face. Danny began to shake.

"I think Ali's having a talk with Kafume," George said quietly.

"Make it stop," Danny whispered.

As if in answer, two shots rang out in rapid succession. Ali walked up to them, tucking his gun away. His shirt was covered in blood and he tore it off and threw it away. His face looked like a carved statue, emotionless but determined.

"We are in deep shit, cousin," George said.

Ali breathed out. "No kidding. No fucking kidding at all."

"Is he dead?" Danny asked.

Ali spluttered and took a step toward him. For a moment Danny thought he was going to strike him. Ali clenched and unclenched his fists and seemed to struggle for the words until they exploded out of him.

"You don't leave someone like that alive, you dumb bastard!" he spat. "If you start it with him, then you finish it. You started it, so I made sure it was over. So, yes, Danny, Kafume is very much fucking dead."

For some reason, the news hurt Danny. No return. No way back. Ali was angry.

"What were you thinking? You just shot one of Gbamanja's main men. You think he'll let that pass?"

Danny felt himself stir from the shock that was trapping him. He had seen the truth of Maria's death in Kafume's eyes as he fired into his leg. This man had organized Maria's death. He was her murderer. Not Winston. Not the other child soldiers already in their graves. Kafume and Gbamanja were the guilty ones. "You know why. He killed Maria. He and Gbamanja did it," Danny said.

Ali walked over and took Danny's face in his hands. His eyes were a mixture of concern and fury, twin emotions battling it out on his face. Danny could not hold his gaze, but if he had, he would have seen the anger slowly burn out and die, losing the fight.

"You did what you did, Danny," Ali said eventually. "He had it coming, I won't argue that. But this changes things for all of us now. We need to move and we need to move fast."

"Where to?" George asked.

"Freetown. But first we have to go back to Bo. I had a little chat with Kafume. A very persuasive chat. He's given me a little information."

"He sounded talkative," George joked coldly.

Ali shot him a glance.

"Look, we need leverage. We haven't got Winston, but I think we can get something else. Rose talked about a file that Maria was collecting. A blue file. I figured maybe it was burned or destroyed when they killed her, but Kafume was a clever bastard. He kept it. That file is in Bo and he told me exactly where. If we can get that file, then we've got leverage again. We can bargain with it and get out of this mess."

"Get into the car, Danny, and wait. George, help me get rid of these bodies," Ali said. Danny meekly walked to the SUV. He pressed his forehead against the cool glass of the SUV's window and watched as George and Ali walked back to where Kafume and the policeman lay next to their battered old Mercedes.

Ali was carrying a green petrol can. Danny knew what was going to happen and he forced himself to look. He watched as George and Ali picked up first Kafume and then the policeman, carrying their sagging bodies like slaughtered game. He watched as they dumped one into the Mercedes's backseat and the other into the car's trunk. Then Ali walked around the vehicle, sprinkling petrol from the can, once, twice, three times, like a religious rite. Ali tossed something through the car's open door and Danny heard the *whumpf* as it caught alight, quickly burning, sending an accusing finger of black smoke into the air.

Danny thought of another burning car, three months ago, burning on a deserted stretch of tarmac and the words of the priest at his father's funeral came unbidden to his mind. "Ashes to ashes, dust to dust." Danny turned his eyes from the fire and looked straight at the road ahead.

THEY PULLED UP OUTSIDE the Hotel Leone. It was lunchtime and the streets were full of people. Ali sat in the driver's seat and gathered himself. He was still bare-chested, having thrown his blood-soaked clothes away.

"Kafume gave Maria's file to the manager here for safekeeping. I have no idea if Gbamanja knew he had it. But we need it. We need it badly," he said. "We need to convince the manager of that."

"You might want to put a shirt on for the occasion," Danny joked to break the tension.

Ali chuckled, and George got out a new top from a bag. Ali looked at Danny.

"This file—if it's here—it is mine, you understand that, Danny," he said.

"It's Maria's," Danny said. "She died for this, Ali. The stuff in that file, the names, the dates. It's what she was living for. It was her life."

"I know that. But it does not matter anymore. You understand that?" he said.

He asked again, his voice like steel.

"You understand that, Danny? This file is for us. It is for me. We use that for our gain. Not for any cause."

There was no argument. There could be none. This was Ali's world. This was a world where, if Winston had been kept Ali's prisoner rather than returned to his mother, he would be still be free. Or alive. It was a world where Maria's quest for justice was rippling out into death after death. It was a world where only the dead and the dying spoke the truth. Where the living bargained their souls away to snatch more precious deals.

Danny nodded. For the moment, Ali was right. But later they would see. He would not abandon Maria yet.

"Right, let's go," he said.

All three of them got out and walked into the Hotel Leone. They had waited until the lobby was empty and there was just a clerk behind the desk.

"Is the manager around?" Ali asked. The clerk looked up and nodded in the direction of a back room. Ali thanked him and they walked in. George stayed in the lobby, leaning over the front desk. The clerk looked at him and George lifted the front of his shirt to show the pistol nestling between his trousers and the folds of his belly. He smiled mischievously and put a finger to his lips.

"Sssshhhh," he said.

Ali and Danny walked into the backroom. An Indian man in a turban sat at a desk poring over a ledger. He looked up.

"Hello, Sanjiv," Ali said. Ali pulled out his gun and marched up to him and placed the barrel squarely in the man's forehead. The Sikh's eyes swiveled inward to look at the gun. He seemed surprisingly unperturbed.

"Hello, Ali," he said, his eyes not moving from the gun. "What can I do for you?"

Ali smiled.

"I'm sorry about this, Sanjiv. I really am. But I need something you have. A blue file. Kafume keeps it with you. Normally, I'd go about this in a more pleasant way, but today I have to be direct."

Ali pressed the gun harder against Sanjiv's forehead. The Sikh slowly rolled his chair backward against the pressure until they bumped into a wall.

"I'm having a shitty day and I'm in a hurry. So I'll be blunt. You give me that file or I will blow your brains against this wall."

Sanjiv remained calm, his hands at his sides.

"Ali. Kafume is a name around here. Perhaps he would be angry at me if I gave it to you," he said.

Ali nodded.

"Let me assure you, you no longer have any need to worry about what Kafume might do."

The implication was clear. Danny knew Sanjiv was like Ali. He was a man who read a situation according to his own needs and did what he must to survive. Looking up at Ali—his face set firm, his gun set firmer—it was fairly easy maths. Sanjiv nodded. A deal.

"It's in my safe," he said. Ali let the Sikh get up. He walked over to a strongbox mounted in the wall. He turned the dial back and forth and heard a metallic *clang* as the door sprang open. Inside were piles of banknotes and leather bags similar to the one Kafume had kept his diamonds in. And a ragged blue file.

Sanjiv looked at Ali.

"I just want the file, my friend. Nothing else," he said. Sanjiv bowed his head and plucked it out, quickly shutting the safe again.

He handed it to Danny. It was bound with rubber bands and wrapped in a see-through plastic bag. Danny expected it to feel heavy in his grasp, this reckoning of the past. But it was not. It was light. Fragile. Just paper after all.

"You know Kafume had people behind him. Powerful people," Sanjiv said.

Ali shrugged.

"I know. But when you tell them who took the file, also tell them that I am a reasonable man. I'm a negotiator. No one needs to get hurt."

"I'll tell them," Sanjiv said. "But they might not listen."

As they left, the Sikh watched them go. He had just been robbed at gunpoint but had not broken a sweat. As the door closed behind them he looked back at his ledgers and began to count his sums again. He was annoyed. He had lost his place. By the time he finally found it again, Ali's SUV was already out of Bo, driving south. Heading to Freetown.

17

[2000]

HENNESSEY HAD LOVED the story of Maria's saved child soldiers. Danny had made no mention of the cash or of the threat of death stalled only by the promise of riches to come. His article had betrayed no hint of what had really happened. Of the full truth. But even as a straightforward rescue mission it had sung from the page, portraying War Child in a heroic light. Danny knew that back in the newsroom, people would begin to talk of awards.

Danny sat in his hotel room reading the emails full of congratulations. It made him feel a strange sense of power, of vindication for being here and taking risks. A gentle rap on the door of his room disturbed him. He said a quick good-bye to Hennessey and walked over to the door. He peered through the spy hole. It was Maria. An ugly bruise mottled her right temple, and she seemed to be staring right back at him, knowing he was watching. She smiled and waved a hand. He laughed and opened the door.

"Room service?" she joked, and then jumped into his arms, giggling. He laughed and buried his face into her thick hair, inhaling her into his lungs. Frantically they began to grab at each other's clothes, tumbling backward toward the bed, half laughing and half serious, until they were naked.

When it was over they lay in each other's arms in a web of limbs, their skin dotted with sweat as the room's air-conditioning lost the battle with their bodies to keep the room cool. They were silent, Maria's head lying on his chest. Danny thought she had fallen asleep and started to gently extricate himself when she spoke.

"Thank you," she said. Then again, yet softer, "Thank you."

He held her tight.

"You risked too much going out in the bush like that," he said.

She was silent for a moment, but when she spoke she did not acknowledge his warning.

"You know, I can't stop thinking about the ones we lost. The boys that bastard took back."

Danny looked at her. He squeezed her naked flesh but could feel her muscles taut beneath her skin. Her eyes were fixed on some part of the far wall, but he knew she was looking out beyond the room, beyond him too, and out into the bush.

"That son of a bitch. We had them and he took them back."

Danny was startled. Then it hit him.

"You're thinking of going back out there? You want to try that stunt again."

She shrugged.

"It worked, Danny. I can be more careful next time. The fact is, five kids who were out there in the war zone are now in our orphanage."

He could scarcely believe his ears.

"Maria. You can't do this," he spluttered. "Apart from anything else, where did you get all that money?"

She was silent for a moment, weighing her answer carefully.

"Danny," she said, "I have been here a long time. I know a lot of people and things that I can't tell you about. Not now. Perhaps not ever. I'm sorry about that. But all that matters to me is that I can get that money. And that money will buy those kids a chance. Nothing else is important."

She was shutting him out again. Keeping secrets from him, and he felt something snap. In a voice that grew louder with every sentence, he told her it was madness. That she would get herself killed. That nothing was worth the risk of losing her. She listened quietly, absorbing his words, stroking his chest. Then, when he was finished, she told him of the five boys they had saved. Of Thomas, stolen from his parents as they worked in the field. Of Mohammed and Ishmael, brothers who saw their family burned alive in their hut. And Samuel and Eka, who were so traumatized that Maria had not yet been able to tease their stories from them. She said it all in a voice quiet and firm.

"They're still just kids, Danny," she said. "And perhaps they can be kids again."

She got up and walked into the bathroom. He watched her naked back and then lay down and stared at the ceiling. He traced the cracks in the stained yellow paint, just as he had mapped out the lines on her body. He knew he could not move her. She was like a rock, and his words were just waves crashing against her.

DANNY DID NOT KNOW WHY Maria was ignoring him. It had been two days of missed calls and unreturned messages and now he had asked Kam to drive him to her office. There was nothing else going on anyway. His story about the rescue had been a huge success, but the daily coverage of what was going on was disappearing fast. A sex scandal had broken out in Britain. A minister caught with his trousers down and his secretary in close attendance. It was dominating the newspapers, pushing Sierra Leone to the back of people's minds.

He walked into her office and spied her behind a mound of paper.

"Hey there," he said.

She looked up at him and in an instant he knew this had not been a misunderstanding. She had not missed his calls or lost his messages. She had been not returning them. She smiled thinly.

"Hi," she said, and then as an afterthought, "Long time, no see."

He moved toward her. She backed away.

"What's wrong?" he asked. They stared at each other, like gunfighters unexpectedly caught in a face-off. Danny had no idea how they had come to this. She seemed almost a stranger to him. What was wrong with her?

Then she spoke.

"I'm sorry, Danny," she said. "I've been so busy."

"Bullshit!" Danny spat, surprised at the venom in his voice. But it worked. Her face fell and he could almost see thoughts racing through her mind. She reached over and took his hand, guiding him to a chair.

"It's your story, Danny," she said. "It's caused some problems for me."

"How? I didn't even tell the truth, I didn't mention the money. Christ, Maria, I broke a lot of rules. I'm supposed to tell the truth, not keep it secret. I only put the story out that way because I thought it would help you. What's really going on?"

Her expression softened and she brushed his cheek.

"It's my fault. I thought the publicity would help. But it's angered

some . . . people. Some people who didn't want that sort of attention."

He looked at her, a red rush of emotion flushing his cheeks. He
shook off her hand and stood up.

"It's about the money? Where did you get it? Who's angry?"

She shook her head.

"Danny. You have to trust me. Please. It's just a little local difficulty.
I'll sort it out. But we can't see each other for a while. This whole country is a seething mess and I'm afraid we've started to add to it. We just
have to take a break. Not for long."

She reached out again. He felt her fingers on his skin. He wanted to
grab them, to pull her body to his. But the anger was too great. He felt
he did not know her. She would not let him know her.

"Please, Danny, trust me," she whispered.

But he had already turned his back and her voice was directed at his
back. He stumbled out of the orphanage and toward Kam, desperately
fighting off tears of rage and frustration. Kam quietly opened the car
door.

"SHE DOES NOT WANT to see me, Kam," Danny blurted out as
they drove back to the Cape Sierra.

Even saying it was painful. Kam threw up his hands, sending the
car swerving slightly.

"Ah, women!" he said. "My friend, you put too much faith in them.
I have many girls here and always they are giving Kam trouble. Even
my wife, she gives me trouble too. It is in their nature to try and push
us men around. It is in our nature to try and push them back. So if
she is ignoring you, I say ha! There are other women for a man such as
you, Danny."

His eyes twinkled.

"Would you like to meet some? Kam has many friends."

Danny had suspected he would get this reaction from Kam. He replayed her words over and over again in his mind. He thought of a million things he could have said; of a million questions he had. He did not even care about her secrets. "I don't want other women, Kam. I just want her."

Kam looked at him.

"Then stay here in Sierra Leone. Win her back. Stay," he said. His voice was serious now.

"I can't, Kam. You know that."

Kam snorted.

"Listen to this, Mr. Danny. I love my wife. I do. I love her. If she asked me to go home, back to Senegal, really asked me. Then I would go."

"Really?"

"That is love. That is what it means to be a woman's husband."

With a bump they drove back through the gates of the Cape Sierra and Danny could immediately see something had happened. Knots of people stood outside the entrance to the lobby and TV crews clustered around, filming correspondents giving their pieces to the camera. He got out and saw Lenny Ferenc. He was holding his head in his hands.

"Lenny, what's the matter?"

The older man looked up. His face was strained.

"There's been an accident," he said. "Kurt and Miguel are dead. Way up-country. They were pushing their luck and ran into an RUF ambush. They're both dead."

Danny went pale. Kurt Schork and Miguel Gil. Two legendary wire journalists. They had been going up the road together for days now, making a daily pilgrimage up-country, pushing the limits to see how far the war had gone. It had been working too. The front line was evaporating in front of them.

"Oh God," Danny said. "What happened?"

"They were in a car ahead of the government army, I suppose. The RUF came out of nowhere. Just shot them down."

Danny bit his tongue. He hadn't known either man well but he had seen them around, chatted casually. They seemed like good men, professional with perhaps an unhealthy love for their job. As agency men they had covered dozens of wars between them.

"I blame the editing desks," Ferenc was saying. "They've been pushing people to go further. It's taking more to get anything out onto the wires or in the papers. Something like this was bound to happen."

It also changed the game. Sierra Leone had dropped so far off Hennessey's radar that Danny had stopped thinking about going out of Freetown. It would be back on now. The death of a couple of foreign journalists would get his attention. There was something unspoken now between himself and Ferenc. It was Ferenc who broke the covenant of silence.

"I'm going up the road tomorrow," Ferenc said. "Care to join me?"

THEY MET AT BREAKFAST the next morning. Danny, Kam and Ferenc. A crew from CNN would be joining them on the road, Ferenc announced, and they would be bringing their own car.

"Safety in numbers," he said.

Not that safety lay in numbers in Sierra Leone. It came from not going down that road. But the deaths of Schork and Gil had invigorated the story. They were not alone in planning their little convoy. It was the obvious journalistic thing to do. The clear-cut victory that they all had told themselves was playing out in front of them was starting to look more frayed at the edges.

"So what's the plan?" Danny asked as they finished eating, with half an ear on CNN in the corner. The CNN correspondent—who was waiting for them outside the hotel—was being broadcast on the television describing the mood of shock among the Freetown press corp. He was an older man, a sort of TV version of Ferenc, with graying hair and a blasé confidence that suggested he had done this sort of thing a hundred times before.

Ferenc wiped his mouth.

"Simple. We head up-country. See how far we can get. Miguel and Kurt were obviously able to get a long way. I don't see why we shouldn't either."

Kam drove them north with the CNN car following The sky hung gray and low, but it did not stop the heat, which radiated through the clouds like a boiler. Danny rolled down his window to let a breeze cool them down. In the back, Lenny, unusually silent, stared out at the passing bush.

"I'd known Kurt for twenty bloody years," he said eventually. "We did Bosnia together."

It had felt like the roadblocks and the soldiers had all become routine. But the deaths of the two journalists made the danger around them suddenly real again. This whole country was a death trap and Danny knew he was not invulnerable. No one was. But talking about it seemed like bad luck. It would have summoned the dead into their car and Danny wanted them kept out.

They began to pass the usual roadblocks and the trip assumed a familiar rhythm. Some checkpoints were manned by the army, who waved them through after a perfunctory nod. Others by militias looking for a bribe of food, cigarettes and booze. Kam handled them with his usual aplomb, doling out goodies like a visiting potentate.

They drove rapidly, eating up the miles. Twenty kilometers from Freetown, fifty, then seventy and a hundred. They were farther up-country than Danny had ever been. Then they came to the final roadblock. Half a dozen cars were already parked there. It was less a checkpoint and more an army encampment. They were waved firmly to the side of the road and they got out and discussed what to do next.

Perhaps it would end up being just a "normal" day. The look on the faces of the government troops said it all. The journalists' deaths had been bad PR. The president had given orders to keep them from the front lines. No more white men can die here. Relieved, Danny sat down.

At that moment another convoy of cars pulled up. Four gleaming silver Mercedes. Danny assumed it was more journalists, those leaving Freetown even later than they had. But as the cars rolled to a halt he saw each was full of men in uniform, stuffed full, in fact, like military sardine tins. Out of one emerged a hefty figure, his army jacket stretched taut over an expanding belly. The soldiers at the checkpoint snapped into salutes.

Danny noticed Ferenc stiffen.

"Hang on," Ferenc said. "I know that fellow."

He jogged up to the checkpoint. One of the soldiers moved in front of him but Ferenc shouted something and the general's flabby features broke into a smile. He waved Ferenc forward and the two feverishly shook hands. Ferenc came back five minutes later and could barely contain himself.

"We're in," he said. "That's General Asimbiye. I interviewed him last week. Now he thinks I'm his best pal. He's going north on a little inspection tour. Says we can just tag along."

Even as Ferenc spoke, the general was getting back into his car and engines were being started. They sprinted back into their vehicles and Kam pulled onto the end of the convoy just in time. Swiftly they moved through the checkpoint, just as the other journalists realized what was happening. They were through. A couple soldiers even saluted smartly as they passed.

"It's like your dad always used to say, Danny. 'It's who you know,'" joked Ferenc, returning the gesture with a royal wave. "It's always who you know."

Now they drove fast down the road through militia and army roadblocks without having to stop. The general's car was well-known and the sight of its approach caused any obstacle in the road to melt away. Ferenc was giggling in the back and Danny could not help but join him. He was scared, yes, but he felt the pull of the story, the thrill of the exclusive. No matter what Maria might think of the end result, this was why he was here.

Gradually the countryside around them became empty. There was no one walking on the roads and no villages could be seen, just the occasional spread of ruins. Finally the convoy slowed as it crested a hill and began a descent into a town about a mile down the road. It was a sprawl of buildings, by far the biggest they had seen, and in several areas patches of smoke could be seen rising into the air. Danny felt his chest tighten.

"Here we go, chaps," Ferenc whispered.

The convoy drove into a town in the midst of jubilant chaos. Troops lounged on street corners, draped themselves off vehicles and crowded in the streets. Through his open window Danny could smell acrid cordite in the air and the tires of the car crunching on something on the road. He looked down and saw that spent cartridges littered the ground.

"They must have just taken this place this morning," he said.

Ferenc nodded.

"That's what Asimbiye said. Rogberi. It fell at dawn and he wanted to see it. I didn't think we'd actually make it, though."

Danny was annoyed that Ferenc had been keeping information from him, but he said nothing as the convoy halted and they saw the general get out. He was mobbed by troops, singing and dancing. As Danny got out he smelled another scent in the air. Stale alcohol. Half of these men were drunk. They leered at them as they emerged, crowding and pressing in. They were happy but there was something unpleasant in the way they came so close, touching and feeling and shouting. There was euphoria here, and booze, and something else, just underneath the surface, the dark, triumphant delight of men who had spent a morning fighting and killing and living to speak of it.

They set about doing interviews, with Kam helping to translate. The CNN reporter and his cameraman began filming and Danny could frequently hear his shouts to keep people out of shots, to calm down and stop waving into the camera. Not that it was much better for Danny either. The presence of a notebook sparked the same reaction. A single interview always drew a crowd and Danny would frequently look up to find himself surrounded by twenty or thirty men all trying to talk. There was something about the situation that had Danny feeling they were walking on a tightrope above a huge chasm. He felt his heart racing and an urge to get out while they were ahead, before the rope snapped and sent them all falling. He began to walk toward Ferenc. It was long past time to go.

Then, from somewhere outside of town he heard a distant pop. Talk died and people froze where they stood. Then the mortar hit earth. It landed two hundred yards away, farther down the road, and Danny could not see if it had hit anyone. But the effect was instantaneous. Men ran in all directions and hoisted weapons as they darted away toward the town's buildings. Then gunfire erupted all around them, deafening outgoing fire and Danny's ears felt as if they would burst. Then he ran too.

He had no idea where he was going. He just ran to the side of the road, tripping and falling as gunfire burst all around him. He was aware of cars roaring into life and two of the general's Mercedes flew by. He waved a hand to try to flag one down, but they sped past, weaving around the road crazily. He looked around in a panic. He could not see Kam or Ferenc, just mobs of soldiers, firing madly into the bush, from where came the short crack of incoming fire and the ping of bullets striking the buildings behind him.

Danny ran again.

He spotted a squat, ruined building and plunged through its open door frame that gaped in front of him like a mouth. It was dark inside and damp but he pressed his back against the firm concrete wall. The wall was thick, easily thick enough to withstand a bullet. He breathed out and tried to take stock of himself. He was slicked in sweat and his heart was racing but he was okay. He checked himself and saw nothing but mud and scrapes. He leaned his head against the comforting wall and breathed out. Outside gunfire still hammered away and Danny prayed—prayed fervently to a God he did not believe in—for it to stop. He swore that he would never come up this road again. If he could just make it back, he would never put himself here a second time. For what? For fucking what?

Then another figure stumbled through the door. It was a young soldier, barely out of his teens. He had lost his gun and was bleeding from his wrist, not a serious wound, but enough to dye his sleeve red. He was breathing heavily and his eyes bulged in his head as he too settled himself against the wall. The two looked at each other wordlessly. Then the soldier spoke.

"The RUF, if they find you here, they will kill you," he said.

It was a simple statement of fact. Danny knew he had to move. He felt so alone. He steeled himself against the clatter of guns outside and peered through the door frame. He saw them. Ferenc, Kam and the crew from CNN had somehow stuck together. They were crouched behind a bunker of sandbags fifty yards away on the other side of the road. He could cover the ground in about ten seconds.

He knew he had to. Though it was breaking all the rules, though he was safe behind these thick walls, he knew he could not stay here. He took one look at the wounded soldier and ran for it.

He emerged into daylight sprinting hard, his eyes fixed on the bunker. He saw Ferenc look up and see him. The tall man raised an arm waving him onward. All around him Danny could hear gunfire and he felt his legs slow, felt as if he were running through treacle. It was comic, he thought. This lumbering across the road, waiting for the bullet to come in a piece of frozen time, immune to terror, just detached and watching from afar. Waiting for the sudden jabbing pain that would end it all.

But it never came.

He flung himself to the ground behind the sandbags and lay there, trying to bury himself deeper, continuing his prayer. "Make it stop, make it stop, make it stop," he intoned.

Then he realized Ferenc was laughing.

"Well done, my son," he said. "I think that's the fastest I've ever seen anyone run. You were like Carl fucking Lewis."

He seemed indifferent to the gunfire, not flinching even at the closest bangs.

"Look," he said. "This is all just noise. Most of this stuff is outgoing. I've hardly noticed anything coming back at us."

The CNN correspondent was equally calm. He sat in an upright position, keeping his head below the level of the sandbags and persuading his cameraman to start filming him for a piece to camera. But the cameraman kept getting it wrong and the two had also collapsed into laughter, like they were on some television out-take show.

This is a madhouse, Danny thought. I am not like these people. I don't want to be like these people.

He did not know what made Ferenc stand up. Perhaps he had seen something. Or perhaps it was bravado. Either way, he clambered to his feet and brushed the dirt off his white jacket, a jacket that stood out so clearly. He peered over the top of the sandbags and put a hand over his eyes to ward off the light. Then he crumpled to the ground, with a barely audible "oof."

Danny thought he had ducked something.

"Careful, Lenny," he said. Then he saw his face. It was pale and in shock.

"Fuck me," Ferenc said. He was holding his hand to his belly and he slowly pulled it away and held it in front of his face. It was dripping with thick, dark blood, like a bear paw plunged into a honey pot. Ferenc stared at it uncomprehending.

"Fuck me," he repeated, and he fell onto his back.

"Lenny!" Danny yelled, and he grabbed his hand. "Lenny!" He felt the warmth of the blood on his fingers. He stared at Ferenc's face. He had no idea what to do. Then he felt himself pushed out of the way. The CNN reporter was leaning over Ferenc, pulling apart his shirt. He exposed his stomach, pale as porcelain, and saw a neat hole in the flesh that was pumping out thick, blackish blood with every one of Ferenc's heaving breaths. For the first time Danny noticed the gunfire had now stopped.

"Get the car! Get the fucking car!" Danny shouted. But Kam was ahead of him, racing off to where they had left their vehicle. A few government soldiers had gathered around, peering into the bunker. Their expressions were puzzled. It was as if they hadn't realized a white man could be hurt, just as they could be. They murmured among themselves as the two CNN men lifted Ferenc to his feet.

Danny took one of Ferenc's arms and looped it over his shoulder. Kam drove up and they bundled him inside. Danny was on the backseat with Ferenc, holding him, feeling him start to shake and shudder.

"Hold on, Lenny," he said frantically.

Ferenc swallowed hard.

"Fucking stupid, fucking stupid," he said. He tried to laugh but a splutter of blood bubbled at his lips. He smiled, showing teeth stained a ghastly red.

"Sorry, Danny," he said.

Danny held him tight. Kam was hurtling the car down the road.

"We'll get you to a hospital, Lenny. Don't you worry," Danny said.

But Ferenc was dying.

Ferenc knew it too. Danny could not believe that there was so much blood in a man. It flowed unceasingly, spreading over the car seat and pooling on the floor. The musty smell of it filled the car. Lenny was pale now, his skin translucent. His breath came in ragged gasps. He was angry and afraid.

"So stupid," he groaned loudly and then softer, "Oh God, oh God."

Fat tears were streaming down Ferenc's cheeks as he moaned and shuddered, ever more faintly, ever more distant. His eyes were glassy and misted. Danny looked into them and knew they were not seeing him anymore.

"Don't let me go, Danny," Ferenc breathed.

Danny didn't. He held him tightly, like a mother with a newborn child, pulling him to his chest, cradling Ferenc, comforting him as he slowly, imperceptibly slipped away. Danny kept his word. He held him close all the way to Freetown, long after he had started to turn cold.

MARIA CAME TO HIM in his hotel room, her eyes red with crying and fury. She slapped him hard across the face.

"You stupid bastard!" she said. "Are you trying to get yourself killed? You can't do that to me, Danny."

Then she fell into his arms, sobbing loudly, and Danny hugged her close and they tumbled to the floor, weeping and crying even as they moved against each other, each devouring the other, staving off death with this act of life. She had come back to him, breaking her self-imposed isolation. It had taken Lenny's death to reach her.

Later, as they lay on the floor, she began to cry again.

"It's not worth it. You think Lenny wanted to die like that? Tell me, when those bullets were flying around, were you really glad to be there? Did you think your stupid little story was worth dying for?"

Ferenc's last moments were burned into his mind. There had been no dignity in that death and Danny wanted nothing more to do with it. But that meant something else too. Danny knew he'd be leaving soon. "I need a break from here," he said eventually. "I need a rest. I'm on a plane out tomorrow."

She nodded but didn't look at him. He took her chin in his hands and forced her eyes to meet his. His own bored into hers, imploring her to open up to him, to ask him to stay. To demand it. To tell him everything about herself. To promise him all of her and forever. But he felt her shrink away from him.

"You know something," she said at last, almost as if talking to herself. "Certain things are worth being here for. When I help my kids, when I change just one child's life. It makes it all worth it. It's just newsprint that isn't worth a damn thing."

He knew what she was saying. She was telling him that she was staying. This was where her life was. She would let him go. She was still an island, aloof and alone.

When she fell asleep Danny watched her. She had promised to see him off at the airport and he in turn had vowed to return to see her, to chart the country's rebuilding. There would be a future for them. Now, with the words fallen silent between them, he traced her body with his eyes, the shape of her hips, the shadows of her breasts. He would be back, he swore. He would be back.

But the next day, when he arose, she was gone. Like the first time they had slept together, there was no note, no last message. Just the mattress that was still warm. He packed his luggage and Kam took him to the helicopter pad. He would wait for her there, he thought. She will come to say good-bye.

So he waited. Two choppers left without him as he stood on the hot tarmac. If he missed the third, he would miss his flight. She did not come. So in the end it was Kam, not Maria, who waved him away, who watched the giant white chopper lift into the sky. It was Kam who kept the vigil until it had become just a dot in the wide open blue, and it was Kam who turned back to Freetown, tears wetting his eyes, with the belief in his heart that he would not see his friend again.

18

[2004]

THE YOUNG AMERICAN girl at the U.S. embassy's front desk made a face like she had just swallowed a piece of sour lemon. She was blond and blue-eyed, what Maria would have called derisively "corn fed," and she preferred things done according to the rules.

"Mr. Benson has appointments all day. He's a very busy man," she said.

Danny insisted. He was there to see Harvey. He would not leave until he had done so. They had a lot to talk about.

"Just tell him Danny Kellerman is here to see him. Now. He'll know what it's about."

He leaned forward and planted his hands on her desk.

"If he finds out that you turned me away and didn't even tell him I had come, you'll lose your job."

That did it. She picked up her phone and snapped, "I am sure he will tell you to make a proper appointment."

But she dialed through nonetheless, cupping her hand as she spoke down the line. He turned his back to her and waited for her to call to him.

"Mr. Benson asks that you go on up," she said, not bothering to hide her anger.

"Thank you. I know the way."

Harvey got up when he entered the room. Two other men were there already. Americans—businessmen, he guessed, or other embassy workers—and Harvey showed them out as Danny entered. Harvey closed the door behind them. The room felt suddenly cold and still.

"What are you doing here, Danny?" Harvey asked. "I told you I'm not going to be any help to you. What is it you want from me?"

"The truth," he said.

"I've given you the truth."

Harvey's voice was world-weary and sad. He sat back in his chair. He looked like he felt sorry for Danny.

"You have to let go of her," he said. "Go back to England, Danny. You're losing it here."

"You have no fucking idea," Danny said.

Harvey stopped talking.

"I know that the child-smuggling story is bullshit," Danny said bluntly. "I know you and Maria traveled to Bo together. I know she was making a file on the RUF leadership, the ones now in government. I know she was going to expose them, screw up their new lives. I know that's why she was killed. She was digging around Gbamanja's past and he is about to become Minister of Mines. I guess he just decided to take her out before she went public and ended his new career."

Harvey didn't blink. He stared at Danny like a wide-eyed fish out of water. Danny saw his Adam's apple move as he gulped.

"What else do you know?" Harvey asked, his voice grating through a throat suddenly dry.

"I know you must have been helping her. You were with her in Bo most of the time," Danny said.

He looked at Harvey, at his pale skin refusing to tan under the African sun. His lank hair and his watery eyes. What had she seen in him?

"I think you had a relationship. You must have loved her," Danny said.

Now Harvey did stand up. He walked over.

"How do you know all this?" he asked.

"I have her file. The blue one. The one where she was collecting war crimes evidence. Proof against men like Gbamanja," Danny said. "I might pick up where she left off." He laughed bitterly. "I told you, Harvey. There was a story in Sierra Leone after all."

Harvey lit himself a cigarette. Danny had never seen him smoke before and suddenly he too craved nicotine. It had been days since he had smoked. Harvey handed him one and then cupped his lighter as Danny inhaled. He felt it surge into his lungs, the familiar dizziness as the nerve endings in his brain got their fix. He blew out a plume of smoke.

Harvey watched him.

"It always bothered me that she loved you," Harvey said matter-of-factly. "Because you're wrong about one thing. She wouldn't have me. Not that I didn't try. Oh God, I did try. I would have loved that woman for the rest of my life and I told her as much. But she made her feelings clear enough."

There was emotion playing across Harvey's face. It was painful and hard and his lower lip began to tremble. He sucked on his cigarette powerfully.

"I couldn't understand it. Why someone like you would leave her. She told me of your last few days together. You barely said good-bye. What sort of man can leave a woman like that behind?"

Danny felt his cheeks burn. This was not meant to be about him.

"Why would you leave someone like her?"

"It was complicated," Danny breathed, feeling the inadequacy of the answer. Harvey shrugged.

"Don't get me wrong. There were others after you left. But she held quite a candle for you, Danny. A special little candle that never went out. I guess that's why she wrote you that letter when she got in trouble."

"And you wouldn't help her? You chickened out?" Danny's tone was accusatory.

"I couldn't help her, Danny," he said. "Not by the end. I tried to persuade her to stop digging when things got dangerous. But she would not listen."

For a moment Harvey's voice cracked slightly, like a fissure opening in ice.

"She never listened. She refused my advice," he said.

"Then help her now," Danny insisted. "I have the file. We can use it. We can do it together. You keep going on about the new Sierra Leone. Well, here's our chance to make it work properly, without all these bastards cashing in. We need to go public with the contents of that file. Ali has it now. But I can get it. We can take Gbamanja down."

Harvey stubbed his cigarette out.

"The new Sierra Leone is already here, Danny. Like it or not, the new Sierra Leone is people like Gbamanja. They are the future here. If you want my help, Danny, I give you the same advice I gave her. Destroy that file. Take it out and burn it and go home."

Harvey gestured to the door.

"It's time for you to go."

"She would have wanted you to help me," Danny said. It sounded like the last desperate pitch that it was.

Harvey just showed him the door. But as Danny walked out he heard him whisper, "I know she would have, Danny. I know."

"I WISH YOU HADN'T done that," said Ali, downing a mouthful of Scotch. "It was not a good idea."

Danny had just told him about going to see Harvey, telling him about how they had found Maria's file, how they knew it was Gbamanja who had ordered her killed and asking him for his help.

"The less people know about this, the better. At least for now. That file is all we've got on our side at the moment."

They were back in Ali's villa. It felt safe here. What happened in Bo seemed like a dream, but Danny knew he had been a part of it, knew he had clubbed Kafume over the head and shot him in the leg. Knew he had listened to Kafume's screams as Ali tortured him.

"I'm sorry, Ali," he said. "I needed to see him. He might help us, I think. Let's give him some time to think it over. He's a powerful ally."

Ali sighed.

"Danny, you don't know what game we're playing here. It's not Harvey who needs time to think. It's me. I need to work out our next step."

He slugged back the glass of spirits and smacked his lips.

"But I can't do any more thinking cooped up in here. I'm going down to Alex's. Anyone care to join me?"

George shook his head. Danny didn't fancy the idea of crowds or conversation either. His head felt like a pressure cooker, on the edge of explosion. He couldn't trust himself to be outside this place of safety, these familiar walls.

"No. I'm going to get some sleep. Or try," he said. Ali picked up his keys and moved to the door. Then Danny called his name.

"I haven't thanked you," he said.

"For what?"

"You shot the policeman. He was going to kill me. But you shot him first."

Ali shrugged.

"It would have been easier to let him kill me," Danny continued. "You had your payoff. You were walking away. So why did you do it?"

Ali looked at him. "You want the truth? I've been asking myself that. If I'd thought about it properly, letting him shoot you is exactly what I should have done. But I didn't think about it. He was going to kill you, Danny. You're my friend. So I shot him instead. It was as simple as that."

He laughed.

"Instincts, huh? They can be a bitch."

Then he was gone. Out into Freetown. Out in search of a few drinks and some distraction.

Danny watched him go and suddenly felt tired. He had barely slept the night before. He had stared into the ceiling fan, watching it swirling around in endless circles. Maria, the file, Harvey, Kafume and Gbamanja. It never seemed to end. He hadn't shut his eyes all night long. He lay his head down on the sofa and surrendered to darkness. He dozed fitfully, rising up into consciousness, until he became aware of someone else in the room besides him. He opened his eyes and saw a figure in the shadows by the door. The man stepped into the light. It was Kam.

Danny felt a rush of happiness at seeing him, but it did not last long. Kam's face was lined with worry.

"Mr. Danny," he said. "Where is Mr. Ali?"

"He's gone out. Why?"

Kam moaned. He took his white cap off and ran a hand through his close-cropped hair.

"Things are bad. Everywhere there is news that Ali is in trouble. That you are in trouble. Freetown is not safe. You must leave. You must get out."

Danny looked at Kam. He remembered George's words about him serving two masters. Had Kam tried to play both sides of the same game and ended up making mistakes? Was that what he was saying? He could not believe it.

"You know George thinks you may have told Gbamanja some things. Perhaps about Winston?" he said.

Kam snorted in anger.

"That George thinks Africans are not to be trusted. But Kam does not betray his friends."

He sat down. His shoulders hunched over.

"I do not betray them," he said.

"I know, Kam," Danny said. "When Ali comes back, he'll have a plan. We can get out of this."

"Ali still trusts me?" Kam asked.

Danny nodded.

It did not seem like much, but for Kam it appeared to be enough. He smiled and got up.

"In the morning," Kam said. "We sort this mess out."

DANNY HAD BEEN AFRAID he would dream of blood and gore and killing. Yet he didn't dream of death. He dreamed of Maria. She was in his bed, lying with her back to him. Her hair covered his face, black and thick. He lost himself in it, reaching for her, and she turned to face him.

"Danny," she said. "Danny . . ." Except it wasn't her voice.

He sat up in a panic It was just after dawn. He took a moment to remember where he was. George was standing over his bed, saying his name. Then he saw the look of fear in George's face and he knew what was coming next.

"It's Ali," George said, his voice strained. "He didn't come back and he's not answering his phone."

He felt a sinking feeling in the pit of his stomach. He jumped from his bed and pulled on some clothes. Kam was already waiting outside in his car. As they headed off to Alex's the roads were just starting to fill with a few early-morning minibuses.

Alex's was shut, as they knew it would be. But George banged on the owner's flat next door until a bleary-eyed Lebanese opened the door, angry and spitting swear words in Arabic. George whispered to him quietly and the man calmed down and the two began to talk. Moments later George came back to the car.

"He left late. Sometime after midnight. Hassan is pretty sure he left alone and that he was going home. He was very drunk though."

There might have been an accident. Ali's driving was bad at the best of times. But a part of Danny already knew it was hopeless. They would not find him like this. They retraced all the possible routes he could have taken. They rang the hospital and the Lebanese embassy. But there was nothing. Then George's mobile rang. He answered it hesitantly. When he turned to Danny afterward, he had already begun to cry.

"That was Hassan. The police have just called him. They've found Ali's car."

They drove to the spot in silence. It was miles from Freetown, down the coast road that led to the end of the peninsula. It was far from any logical route that Ali could have taken. When they arrived they saw the SUV. It had careered off the road and tumbled into a shallow ditch. Its sides were marred by scrapes as if a giant hand had raked its fingernails down its body. Its windscreen was shattered and had collapsed in on itself and the driver's door was yanked open. Two Sierra Leone police cars were parked on the road. Half a dozen policemen milled around. One of them approached them as they parked.

George explained who he was. The policeman shuffled his feet and cast his eyes down.

"I am very sorry, sir," he said. "There seems to have been a robbery."

"Where is he?" said George. Somehow his voice was firm and clear.

The policeman led them through the bush. Danny, George and Kam. It was a funeral march. Ali lay thirty yards from the car. He had been covered with a dirty white sheet but they could tell he was spread-eagle on his back. The sheet was soiled with dirty brown stains that must have been blood. He noticed that Ali's sunglasses, trampled and smashed, lay just beside him.

George walked up and pulled back the edge of the sheet. Danny watched him, careful not to glimpse what lay under the cloth. He saw George's face fall.

"It's him," he said.

Then George pulled the whole sheet off and screamed in shock. Danny looked now. Ali lay on his back, his cold open eyes staring at the bright blue sky, dust smeared across his face. He had been laid out like a cross and—as neatly as if cut by a machine—both of his arms had been cut off just above the elbow. His severed limbs had then been neatly placed at his feet.

He had been given the RUF's short sleeves.

George fell to his knees, sobbing in the dust. Danny felt bile rising in his throat as strong arms grasped him from behind, dragging him backward. A thick African voice shouted in his ear, panicky and hoarse, "Go, Mr. Danny. Go! It is not safe here. Not here, not in the villa. Not in Freetown. Go! Go!"

It was Kam, grasping him firmly as he screamed and yelled, hauling him back to the car.

DANNY WAS BOOKED on the next evening's flight out of Lunghi—the first one available—and the Cape Sierra was about as safe as Freetown got at the moment. Kam had brought him there and checked him in under a different name as Danny lay in the back of his Mercedes, keeping his head down.

"No one else will know you are here," Kam had told him.

Danny stared at Maria's file, which lay accusingly on the table next to his hotel bed. He had insisted they get it back from Ali's villa. It was the cause of all this. He had to protect it. Kam had argued, pleading with him. But Danny refused any other way.

Now here it was in front of him. Him alone. Transcripts and statements, names and dates. All describing horrors and killings. Blood poured upon blood. He looked at the handwriting on its front, wondering when Maria had begun to collect it. Was it before he knew her or after? She had watched as the new Sierra Leone took shape around her. She had listened to Rose's story, and had seen killers morph into ministers, murderers into the police.

He needed to talk to someone. To anyone. He could not be alone like this in his last few hours here. He picked up the phone and dialed Rachel's number, punching the familiar numbers like a priest clutching at a cherished prayer.

"Danny?" she said hesitantly. "Is that you? Where are you?""

He felt relief just to hear her on the line. A flush of warmth filled him. He told her that he was back in Freetown. He had expected anger or surprise, but what he got was sadness, tinged with awkwardness. He felt the warmth start to drain out of him again, a feeling of dreaded uncertainty that he tried to ignore.

"I can't really explain what's going on," he found himself saying. "But when I get back I want to talk. I want to try and sort things out."

He really did, but some inner voice already told him it was too late. He suddenly knew he had lost her for good.

"There's no point, Danny," she said softly. "I want you to come back to England. But not for me. For yourself. I've already got the rest of my stuff from the flat. It's over."

"Where are you staying?" he asked. He was afraid she would hang up and it was all he could think of to keep her on the line. She paused and in that pause, something clicked.

"A friend's place," she said.

She hesitated slightly. She was searching for another word.

"Who?"

He had caught her and she knew it. She sighed down the phone line. Danny wanted it to be a sad sigh, or a guilty sigh. But it wasn't. It was just tired.

"I've met someone else."

He already knew it, but the shock of the words still slapped across his face. "That was quick," he spat.

"No, Danny. It really wasn't."

"How long?" he said.

There was another pause as Rachel guessed his line of thinking.

"I met him a month ago, but nothing happened until after I left you. I know you might not believe that, but it's the truth."

"Why should I believe you?" he blurted. But Rachel was not rising to his bait anymore. He no longer had the power to force her to get angry at him. Instead her voice was firm and measured.

"I could have started an affair, Danny. God knows you'd given me enough excuses. But I really wanted to make things work. I loved you, Danny. But you left our relationship long before I did. You understand that, right? I was the only one keeping it going."

He had had enough. He put the phone down. Two women. One was dead and the other had left him for another man. It felt like a weight crushing down on him. Maria was dead, Ali was dead. Rachel was gone. For a file. A file about men and a country he didn't care about. He'd been chasing ghosts. Running after things that belonged in the past. Suddenly, he felt the room start to collapse in on him, the walls and the ceiling getting tighter and tighter, squeezing him. It was swimming before his eyes and he couldn't breathe. He heaved himself to his feet. He needed to go downstairs and collect himself.

He needed a drink.

THE CAPE SIERRA bar's décor had barely changed. Though it served local beer now, from a brewery that opened the year before. That had been one of the first things Ali had told him. Judge a country's prospects by its brewery. By that token, Sierra Leone was now doing well. He ordered a double Scotch and downed it, wagging a finger at the bartender to keep it full. The man didn't bat an eyelid. He had seen it all before.

Danny sat and stared and drank. The bar filled up with the usual assortment of characters. But it was less frenetic than it had been years before. It was becoming a businessmen's kind of place. There was no Freddie the Fijian mouthing off in the corner. It was men in suits, striking deals and shaking hands. Making money.

He felt a hand slowly run its fingers down his back. He turned and a Sierra Leonean woman stood there. She was young, perhaps in her early twenties and wearing a tight white blouse. She glanced at his glass.

"Mister want to buy me a drink?" she asked.

He began to shake his head. Then he thought of Rachel with her new lover and a deep welling of despair took him. "A drink?" the woman repeated. He looked at her. She was smiling and her face was really quite beautiful, he thought. He ordered a bottle of wine and two glasses from the waiter.

"Let's take this upstairs," he said.

She had to help him out of the bar, but she giggled as she did so. The woman nudged Danny toward the stairs. She was petite and he towered over her as she led him up into his room, digging her hands into his pockets suggestively as he rooted for his room key. He flung open the door and she hauled him in. She took his wallet out of his pocket and pushed him down onto the bed. She took out five twenty-dollar bills.

"This okay?" she asked. He was too far gone to even reply, and she gently tugged at his trousers. He didn't want to do this, he thought. He didn't want to sink any further. But he surrendered to the joylessness of it. He wanted to debase himself. The opposite of what he had had with Maria. Then, sex had been about life and the living. As he moved and writhed within this woman, listened to her crooning in his ear, he knew this was an act of despair.

Then it was over.

She was gone in an instant. Back down to the bar. He had motioned her to stay. He wanted to talk, to hear a human voice that was not the cacophony of anger filling his head. But she had got up, as business-like as a cashier, tucked the dollar bills into her bra and walked out. He began to sob. He so desperately needed to talk.

Danny clawed for his hotel phone and punched in a number. A familiar American voice answered.

"Harvey Benson speaking."

"Ali's dead," Danny breathed. "They cut his arms off."

"Danny? Are you all right?"

"He's dead, Harvey!" Danny shouted.

"Where are you? What's this number? I'm glad you've called. Tell me . . ."

But now Danny was gone. He had wanted Harvey to listen, to hear what he had to say. But all Harvey had were questions. The handset fell from his grasp, his head sagged forward and Danny's freefall stopped, finally hitting bottom on the hotel bed, the stench of whiskey in the room getting stronger with every wretched snore.

DANNY DID NOT wake up the next morning. Rather he bobbed gradually into consciousness, rising from sleep in a series of attempts, coming to the surface, feeling the ache in his head and in his heart, and then sinking back down again. It must have been nine o'clock by the time he sat up straight.

He did not want to think about what he had done the night before. He felt shame, but he would deal with that later. First he had to leave

Freetown. His flight was in the evening. He would hide out in his room all day and then get Kam to take him to the chopper for Lunghi.

He looked at the blue file still on his bedside table. For the first time in days he felt a nugget of hard resolve. He would make it public. Fuck Harvey and his warnings. He had more balls than him. He would do Maria justice. He was the better man. He would take Gbamanja down. Maria had known it and now he would prove it. Then he could rebuild his life.

There was a sharp rap on his door.

"Room service," shouted a voice.

Danny got up. Puzzled. He hadn't ordered anything. He walked over and reached out for the handle, but something stopped him. He peered through the door's spy hole. Four men stood out there. One of them rapped on the door again.

"Room service."

Danny backed away. Oh God. Oh God. How did anyone know he was here? He looked feverishly around the room. There was nowhere to hide. He ran over to the window, but its thick plate glass was sealed shut. He picked up a chair and hurled it against the pane. It bounced off with a crash but did not even scratch the window. The men outside must have heard the noise for the door suddenly shuddered as someone rammed his shoulder against it.

Danny flung the chair again. A spidery snake-like crack appeared in the window. He looked over his shoulder and saw the door bulge as another blow hit it. It would not last long.

He had to call for help. He punched in Harvey's number. He heard his voice, reassuring and in control.

"This is Harvey Benson."

Frantically Danny began to speak.

"Harvey," he screamed as the door shattered behind him. "Harvey, help me, I'm being . . ."

". . . I'm not able to answer right now," Harvey continued. "Please leave a message after the tone."

Harvey's phone was switched off.

"Harvey! Harvey!" Danny screamed, and dived for the blue file, reaching out for it with both hands. But as he did he felt himself roughly yanked back. He writhed and struggled, fighting the men who held him, lashing out even as a heavy fist thrust down onto the side of his head. Then a hand came across his mouth. He tried to bite it but instead a wet cloth was put over his mouth and he smelled something acidic and burning invade his nostrils. He choked, fighting to breathe clean fresh air. But it was too late. He felt his vision fade, his arms stop moving. He was giving up, surrendering, stopping the fight. He began to go limp.

Gbamanja's men had got him, he thought. Like they got Ali. Like they got Maria. He thought of Kam, sitting in the dark in Ali's villa. "Kam does not betray his friends," he had said. And as Danny began to give up, he clung to that memory. He willed himself to have faith in it. It was a rock in his mind as the darkness surrounded him. It felt good to surrender. It felt warm. He let it swallow him whole.

19

IT WAS SO DARK Danny was not even sure he had his eyes open. He twisted his head, barely able to tell which way was up or down. It felt stiflingly hot and something was covering his face, something coarse, like a cloth bag. He could feel his hands were tied around his back and he guessed he was sitting on a chair, but the blackness engulfed everything. The fear crushed his chest like a fist, icy and cold.

"Hello?" he asked of the darkness. "Hello?"

There was no reply and somewhere, unbidden from the depths of his mind, came the fear that he was already dead. He had no memory of how he had got here. He remembered the struggle in the hotel room but he could not summon the faces of the men who had taken him or anything they might have said. He just remembered the bitter smell of chemicals and then a dreamy sleep until he gradually, terrifyingly, realized he was awake. He thought of Gbamanja's villa. Was that where he was? In that horrible lair, full of ex-RUF, full of darkness.

He heard footsteps and someone plucked the bag from his head and suddenly Danny was blinded by light. He shut his eyes, seeing a mass of colors like an oil slick dance in front of his closed eyelids.

"Hello?" he said again, tentatively, plaintively.

"Minister Gbamanja?"

There was a brief laugh. Danny had a vision of Gbamanja standing before him and he flinched. But then came an unexpected voice.

"Hello, Danny," it said. The accent was Midwest American, calm and assured.

Harvey.

Slowly the light became bearable and the view resolved itself in front of him. He was high above Freetown and it was evening. He sat on a secluded terrace to some unknown house. He could see the distant lights of Freetown far below, winking at him, beckoning, laughing. Out of reach. Harvey stood against one wall, leaning on it casually as someone might lean on a lamppost waiting for a bus. His fingers drummed against his hip.

"I told you I was glad you called me, Danny. I had no idea where you'd gone," he said.

Danny stared at him in disbelief. He'd betrayed himself. With a phone call.

"I thought Kam might have . . . ," Danny said.

Harvey laughed.

"Kam? Your driver? No, Danny. Oh, don't get me wrong. He tells Gbamanja a few things, bits and pieces. But he's not got the brains to play this game. He picks a side and stays loyal to it."

Kam had not betrayed him. He had not led them to the Cape Sierra. Not sold him out for fear or reward. The urge to get up and strike Harvey overtook him. He heaved upward and struggled against the ropes that held him but they were plastic and held firm, biting into his skin.

"Don't do that," said Harvey, walking forward. He pushed a hand into the center of Danny's chest and pressed him down into the chair. "You'll end up hurting yourself."

"I'm sorry about this, Danny. It's a bit . . ." Harvey searched for the right word. "Melodramatic? But I wanted . . . no, I *needed* to impress upon you the seriousness of this situation."

Danny gathered his wits. This fucker, this wet fish bastard had him here, looking so cool and so calm and talking about the seriousness of the situation. Well, fuck him.

"Fuck you, Harvey. Let me out of this. I'm a journalist. You can't go around kidnapping reporters. This isn't Hollywood."

Harvey reached into his pocket and took out a packet of cigarettes. He plucked one out and lit it. He inhaled once so that the end flowered into a glowing red coal and he coughed.

"I'm trying to give it up. It's terrible for your health," he said apologetically. Then he casually reached over and stubbed the lit end out on Danny's thigh. It burned through his trousers immediately and sent a molten bolt of pain right through his body. He screamed in agony and stunned shock.

"Now. Perhaps you will realize how serious I am," Harvey said.

Danny could not believe what had just happened. He searched Harvey's face for anything recognizable. But the American seemed a different man, a new version of Harvey. He sensed that it was the real one. He was seeing Harvey for the first time.

"I understand," he said weakly. He desperately wanted to grip his thigh but he could not move his hands.

"I don't think you do, Danny."

Harvey began to pace in front of him. Up and down, up and down, his hands clasped behind his back.

"I tried to tell you. There is a new country being born here. The war is over and it's time to forget the past. This place could be rich, you know? There's diamonds and gold and everything here. It just needs a break from the war so that we can all move on."

It was Harvey's old pitch, but it didn't sound like PR spin anymore. It was an article of faith. Harvey was a believer. He leaned in closer.

"I'm doing good here," he said. "This government needs to work so the country can rebuild. And for this government to work, it needs everyone in it. Even the RUF. Even if some RUF people have—how should we say it?—'questionable' histories. I don't know why you couldn't see that. I don't know why Maria could not see that."

"Gbamanja's a monster," Danny stuttered.

Harvey shrugged. "Yes, but he's going to be my monster." He laughed and then turned serious again. "You have really come close to fucking things up," he said. "You think I like doing this? You think I wanted Ali Alhoun dead?"

Harvey leaned in close and Danny could smell his breath. He turned his face away.

"Do you think I wanted Maria dead?"

Maria? What had Harvey done?

"But you were helping her," Danny said. "You were with her in Bo. You loved her."

Danny blanched at the look that came over Harvey's face and he could hear Harvey breathing heavily.

"What do you know about love, Danny? What do you know about what it feels like to love a woman like that? You know nothing. You didn't have a clue what she was like. You didn't know her at all."

Harvey leaned in close, his teeth grinding together.

"You didn't know her like I knew her," he repeated. His voice was laced with ice but it was the unsaid words that hung heaviest in the air. You didn't love her. You didn't love her like I loved her, was what Harvey had really meant.

The American blinked and then spoke again. He was trying to keep his emotions in check.

"Of course, I was helping her make her file. That's what we do. That is who we are. Maria and I. We make files on people. We dig around. We report. Sometimes we act in our country's best interests. That is our job."

He said the words deliberately and waited for Danny to take them in.

"Maria was working for you? What are you? CIA?"

"Let's not put initials on it, Danny. She had been in her cover job here for years. She knew this place like the back of her hand and she had the balls to take anyone on. She fought for the best interests of America and by doing so, she did what is best for Sierra Leone too. I don't think you can imagine how I felt when I discovered what she was planning to do with our data. Making her own copy that she wanted to go public with. Suddenly becoming some sort of human rights crusader."

Harvey strode over to Danny and struck him firmly across the face. Harvey leaned in close so Danny could feel the spit fleck his cheek as he yelled, "I don't think you can imagine how I felt at all."

Danny's mind was spinning. Maria was CIA? The posting at War Child was just a cover? It seemed madness. But he clung to the one thing that remained true: Maria's file was real. She had wanted justice in the end, and she had died for it.

And Harvey had loved her. Even as he had ordered her to be killed.

"How could you let those bastards near her?" Danny said.

Harvey was breathing heavily again, the sounds of his chest rising and falling filling the air.

"It was not easy to do what I did, Danny. It was hard," he said. His voice was starting to crack just below the surface, a hint of thin ice feeling the strain.

"You let her die. You let her be raped," Danny said.

Harvey stared at him, his hands flexing and relaxing, the veins on his wrist starting to bulge. After a moment the American turned his back to Danny and looked toward the door to the rest of the villa. Danny looked at Harvey's blank back, terrified as to what he would do now. "I did not mean it to end the way it did," Harvey whispered. "Sacrifices have to be made in our line of work. I knew that. She knew that. But as for the way it happened, I did not want that."

He turned to look at Danny again.

"I hope you know that," Harvey said. It sounded like a plea. Danny had no words to respond and Harvey took his silence for an admonition. His mouth cracked into an ugly sneer.

"You know, I have no idea what she saw in a man like you. She knew better than to fall for a journalist, for Christ's sake. All that fake piety. She knew how the world really works. We both did. . . ."

Harvey paused. He seemed to be remembering something—an incident, a moment together, but he kept it hidden behind the mask of his face.

"You know, it was just after she told me that she would never want me as a lover that I found out about your affair."

Danny could scarcely believe what he was hearing.

"Oh, don't look so surprised, Danny. I knew everything. I thought you were just some past fling, but when you appeared here, asking all your stupid questions, that was when I knew we had a real situation on our hands."

Danny looked at him. He knew he had something Harvey would never have and it made Danny feel powerful. Danny had loved Maria and had been loved in return. Harvey had been spurned.

"We were in love, Harvey," Danny said. "I don't care what else you think you know, but you sure as fuck don't understand things like that."

Harvey stepped forward in a flash, his fist rising. Danny flinched and shut his eyes, but there was just stillness and silence. He waited a moment and looked. Harvey sensed he was letting the game get away from him and pulled back from the edge. He reached into a jacket pocket and took out a handkerchief and mopped his brow. He smiled wanly.

"She was the last person I ever expected to start working her own agenda. Her cover job got to her. She believed in it. I should have seen it coming and when I finally found out, it was too late to bring her back. I blame myself, but we had no choice. She was going to be a traitor to her own country as well as this one."

"You're fucking insane," said Danny.

Harvey shook his head. "I should have known something was wrong years ago. When you went with her on that idiotic trip into the bush to buy those RUF children. That story caused a lot of trouble for us. Cover jobs aren't meant to create headlines around the world. We thrive on subtlety, not attention."

He shrugged in a gesture of regret.

"I let it pass then. But I should have known it was a sign of her losing focus."

Danny's head swam with the revelation. He remembered going to Maria's office that day, her shrinking from him, warning that his story had caused trouble for her. He had not really listened to her then. He had just been hurt at her rejection. She had asked him to trust her. But trust whom? He had not even known who she really was.

"Fuck you, Harvey," Danny raged. "This is nothing to do with me."

Harvey snorted in derision and his lips thinned as he leaned in to Danny's face.

"Danny, you're the one who's fucking everything up. Do you think Ali would be dead if you hadn't bothered yourself with this? He'd be sitting in a bar with a whore in his lap.

"Danny!" Harvey exclaimed with an explosive laugh. "*You* are not the good guy here. *I am.*

"Listen," he went on. "If Maria had made her information public, what do you think would have happened? Do you think people like Gbamanja will just put their hands up and come quietly? No, Danny. They'll be back to the bush in seconds, killing more kids and making killers out of others. Back to square one. Back to the war. Do you want that? We can stop this, Danny. Let this country pull itself together."

Danny was silent.

"This is Africa, Danny. Different rules apply."

Harvey looked at him.

"Do you even know why you aren't dead?"

It felt like an ice pick had gone through Danny's heart.

"Because of your fucking newspaper. Undercover agents like Maria go missing all the time. It's part of the job description. A dead Lebanese diamond dealer? Shit happens. But you? A Western reporter, investigating an ex-lover's death. That sort of thing creates a bad smell and we don't like bad smells. So we want to end this now, not with another covered-up death. Christ, why didn't you just buy that Nigerian child-smuggling story and go home?"

He paused for a moment.

"You know, I still think you need more convincing."

Harvey turned around and knocked on the door that led back into the villa. Two burly men—both white—walked out. Harvey said nothing to them, but they moved behind Danny. He frantically twisted his neck, trying to see what was happening, but he just felt his head grabbed in a vise-like embrace. Then another hand gripped his jaw, forcing his mouth open. He noticed Harvey was slowly and carefully putting on a pair of plastic gloves and that something metallic was shining in his hands. He walked forward and straddled him. They were face-to-face, as close as lovers, staring into each other's eyes.

"I am going to give you a choice in a moment, Danny. A simple choice. And you should ask yourself, when you are thinking about your answer, What would Maria really have wanted you to do?"

He moved the metal object close to him, caressing Danny's cheek with its cold steel.

"She loved you, Danny. What would she have wanted you to do?" he repeated. And then he thrust the pliers deep into Danny's mouth and began to pull.

And Danny screamed.

When it was over—finally over—and blood poured down his shirt like a red apron, Harvey took Danny's face in his hand and cradled his chin. And then, in a quiet voice, his eyes flecked with concern, he gave him his choice and Danny began to weep.

THE CHOICE WAS SIMPLE enough. He would be let go. He would go back to London and forget this had ever happened. He would never speak of it again. Maria, the memory of the blue file and what it contained must be put aside. Maria's death would remain a robbery, an aid worker killed in a faraway country. She would have sacrificed her life in vain. Gbamanja would soon become the next Minister of Mines of Sierra Leone. He would be an ally to America and the West. The country would have peace.

Or, Danny could go public. They still would not kill him. They would endure the bad headlines and spin it as best they could. They had been caught in such situations before. But Danny's friends would die.

Every one of them.

Harvey listed them.

"Your driver, Kam, will have an accident. Maybe even his wife and daughter back in Senegal too. George's demise will add to the grief of the Alhoun family. Rose will join her dead children. Winston too. Major Oluwasegun will find the stresses of Lagos too much and be found a suicide. Their deaths will be on your hands, and no one apart from you will know or care. Your death would make headlines, Danny. Theirs will not. Not one of them. That is our surety. Once you are back in London you may be tempted to go public. But every time you are, think of what we will do to your friends."

"You're bluffing, Harvey," Danny had blurted out.

"No, Danny. I am not," Harvey said in a voice as flat and dead as a grave.

Harvey crouched down beside him and picked something up off the floor. He held it up to the light and examined it like a jeweler looking at a diamond. Then he held it up between his thumb and forefinger. It was one of Danny's missing teeth.

"You're not a hero, Danny. Heroes sacrifice themselves and others. Heroes die for their causes. Heroes kill for them. Maria was a hero. But not you. You'll choose to let people live. Just make the right decision here."

Harvey stood up and casually popped Danny's tooth into a jacket pocket.

"If you are ever tempted to break your silence, Danny, think of where your tooth is."

And Danny thought to himself, What would Maria have wanted me to do?

Maria had died for this, and now it came down to him. Everything she had wanted to do, everything she had come to believe in was against this. She may have been CIA but in the end she wanted justice. For Rose, for the thousands like her. How could she exist in a world in which the victims were poor and the murderers grew fat and rich?

She once told Danny that she was saving the world one life at a time. She told him what it felt like to make an impact on individual lives, to know the names of those you helped. He held several lives in his hands now. Kam, Rose, George, Winston. He could keep them safe, but only if he gave up Maria. He would have to surrender her memory, her cause. He didn't want to abandon her again, leave her at the last moment when all she had fought for was in his hands alone.

Yet in the end, the decision felt simple. He stared out over Freetown at night and marveled at the sight, as if seeing it for the first time. The lights, the cars, the boats out at sea. The dirt, the mess and all the trouble in the world. All down there in that city of a million people, a tiny few of whom he now called friends. You choose to save a single life. That had been her way of saving the world. You save those you come to love.

Let Kam live out his days; let him make his wife rich and happy. Let Rose mourn her lost children and die an old woman's death. Let her try to save Winston from his unimaginable demons. Let Gbamanja make his millions. Let Oluwasegun's God look after him. Let George raise a family. Let all those living in peace down there just make the best of it. Let the past be dead. Make it a grave and bury it. Danny looked down at the red stains on his shirt. Too much blood, he thought. It stops now.

He waited for Harvey to come back. When the door opened and

Harvey walked onto the patio, the American looked at Danny's face and smiled. It was a knowing smile, happy and content and relieved.

"You'll let them live?" Danny asked. "All of them?"

Harvey nodded.

"That is my end of the bargain."

"Winston too," Danny said. "Let him go. Get the police to let him go back to his mother. Leave them in peace."

Harvey nodded again.

"He will be with Rose by the morning."

"How do I trust you?"

"You have my word, Danny," Harvey said. "It is all you need. Your silence buys their lives. It is our pact."

Danny believed he was telling the truth. He was no hero, he thought. Harvey was right about that. But Harvey was wrong that he had not made a sacrifice. He had sacrificed Maria and in so doing, he had, at long last, saved a war child. Saved Winston. He looked at Harvey, feeling suddenly strong, despite the pain where his teeth had been, despite the raw taste of blood in his mouth. Harvey looked at him with a raised eyebrow.

Danny nodded once. Their deal was done.

Harvey walked over to him.

"It's over, Danny," Harvey said, and he gently squeezed Danny's shoulder like an old friend, comforting him for his loss. Then, carefully, so as not to hurt him, he slowly untied his hands.

Danny submitted to his grasp and felt his bound hands suddenly free. As he felt the blood return to his fingers, an idea flooded his mind. There was no going back on their deal. But this had begun with a letter, he thought. Now he would see that it ended with one too.

EPILOGUE

[London, Six Months Later]

DANNY KELLERMAN SAT in a café in a back street near Soho and nervously glanced at his watch. She was not late. He was early. But he had already downed one cup of coffee. He signaled to the waiter to bring him another.

"She's a lovely girl," Rachel had told him the day before over the phone. "She's new at my work and she's just your type."

He wondered whether Rachel would be a good judge of that. He was still adjusting to being the latest on the list of ex-lovers Rachel considered close friends. But it felt a good place to be. It felt solid. It felt real. He had told her he was not sure about going on a blind date with one of her colleagues, especially after the circumstances in which their own relationship had ended. But Rachel had just grinned her easy smile and bullied him into it. So here he was, feeling the familiar nerves of a first date. He had placed a copy of a newspaper—as arranged—sitting open on his table to let her know who he was.

He glanced at the open page and saw the News in Brief. The dateline caught his attention. Freetown. A suicide, it seemed, of an American diplomat there. A single shot to the head. Harvey Benson.

His letter had finally done its job.

He had written to Ali's cousin George. He had told him everything that had happened and of the pact of silence that preserved all their lives. But it had not preserved Harvey's. The CIA would still have their new ally in Africa. Gbamanja would get to enjoy his riches. But Harvey was expendable. What had he said about the deaths of agents like him and Maria? "Part of the job description," he had said with a smirk. Well, Ali's family had shown him the truth of those words. His life too could be sacrificed by the CIA for the greater good. He wondered how George had accomplished it. Did they break into Harvey's villa, or trap him in some roadside ambush? But Danny did not want to know the details. It was over now. No one else needed to die.

He wondered what Harvey's final thoughts were. Of Maria, possibly. Still wondering why she had betrayed him. Forced him to do what he had done. Blaming her for her own murder. Or finally, at last, blaming himself.

Harvey had been right, though. Danny had never known Maria. Neither of them had. She had been a brief glimpse of some beautiful, undiscovered country, viewed in a storm. There at the peak of a cresting wave, and gone forever on the next. She had once said she loved him. But he didn't know now if she really had. He thought of her, and of her lost blue file and of all the terrible sins that it had contained. He stared into empty space, suddenly warmed by an African sun, not the weak English version that shone meekly from the sky above.

Then the moment passed.

Danny folded the paper so he couldn't see the headline, and looked out into the crowd. He saw a woman walking toward him, with olive skin and brown eyes and a familiar questioning look on her face. For one last time his heart skipped a beat. But it was not Maria. It was just the pretty girl he was meeting for lunch. She was smiling at him. He smiled back.

He rose to meet her.

ACKNOWLEDGMENTS

I want to thank my agent, Elizabeth Sheinkman, at Curtis Brown. I also want to thank the team at Dutton: Trena Keating, Ben Sevier and Erika Imranyi. Their editing skills have helped craft a much better book. Heartfelt appreciation also goes to friends who read early versions of the manuscript and provided support and encouragement. They are Lee Bailey, Maria Crotty, Kirsty de Garis and Burhan Wazir. Thanks also to numerous editors and colleagues from the world of journalism, especially *The Observer*, for allowing me to have a lot of fun and call it a "career." They are, in no particular order, Tracy McVeigh, Andy Malone, Roger Alton, Paul Webster, Peter Beaumont and Peter Alexander. Final thanks to Simon English, for long years of friendship.

ABOUT THE AUTHOR

PAUL HARRIS is a journalist who has written for Reuters, the Associated Press, and *The Daily Telegraph*. He spent four years in Africa, where he covered the conflict in Sierra Leone. Now *The Observer*'s U.S. correspondent, he lives in New York City. *The Secret Keeper* is his first novel.